Praise for Rowe

"A fast moving, gripping fantasy."
Fantasy Book Critic on
King Rolen's Kin: The King's Bastard

"Rowena Cory Daniells has a
splendidly devious way with plotting."
SFX

"It's a story of kings and queens, beasts and warriors,
magic and religion. If you like any of the aforementioned
things, then you'll probably join me in loving this book."
Den of Geek on *The Chronicles of King Rolen's Kin*

"*The King's Bastard* is a cracking read
and the pace never lets up."
Geek Syndicate

"Royal intrigue, court politics and outlawed
magic make for an exciting adventure."
Gail Z. Martin, author of *The Chronicles of The
Necromancer*, on *The Chronicles of King Rolen's Kin*

"Pacy and full of action and intrigue."
Trudi Canavan, author of *The Black Magician* trilogy,
on *The Chronicles of King Rolen's Kin*

"*The King's Bastard* is a fabulous, rollicking, High
Fantasy adventure that will keep you up at night,
desperate to find out what happens next."
Jennifer Fallon, author of *The Demon Child* trilogy

ROWENA CORY DANIELLS

SANCTUARY

BOOK THREE OF THE
OUTCAST CHRONICLES

SOLARIS

First published 2012 by Solaris
an imprint of Rebellion Publishing Ltd,
Riverside House, Osney Mead,
Oxford, OX2 0ES, UK

www.solarisbooks.com

ISBN: 978 1 78108 015 3

10 9 8 7 6 5 4 3 2 1

A CIP catalogue record for this book is available from the
British Library.

Designed & typeset by Rebellion Publishing

Printed in the US

All my life, I'd been told the Wyrds were ungodly creatures, born without a soul or a conscience. It wasn't until I collated the information on their gifts that I realised they were just people like us, both good and bad. When I was offered the chance to sail with the Wyrds and write the story of their exile, how could I refuse?

Taken from Scholar Igotzon's journal

Chalcedonia and the Five Kingdoms

Prologue

'YOU'RE A TRUE-MAN. What're you doing with the Wyrds?'

He could ask her the same question; she was no more than fifteen, and also of True-man stock. When he had been taken aboard the Wyrd ship, he hadn't expected to find one of his own race living amongst their ancestral enemy. The Wyrds had put them in a cabin together and ignored them, which was not surprising considering the chaos last night.

'I'm making notes to write a history of the Wyrd exile –' He stopped himself. 'Sorry, the *T'Enatuath* exile.'

Her eyes widened. 'You know their language?'

'Only a few words, so far. For instance, they call us Mieren, so don't refer to yourself as a True-man. They'll take insult. We're –'

'Mieren, I get it. I'm not stupid. My husband could do no more than write his own name, but he was awful proud of it. When he caught me trying to make my letters, he hit me so hard I had a bruise for a week.' She held his eyes defiantly. 'After that I practised in secret.'

'Good for you.' Igotzon did not see any point in keeping women ignorant. She seemed determined to learn and he needed an assistant. 'I could teach you to read and write. What's your name?'

They'd shared a bed last night, and he hadn't thought to ask. Not that they'd done anything; he was a scholarly priest and she was the mother of a newborn, which had slept between them.

'I'm Masne.' She followed his gaze to the infant, with the distinctive mulberry eyes and six–fingered hands of a half-blood. 'And that's Soihana. But I suppose she should have a half-blood name, since she's one of them.' Determined blue eyes lifted to him. 'I never lay with a Wyrd, if that's what you're thinking. I swear –'

'You don't have to convince me. Even the best minds don't know why some True-man couples produce half-blood babies.'

'That's what I told my husband.' Tears of anger glistened in her eyes. 'After my pregnancy went beyond six small moons, he beat me. When that didn't bring the baby on, he denounced me before the whole village and turned me out.'

'Typical.' He regarded her curiously. 'Why didn't you hand the baby over to the Wyrds? They take in half-bloods born of True-man parents.'

'And go where?' she countered. 'My village wouldn't have me back. I'd have to go to port and sell my body to buy bread.'

'You could have offered to serve the Mother.' It was the only religious institution that accepted women and, now that he thought about it, it was probably full of women who had nowhere else to go.

'I didn't think of that. Besides...' She raised her chin. 'I couldn't bear to part with Soihana. She's all I have in the world. You understand.'

He didn't. He'd never understood the incoherent emotions that troubled others. For him, the world was logical. Take the True-man – *Mieren* – parents who kept their half-blood sons or daughters, hiding them from their villages. He saw no point. They were always discovered, and the villagers always went hard on them for harbouring the half-bloods. Perhaps by observing Masne with her infant, he would come to understand.

'King Charald's ship approaches.' The cry came through the open cabin window.

Igotzon put his ink and pen away.

'Now what're you doing?'

'Going to watch the handover of Prince Cedon so that I can record my observations for posterity.'

She looked suitably impressed, then frowned. 'After everything that's happened, the Wyrd queen is still going to return the prince?'

'Yes. Look, if you're going to live amongst them, you have to learn their language and their ways. She's not their queen. She's their *causare*. It's an elected position, and she holds it only as long as they need someone to unite them behind a cause.'

'Silverhead ways are strange.'

'Don't call them silverheads and copperheads. The full-bloods are T'En and the half-bloods are Malaunje.'

Masne nodded. 'But their ways are still strange. The way full-bloods divide into brotherhoods and sisterhoods. And the women run things; I would never have believed it if I hadn't seen it for myself. Why do their men let them –'

'They don't *let* them. Power rests with the powerful. T'En women have more powerful gifts than the men.'

'Gifts...' She shuddered.

He was tired of ignorance. 'There are good and bad amongst the T'Enatuath, just as there are good and bad amongst True-men.'

'I guess so, but with their T'En gifts, the bad ones are more dangerous.'

He blinked in surprise. 'Good point.'

'I watch and I learn.' Masne moved closer to him, lowering her voice. 'I like it with the sisterhoods. These two are run by the most powerful of the T'En women. Yet...' She glanced to the cabin door. 'Yet, even they are afraid of the T'En men. If the women are more powerful than the men, why are they afraid of them?'

'They're afraid of T'En men?' He hadn't known this. He scented a mystery, and the chance to uncover the truth. His heart raced with excitement. 'I'll discover things no True-man has ever known. This is an amazing opportunity!'

She stared at him, then laughed. 'I've never met anyone like you.'

'Of course not. I am a true scholar.'

PART ONE

PART ONE

Chapter One

JARAILE WOKE TO a thumping headache and nausea, made worse by the motion of the horse. Above her she could see a canopy of leaves. It was dawn and her breath misted in the cold air, but she was warm in Baron Eskarnor's arms. A surge of panic filled her. 'Put me down.'

Eskarnor laughed. 'Oh, no, my queen, you'd just try to run away.'

'Put me down. I'm going to throw up.'

He stopped the horse and slid off the saddle. She made it three steps before she leaned against a tree trunk and emptied her stomach.

When she lifted her head, he offered her watered wine. She swilled some in her mouth and spat it out, then took a mouthful. Meanwhile, Eskarnor joked with his honour guard. She gathered they'd slipped out of port and ridden all night.

Did the baron suspect she was pregnant? Back in the palace he'd raped her, boasting he planned to sit on King Charald's throne by spring.

'I shouldn't have hit you so hard,' he said, cupping her cheek and tilting her face to the light. 'But you shouldn't have stabbed me.'

No, she should have cut his throat. When he'd thrown her over his shoulder, she'd panicked and pulled the paring knife. Unfortunately the two blows she'd gotten in had done little more than annoy him.

She should have been cool-headed, but she'd been waiting all day for news of her son. In exchange for safe passage to their ships, the Wyrds had promised to return Prince Cedon with his club foot healed. But when the Wyrds had arrived in port, they'd been attacked on the wharf. She'd sent Nitzane with every available man to help them, which left her vulnerable to Eskarnor, who had snatched her from the palace.

Would the Wyrds think the attack on the wharf was evidence the king had broken his word and take out their anger on her son? Her stomach churned with desperation. Sorne said the Wyrds were ruled by women. Surely they would not hurt an innocent little boy? She should be back in the palace trying to organise her son's safe return. Instead she was here, headed for...

Jaraile returned the watered wine. 'Where are you taking me?'

'Somewhere safe.' He grinned, looking younger. 'I can't have someone stealing what I've stolen, Raila.'

'My name is Jaraile. And I have to pee.'

'Go right ahead, but if you think I'm turning my back you're a fool.'

He followed her into the woods and leaned against a tree.

She squatted down, held her pleated trousers out of the way and emptied her bladder. 'They'll come after me.'

'I'm counting on it. I hope they bring every man-at-arms they can muster. I'll choose my ground and I'll rout them. I spent years serving King Charald during the Secluded Sea campaign, studying his every move. Back then, he had a genius for strategy, but the king is not the man he was and Baron Nitzane is more a lap-dog than a wolfhound. The only man who could have stood a chance against me has been banished because he's a half-blood. So resign yourself to becoming my queen, Raila. I promise you won't regret it.'

She stood and adjusted her clothing. She walked past him, keeping her eyes downcast.

He caught her arm. 'They all think you're the sweet, dutiful wife, but I've seen your fire, Raila. I don't know why you're loyal to that cruel old king. I was there the night he wedded and bedded you. I know he bullied your father into giving you away. I could have sworn you hated him.'

She did. But she loved her son, and Eskarnor would have to kill Prince Cedon to put his own son on the throne. She said nothing. The baron led her back to his horse. He climbed astride then hauled her up to ride before him.

'I hate him,' Eskarnor said. 'I was nineteen when Charald invaded Dace and captured my family's estate. My father and older brothers died serving the Dacian king. I had two choices: die pointlessly trying to defeat the Chalcedonians, or turn my coat and survive. I made the only decision I could. But I've never forgiven Charald or his half-blood advisor. So we have a lot in common.'

They didn't. She would kill to save herself, but she didn't kill in cold blood to achieve her goal.

Except... she had told King Charald's manservant to resume treating him, even though Sorne believed the arsenic based medication was slowly killing him. And when the manservant had suggested doubling the dose, she'd agreed.

She was hoping King Charald would hurry up and die, leaving her free to marry Baron Nitzane. She'd planned to make Nitzane believe the child she carried was his and use his wealth and men-at-arms to ensure her son lived to grow up and sit on the Chalcedonian throne.

Instead, she was being carried across the kingdom in the arms of a treasonous war baron, who would be jubilant if he knew she was pregnant with his child. Lucky for her, most mornings she managed not to throw up. Today he had assumed her nausea was due to the blow to the head she had received at his hands. If she could just keep her breakfast down while he was watching, he wouldn't guess.

She had to escape, get back to port and secure the kingdom for her son. Nothing was going to stop her.

Unless the Wyrds had already killed her little boy.

But she refused to entertain that thought.

* * *

GRAELEN HAD PINNED a blanket across one corner of the cabin to curtain off their sleeping area, but it provided very little privacy. While Valendia slept in his arms, he could sense at least twenty T'En adepts sleeping on the other side of that blanket. Only two had devotees like him. These were both young Malaunje men, who'd been accidentally imprinted with their gifts. It was frowned upon, these days. If a T'En's devotee died, he'd be weakened, and if the T'En died, the devotee died with him.

He didn't regret binding Valendia to him. She was the best thing that had ever happened to him. But with so many male gifts packed into a tight space, everyone was on edge. And with Valendia pregnant, his instinct was to let no one near her.

'I miss my pipes,' Valendia whispered. She wasn't asleep after all. 'Would the brotherhood have a spare zither or set of pipes?'

'I can ask.'

The curtain-blanket swung back and Graelen sprang to his feet, going for his knives, his gift rising in response.

The brotherhood's saw-bones lifted his hands palm-up and Graelen sheathed his knives.

'Fast as ever, Grae,' Ceyne whispered and reached out to him. 'My... but it's good to see you.'

And Graelen found himself pulled into an embrace, cheek to cheek. The hug lasted for only two heartbeats yet, in that time, the saw-bones could have tried to create an illusion or plant a compulsion.

But Graelen's mental shields were strong and the saw-bones had made himself just as vulnerable with the embrace. It was an intimacy Graelen had not shared with another T'En man since Paryx had died. Back then, they'd been young initiates together, at sea in the dangerous waters of the brotherhood.

Now he was at sea again, in the waters of exile, with Valendia to protect.

'Let me look at you, lad.' The saw-bones pulled away, tears glistening in his eyes. 'We believed you dead. When they said you'd come back...' He shook his head. 'You look well, remarkably well, considering you've spent a year underground in the crypts.'

'Thanks to Dia.' Graelen helped Valendia rise. 'She's the only reason I'm still alive.'

Valendia smiled with the open friendliness of someone who had never known brotherhood politics, someone who had a good heart. Graelen was terrified for her. Since arriving last night, he'd discovered their brotherhood's leader was more paranoid than ever.

'A devotee, Grae?' Ceyne looked concerned.

'She carries my child.'

'I think I should examine her.'

'I'm fine,' Valendia said. 'As soon as I find something to make music with, I'll be happy.'

Graelen took her arm and Ceyne led them out of the adepts' cabin, picking their way through sleeping bodies, down the passage and into the ship's infirmary. Already there were several patients, those who had been injured in the mad scramble to escape the wharf.

The saw-bones led them through to the bathing chamber, bolted the door and turned to Graelen, speaking in an intense whisper. 'You haven't been locked away in a crypt this last year. You've been somewhere safe. Why did you come back, Grae?'

'I had no choice. King Charald threatened to execute any of our kind who remained behind after winter's cusp. It's not like we can hide amongst them.'

'But with a devotee? Kyredeon will hold her life as surety of your cooperation.'

Valendia took Graelen's arm. 'What going on?'

'Yes, what is going on, Ceyne? I've already reported to Kyredeon and he believes I was locked up for the past year.'

'I've heard the story you spun the all-father. I want to know what happened to Kithkarne.' Ceyne named the old tithe-master, whom Graelen had escorted to collect on the king's debt. 'Last message Kith sent, he claimed the Mieren king was about to negotiate payment.'

'The king never intended to pay off his debt to our brotherhood. In fact, that debt is what prompted King Charald to attack our people,' Graelen said. 'The king kept putting Kithkarne off. When Charald finally agreed to see us, we were drugged. I came round locked up in the crypts. Later, I overheard the priests talking. Kithkarne took five of the enemy with him when he died.'

'Kith...' Ceyne shook his head. He cleared his throat. 'So you escaped with Dia and hid?'

'For a year in the mountains, in a deserted retreat.' Graelen drew Valendia close to kiss her forehead. 'It was the best year of my life.'

She smiled fondly, but she was no fool. 'Grae, you told me the brotherhood leader protected his people.'

'In theory, yes,' Ceyne answered for him. 'But Kyredeon protects his position and he faces a real threat to his leadership.'

'Who from?' Graelen asked.

'You won't know them. Tobazim is a young adept, who spent his initiate years living at a winery. He arrived in the city just before it fell with a core of followers he'd rescued when the winery was attacked. The other is Ardonyx. He's the captain of this ship, and he belonged to All-father Chariode's brotherhood.'

Graelen nodded. 'I heard Kyredeon saved Chariode's people the night the king attacked our city.'

Ceyne looked grim. 'Kyredeon delayed going to the other all-father's aid until it was almost too late. That we saved any Malaunje women and children was down to Tobazim's quick thinking.'

'I see.'

Ceyne nodded. 'Ardonyx was on a voyage of discovery when King Charald attacked. When he returned, Kyredeon accepted him because of his knowledge of the sea. The first thing Ardonyx did was ally himself with Tobazim. They volunteered for the exile-council. They were first to arrive in port. They coordinated operations at the wharf and, last night, they saved the causare, the healer and two T'En children. The causare gift-infused them, by way of thanks.'

'She gift-infused them?'

Ceyne nodded. 'Singled them out for the honour.'

Graelen sat down on the edge of the marble tub.

'What's wrong?' Valendia asked. 'They sound like good men.'

'They *are* good men. That's the problem,' Ceyne said. 'Through their actions, Tobazim and Ardonyx have gained so much stature they could mount a challenge for leadership of our brotherhood. And Grae is Kyredeon's best assassin.'

She laughed. 'But he's not like that. He's changed.'

'You haven't told her?'

She turned to Graelen. 'Told me what?'

'The brotherhood is ruled by force, Dia.' Graelen felt the cold, dead part of him rise again. 'And I'm the knife that kills in the dark.'

She shook her head, taking his face in her hands. 'You don't have to be that person. I know your heart. You're honest, good and true, Grae.'

And when he looked into her eyes, Graelen saw that man.

'Unfortunately, those are not the right qualities to survive in Kyredeon's brotherhood,' Ceyne said.

TOBAZIM FELT WONDERFUL.

He couldn't understand why the others were worried. A warm glow filled his body, and his mind was amazingly sharp. He could hear with incredible acuity. Like now – he could hear them whispering about him.

'Should we take him to the saw-bones?' That was Athlyn, and this was reason enough for him to rejoice. It meant the young initiate had escaped the wharf last night, after Tobazim lost track of him in the mad scramble to evade the Mieren assault.

Although Athlyn was eighteen now and had been with the brotherhood for almost a year, Tobazim felt responsible for him. He'd collected Athlyn from the sisterhood where the lad had been raised, brought him to the brotherhood, saved his life when the winery was attacked and watched over him this last turbulent year.

'Can we trust the saw-bones when Tobazim is vulnerable?' That was Haromyr. Loyal, eager Haromyr. If Tobazim wasn't careful, Haromyr would get himself killed defending their group. 'I know he's been good to us in the past, but Ceyne is on the all-father's inner circle and...' And All-father Kyredeon hated Tobazim.

'Maybe we should ask Ardonyx?' Eryx was more of a diplomat. 'Although he's probably sleeping. The captain stood vigil over Tobazim all night to protect him from the vengeful shades of those they killed.'

'The captain's on deck and will be for a while yet.' Ionnyn was part of Ardonyx's original crew and fiercely loyal to him. Tobazim's gift surged and he saw the brotherhood as a building, constructed of people with different alliances and strengths. His gift was the ability to sense the weights and stresses involved in construction, and it had never expressed itself this way before, nor so clearly. In this moment of revelation, he truly understood the rivalry between Ionnyn and Haromyr; if put under the wrong sort of pressure, it could fracture the group.

'That's just it,' Athlyn said. 'The causare gift-infused Ardonyx too, but he isn't lying in a stupor unable to move. Something's wrong. I really think we should get the saw-bones.'

'If it's a gift problem, we should get the gift-tutor,' Eryx said.

'We should get both of them,' Haromyr said. 'Maric, go fetch them.'

'Right away.' The Malaunje, who had fought alongside them as they escaped from the wharf last night, left the cabin.

There was silence, except for the creak of the ship. Tobazim felt the rise and fall of the deck and realised they were at sea. He knew this was significant, but nothing seemed to matter. He floated in a timeless moment of golden beauty. Visions came to him of buildings: domes soaring high above, lit by shafts of sunlight, bridges suspended over incredible spans... He never wanted to surface.

'I'd heard the causare had gift-infused them both last night, but he still reeks of female power.' It was Ceyne, the saw-bones, yet it felt like no time had passed. Tobazim liked and respected Ceyne, up to a point. He didn't understand how the saw-bones could serve an all-father like Kyredeon.

'Reeks?' Athlyn repeated. 'To me it seems rich and exotic.'

'Of course it does. There's nothing sweeter to us than female gift power. But this is dawn, and he hasn't assimilated her power. It's riding him.'

'That's bad?' Haromyr asked.

'Power is dangerous.' Ceyne's firm hands turned Tobazim's face towards him. The saw-bones gasped. 'That head wound... Why didn't you bring him straight to me last night?'

'You were dealing with life-threatening injuries, and the wound had stopped bleeding,' Maric said. Tobazim felt Ceyne's fingers on his head. He remembered the blow that had sent him to his knees, but he didn't feel any pain.

'I cleaned it,' Maric said. 'Ardonyx told me he was drunk on the causare's power and he'd sleep it off, but he hasn't woken.'

Someone bustled into the cabin. 'Now, what's so urgent you drag an old man from his bed?'

'Deimosh.' Ceyne greeted the brotherhood's gift-tutor. 'Tobazim hasn't come round since the gift-infusion.'

'He was gift-infused when he had a head wound?' Deimosh sounded indignant. 'Why didn't Reoden heal him? She healed the others.'

'He told her he was fine,' Maric said. 'He sent her to heal Ardonyx, then myself. While she was healing me, the causare gift-infused him.'

'Why, what's wrong with gift-infusing someone when they have a head wound?' Haromyr asked.

'Did he complain of double vision?' Ceyne asked. 'Confusion or nausea?'

'He didn't complain at all,' Maric said.

'He wouldn't,' Ceyne muttered.

'What's the problem?' Haromyr asked.

'From the looks of the swelling, he had concussion,' Ceyne said. 'Then the causare bombarded him with power while his gift defences were down.'

'So she's what, made a devotee of him?' Haromyr asked..

'No...' Ceyne sounded hesitant. 'Deimosh?'

'I've never come across anything like this. Each person's gift is individual, and how they interact differs depending on the circumstances. We won't know what she's done until he wakes up.'

'She was honouring him, not injuring him,' Haromyr protested.

The brotherhood elders did not answer.

'Can't you do something?'

'We can try siphoning off some of her power,' Deimosh said.

'I don't have that skill,' Ceyne said. 'You'll have to do it, Deimosh.'

Tobazim felt hands cup his face and the glow drained away. He didn't want it to go. It left an emptiness that went bone deep.

Tobazim tried to push Deimosh's hands away before the gift-tutor could steal... no, it wasn't stealing. They were helping him. It still felt like theft.

'He's coming round!' Haromyr sounded relieved.

'Can you hear me, lad?' Ceyne asked.

Tobazim thrust Deimosh aside and sat up, head reeling. They knelt around him. 'Where is everyone?'

'Out on deck to see us sail through the headlands,' Haromyr answered, then turned to the two brotherhood elders. 'He seems fine.'

Ceyne peered into Tobazim's face. Checked his eyes and asked, 'Can you tell me how many fingers I'm holding up?'

'Two.' He felt unreasonably angry with them.

'Any nausea, dizziness, confusion?'

Tobazim shook his head then winced. 'But everything hurts.'

'And so it should. You fought a rearguard action to escape the wharf last night. Only just got away with your lives. Do you remember the causare gift-infusing you?'

'Of course.'

'Do you feel any side-effects?'

'No. I'm fine.'

'He's back to normal,' Haromyr said, and the others relaxed.

But he wasn't. Tobazim felt as if he'd been robbed. Robbed of his wits by the power of the gift-infusion and then robbed again, when the gift-tutor siphoned it off. Not that he admitted as much; he couldn't reveal weakness.

'You were swamped by female gift power when your defences were down. We don't know what it will do,' Deimosh said. His cheeks were flushed and his eyes glowed with an inner light. The causare's power had done him good. 'If your gift starts behaving strangely, let me know.'

Tobazim nodded, determined to keep his own counsel. For all he knew, Deimosh would run straight back to the all-father to report.

Ceyne put a hand on his shoulder. 'Have something to eat, lad. Then walk about the deck to clear your head. The causare is about to hand over the prince.'

Chapter Two

ARAVELLE PRODDED HIM. 'Wake up, Ronnyn.'

He was warm and he could feel his six-year-old brother, Vittor, sleeping next to him. For a moment, Ronnyn thought he was in their loft bedroom at home. Then it all came back to him. Their cottage had been burned to the ground when the fisher-folk kidnapped his family and delivered them to be exiled along with the rest of their people.

He sat up, heart racing. From the ship's movement, they were underway, but not through the headlands yet. Vittor slept on one side of him and his baby sister, Itania, slept on the other. 'Where's Tam? Is he –'

'Tamaron's fine. At least, I think he is. I haven't seen him since they took him into All-mother Reoden's cabin. Sorry, I didn't mean to scare you,' Aravelle whispered. She was a year and a bit older than him and a half-blood whereas he was T'En, but she was the centre of his world, always had been. 'I just heard them say King Charald is coming to collect the prince. You should go out on deck and see what you can learn.'

He rubbed his eyes. There were others sleeping in the cabin, curled up on bedrolls. He'd gathered they were the remnants of a sisterhood. When the healer collapsed last night, after attending to their little brother, the sisterhood had bundled his family in here and ignored him. 'I heard a newborn crying.'

'I heard him, too. It has to be baby Ashmyr.' Aravelle's mulberry eyes darkened with grief. Neither of them mentioned their mother, who the healer hadn't been able to save. 'Go out on deck, see what you can learn. Look for Sorne.'

Ronnyn nodded. Even though they'd only met the half-blood yesterday, he'd risked his life to save Tamaron.

'If they bring food while you're on deck, I'll save you some,' Aravelle said.

He ducked into the bathing chamber. Hot and cold water, marble tub, silver fittings – he'd never seen anything like it. Hearing his mother's stories of the richness of T'En culture had not prepared him for the real thing.

He relieved himself, then adjusted the loin cloth, made from a strip of his nightshirt. That reminded him of their mother giving birth in the back of a caged-cart. Her last words had been *never forget your Malaunje kin*. Tears stung his eyes. As if he would ever forget Itania and Aravelle.

He needed to strip and wash, but he had no other clothes and no time; he should be out on deck. First he returned to the cabin to find Aravelle sitting guard over their little brother and sister. He was so proud of her, after everything they'd been through. 'I'll need a blanket. It's cold out.'

She nodded and passed him her blanket. He wore it like a cloak as he followed the passage to the mid-deck. The icy planks burned his bare feet.

His father had sailed a small, one-masted fishing vessel: he was familiar with the sea, but his father's boat had been nothing like this seven-masted ship. Shafts of dawn sunlight gilded the segmented sails so that they gleamed like dragonfly wings. There was a high foredeck tucked into the blunt-nosed prow, with cabins where the healer's sisterhood had taken shelter, and across the stern were two rows of cabins. The lower cabins opened off the mid-deck. Steps led up to the lower-rear deck, with a second floor of cabins, and more steps led to the high rear-deck.

Everything was of the finest quality, from the bathing chambers to the cabins with their glass-fronted cabinets and gold-embossed woodwork. He had never seen anything so beautiful, or so frivolous.

Back home, his family had lived in a one-room cottage made of driftwood but they'd lived free of brotherhood interference. His half-blood parents had run away so they could keep him, their first T'En child, and they'd always feared their brotherhood would find them. In the end it was the fisher-folk who...

'Here's the prince, causare.'

Ronnyn turned to see the healer's hand-of-force deliver young Prince Cedon to Causare Imoshen.

The causare smiled and dropped to her knees. 'Show me how you can stand on tip toes, Cedon.'

The small boy balanced on his toes, holding onto her hands. Ronnyn remembered whispered conversations overheard in the cabin last night. People had been indignant; the wharf shouldn't have been attacked, not when they held Prince Cedon as a hostage and certainly not when All-mother Reoden had healed his club foot in return for safe passage to the sea.

Ronnyn looked for Sorne, but couldn't spot him. There was a big T'En woman nearby, who wore the neck torc of a sisterhood voice-of-reason. The gift-warrior who'd brought Prince Cedon onto the deck stood beside her. Ronnyn crept closer until he could overhear what they were saying.

'...king was not behind the attack, Baron Eskarnor was.' The big T'En woman sounded grim. 'Unfortunately, our people have become caught up in a struggle for the Chalcedonian throne.'

'I can run and jump, too,' Cedon announced and proved it by jumping so vigorously he almost toppled over.

Imoshen steadied him with a laugh. 'Keep up your exercises, and every time you do them, think of us. You need to wear your boot to ensure your foot grows straight and strong. Wear it until you grow out of –'

'Where's Ree-ma?' Cedon asked.

'All-mother Reoden is sleeping,' Imoshen said. 'Remember how the bad man tried to swap the other little boy for you?'

Prince Cedon nodded and Ronnyn flinched. The 'other little boy' was his brother Tamaron. Baron Eskarnor had used the attack on the wharf as a diversion, to slip aboard the flagship and take Ronnyn's little brother hostage. He'd tried to exchange Tamaron for the prince. When he realised the Wyrds weren't going to hand over the prince, he'd cut Tamaron's throat and leapt overboard.

And Ronnyn had been helpless to stop him. His hands closed in fists, making his crippled arm spasm in pain.

'The bad man hurt the other little boy,' Imoshen said. 'Ree-ma had to drain her gift to save his life. She'll be all right, but she's worn out for now.'

Cedon's chin trembled. 'Wants my Ree-ma.'

'I know, but' – Imoshen took his hands in hers – 'your father loves you, Cedon. He needs you to grow up big and strong to become the next king – King Cedon the Kind. Remember what we told you?'

He nodded. 'The greater the king, the greater his service to his people.'

'Good boy. I hope one day you'll understand what it means. To lead is to serve.' She kissed his forehead. 'Now, go back to your people.'

She helped him into the sling, which rose up and swung across to the deck of the lower vessel. Ronnyn went to the side to watch. The prince climbed out, then stood uncertainly. An elaborately-dressed elderly man inspected him, made him jump and walk, then hugged him with every sign of joy.

Ronnyn watched, thinking, *so this is the king who broke the three hundred years' truce, captured the Celestial City and exiled us.*

Not far from the king stood a white-haired man. When he turned around to look up, Ronnyn recognised Sorne. What was the half-blood doing down there? He should be sailing with the T'Enatuath.

At first, Ronnyn had been wary of Sorne, with his white hair and missing eye. But as soon as Sorne learnt their mother had just given birth and needed help, he had taken them to the T'En healer. When the wharf was attacked, he'd saved Ronnyn's brothers and sisters. And when Baron Eskarnor grabbed Ronnyn's little brother, Sorne had removed his sword belt and offered himself in Tamaron's place.

Since the fisher-folk kidnapped his family, Ronnyn had felt adrift, lost in a world that made no sense. In Sorne, he'd found someone he could trust.

Now Ronnyn watched Sorne nod to Causare Imoshen. She acknowledged him with a single nod. It was as if they sealed a pact, and Ronnyn realised Sorne might be a half-blood, but he was much more than he appeared. And he was not coming with them.

As the two vessels pulled apart, Ronnyn felt cast adrift. The T'Enatuath were his people, but he didn't know them. If his parents hadn't run away, he would never have known them, or his half-blood sisters. He would have been handed over to a T'En sisterhood, which would have reared him until he was seventeen.

Right now, he needed to make sure Tamaron was all right. He would be frightened without his family by his side. They were all he had ever known.

Last night, the causare had been kind to Ronnyn. Now he tried to approach her, but the big voice-of-reason stepped between them.

'Don't bother the causare. She's been up all night.'

'But I –'

'But nothing. You're the son of runaway Malaunje. She's the leader of our people.' The woman frowned down at him. 'Do you know which brotherhood or sisterhood your parents ran away from?'

He'd heard his mother mention Scholar Hueryx, but he didn't know which brotherhood the scholar belonged to. If the T'En women knew his family had served a brotherhood, they'd send his Malaunje sisters to serve them. 'I don't –'

'How old are you, boy?'

'Twelve, thirteen in the spring.' Back home, he'd done the work of a man. Here he felt like a lost child, and he hated it.

'Go back to your cabin, Ronnyn.'

But he didn't. Instead, he followed the newborn's cries down the passage and peered into All-mother Reoden's cabin. He spotted baby Ashmyr being bathed and clucked over by several T'En women. There were half a dozen small T'En children, all dressed alike in breeches, vests and robes, and several Malaunje servants. He couldn't spot Tamaron, so he pushed the door open a little further.

Strong hands reached for him, dragged him in and threw him up against the wall. 'What're you doing?'

A wave of female gift power swept over him. On instinct, he summoned his defences. The sisterhood's hand-of-force glared down at him from her one good eye, making him wonder why Healer Reoden hadn't saved her other eye.

'Ronnyn!' Four-year-old Tamaron tried to force himself in between them and shove the gift-warrior away.

'He's just a boy. Let him go, Cerafeoni.' One of the women came over. Ronnyn recognised the sisterhood's voice-of-reason, Nerazime. 'He's Tamaron's older brother. They're the children of runaway free Malaunje and don't know any better.'

'Bring him to me,' Healer Reoden said. She was propped in the bunk under the windows, supported by pillows.

The one-eyed warrior seized Ronnyn's arm and escorted him across the chamber. She took such long strides he lost his blanket and by the time he stood before the all-mother he wore nothing but his loin cloth.

'Look at the state of him,' one of the old women whispered. 'Filthy and bruised.'

'It's hardly his fault. They were taken from their home, locked in a cart and transported across Chalcedonia,' Healer Reoden said. 'If anything, the fault is ours for not seeing to his needs.'

Meanwhile, Tamaron caught up with Ronnyn and wrapped his arms around him. Ronnyn hardly recognised his little brother. He'd been bathed and dressed in a miniature version of what the adults wore.

Someone passed the crying newborn to the healer, who opened her bodice. Baby Ashmyr suckled, then cried when nothing was forthcoming.

'Nerazime,' Healer Reoden said.

Ronnyn expected her to fetch a wet-nurse, but the voice-of-reason came over to sit beside the healer.

'Surely it's too soon,' the voice-of-reason said. 'You've barely recovered.'

All-mother Reoden took Nerazime's hand, closed her eyes and concentrated. Ronnyn sensed her gift stir. It made his hearing sharper, colours richer. 'What –'

'Silence,' the hand-of-force snapped. 'Nerazime is sharing power with the healer.'

After a moment, baby Ashmyr stopped crying and started sucking in earnest.

'There...' The healer sighed with relief and kissed Nerazime's cheek. 'Thank you.' Then Reoden lifted her gaze to Ronnyn. 'So you came to check on your brothers?'

He almost asked her forgiveness for ever doubting her, but... 'They are my responsibility.'

Nerazime muttered.

'Leave us,' the healer said.

When Nerazime joined the other women feeding the children, All-mother Reoden patted the bunk near her.

But Ronnyn shook his head. 'I'm filthy.'

Tamaron climbed up next to the healer and wrapped his arms around her. This struck Ronnyn as disloyal to their mother, but Reoden had almost killed herself to save his brother's life.

'I'm sorry I could not save your mother,' Reoden said.

Tears stung his eyes.

'She was worn down with deprivation, then exhausted by the birth. She'd lost so much blood. And then...' The healer rubbed Tamaron's back. 'When they call the all-council, I'll accept you and your brothers as my choice-sons. I'll accept your sisters into my sisterhood's Malaunje. There will be no stigma attached to your birth. It's not your fault that your parents ran away from us. Now, go ask Nerazime for clean clothes, then bring your other brother to me.'

And then they would be separated from Aravelle and Itania. But he wouldn't put up with it. He'd sneak away to see his sisters and he'd make sure his brothers didn't forget their Malaunje kin. He would never abandon them.

ARAVELLE'S HEART SANK when Ronnyn returned. He had been bathed, his hair washed and braided, and he was dressed in fine clothes. She couldn't meet his eyes. He didn't look like her brother any more; she'd lost him to the T'En.

'I saw Healer Reoden. Everything's going to be all right. She's going to take us all in.'

Aravelle looked down and broke the bread in her hands. 'I saved you some.'

'You eat it. I ate with the T'En sisters.'

She forced herself to take a mouthful.

'Even though we're the children of runaway Malaunje, the healer said... Vella?' His forehead crinkled earnestly. 'Why are you crying, Vella?'

'I'm not.' Angry with herself, she brushed the tears away. 'Don't you see? If we become sisterhood Malaunje, once you turn seventeen, you'll join your brotherhood and I'll never see you again.'

Itania climbed into Aravelle's lap and tried to console her. Aravelle hugged the two-year-old and kissed her red-gold curls. They were both Malaunje; it hadn't mattered back home, but here...

'I don't understand.' Ronnyn frowned. 'If we admit we came from a brotherhood, they'll send you two to the brotherhood right now and you won't see baby Ashmyr grow up. This is the best we can hope for.'

It was true. She summoned a smile. 'At least we'll have this time together, and we'll be safe from the Mieren.'

'That's right.' Ronnyn rose and held out his hand to Vittor. 'Come with me. You need to get dressed.'

'What about Vella and Tani?' the six-year-old asked. They'd never been separated.

Ronnyn looked to Aravelle to explain. She had to harden her heart and be strong. 'Go with Ronnyn, Vittor. We'll be fine.'

He was a good boy and did what he was told.

This left her and Itania alone with the survivors of a sisterhood, but at least they were together. Aravelle hugged her little sister who played with their father's cane. He'd carved it after the sea-boar gored his leg, and it was the only thing they had from their previous life.

Soon the ship were beyond the headlands; the deck rose and fell as it ploughed through the waves. Soon there was moaning and then nearly everyone became seasick.

Except for Aravelle. She was used to their family's fishing boat.

A Malaunje woman arrived with mint tea to help settle people's stomachs, and another came in looking for Aravelle.

They were led downstairs to the Malaunje deck, which was overcrowded and chaotic. There Aravelle was introduced to a harassed woman, who shoved a change of clothes in her hands and told her to bathe herself and her sister. Then she spent the next few days cleaning up vomit, until people become accustomed to the pitch and yaw of the deck.

To think she had secretly wished to return to the city so her life wouldn't be filled with drudgery.

Chapter Three

AS HE RODE up from the docks towards the palace, Sorne made sure the people had a clear view of the young prince and future king. The boy didn't know it, but Sorne was his half-brother, the king's eldest, unwanted half-blood son.

'Where's Ma?' Cedon asked, as he rode in Sorne's arms. He'd overcome his lisp and his club foot had been healed by the Wyrds, but he had not forgotten his mother.

'Queen Jaraile wanted to be here, but the bad man took her,' Sorne said, wishing he'd anticipated Eskarnor. The southern baron had outwitted him and that stung. But he'd been focused on coordinating the Wyrd exile and finding his half-blood sister at the time. At least Valendia was safe with Graelen.

On Sorne's right rode King Charald, High King of the Secluded Sea. With one hand on the reins and the other on his sword hilt, you could not spot the trembling that had afflicted him this last year. It had been two days since the seizure that had given everyone such a fright.

As they made their way through the streets, the people cheered their king and prince.

Charald had come to the throne at fifteen, and he was now fifty-seven. In just over forty years he'd made Chalcedonia the most powerful kingdom of the Secluded Sea, and he'd banished the Wyrds. He was a legend in his own time.

He was also a bully, distrustful of everyone and only good for making war.

But King Charald the Great was failing.

When his piss turned the colour of port-wine, he lost his hold on reality. That left Baron Nitzane, who rode on Sorne's left, to hold the kingdom for the young prince. Nitzane was the grandson of the man who'd helped Charald hold the throne at fifteen, and he was the wealthiest, most powerful baron in the kingdom. He was also in love with Queen Jaraile, but Charald did not need to fear him because he was a good man.

Unfortunately, a good man was not what the country needed right now. It needed a great leader, and they did not have one.

Which was why Baron Eskarnor had dared to make a play for the throne. First he had tried to kill the prince to trigger a war between the king and Nitzane, whose son was the next in line for the throne; when this failed, he'd snatched the queen.

The people did not know that their queen had been abducted. They did not know that the kingdom was about to be split by civil war.

Even King Charald did not know. Sorne had advised Nitzane not to tell Charald until after they'd collected the prince, because he feared the king's rage would unhinge his mind.

'Why did the bad man take Ma?' Cedon asked.

To legitimise his claim on the throne, which means he intends to kill you and your father. 'Because he wants to be king. Don't worry. I'll bring her back.' If it was humanly possible.

The little boy twisted to look up at him. 'Why do you have only one eye?'

Hubris. I stole power to gain visions and the respect of True-men, but it made them fear me and they turned on me. 'The Warrior god took my eye to prove I was his servant. He sent me to save your mother.'

The prince accepted this. King Charald believed the Warrior had returned Sorne to get rid of the Wyrds. But, knowing the way the king bent the facts to suit himself, he would probably accept that it was Sorne's task to recover the queen.

They'd crossed the royal plaza now, and entered the stables behind the palace. Sorne dismounted, reaching for Cedon. He swung the boy around, making him laugh, before depositing him on the ground. Unaware of the stable lads and servants watching him, Cedon clamoured for more, jumping up and down as if he'd never had a club foot.

'Look at him. At last I have a son who is fit to sit on the throne,' Charald said. The king took Prince Cedon's hand heading inside, and Sorne hid his contempt for the man who had murdered his mother and disowned him.

'I'm hungry.' The prince had to take little skipping steps to keep up with the king.

'Send for breakfast.' Charald strode into his favourite dining room and came to a stop. 'Where's my table?'

Nitzane glanced to Sorne. Eskarnor had kidnapped the queen from this very room, and carved his challenge into the mahogany table.

'A better one is being delivered, sire,' Sorne said.

'I'll eat on the balcony.' Charald stripped off his riding gloves and threw them on the sideboard. 'Send for the barons. They will bend their knee before Prince Cedon and see for themselves that he is fit to rule. They'll swear allegiance to my line and any who do not come will be declaring for Eskarnor. How dare he try to kill my son?'

Sorne glanced to the prince, who did not need to hear this. 'Sire, the boy needs –'

'The boy needs his mother.' Charald said.

Baron Nitzane sent Sorne a worried look. For as long as Sorne could remember, the king's barons and advisors had been tip-toeing around his rages. Now there was the added fear of unhinging his mind.

'Where is the queen?' Charald demanded. 'Send for Jaraile.'

'The bad man took Ma,' Cedon said, his voice high and clear.

'What?' Charald rounded on Sorne. 'What haven't you told me?'

Sorne ignored the king and took Cedon's hand. 'Go with Uncle Nitzane. He'll make sure you get some breakfast.'

The baron was only too happy to escape what they both knew was coming.

Sorne closed the door on them. 'Sire –'

'Eskarnor took her, didn't he? Couldn't undermine me, couldn't kill my son, so he took the queen.' Charald threw back his head and laughed. Today he reminded Sorne of the king who'd conquered the kingdoms of the Secluded Sea. 'More fool he. She's worthless now that I have an able-bodied heir. In fact, if Eskarnor kills Jaraile, he'll be doing me a favour. She's popular with the people. If he kills her, they'll hate him.'

Sorne blinked. He'd known the king was ruthless, but this was abhorrent, even for him.

'A pox on Eskarnor and his treasonous southern barons.' The king paced, cursing the cunning mercenaries and turn-coat nobles who'd worked their way up to lead companies of men while serving him on the Secluded Sea campaign. 'That's the problem with war barons. They're handy in battle, but greedy in peace time. I rewarded them with Chalcedonian estates. Was that enough? No, they had to covet my throne and plot to crown one of their own king in my place.' Charald rounded on Sorne. 'When is enough enough, for an ambitious man?'

This, coming from the man who had invaded the five mainland kingdoms of the Secluded Sea to make himself high king. Sorne did not know what to say.

'You're lucky you have no ambition,' Charald told him. 'It makes food taste like ash. Nothing is ever good enough.' He sighed and dropped into a chair. 'Growing old is a pain. Everything aches. My back and my stomach...'

'Wine, sire?'

When Charald nodded, Sorne put his back to the king to pour a cup of wine and slip in a soothing powder from Khitan. He'd been doing this for years, whenever the king's rages became too bad. Now he did it for the pain. Not that

Charald knew. He despised anyone who sought pain relief.

The king accepted the wine and tossed it back in one gulp. He rubbed his face and rubbed the small of his back. After a moment he looked up. 'Where's Nitzane? Where's Jaraile? Have you heard back from the Wyrds yet? I want my son back. When they return him, I'll ride through town with him. I'll call the barons in and have them swear allegiance. I know! I'll have a big feast this mid-winter. Is it winter's cusp yet?'

'Soon,' Sorne said, wondering if he should explain all over again.

The king grimaced and shifted his weight on the seat. 'Once, I could spend all day in the saddle, drink half the night away and fuck three women in a row. Now...' Charald looked around the dining room. 'Where's my table?'

'Would you like to lie down, sire?'

Charald shook his head, then reconsidered. 'Yes. Just for a short while. Then I'll be up to riding around the plaza with Eskarnor and Nitzane this afternoon. Have to let the people know I'm still fit and sharp as ever. Send for Jaraile. She can read to me. I used to think it was a waste, teaching the barons' daughters to read, but she has a sweet voice. Always soothes me to sleep.'

Sorne took the king's arm, guiding him to his chamber, where the king's faithful manservant settled him into the chair by the fire and ordered food.

As he did this, Sorne noticed several papers on the sideboard. Wasn't that... Yes. It was the decree he'd drafted on the king's orders, giving four trusted men and the queen authority to rule Chalcedonia and guide Prince Cedon until he became a man. Jaraile had been trying to get the king to sign it, but when he felt well, he refused to discuss it and when he was unwell, he was irrational.

Sorne picked up the agreement and slid it inside his vest, just as the manservant returned and walked him to the door.

'The king was in pain, so I gave him a soothing powder,' Sorne said softly. For a while there, after he told the manservant not to dose him with the arsenic medicine, it had seemed as if the king would rally. But today... 'He was talking strategy one moment, then forgetful the next. We need to keep everyone away from him, Bidern.'

'I fear the news is out,' the manservant said. 'There were already rumours, and too many servants saw him have that seizure.'

Sorne nodded, convinced that what he was about to do was justified.

He went to the king's study, selected a pen and ink and prepared to forge the king's signature. He'd been watching the king sign decrees since he was seventeen. While growing up in the retreat, he'd trained as a scribe and to illuminate manuscripts.

Now he practised several times until he had the right look for the signature of King Charald the Seventh. He made the lettering slightly shaky, as the tremor in the king's hands had changed his signature.

Then he cleaned the pen nib, burned the practice signatures and left the decree on the desk, amidst the papers.

He went to the nursery where he found Nitzane breakfasting with the prince.

'Cedon reminds me of my boy,' Nitzane said. 'They'll both be four in the spring. I should bring Martzane back to court so they can grow up as brothers.'

Sorne drew Nitzane aside. 'I don't think we should leave the prince in the palace. He was taken from this very chamber, and last night the queen –'

'Sweet little Jaraile...' Nitzane swallowed. 'I hate to think of her in Eskarnor's hands. I want to ride north for his estate. I have Captain Ballendin and fifty good men. I can call in at two of my estates on the road north and collect reinforcements.'

Sorne was not so sure Eskarnor had retreated to his estate. 'It's less than ten days since the Wyrds left the Celestial City. I wouldn't be surprised if –'

'Eskarnor's supporters will be at the city. You're right. This is the perfect opportunity to strike at him, while he's separated from the southern barons. I'll pack and leave right now.'

Sorne caught the baron's arm. 'To secure the throne, Eskarnor must kill Prince Cedon. I'm going to hide him. Then I'll go to the Wyrd city and summon the Chalcedonian barons in the king's name.'

Nitzane nodded. 'If Eskarnor has retreated to his estate, I can keep him separated from his supporters and pinned there. It won't be long before he surrenders. By the time you return, I'll have Eskarnor's head for the gate spikes.'

Sorne was not so sure, but he trusted Captain Ballendin to guide the baron.

As Nitzane left, Sorne watched Prince Cedon with an elderly woman. The prince's wet-nurse had died the day he was abducted. This was... 'I know your face.'

'I'm Zurina, the queen's maid. You could take the prince to Baron Kerminzto's estate,' she said, proving she was old, but there was nothing wrong with her hearing. 'His kinsman would protect him.'

'It's the first place his enemies would look.' Sorne had been toying with the idea of taking the boy south to Shifting-sands Bay. One of Nitzane's strongholds overlooked the bay, and he had given permission for the Wyrd fleet to shelter there until winter's cusp, when they were to be exiled. Sorne knew Causare Imoshen would hide the prince and protect him. This plan had the novelty of being unexpected, but it would take several days to ride there and he had pressing duties.

'You could hide him on one of Baron Nitzane's estates,' Zurina suggested.

'Also too obvious.' Port Mirror-on-Sea would be ideal. It was walled and would be on alert, and the palace was protected by the king's guard, but it was impossible to protect someone from an assassin who was ready to sacrifice his own life to kill the target. They needed somewhere close by, but... Sorne had an idea. 'Are you willing to go into hiding with him?'

'Of course. I was nurse-maid to his grandfather and his mother. Poor girl.'

'Then pack your bags and Cedon's, and tell no one of our plans.'

'How can I, when I don't know our plans?'

He grinned. 'I'll be back soon.'

Sorne went to Halargon, commander of the king's palace guard, to share his plan for the prince's safety. The commander was one of the five advisors King Charald had approved to guide his son.

First, Sorne had the commander send word to all the Wyrd estates on Imoshen's list, telling them to travel to Shifting-sands Bay as soon as possible, to join the Wyrd fleet there instead of Port Mirror-on-Sea.

Then Sorne asked for an escort of twelve king's guards for the journey to the Wyrd city. It was a small enough party to travel swiftly, but large enough to deter casual brigands.

'If you can collect the Chalcedonian barons and their men and bring them back here, the port will be defensible,' Commander Halargon said, then grimaced. 'I never liked Eskarnor and the other southern barons. Mercenaries and turn-coats. Men like that have no real loyalty. When Charald returned, I advised him to give them estates far to the north. I thought, with their thin southern blood, the cold would dampen their ambition. I was wrong. It only made them greedier.'

Sorne nodded. Should the baron evade Nitzane, he wasn't going to sit still and let Baron Eskarnor ravage Chalcedonia. Eight years serving King Charald during the Secluded Sea campaign had taught him you took the fight to the enemy, you moved fast and you had to be ready to change your plans at a moment's notice.

'The king is worse today. I fear his lucid periods are growing shorter, and even when he is lucid, he doesn't remember what was said only moments before,' Sorne said. 'Someone needs to go through his study and make sure everything is in order. I'd do it, but I must ride –'

'I'll see that it's done.'

'Best see to it yourself,' Sorne said. 'There could be sensitive documents.'

Halargon nodded.

Satisfied that the decree would be discovered and the government of the kingdom would not suffer, Sorne returned to the nursery, where he found the queen's nursemaid ready with a small bundle. Both she and the boy were hooded and cloaked. Sorne pulled up his own hood.

They slipped down through the back passages and stairs of the palace to one of the many servants' entrances, and out onto the royal plaza. Here they fell in with a party of worshippers visiting the seven churches around the plaza. It took a while – Cedon grew tired, and Sorne had to carry him – but eventually they entered the Father's church.

Once there, Sorne slipped away from the worshippers and entered the private corridors of the religious order. He'd been coming here for years to visit his family, who had been hidden in the secret apartment above the high priest's chambers, so he knew the quiet corridors and the times of prayer.

It was not until he reached High Priest Faryx's outer chamber that he met resistance: a handsome young pup who liked exercising authority.

'Do you have an appointment?'

Sorne flicked his wrist so the sleeve fell away to reveal the ruby worn by the last high priest. By rights he should have returned it, but it had proved useful on more than one occasion. 'Faryx will want to see me. Is he in his chamber?'

The assistant eyed the small boy in Sorne's arms and the elderly woman, then showed them through.

The plump high priest welcomed them to his private study and shut the door.

'You were ready to guide the prince until he came of age,' Sorne said. 'Are you ready to shelter him until his throne is secure, Faryx?' He pushed back the boy's hood. Secure in Sorne's arms, the prince had fallen asleep.

'We heard he'd been returned this very morning,' Faryx said softly. 'But won't the king –'

'The king is having one of his turns.'

'Surely, the queen –'

'Abducted from the palace last night by Baron Eskarnor.'

'Seven save us. I hadn't heard.'

'We're trying to keep it that way. It's up to Nitzane and myself to save her and secure the kingdom. I need to know the prince is safe.' Sorne glanced to the secret apartment above them. 'Is it –'

'Free? Yes.'

'Your assistant saw us come in. Do you trust him?'

'With my life.'

Sorne nodded. He found it strange going up the narrow stair to the secret apartment, which he expected to find empty as it had been the night of the riots when he'd hidden here. But it was fitted out for use, although the kitchen larder was empty. The plants in the raised garden beds on the sheltered balcony had been cut back for the winter.

Sorne did not ask what the high priest had been using the apartment for. While Faryx packed away personal items in the sitting room, Sorne took the boy into the bedroom tucked under the sloping roof.

'What is this place?' Zurina whispered.

'It has been many things over the years. My mother and sister lived her for eleven years, and they were good people. Now it is a safe haven for you and Cedon. I promise you one thing, you won't go hungry. The high priest appreciates good food. And Cedon can run and play on the balcony. Hopefully, you won't be here too long.'

He left the old nurse-maid to unpack and returned to Faryx. The high priest was just sending his assistant away with a basket of belongings.

'He'll return with food to stock the larder,' Faryx said.

'Good. I must ride this very day. I don't know when I'll be back.' Or even if he would survive the war that was coming. 'Can I ask one thing of you? If Eskarnor seizes the throne, he'll hunt the boy down and execute him. Take Cedon into the church, change his name and hide him here. He's young enough not to remember who he really is.'

The high priest nodded. 'Until he is ready to reclaim the throne.'

'No. Let him remain a priest.'

Faryx's eyes widened. 'You don't want him to be king?'

'Enough blood has been spilled and lives wasted in the pursuit of the crown. A king never knows if his friends are true or if the woman who professes to love him loves him for himself or his position.'

Faryx chuckled.

'What?'

'I never took you for a romantic.'

'Me? I am a realist.'

Faryx shook his head.

'Can I ask you something? Why is that you are not offended by my tainted blood? Most True-men find it hard to meet my eyes, let alone acknowledge me.'

The high priest shrugged. 'I think the silverheads are definitely a danger to us. But copperheads have no gift, none of the advantages and all of the disadvantages of their tainted blood. Tell me, do you intend to carry out more sacrifices to gain visions?'

'Not if I can help it. I've seen what lies on the higher plane...' Sorne shuddered. He knew True-men believed the creatures of the higher plane were gods, but in reality they were predators. 'I've been lucky to escape with my life. I don't want to tempt fate again.'

'Then you are no threat to True-men or the church.'

A little later Sorne rode out of Port Mirror-on-Sea with a dozen of the king's guard.

Chapter Four

IMOSHEN'S SHIP WAS about to follow the rest of the fleet through the tall sandstone headlands. Bathed a brilliant red-gold by the dawn sun, the headlands were a thing of beauty, but all she could think of at that moment was Sorne. She'd sent him back to save the last of their people from a kingdom torn by civil war.

Over near the foredeck cabin, Egrayne, her sisterhood's voice-of-reason, was speaking with one of the children who'd been delivered yesterday. Until they held an all-council meeting, the children could not be assigned to a sisterhood. But for now they were safe, sheltered and fed.

She was so tired, she could hardly think. They'd had to bring forward their exile; she'd spent the three days before they left the city madly scrambling to coordinate their departure. Then she'd travelled through rain and mud for eight days to reach the port, and last night she hadn't slept.

Her ship was packed with two sisterhoods – hers and the healer's – along with anyone who'd escaped the wharf during the attack. Despite the over-crowding, she could hear children laughing and Malaunje singing, and smell food cooking. Already she could feel the deck's rise and fall as they left the sheltered bay, and she suspected that soon everyone would be seasick. Then the overcrowding would only compound the problem.

Looking forward to her bunk, Imoshen stumbled up the steps to the rear-deck and went down the passage towards her cabin.

'Choice-mother?' Iraayel opened the door of the shared bathing chamber. At sixteen, her choice-son was half a head taller than her, and just the sight of him made her spirits lift.

'Iraayel.' She smiled, then frowned. 'Is Tancred causing problems?'

They were so cramped for space they'd had to put the big geldr in the same cabin with the lads aged thirteen to sixteen. Tancred would have been born male, but his mother had tried to influence his gender before birth and ruined him. Most days he had the awareness of a five-year-old child coupled with the strength of an adult.

'The lads tease him,' Iraayel admitted. 'But no, it's Dragazim. Somehow he found out how his choice-mother died, and...'

Imoshen's heart sank. The night before they left the city, the sisterhood's gift-tutor had gone down to the crypts below the palace and taken her own life and her devotee's.

Iraayel opened the door to reveal Saffazi trying to console a boy of thirteen who was in tears.

'It's not that she didn't love you,' the seventeen-year-old said. 'It's –'

'She didn't love me. She was always angry with me. She didn't care what happened to me, otherwise why would she kill herself and Ch... Choris?' His voice broke. 'Choris loved me. Now she's gone, too. I hate...' He broke off, seeing Imoshen.

She did not try to lie. 'Your choice-mother was a troubled woman, Dragazim.' Imoshen crossed the chamber and sat beside him on the edge of the marble tub. 'It wasn't that she didn't love you, more that she was afraid of what we would face in exile. Vittoryxe could not bear to leave the Celestial City. She believed the glory of our people was in the past. She didn't understand that exile is a great opportunity in disguise.'

As he blinked, a tear ran down his cheek and Imoshen's gift surged. She was a raedan, able to read people. The glory of the T'Enatuath was all very well, but what this boy needed now was a choice-mother who gave him hope.

She squeezed his shoulder. 'It's time to appoint a new choice-mother for you.' As she stood, she nodded to Iraayel, drawing both him and Saffazi to the door. 'You did well to alert me to his distress. Thank you.'

Then she hesitated. She could hardly take Dragazim into her cabin, it was full of the sisterhood's inner circle and the small T'En children. He would not want them to see he'd been crying. The bathing chamber was the only place they could be private. 'Wait here with him.'

Opening the door, Imoshen discovered Egrayne making her way to their cabin. She stepped into the passage, closing the door after her and lowered her voice. 'We need to appoint a new choice-mother for Dragazim.'

'Vittoryxe's boy?'

Imoshen nodded. 'He learned how she took her own life. Not only has she left us in the lurch with no trained gift-tutor, but she's left the boy without a choice-mother.'

'He's thirteen.'

Imoshen bristled. 'He deserves a choice-mother who will stand by him during his last four years with the sisterhood.'

'Who were you thinking?'

'It has to be someone of equal or higher stature than his original choice-mother, which only leaves the three sisterhood leaders.'

'I'm too old to take on another child,' Egrayne protested. 'And you're not only the all-mother but also causare.'

'It should be Kiane. He's about to begin his training to prepare him for brotherhood life under her guidance. The sisterhood's hand-of-force is –'

'Perfect. I'll fetch her.'

Imoshen returned to the bathing chamber. She glanced around, taking in the marble tiles and gold fittings. It was hardly the dome of empowerment or the sisterhood's formal ceremony chamber, but it would have to do.

'We have a new choice-mother for you,' Imoshen said.

'She won't want me.'

'Nonsense.' Egrayne bustled in with her devotee, who carried the lineage book, and Hand-of-force Kiane. 'You're thirteen,' she told Dragazim. 'Rather than wait until the next empowerment day, let's see if I can find your gift now.'

Dragazim looked up at the T'Enatuath's gift-empowerer with a mix of fear and excitement.

Imoshen gave him a smile of reassurance, then gestured to Kiane. 'And my hand-of-force is here because you'll need a new choice-mother to guide you and prepare you for the challenges of brotherhood life. Who better than Kiane?'

He flushed and dropped to his knees, giving the deep obeisance. 'I am honoured.'

'Very nicely done, Dragazim,' Imoshen said. 'Now rise and prepare for empowerment.'

When he came to his feet, his expression was sober, if slightly worried.

'Dragazim, formerly Choice-son Vittoryxe,' Imoshen said. 'The T'Enatuath's gift empowerer will reach into your mind to identify your nascent gift and quicken it. Do you agree to this?' As if he had a choice; she bristled on his behalf.

The boy nodded.

'Then thank her for this honour.'

He gave the formal obeisance and said the ritual words. Even though he clasped his hands, left over right, Imoshen could see his fingers trembling.

'Concentrate on me, Dragazim,' she urged, as Egrayne stepped around behind him, placing her fingers on his temples.

A shiver ran through his skinny fame.

'I have been doing this for thirty years, child,' Egrayne said. She was more than a head taller than him, and she was not as big as the biggest of the T'En men. Dragazim had a lot of growing to do before he entered the brotherhood. 'This will only hurt if you resist.'

He nodded once.

'Drop your defences.'

Imoshen felt the rise in Egrayne's gift as the empowerer plunged into his mind.

Empowerment always seemed wrong to Imoshen. Her gift had simply arisen, and she had honed it through play and experimentation. In spring next year, it would be thirteen years since she had stumbled into the sisterhood's palace and claimed sanctuary. During that time, she had trained under Gift-tutor Vittoryxe, and she believed the rigid exercises designed to develop the gifts in their prescribed paths actually limited them. Like a limb left unused, other embryonic gifts withered.

If she had her way, Imoshen would put aside this ritual, along with so many other things. If Egrayne only knew her real agenda, she would be horrified.

But Imoshen hid her true feelings as the tension built. It lifted with the suddenness of a silent thunderclap and Dragazim almost fell forward. At the last moment, he steadied himself and blinked sleepily.

'Well done, lad.' Egrayne placed a hand on his shoulder. 'You are a gift-warrior.'

He grinned with delight and met Iraayel's eyes. All the boys looked up to Imoshen's choice-son. He'd led them the night King Charald attacked the city. Under his leadership, they'd held the grand stair, which saved the T'En nursery. Yet no brotherhood would take him, the blind fools.

Egrayne gestured to her devotee. 'Write it in the lineage book, Roskara.'

Imoshen beckoned Kiane. 'Time to make him your choice-son, Kia.'

Dragazim went around behind Kiane, knelt on the floor then crawled between her legs, to symbolise birth.

Kiane reached down and helped him rise, turning him around to face her. 'Welcome, Dragazim Choice-son Kiane.' The hand-of-force touched his forehead with the little sixth finger of her left hand, letting her gift brush his senses. 'I swear to protect your life with my own. I swear to rear you to revere the heritage of the T'Enatuath and protect our Malaunje.'

With the ceremony over, everyone else filed out, but Imoshen caught Iraayel's arm at the door. His father, Irian, had been the brotherhood's hand-of-force, and Iraayel owed his martial prowess and gift to him. But he reminded her of Ardeyne, the brotherhood's clever voice-of-reason. Ever since Iraayel had been empowered, she'd been testing him with glimpses of other gifts so that he wouldn't be limited. Now she'd seen the way Dragazim looked to Iraayel. He was a natural leader. 'You are a gift-warrior, but you are so much more. Don't think a hand-of-force is all you could ever be. Keep up the exercises I taught you.'

He laughed and kissed her forehead. 'My subversive mother!'

He left and Imoshen turned to see Saffazi watching her. Egrayne's choice-daughter had been close to Iraayel, leading him into trouble since he was a child. And this last year their relationship had deepened. They'd faced death together when the city was attacked. Imoshen knew she should explain herself, but she was so tired. All she could manage was a weary smile. 'Come along.'

Head buzzing with exhaustion, Imoshen entered the ship's main cabin to find her inner circle trying to maintain standards while packed into the cramped space. A Malaunje servant was working on Ysattori's floor-length hair, creating the elaborate hairstyles that were a sign of high stature in T'En society. Ysattori's shield-sister waited her turn.

Short of the deep-bond Imoshen shared with Ardonyx, the shield-sister bond was the closest relationship two T'En could share. Unlike the bond between T'En and their devotee, it was an equal pairing of gifts; but if one died, the other often died as well.

The cabin was all bustle as the other sisters and Malaunje saw to the needs of the sisterhood's T'En children. Imoshen's infant daughter had turned one last midsummer. Now Umaleni ran to her.

She was the only sacrare child of the sisterhood. Born of two T'En parents, she would one day be an asset to the sisterhood. But Umaleni was not pampered; Imoshen had seen to that. If her daughter was to grow into a self-disciplined woman who could master her powerful gifts, then she must develop strength of character. Hers would not be an easy path. Iraayel had suffered because of his association with Imoshen, and he was only a man.

Imoshen knelt, scooped her daughter up and hugged her, then smiled at her devotee. 'Have you been good for Frayvia, Uma?'

At the sound of her voice, the other baby girl began to wail and Imoshen's breasts ached. She collected the infant and settled on the bunk under the window to feed her. Umaleni climbed up beside them.

Imoshen noticed a five-year-old boy watching them. He had saved the baby girl's life and carried her across Chalcedonia. Now he drifted over, looking lonely. He was the son of free Malaunje and couldn't speak the T'En language. Imoshen held out her arms and he also climbed up next to her.

Egrayne surveyed the cabin. 'Take the bigger children up on deck to play. The little ones need to sleep.'

As the cabin emptied, she sat on the end of the bunk. 'You can't just make these two children your choice-son and daughter, Imoshen. Their fate should be decided at an all-mother council. The boy will need a brotherhood to go to when he turns seventeen. All the other sisterhood leaders will want the girl. If you take her in without giving them a chance to claim her, they'll resent you.'

Egrayne was right. Few T'En babies were carried to term, and more often than not, they were stillborn or horribly deformed. Healthy female babies were the rarest of all. Every other sisterhood would want the little girl, but... Imoshen looked down at the infant suckling at her breast. 'I've fed her, Egrayne. She's mine now. I'd die for her.'

Egrayne's mouth tightened in a grim line, but she didn't argue.

'Captain Ardonyx tells me it could take four days to sail down the coast to Shifting-sands Bay. We'll hold the all-council when we get there,' Imoshen said. But no one would love these children as much as she did.

'That's another thing, Imoshen. It will be winter's cusp in twenty-six days. Your choice-son turns seventeen two days before that. Since All-father Chariode's brotherhood was destroyed, he is without a brotherhood. Kyredeon took in Chariode's survivors. Have you asked –'

'No, and I won't. There's something wrong with Kyredeon. He's full of fear and hate.'

'Be that as it may, Iraayel has to go to a brotherhood. He's a gift-warrior, and powerful for a male. The sisters won't –'

'He's a good person. He saved your choice-daughter's life.'

'I know. But we are packed on these ships with no privacy. We can't have a powerful young T'En man living alongside us.' She pulled the cover up over the sleeping boy. 'Imoshen, the rest of the inner circle will vote to turn Iraayel out. The Mieren king has vowed to execute any of our people who remain behind after winter's cusp. What will you do?'

If only Ardonyx led a brotherhood. He was Imoshen's secret bond-partner and Umaleni's father. When he and Tobazim risked their lives to save Imoshen's party from the wharf last night, she'd deliberately gift-infused them to augment their power and raise their stature.

Ardonyx feared Kyredeon would fabricate evidence of disloyalty against the pair of them and have them executed. The all-father had made a practice of removing potential threats before they could challenge him for the brotherhood's leadership.

If Ardonyx and Tobazim wanted to survive, they had to move soon. But if they challenged Kyredeon before they had enough support from the rest of the brotherhood's warriors and scholars, they'd be killed.

It would break her heart to lose Ardonyx.

And she would lose more than him, because no other brotherhood leader would accept her choice-son. They hated her, had done ever since the day she'd executed an all-father. She'd had no choice. The sisterhoods had made the safety of her devotee and Iraayel dependent on proving she was not a tool of the brotherhoods.

Surely her kind had enough enemies without bickering amongst themselves? Tears of frustration stung Imoshen's eyes.

'You're tired,' Egrayne said.

'I'm tired of the distrust between the brotherhoods and sisterhoods.'

'Four hundred years of feuding can't be forgotten.'

'There's still time...' Imoshen whispered, as her eyes drifted shut. Less than one small moon, but there was still time for Ardonyx to convince Tobazim to challenge Kyredeon, still time for them to win the brotherhood, save themselves and save her choice-son.

Imoshen heard the door close and knew Egrayne had left her to rest. On the other side of the cabin, old Tiasarone sang the sisterhood's infants to sleep.

Chapter Five

Tobazim gripped the rail of the lower rear-deck, fighting his gift. It was an unusual manifestation of T'En power. Unlike Learon, his childhood choice-brother, his was not a martial gift and he'd always resented this; stature was easy to gain if you were a gift-warrior. But Learon, for all his strength in body and gift, had not survived long in Kyredeon's brotherhood. The all-father had noted him as a possible rival, shamed him before everyone and driven him to seek an honourable death. It had all unfolded so fast Tobazim had not realised the danger. He'd failed his choice-brother, and he carried the knowledge with him like an open wound.

If only his gift had been something martial...

Instead Tobazim could sense the forces and weights of a building and, now that the ship was at sea, he could feel his gift flexing as the ship plunged into the waves and the sails filled above him, driving the ship's prow through the sea. The forces involved roused his gift and he had to reel the power in.

The gift had always seemed to him to be a thing apart from his intellect, a thing that rode his body and drove him, a thing that demanded to be used. His gift seemed to be interested in the ship. He hadn't had this much trouble controlling his power since he'd been in his teens and the gift had surged without warning. He blamed the new surge on the causare's gift-infusion.

'Tobazim, there's–' Haromyr broke off as he joined him and sensed the force of his gift.

However, instead of pulling back, Haromyr drew closer,

basking in the overflow of power. Tobazim wished they'd give him some privacy. What he really needed to do was go through his exercises to balance his mind, body and gift.

'Have you told him?' Athlyn joined him on the other side with Eryx and Ionnyn.

'Told me what?'

'Kyredeon's assassin has come back from the dead,' Haromyr said.

'Ardonyx told me.' Tobazim turned, leaning his elbows on the rail to look up at the high rear-deck, which the brotherhood's all-father, his two seconds and inner circle had claimed. They had also claimed the captain's cabin, relegating Ardonyx to the adepts' cabin. Tobazim just knew there was going to be trouble. At sea, the captain's word was law, but an all-father's rule was absolute. He held the power of life and death over his T'En and Malaunje.

'The assassin's up there now,' Haromyr said. 'Graelen.'

Tobazim let his gaze wander across the elite of the brotherhood's warriors, Hand-of-force Oriemn and his followers. He spotted the new man, a gift-warrior by his neck torc – the most dangerous T'En men always were. Hard of face and lean of body, Graelen fitted right in with Oriemn and his bullies. Contempt burned in Tobazim. Kyredeon's brotherhood knew only one rule, the rule of force for self-advancement. Honour, duty and the protection of those weaker than oneself were values dating from the High Golden Age of the T'En, and had no place here.

'We have to kill him,' Haromyr whispered.

'Kill him,' Ionnyn echoed. In the year that Tobazim had been with the city brotherhood, a core of discontented young adepts and initiates had gathered around him. He feared for them, because if Kyredeon killed him, the all-father would purge all his supporters. 'Kill the assassin before Kyredeon sends him against you and Ardonyx.'

'I won't kill an innocent man.'

'He's not innocent.' Haromyr laughed sourly. 'If half the things they say about him are true –'

'I won't kill just because someone *might* do me harm.'

Ionnyn snorted. 'You can bet Kyredeon won't let scruples stay his hand.'

'Tobazim,' Athlyn pleaded, 'if you die, we are lost.'

It was true, but... 'If I kill on a mere suspicion, I am no better than Kyredeon and we are lost.'

'That's all very well in principle,' Eryx muttered. 'But –'

'But we can't watch you every moment of the day,' Haromyr said.

'You're right,' Tobazim conceded. 'But is that the way we want to live our lives? Strike and counter strike? Living in fear?'

'We want to live free of fear,' Athlyn said. 'Free of Kyredeon.'

The others went very still.

'You speak treason,' Tobazim whispered.

'He speaks what we have all thought,' Eryx said. 'Ever since the all-father drove Learon to seek an honourable death –'

'I'll consult Ardonyx, see what he says.'

'And if he says to kill before the assassin can kill you?' Ionnyn pressed.

Haromyr nodded. For once, he was in agreement with Ionnyn. 'What then?'

'We can't...' Eryx broke off as a beautiful young Malaunje woman came up the steps to the lower rear-deck. 'That's his devotee.'

She was as tall as a T'En woman, all ripe curves and unconscious grace, and when she smiled her face blossomed like a flower.

'Close your mouth, Athlyn,' Haromyr teased.

The young initiate gulped. 'I just don't get it. How could someone like the assassin win someone like her?'

Kyredeon's voice-of-reason was all smiles as he led her into the passage to the captain's cabin.

Tobazim looked up to the assassin, who went to move, but the brotherhood's hand-of-force and his followers hemmed him in.

Tobazim suspected the assassin was as trapped as they were.

But that did not make him their ally.

PRESSED BETWEEN THE hand-of-force and his followers, Graelen could not move. Surely Kyredeon would not hurt Valendia? The bond between a T'En and his devotee was sacred, and she was innocent. But he remembered Kyredeon's irrational hatred for All-father Paragian and his devotee, and feared for Dia.

'Look down there,' Hand-of-force Oriemn said. 'See the knot of brothers together? The one in the centre is Tobazim. Mark him well. Now the all-father wants to see you.'

Oriemn led Graelen down to the captain's cabin under the high rear-deck. When Graelen walked in, he sensed the build-up of aggressive male gift, and his own gift surged in response. As if it hadn't been enough to see Valendia sitting on the desk, between the all-father and his voice-of-reason. In that heartbeat, Graelen would have promised them anything to spare her.

Unaware of the danger, Valendia was playing the zither and singing one of her compositions. Her voice was sweet and pure.

'I heard that your devotee needed a zither,' Kyredeon said. 'So I found one for her.'

Valendia looked up from the instrument. Her eyes sought his, telling him she was aware of the danger and wanted him to reassure her. But what she read in his face made her look down. Shame stung him; what had he led her into?

'You can go now,' Kyredeon told Valendia.

She put the zither down and gave the deep obeisance, hands going to her heart to convey love and to her head to convey duty. 'Thank you, all-father.'

Kyredeon handed her the instrument. 'I make you a gift of this. Think of me whenever you play it.'

Dry-mouthed, Graelen watched her walk out. She looked

back at him once before the door closed. He wanted to tell her to run, but there was nowhere to run to.

'Such a sweet creature, your devotee,' Kyredeon said. 'And she carries your child, the saw-bones tells me.'

'Yes.' He could hardly speak. If Ceyne hoped this would protect Valendia, he did not know Kyredeon as well as Graelen did. Years ago, the all-father had told him if you know what someone values, you know their weakness. Had Kyredeon lived up to his all-father vows, he would have protected Valendia with his life.

'I wonder... Are you loyal, Grae?' Kyredeon said.

'You know I am loyal. All I have ever done is serve you faithfully.'

'There is something you can do for me to prove your loyalty,'

'Name it.'

'There are two trouble-makers on this ship, Captain Ardonyx and Adept Tobazim. I want you to assassinate Tobazim.'

'Not Ardonyx?'

'He's from Chariode's brotherhood, and doesn't have the depth of following amongst the younger brothers that Tobazim has. Tobazim's death will have to look like an accident, so take your time, but... If you should hear that they are planning a challenge, you must bring me word. I will need to purge the brotherhood of his followers.'

Graelen nodded. Anything to protect Valendia.

TOBAZIM WAITED UNTIL the high rear-deck was empty of everyone but the helmsman and Ardonyx, then he went up the steps.

Ardonyx strode over to join him. The pitch of the deck didn't seem to bother him at all. 'You shouldn't be up here. I've already had trouble with Kyredeon today.'

'Over what?' Tobazim asked.

'Tamaron's people. To hear Kyredeon talk, you'd think it

was lack of foresight that sent the all-father and his inner circle on a tour of their brotherhood's estates just before the Celestial City was besieged.'

Tobazim bristled on Ardonyx's behalf. 'You did the right thing, giving his leaderless brotherhood shelter on your ship.'

'Not according to Kyredeon. He begrudges them the space and the food.'

'It won't be for long. Tamaron and the rest of his people will meet us at Shifting-sands Bay and –'

'And then we won't have a ship for him, unless we can buy one from Baron Nitzane.'

'Sorne can negotiate.' Tobazim steered the conversation back to what was worrying him. 'Just before the wharf was attacked, you came to tell me Kyredeon's assassin had returned. What were you going to say?'

'Why? What are the others saying?'

'That I should kill him before he can kill me. What do you say?'

'I say we should not deal so readily in death. This Graelen is a friend of Saw-bones Ceyne. He could be useful to us if...' Ardonyx met his eyes.

'If?'

'You want me to say it?' Ardonyx shrugged. 'It is only a matter of time before Kyredeon strikes out at us. When that day comes, we'll need all the high-ranking adepts we can muster.'

Tobazim's mouth went dry with fear. 'To offer challenge is to be ready to die. Mine is not a martial gift.' And he did not have a shield-brother to support him when they battled the old brotherhood leader and his shield-brother on the higher plane. Tobazim's heart leapt. Was Ardonyx offering this bond?

'Speak with Ceyne. He was on the previous all-father's inner circle. He's known Graelen since he was a lad of seventeen. Don't judge the man by his reputation. In this brotherhood, a bad reputation is a good thing.'

Tobazim grinned. He went downstairs to the infirmary, where he found quite a few adepts and initiates suffering from sea-sickness. And, to his surprise, the assassin's devotee was helping brew a big pot of peppermint tea.

'Almost ready,' she told him kindly. 'A cup of this will settle your stomach.'

He shook his head. What was she doing with a cruel, hard man like Graelen?

Someone moaned and called for a bucket. Tobazim turned to see Athlyn, pale and sweaty. Graelen's devotee held the bucket for him, offered him a drink afterwards and rinsed the bucket. Kind and good-hearted.

Tobazim caught up with Ceyne, who drew him into the bathing chamber so they could speak in privacy.

Tobazim turned to face him. 'What can you tell me about the assassin, Graelen?'

The saw-bones hesitated.

'Is he our enemy?'

'Rather, you should ask, do you have a common enemy?'

'I think I should ask if he is an honourable man.'

Ceyne hesitated. 'Before Kyredeon came to power, Sigorian was all-father. This brotherhood has not had an all-father of substance for over forty years. We have all had to do dishonourable things to survive. The night Graelen gave his vows, he was only sixteen and determined to win stature. That night my apprentice was unjustly accused of spying for Chariode's brotherhood. I couldn't save him. If I'd tried, I would have died, too. I still have nightmares.'

'I'm sorry.'

'Sorry won't save us from Kyredeon's paranoia.'

'PEPPERMINT TEA?'

'Thank you, Dia.' Graelen accepted it. As the day progressed, almost everyone had become seasick. Valendia was one of the lucky ones who seemed immune. She'd been in the sick bay helping Ceyne with the worst cases.

'Doesn't cleaning up after others make you feel sick?' he asked.

She shrugged. 'I nursed my mother when she was ailing. It took her nearly two years to die. Looking after those who are ill makes me grateful to be alive.'

He shook his head. 'No wonder you are wise beyond your years.'

She laughed and went inside. He remained on deck. He much preferred to be outside with the wind in his face. It seemed not many of the others shared his preference; the decks were mostly empty.

He sipped the hot peppermint tea. His stomach was feeling a little better and he was considering trying to catch some sleep when Tobazim came out of the passage to the cabins. Graelen was surprised to see him alone, but his supporters were probably all laid low with the heaves.

Tobazim paused halfway out the door as their eyes met.

Graelen could have bundled Tobazim overboard right then – it was the perfect opportunity – but he didn't.

He turned back to the rail and looked out over the side of the ship.

Tobazim joined him. 'They tell me you are Kyredeon's assassin.'

Graelen schooled his face to reveal nothing. Meanwhile his free hand closed on the hilt of his long-knife.

'They tell me I should have you killed, before you kill me. Ardonyx says you could be useful. Ceyne says –'

'Ceyne?' Graelen was surprised. Was the saw-bones playing them off each other? He must not let Kyredeon's paranoia infect him. 'The saw-bones advises you?'

'I would be a fool not to listen to him. He has advised me since the night we arrived in the palace.'

'And you trust him? The saw-bones has been on Kyredeon's inner circle since the all-father seized power.'

'Ceyne is a good man in a difficult position.'

That was what Graelen had always believed. He released his knife hilt. 'What does the saw-bones say?'

'He says that you are also a good man in a difficult position. Is he right?'

'I don't...' Graelen broke off as several adepts came out onto the deck. He tensed, watching them.

When he turned back, Tobazim was gone. But they had seen them together. If the all-father found out, Kyredeon's paranoia would lead him to assume the worst.

There was only one way to prove his loyalty – kill Tobazim.

IMOSHEN SERVED MINT tea to help settle seasick stomachs. It was evening of their first day at sea, and everyone suffered. She was lucky; having grown up fishing in small rowboats, she had no trouble with the pitching of the deck.

She lit the lamp, turned it down low and hung it from the hook, then surveyed the cabin full of moaning women and small children. It was going to be a long night.

Towards dawn there was a reprieve and nearly everyone had fallen asleep. Her devotee, Frayvia, was just as sick as the rest, but she told Imoshen to rest.

'I think I'll get some fresh air.' She slung her cloak around her shoulders and went out on deck. It was a clear, bitingly cold night, with a faint hint of grey in the east.

Imoshen's heart filled with joy. Exile meant change, and she welcomed it.

Eventually the chill became too much and she returned to the cabin to find all was quiet. Frayvia had taken the chance to dress for the day and was kneeling next to her chest. When she noticed Imoshen, she rolled something up and went to put it away.

'What's that?' Imoshen whispered.

'A gift from Sorne,' she said, after a moment's hesitation. Imoshen's gift surged; Frayvia's reluctance to reveal the object sprang from the depth of her feelings for Sorne. 'It belonged to his mother. It's the only thing he has of hers.'

'Then it is a very rich gift, indeed,' Imoshen said. 'Can I see?'

Frayvia placed the neck torc in her hands.

'I don't recognise the design.'

'He believes it came from across the eastern mountains.'

'That explains the stone. I've never seen anything like it. Such a vivid blue.'

Frayvia flushed. 'Sorne used to wear the torc when King Charald asked him for a vision. It would glow when the predators from the higher plane came through.'

'Sorne...' Imoshen hesitated. As a Malaunje, Sorne had no innate power. She believed, had he been born T'En, he would have been a seer, capable of calling up visions. Being Malaunje, Sorne had siphoned off power from the empyrean plane to trigger his visions, but to do this... 'He risked death each time he had a vision. He's lucky the empyrean predators he summoned were satisfied with the offerings he made. The gift residue in T'En relics would not have been enough for the really dangerous beasts. They could have –'

'I know.' Frayvia shuddered. 'He's promised not to seek any more visions.'

'I'm glad.' Imoshen hugged Frayvia and returned the torc. 'I think you should wear this with pride.'

Frayvia smiled and fastened the torc around her neck.

Imoshen was glad Sorne no longer risked his life to gain visions, but with the T'Enatuath sailing into exile, her people could have used the guidance of a seer. There had not been one born for hundreds of years.

They did have a scryer, who was able to search for possible future paths, but their scryer had been injured the day All-mother Reoden's daughter was murdered. The scryer could not forgive herself for failing to foresee the attack, and her gift had been blocked ever since.

One of the children moaned in their sleep, woke up and vomited. This disturbed the others and set them off. Imoshen hoped, for all their sakes, they would find their sea-legs soon.

Chapter Six

JARAILE HAD NEVER seen the Wyrd city. She'd heard it described as a cesspit, and also as one of the wonders of the world. Approaching it that afternoon, after three days' muddy ride from port, it certainly lived up to its reputation for beauty. It stood on an island in the lake. A ribbon of white causeway stretched out to the city. The walls and buildings were a brilliant white. There were gardens on the roofs, mostly barren now, except for the occasional pencil pine.

'The closest end, the low end, is where the brotherhood palaces are. They were given to the barons as a reward for their loyalty. Apparently they drew lots when the Wyrds left,' Eskarnor told her. He adjusted her buttocks across his lap and she could feel him pressed into her flesh. She knew what he would do once they were alone in the palace. 'Beyond the next wall are the shops, theatres, eateries and a park. Behind the last wall, on the peak of the island, are the sisterhood palaces. Charald had declared them his, but by tomorrow morning, I'll be claiming them.'

'The Chalcedonian barons won't swear loyalty to you.'

'I think you underestimate how much they hate your husband. There is not one baron amongst us who hasn't felt the force of his irrational rage. Fear is all very well for keeping men in line, but when a man does not know if his king is going to turn on him in a rage, then fear becomes a goad to action.'

Jaraile suspected he was right. The king had always had a temper and bullied his way through life, but these last few years, she'd seen even Charald's trusted advisors recoil in horror.

They rode down the causeway towards the gates.

'Your men-at-arms were sent –'

'– to my estate, which lies far to the north. It's huge, but that's because it's so barren. Frankly, it's an insult, considering my service to King Charald.' Then he laughed. 'Sorne had men watching the port for signs of my warriors gathering, but he didn't bother to watch the army besieging the Wyrd city. And he wouldn't have thought anything of it, if he had, because I was entitled to a contingent of men to claim my palace. The rest have slipped back and been secreted throughout the tents of my loyal barons.'

Jaraile's mind raced. If Eskarnor had been allowed to retain a contingent of men here, then Nitzane must have men here, too. If she could just work out which palace was his and escape, she could claim sanctuary with them.

By the time they rode through the gate, one of the baron's men was waiting to escort Eskarnor to his palace.

'Captain Pataxo,' Eskarnor greeted him with a laugh. The baron was so different from Charald – ruthless, yes, but also ready to laugh, especially now that his plans had finally come to fruition. 'Where's my palace?'

'It's the last one on the north side of the city.'

'Good. I want all the barons and their honour guards invited to tonight's feast,' Eskarnor said.

Pataxo's gaze skipped over Jaraile, but it was clear he knew who she was. 'It will be done. We're lucky we didn't get the ruined palace. Nitzane's man drew the short straw.'

'Which palace is that?' Jaraile said.

Eskarnor pinched her. 'Don't even think it.'

She looked up at him, startled.

'I'm no fool, Raila.' Eskarnor grinned. 'Besides, if you took refuge with Nitzane's men, I would have to kill the lot of them. You don't want to be responsible for their deaths, do you?'

She sank down. He had outsmarted Sorne, who was the

smartest man she'd ever met. Perhaps there was no hope. Perhaps she was destined to be the prize of cruel bullies.

No. She had her son to think of. She must not give up hope. But she could let Eskarnor think she had. She slumped in his arms, as if dejected.

That evening Jaraile dressed in looted finery. Eskarnor decked her in silks and brocades. Above her, on the rooftop garden, she could hear the feast getting underway, with much singing and drinking.

It was dark by the time Eskarnor escorted her onto the rooftop garden. From the roar of laughter and voices, the wine had been flowing freely. Lanterns strung from poles gave the event a festive air. Long tables had been carried up and a set for the feast. Musicans played a Dacian air on instruments Jaraile was unfamiliar with. She could hardly hear the music for the rowdy singing.

But as Eskarnor led her between the tables to the high table, the singers faltered and the musicians lowered their instruments. She saw her cousin, Baron Kerminzto, go very still and wished she could get a message to him. She tried to tell him to run with her eyes, but he just looked grim. Did he think she had willingly abandoned King Charald and her son?

Eskarnor led her around behind the table, then climbed onto a chair and drew her up beside him.

'You will have all heard the rumour concerning King Charald's mental state,' Eskarnor said. 'The king's mind is going. Why, not so long ago, he held a conversation with Queen Sorna, who has been dead these thirty years.'

Jaraile glanced to Eskarnor, horrified. How had he known? He hadn't been there that day. Someone must have betrayed Charald.

'Yes, the secret is out, my queen,' Eskarnor said, taking her hand as if consoling her. Jaraile had just confirmed his claim.

He tucked her arm through his. 'For over forty years, Charald has bullied his own kingdom and all those around the Secluded Sea. You know why he hates the Wyrds?'

'Because the one-eyed half-blood is his son!' Captain Pataxo yelled.

'Worse.' Eskarnor was enjoying himself. 'Because the rumour about his twin is true. Charald was born with a half-blood twin. Talk of tainted blood!' Eskarnor shook his head. 'Charald should never have sat upon the throne. Tonight, I come here with Queen Jaraile to offer an alternative to a cruel, irrational old bully. Unite behind us and we will free Chalcedonia from King Charald the Tyrant. No more handing over your best men to go off and fight his campaigns against subject kingdoms that have revolted. Tonight, choose freedom and a new start for Chalcedonia. All barons who swear loyalty to me will keep their lands and titles.'

'What of Nitzane?' Pataxo called.

'That lap-dog? He's no warrior. United, we are more than a match for him.'

'What of Prince Cedon?'

'The Wyrd wharf was attacked by slum-dwellers. The Wyrds cut the boy's throat to...'

Jaraile's head buzzed. This was what she'd feared. The lanterns spun and she toppled. Eskarnor caught her, sweeping her off her feet.

'Poor thing. The shock's too much for her in her condition. Charge your glasses. The queen carries my son, heir to the throne.'

Jaraile stiffened in his arms.

Eskarnor laughed and kissed her, holding her tightly.

'Did you think I wouldn't notice how you pick at your food and force it down?' he whispered. Then he raised his voice. 'I vow before you all here tonight, King Charald will be dead by summer so I can marry the queen and make my son legitimate. Step forward now and give your oaths of loyalty.'

In the cage of his arms, Jaraile could only watch as the rooftop crowd erupted. She saw her cousin try to fight his way to the stairs. She saw Eskarnor's men drive their enemies against the rails and over so that they fell to their deaths, four storeys below.

The struggle surged towards them at the high table.

'Wait here.' Eskarnor sat her in the chair, placed one boot on the table and jumped over it to join the fighting.

To her disgust, she saw at least two of the Chalcedonian barons turn on the others, uniting against the very men they'd sworn to support.

But all she could think of was her sweet little Cedon, dead. She'd failed him. He'd died alone and frightened. Had he called for her right at the end?

Could you die of grief?

How could she go on after this? Why go on?

'Traitor!' Baron Dekaitz charged the high table, bloody sword raised to strike her.

She threw herself backwards. The chair tipped. She slammed on the tiles, rolled onto her hands and knees, and tried to scramble away, but he caught her from behind.

Dekaitz grabbed her by her hair, pulled her head up and brought his sword to her throat.

She screamed, infuriated by the injustice of it.

Then screamed again as Dekaitz was hauled aside, jerking her head and tearing her hair out by the roots. She crawled away, blood trickling down her forehead into her eyes. Stunned, she pressed up against a raised garden bed and turned in time to see Eskarnor run Dekaitz through.

The man dropped to his knees. Eskarnor grabbed him by his hair and sliced his head clean off. Lifting the severed head by the hair, he turned to display it to the others. 'This is what happens to those who threaten what's mine!'

And he deposited the head on the table. Meanwhile, the screams of the dying and the curses of the fighting men gradually faded.

Satisfied, Eskarnor returned, lifted Jaraile and took his seat at the high table with her in his lap. He inspected her head. 'A few patches of torn scalp, that's all. You'll be fine.'

Through her tears and the blood she saw the two

Chalcedonian turncoat barons, Ikor and Unaki, take the heads of Barons Dittor and Rantzo. They strode over and deposited them on the table with Dekaitz's head. These three unfortunate barons had been Nitzane's firm supporters.

Ikor and Unaki dropped to their knees to give their oath of loyalty to Eskarnor, buying their place in his ranks with the heads of men they'd sworn to serve alongside.

She would not trust them. Ever.

That only left her cousin, Kerminzto. She hoped he'd escaped, hoped Eskarnor would...

'Where is Kerminzto's body? Bring me his head,' Eskarnor ordered. As his men searched the dead, Eskarnor gestured to the wine. 'Pour me a glass.'

Amazingly, the bottle had not broken during the fighting. She righted a goblet and poured wine for him.

'And one for yourself. I'm not like these Chalcedonian men, who treat their women like slaves,' Eskarnor said. 'You'll drink alongside me and you'll rule alongside me.' He bared his teeth in a feral grin. 'As long as you prove loyal.'

Terror made Jaraile's hand shake.

He steadied the wine bottle and tilted her goblet to her lips. 'Drink up. You need something for your nerves.'

She gulped a mouthful, not sure if she could keep it down. It was Dacian, stronger than she was used to. It made her cough and her eyes water.

He laughed, drained his goblet and called to the servants. 'Serve up the meal.'

Meanwhile the heads of three barons sat on the table in front of her. She tried not to look at them.

'No sign of Baron Kerminzto,' Captain Pataxo reported.

Jaraile's heart soured, but she kept her eyes lowered.

'Double the guard on the causeway gate,' Eskarnor said. 'I want his head by dawn tomorrow.'

The meal arrived: rare roast beef, oozing blood.

Jaraile took one look, lurched to the side and threw up.

Eskarnor rubbed her back, then gestured to the table.

'Clear these heads. We are not barbarians. Fix them to the spikes above the causeway gate.'

'I don't think there are spikes above the gate,' Pataxo said.

'Then fix some in place. You'd think the Wyrds would have gate spikes.' Even as he said this, Eskarnor offered her more wine.

Jaraile gulped a mouthful. Heat raced all the way down to her toes and up again. She pushed the goblet aside. 'My s-son, are you certain the Wyrds killed him?'

Eskarnor wiped the tears from her cheeks. 'I didn't tell you because I didn't want to distress you. Not when you're in a delicate condition.'

He adjusted her on his lap and cut off slivers of meat to tempt her.

Meanwhile the puddles of blood where the heads had sat congealed. It felt as if she was fifteen again, at the mercy of King Charald. Eskarnor was every bit as much a monster as the king was.

But she suspected he was smarter.

SORNE WOKE WITH a sword to his throat. Blinking, he made out Baron Kerminzto's features in the pale light of dawn. He sat up slowly as he tried to work out what was going on. They were less than a day's ride from the Celestial City and his dozen king's guard were surrounded by at least forty of the baron's men.

'Your sentries need to be more alert,' Jaraile's kinsman told Sorne. At Kerminzto's signal, the two sentries were sent to join the rest of the king's palace guard and one of Kerminzto's men built up the fire.

The baron sat opposite Sorne, perching on a fallen tree trunk. The sword tip did not waver. 'I'm going to ask some questions and I want honest answers, Warrior's-voice, or whatever you're čalling yourself now.'

'Sorne will do.'

'Sorne, then.'

Kerminzto was around forty years of age, and he had come to the barony within the last two years, when Jaraile's father dropped dead unexpectedly. Sorne didn't know much about him. During the Wyrd Campaign, Kerminzto had kept quiet, not drinking to excess and not presuming on his relationship to the queen to claim favours. He'd struck Sorne as a sensible man. It was precisely because he did not presume on his relationship with the queen that Sorne had recommended Charald name him one of the five people to guide Prince Cedon in the event of the king's death or, as appeared more likely now, if the king became incapable of ruling.

'Are you King Charald's unwanted half-blood son?' Kerminzto asked.

'Yes.'

'Was the king born with a half-blood twin?'

'So his enemies claim. I can't vouch for the truth of it.'

'Is Prince Cedon dead?'

'No. The Wyrds returned him with his club foot healed. He's fit to take the throne.'

'Has King Charald lost his mind?'

Sorne hesitated.

The sword tip dug into his throat.

'His wits come and go. When his piss turns the colour of port-wine, he raves.'

Kerminzto nodded. 'Can the saw-bones –'

'He refuses to see one, and the apothecaries offer cures based on arsenic, purges and blood-letting, all of which leave his pockets lighter and him worse off than when they started.' Sorne thought he saw a glimmer of amusement in the baron's grey-blue eyes. 'Why –'

'I ask the questions, half-blood. What are you doing on the road to the Wyrd city?'

'Nitzane sent me to summon the barons in King Charald's name. He's leading a strike against Eskarnor's estate...'

Kerminzto laughed bitterly. 'You're too late. Eskarnor

didn't ride north to his estate. He took Jaraile to the Wyrd city. He invited all the barons to a feast and killed off any who would not give their oath of allegiance.'

'How many joined him?'

'How would I know? I was fighting for my life.' Kerminzto spat in disgust. 'I imagine that by now Eskarnor will have given our men-at-arms a choice – swear loyalty to him or die. I'm expecting many will desert, when they get the chance.'

'How many escaped?'

'Again, I can only speak for myself. I'd sent the majority of my men home to bring in the harvest.' Kerminzto gestured to himself and his men. 'There's us, and I have several watching the road. I only escaped with this many because we left the city via my palace's lake gate and swam for it. A few of my men couldn't swim. They'll be spying for me, if they get the chance to send word of Eskarnor's movements.'

Sorne's head spun. 'Do you know his plans?'

'I know his plans for me.' Kerminzto gave another bitter laugh. 'There's a spike on the causeway gate waiting for my head. And Jaraile believes her son is dead.'

'Poor Jaraile.' Sorne had promised the queen Prince Cedon would be returned whole and healthy. Now she'd think he'd failed her. Which he had. Sorne should have anticipated that Eskarnor would take her. 'But Eskarnor won't hurt her as long as she's useful –'

'Oh, she's useful, all right. She carries his child. But I know Jaraile, she's a good girl. She'd never let Eskarnor into her bed.'

'She didn't, not willingly.' Sorne winced, recalling Nitzane's furious, tearful confession. The baron had failed to protect her, and it was eating away at him. Sorne didn't know how Eskarnor could use a woman's body as a battlefield for the crown, but Charald had been the same, seeing his queens as fields to be ploughed so he could reap sons. 'I need you to send one of your men to let Jaraile know her boy lives. She must hold onto hope.'

'Very well.' Kerminzto sheathed his sword.

Sorne opened his travelling kit and wrote a short note for Jaraile, signing it with an S.

Kerminzto accepted the message. 'But I don't know if my man will be able to get near her. Likely Eskarnor will have her locked up in his palace. And there's more important things at stake than Jaraile's soft heart. There'll be no throne for Prince Cedon if we don't quash this rebellion and execute Eskarnor. How did it get to this point? Last time I saw King Charald, he was hale and hearty, and he'd taken Nitzane and Eskarnor to the port with him to keep an eye on them.'

'Nitzane's loyal –'

'Nitzane's a fool.'

'He means no harm and he has a kind heart.'

'Then he's useless against Eskarnor.' Kerminzto spat again.

'Eskarnor could shut the gates of the Wyrd city and sit tight, but that would put him in the same position as the Wyrds were. His estate and the estates of his loyal barons would be vulnerable.'

Kerminzto grimaced. 'I won't sanction the killing of innocent women and children.'

Which was a relief for Sorne, but... 'I doubt Eskarnor has such scruples. Three nights ago, I saw him cut the throat of a four-year-old boy to make his point.'

'Are you saying we should use Eskarnor's own tactics against him?'

'It would be a mistake. If a man has no hope, he'll fight to the death. If he has hope, he'll reconsider his allegiances. We need to hold the rebel barons' families hostage.'

'Hold them where?' Kerminzto gestured around him. 'Eskarnor has thousands of men. We have around fifty between us.'

'Eskarnor must kill the king and his heir if he is to win the throne, and they're both in Port Mirror-on-Sea. Eskarnor doesn't own a fleet. He can't blockade the harbour.'

'We can hold the port,' Kerminzto agreed. 'But what does that benefit us if we lose the kingdom? We need an army.'

'None of Eskarnor's barons will be at full force. Charald ordered the barons to maintain a skeleton army on the siege, and send their men-at-arms home to bring in the harvest. The rebel barons will have kept their most trusted men with them, those who served them down south, and sent the rest back to their estates. As far as the men on the estates know, they still owe their loyalty to King Charald, and those men are Chalcedonians whose real loyalty lies with King Charald, not a southern baron who has lorded it over them these last four years. If we ride to the rebel barons' estates and summon the men-at-arms in the name of King Charald, they'll come.'

Kerminzto's deep-set eyes gleamed. 'I always said you were a canny one.'

Sorne pulled a stick from the woodheap and sketched a map of Chalcedonia. 'Here's the Wyrd city and here's the port, due west. A fast rider can make it to port in three days. The Wyrds took eight days, due to the state of the roads and the weight of the wagons. It's been a wet autumn, wagons get bogged and churn up the roads. The more men Eskarnor has, the more supplies he needs to bring with him and the slower he'll travel.' Sorne knew from bitter experience what was involved in moving men, supplies and machines of war. But then so did Eskarnor. They'd both served under King Charald.

'You're saying we have a few days up our sleeves?'

Sorne nodded. 'The commander who acts swiftly and decisively will win the campaign for Chalcedonia. We're headed into winter. Once the snows settle in, north of us nothing will move. Even in the south, travel will be problematic.' Sorne gestured. 'Two thirds of Chalcedonia lies north of us, but it's barren and less populated, especially to the west. I'll take the south, where most of the Chalcedonian barons live. You take the north. We'll ride into the barons' estates and demand as many men-at-arms as they can muster in the name of King Charald.'

'That'll work for the southern rebel barons and the barons who've stayed loyal to King Charald, but what of the Chalcedonian barons who have sworn fealty to Eskarnor? Their men will desert us when they learn that their barons have chosen the rebel side.'

'That's if any of the Chalcedonian barons turned coat.' Sorne frowned. 'We need to know which of them, if any, swore loyalty to Eskarnor. Civil war is a messy thing.'

'And what of the rebel barons' families?' Kerminzto prodded. 'Their wives may know of their husbands' plans to unite behind Eskarnor. I don't want to be dragging weeping women and children across Chalcedonia with me. They'll escape the first chance they get and betray the real state of affairs.'

'That's tricky. Most of the rebel barons' wives are Chalcedonian, and were forced to marry to legitimise the southern barons' claims on their estates. Even if the wives are loyal to their husbands, they won't know that Eskarnor has made his move. Tell them King Charald plans to celebrate the safe return of his heir in Port Mirror-on-Sea and all the nobility are expected to attend. It's what he planned.' Sorne shrugged. 'If the estates are within a couple of days' ride, send the barons' wives and families straight to the palace. Otherwise, send them to one of these harbours.' Sorne marked the four harbours north of the Port Mirror-on-Sea. 'I'll ride for Shifting-sands Bay, here.' He marked a spot south of Port Mirror-on-Sea. 'Nitzane runs a small fleet of merchant ships. I'll send one of his ships to the northern harbours with orders to pick up the barons' families and deliver them to Port Mirror-on-Sea. I'll collect the Chalcedonian barons' families and send them to port, while gathering their men-at-arms.

'If we can delay Eskarnor's attack until spring, we can prepare the kingdom by securing the rebel barons' families as hostages and gather an army.'

'And if we can't?'

'Then Eskarnor has the advantage. His men are already at the Wyrd city. All he has to do is prepare to march. If he does take the bait and besiege the king in port, then he'll have to protect his back. We can strike his camp and disappear into the countryside.'

'My family's estate lies to the west,' Kerminzto said. 'I was about to turn off the port road and skirt the lake when we spotted your camp. I'm going to my estate first. Collect my family and men-at-arms.'

'Send your family to Shifting-sands Bay. They can sail up the coast so there is no chance of them running into Eskarnor on the way to port.'

'You seem pretty certain he will make for the king.'

'He has to. As long as there is a viable ruler, his claim will not be legitimate. Once Charald and Prince Cedon are dead –'

'There's still Nitzane's son.'

'Good point.' Sorne had forgotten young Martzane. Baron Nitzane had said he didn't want to claim the throne for his son. But if his son was the only heir left, and the boy's continued survival depended on killing Eskarnor, then Nitzane would pursue the crown on his son's behalf. 'I'll send a message to the King of Navarone. The boy is being fostered with his uncle.'

'Fair enough,' Kerminzto said. 'Once I get my men, I'll ride north.'

'Nitzane's ridden to collect the men from two of his estates on the road north and attack Eskarnor.'

'If I run into Nitzane, I'll tell him the plan. Hopefully, we'll have all the rebel barons' families as hostages and a sizeable army back here before the snows make travel impossible.'

'If you make Port Mirror-on-Sea before I do, hold the port. I'll coordinate the harassment of Eskarnor's besieging army.' Sorne stood up and used his boot to smear the map. 'Information is the most important thing. We need to know who's turned coat to support Eskarnor, and who he murdered. Fast horses could win this war.'

'And loose tongues could lose it.'

Sorne nodded. 'King Charald named five advisors to guide the prince until he's old enough to rule. I recommended you.'

'Did you now?' Kerminzto rubbed his jaw, his fingers rasping across a day's growth. 'Well, don't expect me to thank you.'

Sorne laughed. He'd been right; Kerminzto was a sensible man. 'I hope Prince Cedon takes after you.'

'I hope he doesn't have Charald's rages. Jaraile's nature with some smarts and some spine would be good.'

'Oh, I think you've all underestimated Queen Jaraile.'

Luckily for them, one of Kerminzto's men arrived before they parted, with news from the Wyrd city. Of the Chalcedonian barons, only Barons Unaki and Ikor had turned against King Charald. The rest were dead, which meant their sons, cousins and younger brothers had assumed the titles.

Chapter Seven

SORNE REACHED BARON Aingeru's estate mid-afternoon. Originally from the southern kingdom of Maygharia, Aingeru's loyalty was to Baron Eskarnor. But Aingeru was still in the captured Wyrd city with his band of ex-mercenaries. As far as the people of Aingeru's estate knew, their baron was loyal to King Charald. The estate's workers had lived here for hundreds of years, and if put to the test, Sorne suspected their loyalty would be to the land, not the baron.

So he rode across the late autumn countryside into an enemy baron's estate, accompanied by only two of the king's guard in full dress uniform, trusting that he was ahead of Eskarnor's news. By the way the people in the fields waved and turned back to work, it looked like he was right.

Although winter's cusp was not far off, the day was fine and warm. It was a busy time of year. Herds had to be culled so the best stock could be nursed through the winter. The meat would have to be preserved. Some fields had already been harvested while others were covered in people cutting and threshing.

Clearly, the call to bear arms would not be welcome.

Come to think of it, there was a good chance the war for the Chalcedonian throne could be fought on the fields of this estate. A day's fast ride from the Wyrd city and two from the port, it would be right in the path of the opposing armies.

One of which he was in the process of gathering.

He had sent the rest of the king's guard to the estates

of Barons Dekaitz, Ikor, Rantzo and Dittor, all of whom belonged to the old aristocracy of Chalcedonia. Ikor had turned against King Charald, but his people did not know it. The families of these four barons were to ride to Nitzane's stronghold at Shifting-sands Bay and sail up the coast to Port Mirror-on-Sea. They would be safest in port and would be told the true state of affairs, but he could not tell Aingeru's wife. She was loyal to her husband, and he was loyal to Eskarnor.

Baroness Aingeru would have to be lured to the port. Once she and the children were hostages, there was a good chance Aingeru would reconsider his allegiance. He was respected and led a company of well-disciplined Maygharian ex-mercenaries. If he could be turned, other rebel barons might also reconsider their allegiance.

Meanwhile, the Chalcedonian barons' men-at-arms, under the leadership of the guards, would head straight to Nitzane's other south Chalcedonian estate at Riverbend, and Sorne would meet them there.

Sorne had given the oldest and most experienced of the king's guard these tasks, leaving him with two seventeen-year-old youths. He turned in the saddle to speak to Vighir and Lazandor. 'We will be treated as honoured guests. As far as Baroness Aingeru knows, her husband is still loyal to King Charald. Only we three know the true state of affairs. Watch what you say. Tomorrow morning, I want the baron's wife to ride out of here with her children, unaware that Eskarnor has made his move.'

They nodded. Sorne beckoned the man supervising the threshing and leant forward in the saddle, elbows resting on the pommel. 'Where's the baroness?'

'Over in the orchard.'

Sorne nodded his thanks and headed that way.

Before he reached the orchard, he found Aingeru's wife and children picking blackberries in high spirits.

Zaria's long black hair tumbled down her back as she crawled out of a blackberry bush with a laugh. 'I have it!'

She displayed the berry and dropped it in the basket.

'Strangers, Ma,' one of the twins reported.

Zaria straightened and shaded her eyes to study them as they walked their horses towards her. She had been a camp follower, a poor thirteen-year-old plucked from a street corner in Khitan because of her pretty face and swept along with the army. But she'd been lucky. Aingeru had taken a fancy to her, married her and got himself twin boys within a year. That had been nearly ten years ago.

Aingeru could have put his camp-wife aside when he was made a baron, but he'd kept her by him. Sorne believed Aingeru loved her.

A little girl of five ran over and hid behind her mother's skirts. A boy of about three promptly sat in the grass and helped himself to his sister's basket of berries, stuffing them into a mouth already stained with juice. Meanwhile the twins studied Sorne and his two companions. The boys were about nine and identical, with the olive skin and flashing black eyes of southerners.

'Baroness Zaria,' Sorne greeted her.

'Warrior's-voice.'

'Not any more. I'm the king's agent. And I bring good news.'

One of the twins whispered, 'Why does he have only one eye?'

'That's what happens if you don't listen to your mother and play with sticks,' Sorne told him.

Zaria laughed. 'Aingeru sent me a message to say the king has taken the Wyrd city.'

'Yes. We have the city, but my news is about the king's heir. Prince Cedon has been returned whole and healthy.'

'Oh, I'm so glad. Jaraile will be relieved.'

Sorne knew a moment's shame. When he'd suggested the Wyrds take the prince hostage, he hadn't thought how the prince's mother would pine for him. And they were still apart. He cleared his throat. 'The king is planning a great feast. All of the barons and their families are to attend.'

'What, the children as well?'

Sorne nodded. 'King Charald wants his son to meet his future barons. Prince Cedon will be four in the spring. Bring the little ones. The king plans all manner of delights for the children, and feasts and masquerades for the grownups.'

'A trip to port?' One of the twins cried. 'Say yes, Ma. Please say yes.'

Sorne smiled. 'You'll stay in the palace as King Charald's guests.'

'Can we see the ships?' the same twin asked.

'Can I ride my pony to port?' the other wanted to know.

'We'll see.' Zaria looked up at Sorne with a smile. 'You'll stay for the night?'

And make sure she left the next day. 'Yes.'

'It will be good to see Jaraile again,' Zaria said.

Sorne hesitated. An unlikely friendship had sprung up between the camp follower and the queen, daughter of an old Chalcedonian family.

One of the twins tugged on Sorne's arm. 'Can I ride your horse?'

He looked to Zaria, who nodded.

By the time they turned to go back, four children were riding the horse, while Zaria carried the baskets of blackberries.

GRAELEN WRAPPED HIS arms around Valendia as the fleet made its way through the long, narrow headlands into Shifting-sands Bay. With the sun setting behind them, the sails were gilded and the sandstone towers of the stronghold glowed on the cliff top. A cold wind blew in from the sea, pinning his cloak to his back.

He shielded her from the chill with his body, and wished he could shield her from the machinations of the brotherhood. Kyredeon was up to something. He'd interviewed two of the refugees from All-father Tamaron's brotherhood.

'Everyone's just gotten over their seasickness, now we're back in port,' Adept Haromyr said. He stood beside Tobazim, and as their companions laughed, Haromyr caught Graelen's eye with a challenge. *See*, he seemed to say, *we have many supporters. Move against us and we will strike you down.*

On the mid-deck, the Malaunje of Kyredeon and Hueryx's brotherhoods mingled. Both the foredeck and the two rear-decks were packed with T'En and a sprinkling of devotees, but a small space had been left around Graelen and his devotee; there were no brothers he could call his friends. After Paryx's death, he'd lost contact with the young adepts and initiates.

He didn't mind. Moments like this gave him privacy.

'You've been very quiet,' Valendia whispered.

'And you don't play the zither.'

'Because every time I look at it I think of *him* and my skin crawls.'

He could sense her indignation. It was a pure, clean emotion and it made him smile.

'The all-father and his two seconds asked something of you that day, Grae. What was it?'

'You don't want to know.'

'They told you to kill Adept Tobazim and Captain Ardonyx,' she said, proving there was no point trying to hide things from her. 'And they threatened me.'

'They didn't need to threaten you.'

She turned in the circle of his arms. 'I've only lived with the brotherhood four days and I can't stand it. Everyone is afraid of the all-father and his seconds, and afraid of each other.'

'Because Kyredeon has spies.'

'How can you bear it?'

'It was not this bad in the city. We had the whole palace, and the free quarter to roam.' But even so, he had found it claustrophobic, and had welcomed the chance to go to port.

'Ceyne says –'

'You've been spending a lot of time with him. Should I be worried?'

'He needed an assistant, as you very well know.' She thumped his chest, then grew serious. 'The saw-bones says the all-father sets the tone for the brotherhood. He says Kyredeon came to power through deceit and has held onto power through coercion and intimidation. Ceyne told me Paryx's gift went bad because he could not bear the things Kyredeon made him do. Oh, Grae...' Tears glittered in her beautiful wine-dark eyes. 'I can feel you drawing away from me, growing cold. I couldn't bear it if I lost you.'

He kissed her forehead. 'You won't lose me.'

'There are more ways to lose you than in death. Don't do this thing for Kyredeon, Grae. It will kill something in you.'

He could not give her the answer she wanted so he said nothing.

'Ceyne says –'

'That saw-bones has been saying far too much.'

'He counts you as his friend, Grae. Perhaps it is time for Kyredeon to step down –'

'All-fathers don't step down, Dia. They are challenged for the leadership, and they either die defending their position or they kill their opponents and retain it.'

She nodded. 'Can you bear to go on serving an all-father you don't respect?'

Graelen swallowed. After speaking with Tobazim, he had been watching the brotherhood alliances, weighing up who had the power and the numbers. 'Tobazim is not powerful enough to defeat Kyredeon. If he mounts a challenge and loses, all those who supported him will be purged. I could not risk you –'

'Would you rather lose me by degrees?' She pushed his arm aside and walked away, returning to the infirmary.

Graelen gripped the rail as the alternatives went round and round in his mind. He knew who he would rather serve as all-father, but for Valendia's sake, he had to back the winner.

As he watched the ship drop anchor, Tobazim came out of the cabin and began to go through his exercises with the kind of dedication more often seen in a warrior than a scholar. He moved with grace and precision.

Someone came up behind Graelen and he turned, hand going to his knife hilt.

The brotherhood's voice-of-reason glanced down. 'You'd better not draw that against me.'

Graelen forced his hand to release the knife hilt.

'The all-father wants to see you.'

Had word of his conversation with Tobazim filtered through to Kyredeon? Graelen followed the voice-of-reason down the passage, thinking that if the worst came to the worst and it looked like they'd execute him, he would ask Ceyne to try to save Valendia. But he doubted there would be time.

As Graelen stepped through the cabin door, the hand-of-force caught his arm, shoved it up behind his back, and forced him to his knees.

'Why didn't you tell me about the gift-benediction?' Kyredeon demanded.

Graelen gaped in surprise.

'He has no idea,' the voice-of-reason said. 'I told you –'

'You used to be so good at bringing me information.' Kyredeon signalled Hand-of-force Oriemn to let Graelen up. 'What happened?'

'I used to go drinking with the initiates and young adepts.' He stood, shrugging his shoulder to ease the pain. 'But Paryx is dead and I've been away from the brotherhood for too long. No one trusts me now that they know...' Graelen glared at Oriemn and his three gift-warriors. Kyredeon's first hand-of-force hadn't liked him, but Graelen suspected this one hated him. 'It used to be only a whisper, but someone let my true identity and role in the brotherhood become general knowledge. It's hard to blend in, if everyone says, "look, there goes Kyredeon's assassin."'

'So you're useless?' Oriemn said.

'If you know nothing of the gift-benediction, step aside and keep quiet,' Kyredeon told Graelen. He nodded to his hand-of-force. 'Send for my inner circle, then fetch Ardonyx. Rough him up a little and make sure everyone sees.'

After Oriemn and his followers walked out, the voice-of-reason asked, 'Why not send for both Tobazim and Ardonyx?'

'Because I want to provoke Tobazim into defending Ardonyx. On its own, the fact that they performed a gift-benediction without my permission is not enough to punish them.'

'But it was performed on one of All-father Tamaron's Malaunje.'

'The Malaunje woman had been raped by Mieren. She came to them for help, requesting the gift-benediction because it improved the chances of her baby being born Malaunje. If anything, they have won stature for the brotherhood.' Kyredeon gave a cunning grin. 'But if I can make Tobazim think Ardonyx is under threat and force him to strike before he's ready, I can cripple him before he grows too powerful. If I'm lucky, I can kill him and a few of his supporters and claim it was self-defence.'

TOBAZIM COMPLETED THE exercises and came back into a ready stance. Sweat dripped from his eyebrows, stinging his eyes. His muscles burned and trembled, and his heart raced.

But he could still feel it – the craving for the causare's gift. It had started the second day after the effect of the gift-infusion faded, and it had not let up. He'd told no one. Not even Ardonyx, who had asked only this morning if something was wrong. He didn't dare admit his weakness.

'Are you done?' Haromyr asked. 'They'll be serving up

the evening meal soon. I don't know about you, but I'm hungry.'

'It'll be good to eat a meal that doesn't try to get away from us,' Eryx said.

'Or come back up again,' Athlyn added. 'Why did I have to throw up in front of Valendia?'

The other two laughed.

They'd appointed themselves Tobazim's bodyguards. He let them think his strict exercise regime was a ploy to warn off attackers, rather than a desperate attempt to rid himself of this compulsion to go to the causare.

'I'm done.' He'd bathe, then eat. Hopefully, he'd be so exhausted, he'd be able to sleep.

The bathing chamber was wreathed in steam, and the last few initiates left hurriedly when they saw who it was. Tobazim couldn't decide if they were afraid of him, or showing deference. His gift surged and he saw the initiates at the base of the brotherhood pyramid; they were showing deference. This new aspect of his gift unsettled him.

He stripped and stepped into the bath, which was decidedly cool. All the better; it would sharpen his senses.

'Go save us some food,' Haromyr told Athlyn, who hurried away.

The causare's gift was the ability to read people. Tobazim had always been able to judge stresses in the process of construction. It seemed her gift-infusion had roused a new aspect to his gift, making him something between a raedan and a builder. He'd only ever heard of new facets of a T'En's gift arising after a life and death experience on the higher plane.

Tobazim rose from the bath, rubbed himself dry and dressed in breeches and undershirt. The three of them stepped out into the young adepts' cabin where the others were eating, sitting cross-legged on their bedrolls.

'Where's Athlyn?' Haromyr muttered. 'I swear if I miss out on dinner, I'll –'

The cabin door opened and Athlyn peered in. His gaze

raked the gathering. As soon as he spotted Tobazim, he jerked his head, beckoning him.

Tobazim crossed the cabin.

Haromyr and Eryx followed, hands going to the hilts of their knives. The general chatter died down. All three of them went to the door, stepping out onto the passage and then onto the mid-deck, where Ionnyn waited with one of the gift-warriors from All-father Tamaron's brotherhood.

The large sailor radiated gift aggression.

'What's wrong?' Tobazim asked.

'They've snatched Ardonyx,' Ionnyn said. 'We have to save him.'

Tobazim glanced to Athlyn. 'Why did they take him?'

Athlyn glanced to Gift-warrior Norsasno.

The big adept from Tamaron's brotherhood shrugged. 'I don't know if this has anything to do with it, but Kyredeon sent for Lysarna and Imokara. They say he interviewed them about the gift-benediction you and Ardonyx performed not long after you first arrived on the wharf.'

Haromyr swore softly.

'It's four days since Kyredeon arrived in port. I'm surprised it took so long.' Tobazim bluffed. 'Has he sent for me?'

'No. He sent for the assassin –'

'And his hand-of-force just grabbed Ardonyx from the rear-deck.' Ionnyn bristled. 'Even though the captain didn't resist, Oriemn's followers beat him.'

'This can't be about the gift-benediction,' Tobazim said with as much conviction as he could muster. He caught Norsasno's eye. 'Scholar Hakonnyn hasn't complained about our role in it, has he?'

'No. Our Malaunje women approached you and you did our brotherhood a service. If anything, you've won stature for your brotherhood.' Norsasno nodded. 'Hakonnyn said you did what only high-ranking initiates could do.'

'Then why did they beat Ardonyx and take him?' Ionnyn countered.

'Io is right,' Haromyr said. 'We need to defend Ardonyx.'

Norsasno caught Tobazim's eye. 'It doesn't add up.'

Tobazim's body tensed and his gift surfaced in anticipation of trouble. 'They're in the captain's cabin?' He refused to call it the all-father's cabin. It should have been Ardonyx's.

'You want me to come with you, to put forward our brotherhood's position?' Norsasno asked.

Tobazim was surprised by the offer. 'No, it's all right. Kyredeon wouldn't take kindly to having another brotherhood interfere. No offence meant.'

'None taken.'

'Do you want me to gather the sailors?' Ionnyn asked.

'You want me to get the others?' Haromyr offered.

There were at least a dozen, maybe twenty young adepts and initiates who would spring to his call, but Tobazim didn't want them risking their lives over this. It shouldn't get that far.

Athlyn looked frightened but determined. The young initiate had shared the same choice-mother as Tobazim and Learon, and was the last link to his old choice-brother. Too many people's lives depended on Tobazim for him to make rash decisions. He gestured to Haromyr, Eryx and Athlyn. 'Return to the cabin. Go back to your post, Ionnyn.'

The big adept did not look happy.

'What if you need us?'

'If I need you, it's already too late.'

As Tobazim climbed the steps to the rear deck, he wondered if he'd done the right thing. The low sun threw long shadows across the deck. Nearly sunset.

Was he walking to his death?

He hoped he could talk his way out of this, because he wasn't strong enough to challenge Kyredeon.

As he approached the door of the captain's cabin, Tobazim sensed gift aggression. His own gift surged, sending waves of prickling awareness across his skin.

He knocked. For a moment no one answered, then the

door swung open and Ceyne stood there. His expression held warning.

'You were right, all-father.' The saw-bones sounded like a gift-tutor chiding a student. Tobazim suspected he was trying to defuse the situation. 'It's the other half of that pair of trouble-makers.'

'Saves me sending for him,' Kyredeon said, sounding too affable for Tobazim's peace of mind. He gestured. 'Come in.'

Tobazim took in the scene. Ardonyx knelt on the floor. Kyredeon and his inner circle stood over him. Graelen was amongst their number; it was clear where his allegiances lay.

Unless he, like Ceyne, was an unwilling witness. But Ceyne had admitted he'd once stood back and let his apprentice go to his death, rather than risk his own life.

Tobazim crossed the chamber and sank to his knees, performing the correct obeisance. When Ardonyx cast him a swift look of warning, he caught sight of his brother's bleeding nose. His gut tightened and his gift readiness rose another notch.

Their all-father leant against the desk and folded his arms. 'Not only am I stuck housing half of Tamaron's brotherhood, but now I hear you two have performed a gift-benediction on one of All-father Tamaron's Malaunje. The female in question acknowledged your stature and thanked me.' Kyredeon's voice was heavy with sarcasm. 'A gift-benediction, no less?'

'We had no choice,' Tobazim said. He went to lift his hands in the gesture of supplication, but Oriemn stepped behind him, pinning his arms. Tobazim repressed a surge of anger, fighting to keep his voice neutral. 'Brigands had raped Imokara. The sooner the gift-benediction was carried out, the more chance she had of birthing a Malaunje baby. Ardonyx was injured, so I –'

'It was only by combining our skills that we were able to perform the benediction, all-father,' Ardonyx said. 'As it was, we struggled.'

Tobazim glanced his way, for it had not been a struggle.

They had gift-worked perfectly together, understanding each other intuitively. His gift surged and he sensed the stresses in the confrontation. Ardonyx was lying to make them seem less capable.

'And you completed the gift-benediction without breaching the woman's defences? That requires great skill indeed. Next you'll be telling me you've both mastered gift-tutoring,' Kyredeon mocked. 'All-father Tamaron will arrive any day now and, when he does, he could take offence. Give me one good reason why I shouldn't hand the pair of you over to his hand-of-force?'

Tobazim could come up with a dozen reasons, but if Kyredeon was being reasonable, he would have been congratulating them for making All-father Tamaron beholden to him.

In the corner of Tobazim's eye, sunlight glinted on Kyredeon's sculpture of the Celestial City. During the last season before their exile, the all-father and his voice-of-reason had combined their skills and gifts to create this tribute. Made of blown glass and wrought silver, it stood waist-high and was a work of art. Farodytor was the silversmith, Kyredeon the glassblower.

To Tobazim, this sculpture of the Celestial City represented the true ideals of the brotherhood. To protect in honour.

'Your presumption deserves punishment,' Kyredeon said. 'Oriemn –'

'We invoke the sacred vow,' Tobazim announced.

'What?' Kyredeon straightened up.

'We took a vow to protect Malaunje, *all* Malaunje,' Tobazim rushed on. 'Imokara came to us for help. We had no choice.'

'That vow is sacred to all T'En,' Ardonyx said, picking up his line of argument. Tobazim sensed a little push of power, but wasn't sure where it had come from. 'It is why the Malaunje serve us, because we offer protection. We could not dishonour our vow.'

'They speak truly,' Gift-tutor Deimosh said. Ceyne nodded agreement.

The others kept their silence, watching the all-father to see how he would react. Kyredeon looked like he had bitten into an apple and found a worm. His eyes narrowed.

Before he could speak, someone knocked on the door.

'Come in,' Kyredeon called.

The Malaunje servant entered, dropped to both knees and delivered the message. 'Causare Imoshen has called an all-council on her ship.'

Kyredeon dismissed the messenger with a wave of his hand.

'You can count yourselves lucky,' he said. 'But this is not the end of it. Get out.'

Tobazim came to his feet, dizzy with relief. In the hall, Tobazim's knees wavered. Ardonyx slung an arm around his shoulders and led him up onto the high rear-deck, where they could speak privately. A Malaunje sailor was at the wheel. He looked relieved to see Ardonyx.

'What just happened?' Tobazim whispered.

'I think Kyredeon expected you to panic, but you kept your head.'

'I'd rather have a martial gift than a cool head.'

'A cool head may prove more useful, in the long run.'

'I should go back to the cabin and make sure Haromyr doesn't do something stupid.'

Ardonyx nodded.

Tobazim rubbed his face. He felt detached and slightly drunk. 'From the way Kyredeon reacted, you'd think we'd formed the deep-bonding with a T'En woman and betrayed all our brotherhood secrets to her!'

Ardonyx looked grim, and Tobazim left him.

Chapter Eight

'PUT THE BRAZIER here,' Imoshen told the burly Malaunje, who manoeuvred it into place. She stepped back, closer to Egrayne. 'We'll hold the all-council on deck, under the moons and the stars.'

'It's not like we have much choice,' Egrayne muttered. The harbour-master had not been pleased with Baron Nitzane's authority to give them safe harbour, and they were confined to their ships.

Imoshen grinned. 'My flagship, my rules.'

'It won't help you if the brotherhoods declare they have no confidence in you and force another causare election. Even with Chariode's loss, the all-fathers still outnumber the sisterhoods, eight to six. You can't win if they unite against us.'

'What are the chances of that?' Imoshen asked. But they both knew it had happened before. When All-father Rohaayel was about to be executed for breaking the covenant, the all-fathers had sent their hands-of-force to avenge his death.

And Imoshen had defeated them.

'You never told me how you killed all those gift-warriors,' Egrayne said. 'Without training on the higher plane it should have been impossible. Your gift is the ability to read people, it's not a martial gift.'

'No one has ever asked me how I did it. Why not?'

'We were shocked to learn the all-fathers had sent their hands-of-force. Had it been one or more of the all-mothers conducting Rohaayel's execution and not you, they would

have been killed. We could have had a brotherhood
uprising on our hands. Instead, we discovered we had the
most powerful sister since –'

'I'm not powerful,' Imoshen said. 'When the gift-warriors
struck, Rohaayel was as surprised as me. He protected me,
killing four of them.'

'But... but his gift was crippled by the loss of his shield-
brother.'

'He used the higher plane's hunger for our power. I'd
formed the plane in the shape of my island and he threw
himself into the sea, taking them with him. The sea
devoured them. I was left trapped on a rock with the waves
crashing around us, or so they thought.' Imoshen shrugged.
'I knew that every sixth or seven wave was bigger than the
rest. I saw it coming and lured them onto a rock that I
knew would go under. I let them think they had me. At the
last possible moment, I leaped to safety. They were washed
to their deaths and the empyrean plane devoured them. I
didn't kill a single one of them. I'm a fraud, Egrayne. All
these years, everyone has thought me powerful, but –'

'Using the danger of the empyrean plane is a legitimate
duelling technique.' She squeezed Imoshen's hand and
let a little of her gift warm her. 'Considering you had no
experience of the higher plane, you –'

'Oh, but I did.' Imoshen was tired of lying. 'I'd been
segueing to the higher plane since I was thirteen. I used to
have waking nightmares where reality would shift and I
could see the empyrean plane superimposed over this one.'

Egrayne pulled away. 'But only gift-warriors have that
ability.'

Imoshen met her eyes. 'I believe –'

'They're here, causare,' Kiane said. 'Do you want me to
keep the all-fathers down on the mid-deck until the all-
mothers have arrived?'

'No. Send them up. Have the motherless children wait
on the lower rear-deck.'

The Malaunje unrolled a circular carpet and hung the

last of the lanterns. They'd just finished when the first of the sisterhood leaders arrived with their seconds and Malaunje servants.

Imoshen smiled as Reoden joined her.

'Are you recovered, Ree?' Imoshen took the healer's hands and kissed her cheeks. 'I've hardly seen you since we set sail.'

'Blame it on seasickness.'

'You've been seasick?'

'No, but everyone else has.' Reoden grew serious. 'I saved Tamaron's life. He and his brothers – all the children of that family – are mine to protect, Imoshen.'

'I wouldn't dream of taking them away from you. But...' She glanced to the healer. The thought of sending Iraayel to the brotherhood tore the heart right out of her. 'Four boys, Ree?'

'Imoshen, Ree.' The gift-wright, Ceriane, joined them. 'No more interesting empyrean wounds for me to heal?'

The thin gift-wright had helped save Sorne's life. Imoshen smiled, then sobered. 'My gift tells me something is wrong with Kyredeon. Is his power corrupting?'

'Not that I've sensed, but it would not take much to tip him over the edge,' Ceriane said.

'What do we do if an all-father's gift corrupts?'

'Usually, his brotherhood kills him and a new all-father takes his place.'

'What's this about a new all-father?' Athazi asked. She glanced to the gift-wright. Athazi had always resented the high stature of Ceriane's gift. Unaware of this, Ardonyx had assigned them to the same five-masted ship. 'Has the gift-wright heard something we should all know?'

'No, we were just discussing Kyredeon,' Imoshen said. 'Here's Mel.'

Imoshen's gift surged as she read Melisarone. The old all-mother carried a bone-deep sadness within her. Leaving the city where she had spent ninety years had torn out her heart. She would not live long in exile.

The sisterhood leaders were missing All-mother Parazime, who had been visiting one of her estates when the king attacked. She had been planning to meet them in Port Mirror-on-Sea, but now she would have to travel further south to join them here. Hers was the smallest of the sisterhoods, and Imoshen had given the remaining sisters shelter on her ship. Parazime's old historian had come to represent her sisterhood in the leader's absence. The brotherhoods were also missing one leader. All-father Tamaron had been stranded on one of his estates.

'Here come the brotherhoods,' Athazi whispered, her voice an odd mixture of longing and resentment.

As the powerful T'En men approached, the sisterhood leaders edged back and Imoshen realised Kiane had held the men back, to give precedence to the T'En women. The all-fathers would resent this reminder of their subservience.

Despite the cold, the men went bare-chested, to reveal their duelling scars. Their pleated breeches hung low on their hips, held up with jewelled belts. Soft boots and knee-length, sleeveless brocade robes completed their formal costume. Around their necks, they wore their torcs of office, each a work of art inlaid with precious stones, set with their brotherhood symbols. Kyredeon's symbol was the eye, because the first leader of his brotherhood had been a seer.

'You can expect a challenge tonight,' Egrayne warned Imoshen softly. 'We fled the port with our tail between our legs.'

Imoshen's gift surged and she read each brotherhood triumvirate as they approached. Kyredeon and his seconds were primed for violence. They radiated anger, which seemed to be directed at the world in general, although its focus narrowed on her when they saw her.

They were followed by Hueryx, who had stood against her for the causareship. He'd been his brotherhood's historian. It was unusual for an all-father to come from the ranks of the scholars. More commonly the voice-of-reason was a scholar and the all-father and his hand-of-force both had martial gifts, or all three had the martial gifts.

The thin all-father was wound tight as a coil and he took a place as far as possible from Kyredeon. That's right; his brotherhood shared Kyredeon's ship. Hueryx's hand-of-force leaned close to say something and the all-father glanced to Imoshen. In that moment she read his intention. He was going to confront her.

All-father Paragian and his seconds joined them. Paragian had also stood against her for the role of causare. He was popular and it was only because the brotherhoods had split their votes that she had won the role. From Paragian's triumvirate she sensed determination.

Brash young All-father Saskeyne and his seconds were one step behind Paragian. She sensed no menace from him, but he had sent his warriors out to steal the banners of King Charald's army. This had triggered reprisals against their estates. Saskeyne was swift to act and did not consider the ramifications.

That was all the large brotherhoods, leaving only the four lesser brotherhoods, three more all-fathers and Scholar Hakonnyn, who represented Tamaron's brotherhood. These three triumvirates were on edge. The lesser brotherhoods were always defending themselves against takeovers by one of the big four.

The brotherhood leaders shifted, eyeing each other uneasily. Imoshen didn't need her gift to know the over-crowding on the ships would trigger duels and rekindle old feuds.

Hueryx drew breath to speak and she knew he was going to challenge her leadership.

'I propose we make a vow for the duration of the voyage,' Imoshen said, forestalling him.

'What kind of vow?' Paragian asked.

'No inter-brotherhood or sisterhood rivalry.' She knew this would please the lesser brotherhoods and protect Hueryx from Kyredeon.

'I support this vow,' Hueryx said.

'I'd give this vow,' Paragian conceded, 'but only if all of us give it.'

'We must be united. Distrust breeds distrust,' Imoshen said. 'We must all make sacrifices for the good of the T'Enatuath.'

The brotherhood leaders stiffened. The jewelled clips that held their long hair in place glinted in the lantern light. Imoshen's heart sank as she read them. They were too intent on personal stature and the fate of their brotherhoods to see the fate of the T'Enatuath. Although they'd had half a year to come to terms with exile, they did not want to make concessions, let alone sacrifices.

Once before she had confronted them about this, and now it was time to make her point.

Imoshen stepped forward.

The others drew in a collective breath as she took her ceremonial knife from her belt. Reaching around behind her, Imoshen grasped her long plait. The T'En only cut their hair when they believed they were going to die in battle, or when a choice-mother sent her son to his brotherhood. On that day, she cut his hair to symbolise that he was dead to her.

Imoshen's hair was down to her knees, but to be truly fashionable, it should have been long enough to walk on. The elaborate styles which took so long to create were a sign of the T'En's high stature.

Holding the braid at breast level, she began sawing through her hair.

'With this sacrifice, I mourn the loss of the Celestial City,' she said. 'I mourn the loss of the warriors who fell protecting us, and the scholars who remained in the crypts because they could not face exile. I mourn the Malaunje innocents, who were murdered the night the Mieren invaded the city. I mourn our people who did not make it to Port Mirror-on-Sea but were murdered on their estates or on the road. I mourn those who died to defend the wharf when the people of the slums attacked us.'

Finally the knife severed her hair and she lifted the long plait, holding it in front of her.

Imoshen walked over to the brazier. Her short, uneven hair sat around her shoulders, stirring in the updrafts from the brazier like a living thing. Her gift sang under her skin, riding a wave of emotion so thick she felt as if she would choke on it.

'Exile is not death, it is a new start. I rename my ship the *Resolute* because that is what we must be,' Imoshen said. 'The T'Enatuath will endure, but to endure we must make sacrifices. Tonight I honour our fallen and, in their memory, I say there must be no more rivalry between the brotherhoods and sisterhoods. We share a common enemy in the Mieren.'

She dropped her plait into the fire. The sickening smell of burning hair filled the air and she felt their gifts rise. 'I offer to share my flagship with All-mother Reoden's sisterhood. And before all of you here tonight, I declare she will not be beholden to me. '

'I am honoured, T'Imoshen.' Reoden surprised her by using the causare honorific, which only Egrayne had ever used. When Imoshen met the healer's eyes, she read admiration and determination.

Reoden stepped closer. She held out her hand for Imoshen's knife.

Imoshen hesitated. Back when they had been secret lovers, she had rolled naked in Reoden's hair, feeling its gift residue race over her skin.

'Causare.' Reoden lifted her hand.

Imoshen passed her the knife.

Reoden took her long plait and began to cut through it. 'I honour our fallen. Exile is not death. I vow to turn my warriors only against enemies outside the T'Enatuath. United, we will survive.'

She was still sawing at her hair when old All-mother Melisarone stepped forward. She had been a warrior before she became a sisterhood leader, and she carried her own long-knife which she used on her hair, as she honoured their fallen. Hers was a small sisterhood, and the ship they had been assigned was one of the smallest: a three-masted vessel, purchased from the Mieren. She named her ship the *Hope*. 'Following T'Imoshen's example, I offer All-mother Parazime's sisterhood a berth on my ship, without obligation. And I vow to turn my warriors only against enemies outside the T'Enatuath. United, we will survive.'

Everyone looked to All-mother Athazi. Imoshen could tell she was furious, but the sisterhoods had to present a united front before the brotherhood leaders.

The plump little all-mother stepped forward. With sharp, vicious tugs, she unpinned her hair and quickly cut through it. She gave the same oath and... 'I will share my ship with All-mother Ceriane. She will not be beholden to me. I rename my ship the *Endurance*.'

Ceriane, the only gift-wright of the T'Enatuath, stepped forward, used the honorific and cut her hair, accepting Athazi's offer to share the ship. Not by the slightest gesture did she reveal the rift between herself and Athazi.

Imoshen was proud of her; proud of all the sisterhood leaders.

Their side of the impromptu ceremony complete, the all-mothers stepped back. Imoshen looked across the brazier's leaping flames to the brotherhood leaders. Her gaze went from face to face, until she found All-father Paragian. The day he'd stood against her for the causareship, she'd read him. He had the best interests of their people at heart.

He swallowed, came forward and beckoned his voice-of-reason. 'Take down my hair.'

The styles the men wore were as elaborate as those worn by the women. He stood still as his second unpinned his long hair. This done, Paragian drew his knife. Twisting his hair to form a thick rope, he sawed through it. 'I rename my ship the *Triumphant*, because we will not be beaten. As Causare Imoshen has done, I vow to turn my warriors only against enemies outside the T'Enatuath. United, we will survive.'

Imoshen did not care if the all-fathers refused to use her honorific, as long as they cooperated.

He rolled up his hair and threw it onto the fire, meeting Imoshen's eyes across the flames. Paragian cleared his throat. He and Kyredeon had run trading fleets and owned most of the ships the brotherhoods were using. 'Since All-father Saskeyne's brotherhood is already sharing my flagship, I say he is welcome and will not be beholden to me.'

The young all-father looked relieved, if a little surprised. He cut his hair to mourn their dead, accepted Paragian's generosity and gave his vow. As Saskeyne did this, Imoshen sent Paragian the slightest of nods and looked to Kyredeon.

The all-father managed to keep his anger contained as he stepped up to the fire and cut his braid. He renamed his flagship the *Victorious* and offered Hueryx's brotherhood a place on it. Now, if he broke his vow, he would be foresworn before all of the T'Enatuath's leaders.

Imoshen looked to Hueryx. His brotherhood was safe, or as safe as she could make him. Her gift surged and she knew he understood what she had done and why, as he sent her the slightest of nods. He gave his vow, accepted Kyredeon's offer and sacrificed his hair in mourning.

When this was done, All-father Abeliode cut his hair and renamed his ship, purchased from the Mieren, the *Conquest*, but he did not offer to share the three-masted vessel with either All-father Dretsun or Tamaron. She could understand why. His was the largest of the lesser brotherhoods. The *Conquest* was barely big enough for his brotherhood, let alone another.

Imoshen looked to old All-father Egrutz. It was rare for an all-father to grow old. She had heard he was training his replacement. Egrutz had the use of one of Paragian's five-masted ships. He met her eyes and gave a nod. Stepping forward, he cut his hair, mourned their dead, made his vow and renamed his ship the *Perseverance*, then offered to share with Dretsun's brotherhood.

As Dretsun sacrificed his hair, Imoshen marked the

difference in the names the brotherhoods and sisterhoods gave their vessels. The all-mothers had named their ships for the attributes they valued: hope, resolution and endurance. While the all-fathers had chosen names like *Victory* and *Conquest*. Only old Egrutz had broken the pattern when he named his ship the *Perseverance*. But then he was nearly ninety and had lived long enough to know that the striving for stature and power was never-ending.

That left All-father Tamaron's brotherhood without a ship.

'I'll send a message to Baron Nitzane and see if he will sell us one of his ships,' Imoshen told Scholar Hakonnyn. 'Now we must assign choice-mothers for the T'En children, and allocate brotherhoods for the boys.'

'No,' Dretsun said.

As the all-father stepped forward, Imoshen read him. She'd expected a challenge, but thought it would come from Paragian or Hueryx, or even Saskeyne; not Dretsun, leader of a lesser brotherhood.

Dretsun gestured to Imoshen. 'I say this causare has led us badly.'

The atmosphere turned icy as the sisterhood leaders stepped closer to Imoshen.

Dretsun looked around at the gathering. 'I say we had to rush our departure from the city –'

'To avoid Baron Eskarnor attacking our people on the road to port,' Imoshen said. 'But we outmanoeuvred him and reached port safely.'

'You call that safe?' Dretsun sneered. 'We were attacked on the wharf while under the king's protection.'

'King Charald has grown frail since we made the bargain back in the spring, which is not something I could have anticipated. I've arranged for our fleet to shelter here under the protection of Baron Nitzane while we wait for the last of our people to come in from their estates. Or were you going to sail off and abandon them?'

Dretsun bristled. 'I say this causare has failed in her duty to protect the T'Enatuath. And I nominate myself for causare.'

Both Paragian and Hueryx objected, but Imoshen read the leaders of the lesser brotherhoods and realised Dretsun had their backing. It was a clever ploy: the lesser brotherhoods were vulnerable to the great brotherhoods, but if they united under one leader, they were easily bigger than any of the larger brotherhoods alone.

'If we are doing this, then it must be done properly,' Paragian said. 'We must call for a vote of no confidence in the causare, then call for nominations.'

'Certainly,' Imoshen agreed. 'But first let's hear what All-father Dretsun would do if he were causare. I take it you have a plan to save our people, Dretsun? You know of somewhere we will be safe? Because we cannot stay here after winter's cusp, and when the winter storms strike, the Secluded Sea will not be safe for our fleet. Where will we go, Dretsun? Where?'

She was betting that he had been so focused on unseating her that he had not thought this far ahead.

His mouth opened then closed and he glared, as he realised he had fallen into her trap.

'Because I have a plan. I know where we can go.' She paused and looked around the circle. 'Back in the Celestial City, like you, I was trying to come to terms with exile for my sisterhood, but I was also thinking ahead. I sent a message to the Sagoras of Ivernia.'

'The Sagoras?' Dretsun's eyes narrowed. 'But they are Mieren. Why should Mieren offer us sanctuary? What bargain have you struck?'

'No bargain, yet. But I offered to trade the one thing we are richly endowed with: knowledge. It is the one thing the Sagoras prize, above all else.'

There was muttering from the brotherhoods and silence from the sisterhoods. Imoshen knew, the moment the men left, the women would be berating her for not consulting them. While it was true she had sent a message to the Sagoras, as yet there had been no reply. But now was not the time to reveal this.

'It was not your right to bargain away the knowledge of the T'Enatuath!' Dretsun protested.

'I offered to strike a bargain, no more. The details are yet to be negotiated.'

'We can't give them access to the higher plane,' Dretsun stated, and though he did not know it yet, she had defeated his challenge. 'The dangers are too great –'

'I agree,' Imoshen said. 'So between now and when we reach Ivernia, we must decide what knowledge, both practical and theoretical, we can offer the Sagoras. All-father Dretsun, can I rely on you to put together a list for barter?'

He nodded, pleased that his stature had been acknowledged.

And she had diverted a causare challenge.

'Time to see to the children.'

Chapter Nine

ARAVELLE TOOK HER little sister's hand as they waited on the lower rear-deck. Her brothers were already there, with a T'En boy of five or six holding a small baby. Ronnyn held their newborn brother, Ashmyr; he, Vittor and Tamaron were all richly dressed in velvet and brocade. Their long, white hair had been styled more elaborately than their mother had ever managed, even on feast days. They didn't look like her brothers any more. Resentment burned in her.

'Tani!' Tamaron spotted them and ran over to hug Itania, lifting the two-year-old off her feet. Her happy laughter carried.

'Vella.' Ronnyn's eyes widened. 'You look... grown up.'

She sensed he'd been going to say something else. She wore simple pleated trousers, a long-sleeved knitted vest and a thigh-length smock. The clothing was finer than anything she'd ever owned, but it marked her as a servant.

'You have father's cane.' He looked relieved. 'I thought I'd lost it.' And he held out his hand as though it belonged to him.

She didn't want to give up the cane – it was all she had of their old life – but she handed it over. He was still her brother.

'Here. Enough of that.' An elderly T'En woman separated them. 'T'En don't acknowledge their Malaunje kin.'

Behind the woman's back, Ronnyn sent Aravelle a cheeky grin that crinkled his forehead, and mouthed, *later*.

Vittor and Tamaron started to protest, but they were sent up to the high rear-deck, where many beautifully-dressed

T'En men and women were waiting. Amongst them were Malaunje servants, who were almost as magnificently dressed, each holding a large leather book.

'These are the children of Malaunje loners and runaways, so they don't know our customs,' Causare Imoshen said. 'They must be assigned choice-mothers, and brotherhoods must be allocated for the boys when they reach seventeen.'

Aravelle picked up Itania, who was tired and starting to grizzle. She felt the grownups watching her, judging her and her parents. She told herself that she didn't care what they thought, but her family had to live with these people.

The little boy with the baby was led onto the centre of the carpet. Even though she resented his T'En blood, Aravelle's heart went out to him, as he tood there so small and alone.

The boy looked up at the causare. On the other side of the brazier, the T'En men shifted and mumbled, while the T'En women whispered. Aravelle understood what the muttering was about when the boy glanced her way. A streak of copper hair grew from above one ear. She did not know what it meant, but she knew the T'En would regard it as a flaw.

'Tell us what is known of this child, Egrayne,' the causare said.

The tall woman beckoned a Malaunje and consulted a book the servant held open for her. 'He says he is five years old and speaks only Chalcedonian. From what we can gather his parents lived in a mountain village, inhabited only by other Malaunje. We believe his Malaunje parents were the children of Mieren, who ran away to the mountain village. As the child of loners, he has no affiliation with any brotherhood.'

'And the babe?' the causare asked.

'A female T'En, less than half a year old. No blood kin to him, she's also the child of Malaunje loners, with no affiliation to any sisterhood.'

An eager murmur of longing came from the T'En women.

'She's mine,' the boy said, his arms tightening protectively.

'I found her hidden in a chicken coop. Let her suck raw egg off my fingers.'

'That was clever,' Ronnyn whispered to Aravelle and she realised her brothers had edged closer to her, even though Voice-of-reason Nerazime was with them.

'Which brotherhood will take this boy?' The causare raised her voice.

No one spoke.

'Come, he may be the child of loners, but he has shown ingenuity and responsibility.'

No response.

Then one of the men raised his hand. 'I'll take him.'

'All-father Kyredeon.' The causare acknowledged a battle-scarred male with a hint of reluctance. Apart from his face being more deeply scarred than any other man's, he seemed no different from the others to Aravelle. Perhaps the causare read something in him that only a raedan could. Aravelle reminded herself that the boy was T'En; at least he wouldn't have to spend his life as a servant.

'Make a note in my brotherhood's lineage book,' Kyredeon said to two Malaunje behind him.

'Which sisterhood will have the honour of rearing the boy?' the causare asked.

No one spoke.

'Come,' she pressed. 'I know our ships are over-crowded, but one child will not make a difference. Which sisterhood will rear this boy?'

No one stirred.

'Is the copper streak so bad?' Ronnyn asked softly.

'That is one mark against him,' Nerazime said. 'But he has also shown defiance. Caring for T'En males of dubious lineage and great spirit is hard work. All that effort, only to give him up at seventeen.'

'I will take the female child,' an old T'En woman announced. 'My sisterhood –'

'No. *My* sisterhood –' a sour-looking plump woman interrupted.

As the women argued, the boy took a step back, arms tightening around the infant.

'Since no one will take him, the boy will be my choice-son,' the causare announced to a ripple of surprise, 'and since he protected this baby and cared for her all the way across Chalcedonia, I cannot part them. My daughter needs a younger sister to teach her responsibility. Make a note in our lineage book.'

The T'En women muttered, but no one dared object.

While the Malaunje wrote in the lineage book, Voice-of-reason Egrayne led the boy around behind the causare. The baby was passed through the thick folds of the causare's pleated trousers. She lifted the infant up and kissed the babe's forehead. Then the boy's head appeared as he crawled through.

'Welcome, choice-son.' The causare helped the boy to his feet and returned the baby to his arms. She touched the tip of her left hand's sixth finger to his forehead, then to the babe's. 'I swear to protect your lives with my own. I swear to rear you to revere the heritage of the T'Enatuath and protect our Malaunje.'

'Causare, what names shall I put down?' the Malaunje asked.

Imoshen focused on the boy. 'We cannot use your Chalcedonian name, so I will call you... Deyne.' She hesitated as if she might explain the name's origin, but when the causare continued it was to discuss the baby's name. 'As for the girl –'

'I don't know her name,' the boy admitted. 'I called her Little Chicken because of where I found her.'

'Well, we can't call her that.' The causare's voice held a smile. 'We'll call her Arodyti, after my brave and loyal hand-of-force.' Her voice grew husky with emotion. 'May this little one live up to her memory.'

The causare called a Malaunje woman over and her new choice-children were led away.

Voice-of-reason Nerazime took Ronnyn by the shoulders.

'Your turn, lad. If she asks you a question, you address her as "causare" or "T'Imoshen." Off you go.'

Nerazime indicated that Aravelle was to stand behind her T'En brothers, reminding her of her place. In her arms, little Itania slept on, impervious to the insult.

Even though Aravelle knew the healer would accept them, she felt nervous.

'What is known of these children?' the causare asked.

Healer Reoden stepped forward. 'There are four male T'En, one of them a newborn, and two female Malaunje, all from the same parents, both Malaunje.'

Aravelle was close enough to hear Egrayne whisper to the causare. 'Four healthy T'En from the one set of Malaunje parents. The T'En blood will run strong in those girls.'

Aravelle bristled. They were not breeding cows.

'I was too late to save the mother,' Reoden continued. 'They speak our language, so their parents must have run away from a brotherhood or sisterhood. They don't know which one.'

The causare stepped closer to Ronnyn, which made Aravelle realise she was the same height as her brother. 'Think back. Did your parents ever mention a name of someone from their brotherhood?'

Ronnyn hesitated. Aravelle knew it was not in his nature to lie.

When there was no response, the causare turned to Vittor. 'Where did you come from?'

'The island,' Vittor said. 'Mieren came. They killed Da. They burned everything and took –'

'...us prisoner,' Aravelle said quickly, before Vittor could reveal the beautiful torc Scholar Hueryx had given their mother. 'Then they threw us in a caged-cart and –'

'The causare was not speaking to you, girl,' Egrayne reprimanded Aravelle, then added to Imoshen. 'For all that they speak T'En, they might as well be the children of loners.'

Aravelle's cheeks burned.

The causare raised her voice. 'It's not their fault they were raised by runaway Malaunje. The boys need a brotherhood. Which all-father will take them?'

She waited, but no one stepped forward.

Aravelle stiffened, lifting her chin to hide the pain of rejection.

'Come, all-fathers,' the causare urged.

'There's something wrong with the eldest boy's arm,' one of the T'En men said. He was not as big as some, but he was certainly sharp-eyed. 'Show us, boy.'

Ronnyn passed their baby brother to Vittor and the cane to Aravelle. Then he lifted his bad arm to reveal the scars and knotted muscles.

There was an intake of breath from the women and muttering from the men.

Aravelle bristled. She wanted to shake her brother. She wanted to tell them all how brave he'd been, how hard he'd worked to regain the use of his arm, and how he'd trained his right hand so that he could use it instead of his left. But she couldn't. It would shame Ronnyn to be defended by a Malaunje.

'It was a stink-badger,' Vittor said. 'He killed it to save me. He was amazing. Blood went everywhere.'

The men grinned.

'Why didn't you show me?' the healer asked.

'You were busy,' Ronnyn said.

She took his arm in her hands. As her fingers probed his muscles, she frowned.

'You took on a stink-badger with your bare hands?' the sharp-eyed man asked.

'I had an axe. And' – Ronnyn glanced over his shoulder – 'Vella and Vittor helped. But it wasn't the first stink-badger that did this. It was the second, that came in from the side. I didn't spot him in time.'

'But he killed it, too,' Vittor said, his voice full of pride.

This time the men chuckled.

'Can you heal him, Ree?' the causare asked.

'With time, I can repair some of the damage. But this is too old to heal properly now. It's a wonder he can use his arm at all.'

'Vella massaged it every day,' Ronnyn said.

Both women sent Aravelle assessing looks, as if she'd suddenly proven useful. She looked down, face hot. Back then, Ronnyn's gift had already been manifesting and every time she massaged his arm, he'd tried to slip past her defences.

'And the broken nose?' the same man asked.

'Mieren,' Ronnyn said.

That drew more mutters. But the tone was different now. Aravelle could tell the men approved of her brother.

'I'll do what I can for the boy's arm,' the healer said. 'It won't be perfect, but it will be better. I should reveal that I am honour-bound to rear these four boys and watch over the girls. Their Malaunje mother placed a geas on me with her dying life force.'

'A Malaunje with such an affinity for the gifts,' Egrayne whispered to the causare. 'What a waste!'

A ripple of annoyance and respect raced through the T'En, and a bud of desperate dignity unfurled in Aravelle. She squared her shoulders, lifted her chin and whispered, 'Stand tall, boys.'

'So I will take the Malaunje girls into my sisterhood,' Reoden said. 'And –'

'Wait.' The sharp-eyed man left the brotherhood ranks. He moved with coiled tension and radiated concentration as he studied Aravelle's family.

'All-father Hueryx,' the causare acknowledged him. 'What is it?'

Ronnyn glanced over his shoulder to Aravelle, his forehead crinkling. She knew what he was thinking. Was this the same Hueryx their mother used to tell stories about? Were their parents' transgressions about to be revealed?

Hueryx left Ronnyn and came around to study Aravelle. She lifted her chin. Even if it was the same Hueryx, he would never recognise them. She'd only been a baby and Ronnyn hadn't been born when their parents ran away.

Hueryx lifted a hand to Aravelle's bruised eye. 'How...'

She sidestepped him, glaring.

He chuckled, muttering under his breath. 'I swear it is Sasoria all over again.'

Aravelle gasped to hear mother's name.

Hueryx turned to Ronnyn. 'And you... I thought I'd lost you.' He shook his head in wonder.

Aravelle was aware of the causare and Reoden exchanging worried looks.

'You know these children?' the causare asked.

Hueryx nodded. 'They are as alike as peas in a pod and they all have the impudent look of a very valuable, but wilful, Malaunje scribe who went missing under strange circumstances nearly thirteen years ago. I am honour bound to take the boys when they turn seventeen and protect the girls right now. They are brotherhood-born.'

Aravelle's heart sank. Now she wouldn't see her brothers until they were all grown up. Ashmyr would never know her.

'But I must fulfil the geas,' Reoden protested, glancing to the causare for support.

'Do it by rearing the boys,' Hueryx said. 'I'll have them back when they are ready for the brotherhood. The girls are mine. I'll take them now.'

Vittor shuffled closer to Ronnyn and Aravelle. Her brother glanced to Nerazime, who gave the slightest shake of her head and nodded towards the causare. She would decide. Aravelle focused on her.

'They are brotherhood-born, causare,' Hueryx reminded her. Although he spoke softly, his tone held a warning. 'Would you deny the brotherhoods their due?'

'This is easily resolved. Where is your brotherhood's lineage book?' the causare asked.

Hueryx beckoned a Malaunje, who hurried over with a large, leather-bound tome.

While the all-father flicked through this, looking for the right page, the causare turned to Ronnyn. 'Name your Malaunje birth parents, if you can.'

'My mother was Sasoria and my father was Asher,' Ronnyn said. Then he added, as if he could not help himself, 'My father died trying to protect us. We had to leave his body for the wild dogs.'

Aravelle felt hot tears sting her eyes. Vittor gave a soft sob, but she refused to cry.

'It must have been hard to leave him,' the causare said and her hand cupped their cheeks one after the other. Inexplicably, Aravelle felt a weight lift from her chest with the causare's touch.

'Sometimes we have to do hard things,' the causare said, holding her eyes. 'They shape us, but they should not cripple us.'

Then the causare turned to All-father Hueryx. 'Are the children's birth parents listed under your Malaunje?'

He smiled and gestured for the Malaunje servant to show the causare the open page.

She ran her finger down the list of names. 'Here they are. Sasoria, scribe and Asher, illuminator.'

Aravelle blinked. Her father had illuminated manuscripts? He had been an artist?

Of course he had, just look at the cane.

The causare dismissed the servant.

'As if that is not enough, this speaks for itself,' Hueryx said and held out his hand for their father's cane.

Aravelle didn't want to give it to him. She just knew he was going to use it against them in some way. But she had no choice. When Hueryx lifted the cane to study the carved snake on the handle, she realised the same symbol was central to the design on his neck torc. A snake swallowing its tail.

The all-father raised his eyes to her brother. 'Where did you get this, Ronnyn?'

'My father carved it, after the sea-boar gored his leg.'

'Stop calling him father.' Hueryx pounced on that word. 'He wasn't your father, boy.' He turned to the causare, displaying the cane triumphantly. 'This cane proves it. They came from my brotherhood, and the boy is my son. When his mother knew he was going to be born T'En, she ran away.'

There was a hushed murmur of disapproval from the rest of the T'En.

Aravelle opened her mouth to object, then bit her tongue.

But Hueryx noticed. He raised his brows, crinkling his forehead in challenge. At that moment he looked so like Ronnyn, it took her breath away.

It was true. All true...

A rushing filled her head. She hated All-father Hueryx. He'd destroyed everything she believed. Her mother had lied to them, letting them think they all shared the same father.

Hueryx gestured to his lineage book. 'See that it is written. Ronnyn, son of All-father Hueryx.' Those sharp eyes returned to the causare. 'Do the sisterhoods acknowledge my claim?'

Aravelle was close enough to see the look of apology the causare sent Healer Reoden before she spoke.

'We acknowledge All-father Hueryx's claim on Ronnyn and his brotherhood's claim on all these children. All-mother Reoden, consider your geas fulfilled where the Malaunje girls are concerned. You will have the boys to rear until they turn seventeen.'

'Nerazime, enter the boys in our lineage book,' Reoden said. 'Mark them as destined for Hueryx's brotherhood.'

While the sisters consulted over the book, Hueryx returned the cane to Ronnyn. 'Fine workmanship. I see Asher never lost his touch. But then he always did appreciate the finer things in life.'

There was such anger in his silky voice that Aravelle shivered.

It reminded her of something she'd overheard her father say, back on the island. When he'd spoken of Scholar

Hueryx, there'd been an undercurrent of anger in his voice. And she just knew Asher had been forced to stand aside when Hueryx claimed her mother, but he had reclaimed her when they ran away. How that must have infuriated the all-father.

Yet Asher had been the one to suggest returning to the Celestial City so that Ronnyn's gift could be trained. Even knowing what awaited him, Asher had been willing to return to the brotherhood. Now that was love. She felt proud to have him for a father.

Hueryx beckoned another Malaunje servant. He was a warrior by his bearing, although his jaw was beardless. 'Saskar, see to the Malaunje girls.'

Saskar gave his obeisance and took Aravelle's elbow to guide her towards the brotherhood side of the carpet. 'This way.'

It was all happening too quickly. She looked up to Ronnyn. He went to go to her, then stopped himself. In that instant, she both hated and loved him.

Hated him for being T'En, and All-father Hueryx's son.

Loved him for still wanting to acknowledge her, a lowly Malaunje.

But he was wise to hold back.

Vittor and Tamaron had no such reservations. They ran to her, sobbing.

Awkwardly, with the newborn in one arm, Vittor flung his free arm around Aravelle's waist. Tamaron clamoured to be picked up; his cries woke Itania, who responded with tears of her own. Her cries cut Aravelle to the core. It was too much. Ronnyn tried to join them then, but Hueryx was already drawing them apart.

'Here, none of that,' the all-father admonished. 'They're Malaunje, boy. Think of your stature.'

Vittor's eyes blazed and he would have objected, but Aravelle sent him a fierce, warning look.

He took her meaning and retreated a step to rejoin Ronnyn.

'Tamaron,' Reoden said, opening her arms. He went to her and she scooped him up in one arm. Her free arm settled protectively around Vittor and Ronnyn's shoulders.

'They've been living wild, Hueryx,' Reoden said, 'and don't know any better.'

His eyes narrowed. 'Oh, I know what's been going on. More so than you, I think. I'd watch out for those boys if I were you. If they are half as daring as their mother, they'll be trouble!'

'I'm more than ready. I felt the force of the mother's will.' The healer's beautiful wine-dark eyes fixed on him. 'A scribe with such keen affinity for the gifts? You should have taken better care of her.'

'Hard to take care of someone when they won't let you!' A spasm of anger tightened the all-father's features as he gestured to Ronnyn. 'At least I've claimed him. Malaunje women keep their counsel, and we count ourselves lucky if they acknowledge us as the fathers of our own children. Then you T'En women take them away and rear them. And we might see them once or twice in seventeen years.'

'This is the way of the T'Enatuath. It has always been so.'

'That does not mean we have to like it!'

For a heartbeat, the all-father and all-mother faced each other over Aravelle. There was a divide within the T'Enatuath that her mother's stories had only hinted at. What else had she glossed over?

'Now that the matter is resolved, let us move on,' the causare announced, her voice clear and forceful.

'All-mother,' Hueryx offered Reoden obeisance, one hand going to his forehead and out, though the gesture held a bitter edge.

'All-father.' She inclined her head as Hueryx backed away.

Aravelle felt the Malaunje warrior tug on her arm, and she went with him as he drew her away from her brothers and into the brotherhood ranks.

She held Ronnyn's eyes until Hueryx stepped between them, blocking her view. From behind a wall of tall T'En men, she heard her brothers become Healer Reoden's choice-sons.

The sisterhoods had claimed her T'En kin, just as her mother had always feared.

Her mother... who had refused to give up her children, who had lied, who had never stopped loving them...

It was all too much. Aravelle's head swam and she just wanted to hide somewhere safe and cry herself to sleep.

'Tomorrow we will have to repack the holds and negotiate to buy the stores we lost,' Imoshen said. 'But tonight, we celebrate our escape from the wharf and finding safe harbour.'

As Aravelle waited to be rowed across to the brotherhood ship, the sisterhood Malaunje came up on deck, bringing food and musical instruments.

Chapter Ten

ARAVELLE IGNORED SASKAR'S offer of help and picked up sleepy Itania. They had just climbed aboard the all-father's ship. Only it wasn't Hueryx's ship, it belonged to All-father Kyredeon; and the celebration had already begun. Someone started to play pipes and towards the rear of the ship people came out on deck, talking and laughing. The noise woke Itania, who whimpered and clung to Aravelle.

'There you are,' Hueryx thrust through the crowd. 'Saskar, take Aravelle to...' He broke off, spotting someone behind her. 'Charsoria, come here.'

All-father Hueryx greeted a broad-shouldered Malaunje woman who looked a few years older than Aravelle's mother. He leaned closer to Aravelle, raising his voice above the music. 'This is the leader of my brotherhood Malaunje, Vella.'

'Charsoria, this is Sasoria's eldest daughter, Aravelle. Accord her the stature due my Malaunje daughter.'

Aravelle's gaze flew to Hueryx's face. He sent her a knowing smile, that was familiar because she'd seen it on Ronnyn's face so many times.

She'd accepted that Hueryx was Ronnyn's father. But hers? She felt sick, betrayed by her mother yet again. The bedrock of her life was built on sand. For all that he had treated her like his daughter, Asher was not her father.

But he would always feel like her father. It was this sharp-eyed T'En man who was the interloper.

'Welcome to the brotherhood, Vella,' Charsoria said. 'You will address me as the all-father's-voice.'

'All-father's-voice Charsoria.' Aravelle shifted Itania to her right arm, freed her left and gave her obeisance. 'My name is Aravelle, not Vella.'

Charsoria stiffened.

'Just like her mother.' Hueryx grinned. 'The little one is Sasoria's child, too. And she produced four T'En boys, Chara.'

'Four? The T'En blood runs strong in this family. The girls will be a great asset, all-father.' Charsoria's mouth was tight and thin, as though the words left a bitter taste on her tongue.

Aravelle was not going to be an asset to anyone, not if she could help it.

'I don't see Sasoria. Where is my half-sister, all-father?' Charsoria asked.

Aravelle bit back a gasp. She hadn't known her mother had a half-sister. Sasoria's stories had mostly been of the brotherhood's past glories, and of Scholar Hueryx, who had featured as a clever trickster, always confusing his opponents.

'I'm sorry.' His expression clouded and his voice broke. 'Sasoria died the day we reached the wharf, Chara. All-mother Reoden's fostering the boys. The girls will be your choice-daughters, as befits their stature.'

Charsoria gave her obeisance. 'It will be so.'

But not because she wanted them, Aravelle could tell.

'This way.' Charsoria went to leave.

But Hueryx caught Aravelle's arm and gestured to the bruises on her face. 'The Mieren who captured you, did they rape you? Did they hurt you, Vella?'

Tears of fury threatened, but she would not cry. She raised blazing eyes to him. 'They raped me, but they could not hurt me!'

His eyes widened.

She jerked her arm from his slack fingers, stepped back, then turned to follow Charsoria.

The all-father's-voice gestured to the hatch leading below-deck.

Aravelle climbed down carefully, with Itania in one arm. Charsoria followed. The middle of the lower deck was full of men and boys older than Ronnyn. All were Malaunje, and all were dressed like princes. The floor was a satiny wood, the fittings polished brass. Real glass gleamed in the windows. Rich carpets covered the floor. Piles of belongings were stacked everywhere.

The all-father's-voice gestured to the bow of the ship. 'All-father Kyredeon's brotherhood lives in the stern. This end is ours.' And she led Aravelle to the prow, where cabins were tucked into the ship's blunt nose.

A girl of about Aravelle's age came out of the passage door, carrying bedding.

Charsoria grabbed the girl's arm. 'Make up two meals. Nariska, bring them to my cabin.'

Aravelle followed Charsoria into the passage, walking past two cabins. Their open doors revealed women settling young Malaunje children for the night. These cabins also contained gleaming paintings, richly coloured wall-hangings, carpets, and chests with shining brass handles. Aravelle had never seen such wealth.

Charsoria opened the last door and stepped into the cabin. This room was decorated even more richly. Aravelle could not take in the opulence. If this was how the Malaunje lived, how did the T'En live?

Several older women and more than half a dozen children looked up. They were all well-dressed.

'My new choice-daughters. Sasoria's girls, Aravelle and Itania,' Charsoria said. 'These are my inner circle and their children.'

The oldest of the women cast Aravelle a wary glance. The middle-aged one came over to join Charsoria. Now that Aravelle saw them together, she saw the similarity in their faces. These two were related.

Charsoria beckoned to the oldest woman. 'Redravia, take the little one.'

'I can look after Itania,' Aravelle said.

'And you will,' Charsoria agreed. 'But first I want to talk to you.'

Redravia approached and held out her arms. Aravelle passed Itania across, with soft assurances that everything would be all right.

As she turned around, Charsoria slapped her across the face.

Caught off balance, she fell, hitting the floor heavily. Her swollen lip split again, filling her mouth with blood.

Tears of shock obscured Aravelle's vision.

'No, don't get up. Stay there and listen.' Charsoria stood over her, hands on her hips. Behind her the middle-aged woman watched, eyes bright with malicious delight. 'Don't you shame me, girl. You might be Hueryx's acknowledged child, and Sasoria's daughter, but I am your choice-mother now. And I've worked too long and hard to have you lower my stature by your behaviour. Don't you shame me like your mother did!'

'She reminds me of her mother,' the middle-aged woman told Charsoria. 'She has the same impudent look.'

Charsoria's eyes narrowed. 'I'll be watching you.'

Itania whimpered.

Charsoria ignored the toddler, focusing on Aravelle. 'The Mieren raped you?'

Aravelle nodded.

'Are you bleeding?'

She touched her lip; of course she was bleeding.

'No. I meant, are you likely to fall pregnant? We don't want any Mieren brats born to our women.'

The idea hadn't occurred to Aravelle and she shuddered with horror, then shook her head, grateful that she was not yet a woman.

'Then get up.'

Despite Aravelle's best effort not to cry, tears ran down her cheeks. It was the shock of the blow, not the pain.

'Stop your snivelling. You're not the only one who's been raped. The Mieren do it to teach our women a lesson, to make us lesser beings like their women. But we aren't like them. We choose our lovers. We decide who will father our children and whether we acknowledge them as such.' Charsoria's mouth thinned. 'And don't think to go whining to All-father Hueryx. He has enough on his hands now that we have to share the ship with Kyredeon.'

There was a soft knock on the door. Charsoria glanced at it then back to Aravelle. 'Well, get the door, girl. That'll be Nariska with your food.'

Aravelle wiped her face and answered the door.

Nariska entered with a tray.

'You can eat once you're clean. Strip,' Charsoria ordered. 'Strip your sister and yourself. Those clothes will be returned to the healer. We don't want her charity. Then scrub yourselves. We don't want any sisterhood gift residue. See that they do it properly, Hariorta. I have work to do.' And she went to the desk, leaving them under the middle-aged woman's malicious care.

'Bring them, Redravia,' Hariorta ordered and went through to the bathing chamber and stood over them as Aravelle took off Itania's clothes, and then her own.

The old woman ran some water in the tub. This bathing chamber was finer than anything they'd had at home. The thought made Aravelle's chest ache with sorrow. She soaped herself and Itania under Hariorta's watchful eye, then rinsed them both.

'Check their hair for lice, Redravia.'

Shame and fury made Aravelle's cheeks burn as the old woman ran her fingers through Itania's hair, searching her scalp, then straightened up. 'I don't see any –'

'They've been with Mieren.' Hariorta handed Aravelle a bottle. 'Use this. Be sure to do a good job. I won't have filthy lice infecting our people. Redravia, bundle up the healer's clothes and send it all back.'

Itania howled as Aravelle rubbed the foul-smelling lotion through her hair. She felt like howling herself, but bit her bottom lip until it started bleeding again. She would not cry.

If nothing the Mieren did could break her, then nothing her mother's half-sister did would break her.

A few moments later, they were dressed and back in the main cabin, sitting in front of the brazier. Aravelle combed Itania's fine, curly hair as it dried. Combing it was always a chore.

'There.' Aravelle finished twirling the last long ringlet around her finger and sat back on her heels. 'Let's see you.'

Obediently, Itania turned around with one chubby little hand still clutching a piece of bread.

'There. Pretty as a picture and clean as a whistle.' It was what her mother always said.

Itania smiled, then stuffed the last piece of bread into her mouth. Aravelle brushed crumbs off her sister's nightgown. She suspected it was the poorest Hariorta could find, but to her it was luxurious. All she'd ever known was their father's old shirts cut down and remade into nightgowns.

Leaving Itania to lick her fingers, Aravelle unwound the cloth that held her own wet hair up, and began to run the comb down its length, almost to her knees.

'What's this?' Hariorta demanded. She clutched Aravelle's arm and spun her around. Itania whimpered and tried to hide, but one of the other women caught her and lifted her off her feet. 'Look at this, Charsoria!'

Aravelle had no idea what she'd done wrong.

Charsoria came over and inspected Aravelle. She caught Aravelle's long wet hair, wound it around her hand and tugged sharply. Tears of pain stung Aravelle's eyes.

'What's this?' Charsoria tugged on her hair again.

'I've done as you said and washed it.'

The back of Charsoria's free hand cracked across her cheek. 'Don't give me cheek, girl!'

Charsoria leaned close, her hard eyes pinning Aravelle. She saw that Aravelle did not understand, and gave a bitter laugh. 'I knew it. I knew Sasoria thought she was better than us. Look what she's done.' And here she gestured to the rest of the women, drawing them over to look.

Another four Malaunje women had come in since Aravelle arrived. Clearly warriors, they'd been divesting themselves of leather arm guards and boots.

'She's let her daughters' hair grow as long as one of the T'En's!'

All the women muttered their disapproval, clucking their tongues against the roofs of their mouths. It was only now that Aravelle noticed none of them wore their hair longer than their waists.

'We can't have a Malaunje with ideas above her station, Charsoria,' Hariorta said.

'Exactly.' Charsoria snapped her fingers. 'Fetch me the scissors, Nariska.'

The girl ran to obey.

'Turn around,' Charsoria ordered with a malicious tug of Aravelle's long hair. 'No Malaunje...' *tug* '...may grow their hair longer...' *tug* '...than waist length.' Charsoria pulled with unnecessary vigour as she gathered Aravelle's hair behind her. 'Cut it, Hariorta.'

The grate of metal on metal grated in Aravelle's nerves. She gritted her teeth as they hacked off her hair. That this was her own mother's half-sister made it even harder to bear.

Lifting her chin, Aravelle stared beyond the women's heads. She would not cry.

But she did.

She cried when Charsoria ordered Hariorta to cut Itania's hair, cried as those red-gold baby curls drifted to the floor.

When it was over, Charsoria told Aravelle to gather up their hair and throw it in the brazier.

And when the smell of burning hair filled the cabin, she blamed Aravelle then ordered the windows opened.

Aravelle did as she was told, plaited her hair, which was now barely waist length, and then gathered Itania in her lap and sang her to sleep. Charsoria was not going to break them.

Nothing would break them.

*   *   *

SORNE HAD SPENT all evening helping Baron Aingeru's wife organise tomorrow's departure. The children had been fed and put to bed, the travelling chests were packed, the carriage was cleaned, and the horses' traces oiled and repaired. They'd eaten and just about everyone had gone to bed for an early start on the morrow.

He had been partially undressed and about to climb into his bedroll when a thought occurred to him. The road to port was in a bad state, thanks to the rain and the heavy traffic caused by the Wyrd exodus. He was worried Zaria and the children might be delayed. If Eskarnor sent scouts on ahead, they could get caught up with the army. An army was no place for children. Sorne would offer them the alternative of sailing up the coast. One twin was mad for horses, the other was mad for ships. This way both of them would be delighted. So he pulled his robe over his shoulders and returned to the family's private dining room, hoping to catch Zaria before she went to bed. He'd left her discussing preparations for the winter with the estate manager.

Instead, he heard voices speaking Maygharian, which meant Aingeru's ex-mercenaries were here. Sorne had spent a year in Maygharia in the king's service and had become fluent in the tongue.

'It's a day for messages,' Zaria said. 'First the king's half-blood advisor, now my husband sends you to –'

'The king's half-blood advisor is here?'

'He arrived this afternoon,' Zaria said. 'Prince Cedon has been returned safe and we're invited to the palace for the festivities. Why?'

'Where is the half-blood now, and how many men does he have with him?'

'Just the two. I put them in the guest chamber. What is this about?'

A child's soft grizzle reached Sorne.

Geruso, the three-year-old boy, came down the passage, rubbing his eyes. Sorne took four steps and picked him up to hush him.

Too late. He turned to find that Zaria had come to the doorway.

Sorne was unarmed. One word from her and he would be dead.

Zaria's eyes widened.

'What is it?' one of the men asked, stepping into the hall behind Zaria. He cursed, drawing his sword.

A second man joined him, shoving her back.

'Geruso,' Zaria whispered, eyes fixed pleadingly on Sorne.

He was not Eskarnor. Sorne put the boy down and ˜urned and ran. The ex-mercenaries charged after him.

'Wait,' Zaria cried. They ignored her.

Sorne hoped Aingeru had sent no more than two men.

He flung open the door to his room. 'Grab your weapons. We're under attack.'

The two youths scrambled out the far side of the bed, fumbling for their swords.

Darting across the chamber, Sorne made for his weapons. By the time he'd snatched up his blade, both ex-mercenaries were through the door. Sorne threw his scabbard aside as Aingeru's men split up. One of them came for him, the other went around the bed after Vighir and Lazandor. The king's guards, for all their training, were inexperienced youths, and these were veterans of the Secluded Sea campaign.

The ex-mercenary charging Sorne kicked a chair aside. It was a long time since Sorne had to fight for his life, and his mouth went dry with fear. Then the man swung his sword and Sorne's training took over. Block, divert, counterstrike.

A shrill cry came from one of the youths.

Sorne glanced that way and felt a blade whistle towards his head.

He lurched back, leaping over a chest as he sought to put more space between him and his assailant. From the hallway came the sounds of men shouting and running. Sorne's attacker smiled and closed in on him.

But his strike was overconfident. Sorne blocked, let his

blade skip over the mercenary's sword and ran him through.

Sorne pulled his sword free and went to help the youths, but found the second ex-mercenary was dead. One of the youths swayed on his feet while the other cleaned his sword with shaking hands.

Four of the castle's men-at-arms appeared at the door, weapons ready. Zaria stood behind them with a lantern. They took in the overturned furniture and bloody corpses and were about to charge in when Zaria called them off.

'Wait.'

'But they killed –'

'I know,' she snapped. 'I have questions.'

Zaria walked in and the men-at-arms followed, spreading out with weapons drawn. Behind them, servants crowded the doorway.

'Why did my husband's men attack you, Sorne?'

'Because Baron Eskarnor has betrayed the king.'

Zaria's eyes widened. 'Why would Eskarnor turn on King Charald?'

'The king grows weak with age, so Eskarnor no longer fears him. He abducted Queen Jaraile and plans to legitimise his claim to the Chalcedonian throne through her.'

Horrified, Zaria stared at him across the bodies of her husband's men.

Sorne was sure that if he fell here, the kingdom fell to Eskarnor. He had to convince Zaria to take the opposing side to her husband.

'You know Eskarnor, Zaria. You know what he's capable of. Four nights ago I saw him cut the throat of a four-year-old boy because the Wyrds refused to hand over the prince for him to murder.'

She flinched. 'You forget, I saw what Charald did to Khitan, what he did to all the other kingdoms of the Secluded Sea. The king's no better.'

'The king spends his days locked in his bedchamber, raving.'

'He does? We'd heard rumours...'

Sorne nodded. 'Queen Jaraile, Baron Nitzane, and three others have been appointed Prince Cedon's guardians. The choice is not between Eskarnor and Charald, but between –'

'Leave us,' Zaria ordered.

The men-at-arms were inclined to argue, but she told them to remove the bodies, then turned to Sorne. 'Aingeru –'

'Would change sides if he thought you and the children were hostages in the palace. And quite apart from that, you really would be safer in port. Eskarnor is going to march his army through here. I bet your husband sent word for you to go to the Wyrd city.' Her expression told him he was right. 'Aingeru doesn't trust Eskarnor's army to keep their hands off you.'

Lazandor moaned softly and Vighir caught him as he passed out.

'What a mess this is,' Zaria muttered. 'Put the lad on the bed.'

Sorne helped carry the youth.

'Bring the lantern closer.' Zaria rolled up her sleeves, inspected the wound and applied pressure to slow the bleeding. 'Vighir, go tell the servants to bring my healing bag.'

After he left, Zaria looked over the wounded youth to Sorne. 'Eskarnor will kill my husband if he suspects he's disloyal.'

'While Eskarnor was a guest in the king's palace, he raped Jaraile and tried to have Prince Cedon killed. When that failed he abducted the queen. If he wins the throne, he'll be worse than Charald.'

She gave a bitter laugh. 'Once I would have said that was impossible, but...'

Vighir returned with her healing kit and she concentrated on sewing up the wound.

Sorne watched, cautiously optimistic.

Zaria finished binding the wound and mixed a draught. 'He'll wake before dawn, in pain and possibly feverish. When he does, give him this,' she told Vighir. 'It will soothe him and aid the healing.'

'Thank you, baroness.'

Zaria packed up her things, then turned to Sorne. 'We can't leave him here. Eskarnor will have him killed. He'll have to come with us.'

Sorne went to speak, but she held up her hand.

'You lied to me. I understand why, but I don't like it.'

'Then you should know I don't plan to ride to the city. The rain has stopped, but the Wyrds' wagons turned the port road to a quagmire. I plan to take us south to Nitzane's stronghold at Shifting-sands Bay, then send you up the coast by ship to Port Mirror-on-Sea. We'll make better time if we ride and you should tell your people they're in the path of war.'

'How long do we have?'

'I don't know. It depends on how organised Eskarnor is.'

'Aingeru...' She covered her mouth as a sob escaped her. 'Aingeru has no love for Eskarnor, but he hates Charald after what the king did to Maygharia.'

'The king is dying. Queen Jaraile will need strong barons around her.'

'If I send Aingeru a message, he'll support Jaraile. I'll tell him we're going to port and he is to meet you...' She looked at Sorne. 'Where will you be gathering your forces?'

He hesitated. If Aingeru did not do what Zaria expected, he could hand his wife's message over to Eskarnor and...

'Riverbend Stronghold is in the middle of South Chalcedonia,' she said. 'It makes a good gathering point for the barons. That's where you're rallying the army, isn't it?'

Sorne nodded. He was not surprised she'd guessed. Zaria had spent her teens listening to men talk tactics.

She nodded to herself. 'I'll tell our men-at-arms to march for Riverbend.'

Sorne wondered if he had just won a powerful baron and weakened Eskarnor, or lost the war.

Chapter Eleven

ARAVELLE TURNED AROUND, her stomach cramping with fear.

'Vella? Vella, come here.'

The oldest of Charsoria's inner circle beckoned from the galley door. Aravelle had spent her first morning with the brotherhood scrubbing pots. To think she used to long for the beauty and culture of the Celestial City. She would probably have scrubbed pots there, too.

Aravelle glanced to the cook, who sent her off.

She wiped her fingers on her cleaning smock and hurried over. 'Is Itania all right?'

'She's fine, but she does miss you.' Redravia shuffled down the hall, speaking over her shoulder. 'You've been called to serve the all-father.'

'Why?'

'How would I know? Charsoria wants to see you first.'

Aravelle braced herself and stepped inside the cabin. 'You sent for me, all-father's-voice?'

Charsoria looked Aravelle up and down, her eyes narrowing in annoyance. 'This will not do. You can't go before the all-father looking like a kitchen drab.'

Since these were the garments she'd been told to wear and Charsoria had sent her to the kitchen to work, Aravelle bit her tongue. As she took off the smock, Itania broke away from the other small children and ran to her. Aravelle hugged her little sister.

'Hurry up,' Charsoria snapped. She opened a chest and began sorting through various items of clothing.

A toddler bumped into Nariska, who was clearing away

the breakfast things. The fourteen-year-old dropped the tray, and bowls and plates shattered. Children yelped with fright as the women hissed with annoyance.

'Stupid girl.' Hariorta clipped Nariska over the ear. 'Now you'll have to clean it all up!'

The girl dropped to her hands and knees to pick up broken crockery.

'Stay here.' Aravelle put Itania on a bunk and knelt to pick up pieces of broken crockery. Nariska sent her a surprised look.

'What are you doing, Vella?' Charsoria caught her arm, hauled her to her feet and thrust some clothes at her. 'Get dressed.'

Aravelle dropped her drawstring pants and stepped out of them.

'At least you're not pregnant,' Charsoria said, gesturing to her thighs.

Aravelle glanced down to see blood smeared on her inner thigh. That explained the stomach cramps. Her mother had promised that Father would build a room for her when she became a woman. But here she was...

An angry sob escaped Aravelle.

'Here, now. No call for tears,' Redravia said. 'Your first time? Feeling crampy?'

Aravelle could only nod.

'I'll brew some soothing –'

'No time for that,' Charsoria snapped. 'Show her where we keep the rags.'

Soon Aravelle was dressed in soft woollen trousers, vest, and a rich tabard of deepest indigo. The brotherhood symbol of a snake swallowing its tail was embroidered in buttery yellow thread along the hem. All her clothes came from the communal chest. From now on she owned nothing; not even her own privacy, it seemed.

'Let me see you,' Charsoria ordered.

Aravelle turned.

The all-father's-voice frowned. 'I can't do anything about

that split lip or the red eyes. Stop moping, girl. Your first blood is a time to rejoice. Your hair should be neater.' She turned Aravelle around with a sharp jerk and ruthlessly plaited her waist-length hair, tying it off with a leather thong. 'There. Now for shoes. Can't have you going before the all-father barefoot like a Mieren street brat. Let me see your feet.'

Aravelle lifted the hem of her trousers to reveal pale, scratched feet.

'She looks about your size, Redravia. Give her yours. I'll have another pair made for you.'

The old woman sat to remove a pair of simple black slippers.

Aravelle slid her feet into them. They were still warm and... 'Too small.'

'They'll do for now. Now, look at me, girl. I don't know what the all-father wants you for, but don't you shame me by giving him any lip. Now, go.'

Aravelle hesitated. 'I don't know where...'

'Show her the way, Redravia.'

With a quick hug for Itania, who began to wail despite Aravelle's entreaties for her to be good, they hurried off. Itania's accusatory cries followed them out the door and down the passage. Up on deck, Aravelle found Malaunje from both brotherhoods hard at work. It was a fine morning, and they were taking stores out of the hold and reorganising them.

She wriggled her toes in the too-small slippers. It seemed she could do nothing to please the all-father's-voice.

'Why does Charsoria hate me? And who is Hariorta, her mother?'

Redravia gave a hoot of laughter. 'Don't let Hari hear you say that. She's Charsoria's older half-sister.'

'She's also my aunt?'

'No, different mother. One day I'll show you in the lineage book. Your mother and Charsoria share the same mother, and she was the last all-father's-voice. Charsoria only has the position now because your mother ran away.

Hueryx has forced her to honour you and Itania as her choice-daughters. Worse, she has produced only sons, so when the time comes and she must look for a suitable girl to train, the all-father will expect it to be you.'

'Oh...' No wonder Charsoria and Hariorta hated her. 'But I don't want to be all-father's-voice. I'll tell her.'

'You'll do no such thing.' Redravia sniffed. 'Besides, she'd never believe you.'

'It's not fair.'

'Who said Malaunje life was fair?' Redravia entered the passage under the foredeck, stopping at the last door. 'You go ahead. And remember' – her faded mulberry eyes fixed on Aravelle – 'you have rights. You cannot be forced to do something you don't want to do. You should have been trained to resist their gifts, but...'

Aravelle's stomach churned. 'They won't –'

'They won't force anything on you, but watch out for their honeyed tongues. If you're not careful, you'll end up doing what they want and being grateful for it.'

Heat rushed up Aravelle's throat and over her cheeks. Other than warning her to beware the wiles of brotherhood T'En, her mother had not prepared her for this. But she hadn't had any formal training, and somehow she'd resisted Ronnyn's power all last summer. Even so, he was a boy; these were the brotherhood's most powerful T'En men. She fought the first flutterings of panic.

One glance over her shoulder told her Redravia was headed for the door to the mid-deck. 'Thank you,' Aravelle called softly.

The old woman paused then shook her head. 'Sasoria should never have deserted us.'

Aravelle swallowed and knocked.

The cabin door swung open and three young T'En men strode by, brushing past her as though she was invisible.

'Come in.'

Aravelle stepped into the dim cabin. A row of windows, larger than the ones in Charsoria's cabin, ran along the far wall. Their light silhouetted three men kneeling on cushions, and illuminated richness beyond anything Aravelle had ever seen. And she'd thought the Malaunje quarters opulent.

So many things gleamed: copper, pewter, crystal, gold and silver. All the colours were incredibly vivid, blues and purples, a red richer than blood. Her gaze was drawn to a banner hanging on the wall. It was as tall as her and a snake swallowing its tail was picked out in gleaming gold thread on an indigo background.

But what hit her most was the smell.

It made her nostrils sting and her heart race. It spoke of danger and it promised everything. With a start, she realised it wasn't a smell at all.

The T'En had been gift-working.

'Don't stand there, come in and shut the door,' All-father Hueryx said.

With Charsoria's admonition to keep her tongue between her teeth, and Redravia's more cryptic warning still ringing in her ears, Aravelle stepped cautiously into the cabin.

'She's been knocked around but, even so, I can tell she's pretty rather than beautiful.' The one on the left sounded petulant, as if life had proved a disappointment to him.

'Is my all-father's-voice treating you well?' Hueryx asked.

The irony of this made her smile and she heard a soft gasp from one of the men.

'Come closer,' the one on the right ordered. He was big and he spoke with a soft lilt. Had to be the brotherhood's hand-of-force.

She picked her way through the discarded bedding and heaped clothes. A chest of weapons had been opened and scattered about as though someone had been looking for something.

When she was about a body length from the men, she stopped and waited with her left hand folded over right, both clasped in front of her. As was appropriate, her gaze remained on the floor. She could pretend to be the perfect Malaunje servant if she had to.

'You should punish her, not reward her,' Hueryx's voice-of-reason advised. 'Malaunje who run away should be –'

'No one will be running away now. And Vella was an infant. She had no say in what her mother did.'

'Sasoria stole your T'En son.'

'And now he is returned. Besides, no one looking at Ronnyn could deny he's mine.' The all-father returned his attention to Aravelle. 'You must be, what, nearly fourteen?'

She nodded. 'Just after winter's cusp.'

The hand-of-force cleared his throat. 'What will you do with her?'

'Do you read and write, Vella?' the all-father asked.

'Of course.'

The voice-of-reason stiffened. 'The insolence!'

'Don't you get tired of insincere subservience, Dragomyr?' Hueryx countered.

'What will you do with her?' the hand-of-force asked again. Even kneeling, he seemed to radiate energy.

'I hear the causare has a renowned Mieren scholar on her ship, who set sail with us specifically to write our history,' the all-father said. 'I am going to write a history of the last thirty years. If I don't, only the sisterhood version of events will be remembered. Vella can scribe for me.'

'Very well. But if she is going to be underfoot, she can be useful,' Voice-of-reason Dragomyr announced. He was stockier and very fair. His lashes and eyebrows were so pale he had a slightly unfinished look. 'I want this cabin cleaned.'

'I live to serve.' Aravelle gave the appropriate bow.

She heard the softest of chuckles from All-father Hueryx and felt a tug of like to like. She shut it down immediately. She hated him. He was the reason her mother had fled, which meant he was the reason Charsoria hated her.

'Make yourself useful,' Dragomyr told Aravelle.

'But first she can make us some spiced wine,' Hueryx announced. 'Do you know the spiced wine ceremony, Vella?'

She nodded, glad her mother had taught her.

'Show me.'

But she did not know where anything was.

There should have been a garden or another chamber where the men could admire art or poetry, lulled by music or sublime silence. As the host, All-father Hueryx should have selected a poem with accompanying artwork to be the theme of the ceremony. Nothing was as it should be. Panic welled up in her.

'Our spiced wine chest is on the desk,' Hueryx told her. He came to his feet, opened another chest and selected a small statue, unwrapping it and placing it on the centre of the low table.

The three of them knelt at the table and placed their hands on their laps, fingers interlaced to form cups, their gazes on the statue. They prepared to meditate.

Aravelle opened the chest. It was a more ornate version of the one back home, with individual layers that lifted to reveal drawers beneath. Everything was exquisitely made, from the cups to the herb jars.

For some reason, it was very important to Aravelle that she do this right.

She prepared the scented water for the brotherhood leaders to cleanse their hands and faces. A pot of water was already warming on the brazier. But first she placed the ceramic pot over the stove and poured in the wine. Then she measured the herbs and spices: dried orange rind, ginger, honey to taste, a cinnamon stick, cardamom and a little brandy. She used the recipe her mother favoured.

Once the spiced wine was heating, she made up three bowls of warmed scented water and selected three fine cloths. These she presented to the brotherhood triumvirate in order of rank. Each man took a bowl, washed his face, then his hands and patted himself dry before handing back the utensils.

She gently stirred the wine, enjoying the familiar scent. Judging it ready, she removed the pot from the heat and poured a small measure of wine into three glasses before placing them on the tray. Again, she served them in order of rank.

Hueryx inhaled, sipped his wine and smiled. 'Just the way I like it.'

'Piquantly pretty and accomplished.' The hand-of-force raised his wine to salute her.

Aravelle wasn't sure what he meant by 'piquantly pretty.'

'Bring the pot. I will pour,' Voice-of-Reason Dragomyr said. She noted that, after that first polite sip, he did not touch his spiced wine. 'You may start work as long as you are quiet.'

She knelt and bowed before coming to her feet.

The cabin was a mess. Where to start? The simplest and most silent thing to do was pick up the bedding and fold it.

While she worked, the all-father and his two companions speculated on what was going on in Kyredeon's brotherhood.

'If it were possible, I'd suggest you assassinate him,' the hand-of-force said. 'Strike him down, before he can strike at you.'

'Reyne...' Hueryx shook his head fondly. 'We made a solemn vow not to attack our fellow leaders.'

'You think that's going to stop Kyredeon?'

'Thanks to Imoshen, he'll be an oathbreaker if he moves against me.'

'When we went into that all-council you were going to denounce her for the debacle on the wharf,' Dragomyr said. 'I was all set to call for a vote of no confidence and then nominate you, but I didn't get your signal.'

'Imoshen anticipated me and moved to counter my greatest fear for our brotherhood, and she did it in such a way that...' He shook his head. 'Did you get shivers when she cut her hair and swore that vow to unite us?'

'With her short hair she looks like a common Mieren,' Dragomyr muttered. 'Yours will take years to grow back.'

'Drago...' Hueryx shook his head. 'You have no vision.'

The hand-of-force chuckled, which seemed to incense Hueryx's voice-of-reason.

'If you admire her so much, why don't you offer to tryst with her? Or have you already...?' Dragomyr's brown drew down in suspicion. 'The other day, when I was speculating on the identity of her sacrare's father, you said nothing. Are you the father? Did you tryst with her in secret and keep it from us?'

Hueryx threw back his head and laughed.

Dragomyr bristled. 'She's the most dangerous sister alive today. Do you have a death wish?'

'No. But one of the all-fathers does. As much as I would like to claim that honour, I am not the father of the sacrare. Imoshen very wisely hid his identity and I have not been able to guess it. If Kyredeon knew, I shudder to think what he would do. And it is just as well I did not offer formal challenge. You saw the way she demolished Dretsun's challenge? His stature may never recover. She thinks ahead. Applying to the Sagoras for sanctuary is exactly the move I would have made.'

'What are you staring at, insolent girl?' Dragomyr waved a hand at Aravelle. 'Get back to work.'

After that, she kept her head down and collected discarded clothing. Each item held the gift-enhanced scent of the wearer, making her feel dizzy and yet covetous at the same time. This was awful. How did the Malaunje protect themselves? How had her mother worked beside Hueryx without...

She hadn't; she'd become his lover and produced two children. But then she had run away. The complexities of her mother's motivations dawned on Aravelle. Now she understood why, when Sasoria spoke of Scholar Hueryx and the Celestial City, her voice had held equal parts longing and resentment.

Aravelle had finished putting the weapons away and was returning silver chalices to their case when the all-father and his seconds spoke of death.

'...be seventeen soon, and her sisterhood will turn him out, but no all-father will take him, not when Imoshen the All-father-killer is his choice-mother, not when it means the all-father would earn the enmity of all the other brotherhood leaders,' the hand-of-force said. 'When that day comes, we'll have to execute him.'

'The causare will come up with something,' Hueryx said. 'She won't let us kill her choice-son.'

'I think you have an exaggerated idea of Imoshen's power,' Dragomyr said. 'No all-father will take him, and he can hardly go back to Chalcedonia.'

Someone tapped on the door.

Hueryx gestured for Aravelle to answer it.

'All-father.' Saskar gave his obeisance from the doorway. 'Captain Ardonyx is reorganising our stores.'

They bristled like dogs whose territory had been invaded, left their spiced wine on the table and went out to see what was going on. Feeling relieved, Aravelle continued to pick-up and put away.

When the door swung open again, she flinched, but it was only Saskar. He came straight across the cabin to her.

'What did they want with you?'

'All-father Hueryx plans to write a history. He wants me to be his scribe.'

'He can read and write perfectly well.'

Of course he could. Alarmed, she met Saskar's eyes.

He nodded grimly.

'Then why would he need me?'

'I don't know. But I did hear Hueryx was furious when your mother ran away with Asher.'

She shivered.

'Don't worry. Hueryx is a much better all-father than Kyredeon.'

'The voice-of-reason doesn't approve of me.'

'Dragomyr doesn't approve of much. His all-father is smarter than he is, which is hard for a voice-of-reason to take.'

'Then why is Dragomyr Hueryx's voice-of-reason?'

'The last all-father lost control of the brotherhood when one of his supporters killed himself, this upset the balance of power. To make the challenge, Hueryx had to move quickly. He needed the backing of two strong seconds. Dragomyr might not be as smart as Hueryx – few are – but he is loyal. Hueryx's hand-of-force is also loyal, and ambitious for stature. Keep out of Reyne's way.'

Aravelle frowned. 'I don't see why you're telling me all this.'

'My Mieren parents raised me until I was eleven before our village forced them to turn me over. It's hard coming in from the outside. I know. I've spent the last seven years trying to make sense of the T'Enatuath. There are two ways of doing this, Vella. You can make waves and get swamped, or you can ride it out. So keep your head down and stay out of trouble.'

'Charsoria hates me already. When she learns I'm to scribe for Hueryx...'

'She'll be furious. But there's nothing she can do.'

Aravelle rolled her eyes. 'You only think that because you've never had to live in the same cabin with her.'

He grinned. 'If she's going to take out her spite on you, you might as well enjoy the benefits of your new role.' Without asking, he took the remainder of the spiced wine and poured it into two cups, giving her one and raising his. 'Here's to Aravelle, the all-father's scribe.'

Together they polished off the spiced wine. Her stomach no longer ached and she felt lighter of heart. Nothing had changed for the better, but now she had a friend. 'Thank you. I should get back to work.'

'I'll help.'

'You don't have to.'

'Oh, but I do.' He grinned. 'You're doing my job.'

So they began to clean up. While working alongside Saskar, she wondered why he had to clean the cabin when he wore the leather breeches and vest of a warrior.

As she picked up the bronze statue to return it to the chest, she was struck by the pathos of the figure. It depicted a wounded warrior and his two friends who stood over him, ready to defend him to their last breath. The force of their emotion, captured in the lines of their bodies, was so powerful that it brought tears to her eyes.

'It's by Iraayel,' Saskar said. He saw she did not understand. 'All-father Iraayel, the great sculptor. It's called the 'Fallen All-father.' It's not the original, of course. That stood twice as tall as us and was made of marble.'

He came over with a cloth and wrapped the small statue reverently. 'There were so many precious things that we could not bring them all. We made copies and hid the originals. One day...' He had to clear his throat. 'If our people ever return to Chalcedonia, they'll reclaim our heritage.'

Loss made Aravelle feel cheated and hollow. She'd never seen the Celestial City. All she had were her mother's stories.

He put the bronze in a chest and handed it to her to put away, but caught her arm. 'Don't be taken in by Hueryx. He can be charming, but he always gets his own way.'

'Don't worry,' Aravelle said. You had to like someone to be taken in by him, and she hated the all-father. 'I cannot be charmed.'

Chapter Twelve

RONNYN HAD NEVER felt more constricted in his life. The T'En children were only allowed out of the cabin at certain times of the day, and only allowed in certain places. The Malaunje used the mid-deck and the below-decks. The T'En had the foredeck and rear-decks, except when the big lads practised their combat training: then they claimed the mid-deck and everyone kept out of their way.

This was the first chance he'd had to see the lads go through their exercises. They ranged from boys just a little bigger than him to youths taller than Hand-of-force Cerafeoni. In preparation for their role as brotherhood warriors, they had memorised sequences of strikes and counter strikes. As they performed these patterns with wooden long-knives, Cerafeoni observed closely, interrupting to correct the angle of a deflection or their stance.

When she saw Ronnyn, she said, 'Stand back. Empowered lads tend to be a bit wild at this age, that's why we keep them segregated.'

Watching the warriors made him restless to begin his own training. Instead, he was stuck with the children, who were all Vittor's age or younger. The little ones spilled out of the passage, crowding around him.

'That's it for today,' Cerafeoni called. 'Back to your cabin.'

As the trainee warriors walked past, joking and laughing, an aura of roused male gift enveloped Ronnyn, making his heart beat faster. Surrounded by small children, he felt inadequate; shame burned in him.

Just then, the scarred T'En woman and her shield-sister herded the children up onto the foredeck and started the lesson. When it become clear Ronnyn already knew most of what the sisters were teaching, they told him to go and keep out of trouble.

He was used to working from sun-up to sun-down at home, and he looked about for something to do. When he heard his baby brother cry, he headed for the cabin. There he found the all-mother's Malaunje servant woman clucking over his little brother. She greeted Ronnyn with a smile.

Wrapping the infant in a shawl, she took him out to find the all-mother.

At a loose end, Ronnyn looked around the cabin and spotted the chest where the sisterhood kept their books. They'd only had one book at home. Now he went to the chest, opened it up and took them out one by one. The weight of the leatherbound covers, the richness of the paper, the illustrations with their brilliant inks and glowing gold leaf... he felt like each one was a treasure, and that was without even reading them.

Choosing one, he made himself a nest in the far corner and became lost in the T'Enatuath origin myth. He wasn't sure how much time had passed when a noise made him look up. To his surprise, a panel in the far wall opened.

Ronnyn went absolutely still as a T'En child about his own age darted out. Although partially obscured by the desk, he could see they were richly dressed, same as him. Then he caught a glimpse of her face and almost gasped. From the arch of her eyebrow to the line of her lips, she was beautiful.

Ronnyn swallowed.

As if afraid of discovery, she made straight for the chest, selected a volume and returned to her hidden nook. It all happened so quickly, he didn't have time to call out.

Now that he'd seen the panel open and close, Ronnyn realised one corner of the cabin had been walled off. A

small grille near the ceiling meant the prisoner could hear
what was going on.

Ronnyn put his book aside, quietly collected a chair
and went over to the false wall. He climbed up and peered
down through the grill into the private nook. It was wide
enough for a bunk and little else. There was one small
window. Under this the girl sat reading, cross-legged. He
could see the crescents of her eyelashes on her cheeks and
he wanted her to look up so he could see her face again.

He wanted to help her. 'Why aren't you allowed out?'

The girl looked up, startled to find him peering through
the grille. 'Go away. If they knew you'd seen me, I'd be in
trouble.'

'That's not fair. They shouldn't shut you up like this.'

'It's all right. It's for my own good,' she said.

But she looked so sad Ronnyn's heart went out to her.
'I'll speak to the all-mother –'

'She's the one who put me in here.'

Ronnyn felt betrayed. He'd instinctively trusted the
healer. 'How can I help?'

'No one can help me. They've all tried.'

'There must be something I can do.'

The girl blushed furiously, put the book aside and came
to stand under the grill. She looked up earnestly. 'Please go
away. You'll only make things worse.'

'Do you need anything?'

'I have everything I could want.'

'Except freedom.'

'Who is truly free? Not even the all-mother, she's bound
by tradition. None of us are truly free.'

Ronnyn laughed. 'I'm free.'

'Not if you belong to the T'Enatuath.'

'I grew up free,' Ronnyn said. 'And I'll be free again one
day. You wait and see. And when I go, I'll take you with me.'

She rolled her eyes. 'You don't know what you're talking
about. I can't leave.'

'Why not?'

She looked down. 'Go away.'

'I'm only trying to help.'

'No one can help.'

'I promise I'll find a way to set you free. I will. I'll –'

'If you ask about me, you'll get me in trouble. You might even put me in danger.' She wrung her hands. 'Just go away and forget you ever saw me.'

Ronnyn didn't want to distress her, so he climbed down off the chair. But he couldn't forget her.

IT WAS DUSK, and Imoshen stood on the high rear-deck, feeling the gentle rise and fall of the ship under her feet as it lay at anchor in Shifting-sands Bay. She lowered her shields, opened her gift awareness and sensed the build-up of a storm in the air. It reminded her of when she was growing up on Lighthouse Isle.

'Choice-mother?'

Imoshen turned to see five-year-old Deyne sprinting across the deck towards her. Tiasarone followed at a more sedate pace with baby Arodyti in her arms, while Frayvia, Imoshen's devotee, carried Umaleni, who wriggled, eager to be put down so she could chase after Deyne.

Imoshen held out her arms. 'Deyne.'

The little boy covered the distance between them. She laughed and caught him. Lifting him off his feet, she spun in a circle, then put him down as he was too heavy to hold for long.

'These children will be the death of me,' Tiasarone complained, but she did not hand Arodyti over, even though Imoshen offered to take the infant.

Frayvia and Imoshen shared a smile, and the devotee passed Umaleni to her.

'Have they been good children?' Imoshen asked.

'Always,' Deyne insisted and Frayvia laughed.

Imoshen was not surprised. This was what her gift had told her. His nature was true and loyal.

Umaleni wriggled with delight. Imoshen kissed her daughter's forehead and studied her dear little face. Every day Umaleni grew more like her half-cousin Iraayel. Which was lucky, as no one would be able to guess her T'En father's identity from her features.

'What brings you up on deck?' Imoshen asked.

'You didn't come to say good night to the children.'

'And we knew you meant to,' Deyne said earnestly.

Imoshen blushed.

Five nights. She had tucked him into bed five nights and in that time he'd laid claim to her heart by giving his without equivocation.

'So I did,' Imoshen agreed. 'But I was distracted by the blue fire.'

'Fire isn't blue,' he told her kindly.

There was a snort of laughter and Imoshen looked up to find her sisterhood's voice-of-reason had joined them.

'Fire isn't blue,' Deyne repeated. 'Fire's yellow and red.'

'This fire is blue.' Imoshen knelt and put Umaleni down. Then she opened her gift senses and called the foretaste of lightning to her. It was a trick she used to perform for Iraayel. Back when they had lived on the island, they would stand at the top of the lighthouse and she would make the blue flames dance on her fingertips.

Now she smiled as Deyne and Umaleni gasped and laughed with delight.

'You didn't tell us you had control of fire.' Egrayne sounded annoyed.

'It's not real fire. It can't burn,' Imoshen said, transferring the flames from one hand to the other. 'It's what's in the air before a storm. There's a lot of it around tonight. Can't you sense it?'

Tiasarone and Egrayne glanced to each other, then shook their heads.

'It's nothing.' Imoshen shrugged. 'A harmless child's game.'

'If you can call this, can you call lightning and thunder?' Tiasarone asked.

'No.'

'Maybe even a storm?' Egrayne pressed.

'I'm no weather-worker. I can't call up the slightest breeze. Believe me, I've tried.' Thirteen years ago this midwinter, they'd fled the lighthouse island. If she could have called a fog to hide their flight, she would have. 'All I can do is call this useless blue fire.'

'Pretty.' Deyne reached out to touch it.

Tiasarone pulled his hand back.

'Don't worry. It won't burn,' Imoshen said.

'It's the sea god's sign,' a man whispered.

They all turned to see the Malaunje ship's master. He was a dour veteran of many voyages, but right now he looked stunned and more than a little fearful. He backed up a step, eyeing Imoshen warily.

'It's harmless,' she told him.

He shook his head. 'The Mieren say the sea god manifests as blue fire. He blesses a ship by dancing on the masts. Sometimes he warns if a storm is coming. And sometimes, he appears in a ball of light that can burst and claim a sailor's life.' He swallowed. It was more than Imoshen had ever heard him say. 'I've always wondered...'

'Well, now you know it has nothing to do with gods,' Egrayne snapped. She turned back to the others, muttering. 'Really. Malaunje are as bad as Mieren, sometimes!'

The ship's master stiffened and retreated.

Imoshen felt for him. She'd grown up surrounded by Malaunje, with regular visits from her covenant-breaking father and his seconds, and she knew how much the halfbloods resented the T'En.

'I'm sorry.' She rose, brushing her hands to disperse the flames. 'I thought all T'En could call blue fire. It was a game I played for Iraayel back on Lighthouse Isle.'

Egrayne and Tiasarone exchanged looks.

Imoshen's raeden gift read their silence. She'd reminded them of her unorthodox upbringing and made them uncomfortable. Surely they trusted her after all she'd done:

executing her own father, birthing a sacrare daughter, accepting leadership of the sisterhood and then taking on the causareship.

'Up!' Umaleni tugged on her hand.

Eager to hide her true feelings, Imoshen bent down, lifted her daughter and buried her face in the toddler's chubby neck. Umaleni wriggled with pleasure, then gave a wide yawn, revealing her brand new baby teeth.

'The children should have their wash and their dinner,' Tiasarone announced.

Imoshen smiled down at little Deyne. 'Let's go.'

He beamed and, with all the dignity of a great all-father, offered Imoshen his arm. She accepted it, sure no one could resist his grave courtesy, and headed for the steps.

'What a pity you're not a weather-worker,' Egrayne said, falling in with her. 'We could use a good wind when we set off for Ivernia.'

'Oh, if I could summon the wind things would have been very different.' She would not have lost her first bond-partner, Reothe, and her sacrare son the night they ran away. A fog would have hidden them all and Reothe would not have had to fight off their pursuers, so she could escape with their son, four-year-old Iraayel and Frayvia.

If Reothe had escaped with her, they would have run to one of the islands and made a home for themselves, free of brotherhood and sisterhood interference. Together and free. They'd been so young and so much in love...

Tears stung her eyes. Thirteen years this midwinter and she could still weep for them and their ill-fated dreams.

Imoshen hoped she never forgot.

JARAILE HAD THOUGHT the brotherhood palace luxurious, but the sisterhood palace surpassed it. Naturally, Eskarnor had claimed the biggest and best palace for himself then selected chambers for her. She had her own balcony looking west across the city to the lakeside town. It was so high above the city, it gave her vertigo.

She had a suite of bedrooms, her own private bathing chamber and a reception room, every possible luxury, but it was a gilded cage.

Now it was dusk and she wandered along the balcony, wrapped in furs. She was naked underneath, having just come from the bathing chamber and, before that, Eskarnor's bed. It did not matter how often she washed, she could not wash the smell of him from her skin. She hated the way he made her feel.

She consoled herself with the fact that her kinsman, Baron Kerminzto, had escaped. In a way, this was what had saved her life. The first night up here, her second in the city, the thought of her little boy dying alone without her and been more than she could bear. She'd been prepared to jump off the balcony when Eskarnor was called from the bed and Captain Pataxo reported that they had closed the gates and searched the city, but Kerminzto had eluded them. How Eskarnor had raged.

Now she spotted people coming up the stairwell from the grand hall: Pataxo and one of the barons. She thought it might be Aingeru. She slipped inside to where Eskarnor lay sprawled on the bed, his big hairy chest rising and falling as he slept. The moment she knelt on the bed his eyes sprang open.

He slept like a warrior, always alert. She'd learnt that the first night.

'Someone comes,' she said.

A moment later there was a knock on the door.

Eskarnor swung his legs off the bed, found his breeches, pulled them up and laced them closed. He drew her close, sliding his hands under the fur.

'Your skin's so soft,' he muttered, calloused hands running over her thighs and belly. 'Look what you do to me.' He took her hand and cupped himself. 'Don't get dressed. I'll be right back.'

Waiting a few moments, she went to the adjoining bathing chamber; she had discovered that the air vent here carried sound from the passage. She stretched out on the floor to listen.

'...taken my wife and children to the palace,' Aingeru was saying. 'He's holding them hostage. She managed to get a message to me. Here it is.'

'A pox on that half-blood. I don't know why he's loyal to Charald,' Eskarnor said. There was a pause as he read the message. 'Sorne's gathering an army. He's calling up the men the barons sent home to bring in the harvest, calling them in the king's name, the devious, conniving...'

'They're to meet him at Riverbend Stronghold. If you send me and my men, I can lie in wait for him, pretend to go over to his side and murder him in his bed. Wipe out the nest of rebels,' Aingeru offered.

'So you can... Prepare your men and ride out tomorrow.'

She heard the sound of footsteps going down the long passage.

'Aingeru is mad for that wife of his,' Pataxo said. 'I can't see him risking her life. And there's the children, three fine sons. A man needs... What if the half-blood has kidnapped all the barons' families?'

'Good riddance to mine,' Eskarnor muttered. 'All she's given me is a daughter. I need a son and heir. If the half-blood kills her, he'll be freeing me to marry the queen.'

'But the other barons –'

'Don't you say a word about this to them.'

'Aingeru's men will know. They'll talk.'

'So they will. But the half-blood is only one man. He can't have ridden the length and breadth of Chalcedonia in five days. Tomorrow we leave for port. Once we have the king and the prince under siege...'

Jaraile's head buzzed as her heart raced. Did he just say what she thought he'd said? Her son lived?

'...cut off from his commander. The half-blood'll be too busy trying to work out how to break the siege and save Charald and Cedon to take any more of the barons' families hostage. Send Ikor to me.'

'Why?'

'He can prove he really is my man. I'll send him and his men with Aingeru. If Aingeru lets his cock decide his loyalty, Ikor can bring me his head.'

'Ikor's estate lies to the east on the coast just south of the port, won't he be tempted –'

'I'll tell Aingeru to watch over him and at the first sign of disloyalty to bring me his head. They'll both be so busy watching each other, they'll stay loyal!' Eskarnor laughed, pleased with himself.

Booted feet strode off.

'Oh, and Pataxo?' Eskarnor called. The boots stopped. 'I'm leaving you with two hundred men to hold the Wyrd city.'

'But –'

'But nothing. I'm trusting you with the queen. She carries my child. She legitimises my claim to the throne. The people love her. Hold onto this city and hold onto her, or you won't hold onto your head.'

Jaraile sprang to her feet, mind racing.

Her son lived.

The Wyrds had not killed him. Tears of joy streamed down her cheeks.

'Raila?' Eskarnor called.

She dropped her fur and stepped into the sunken bath, running more hot water.

She ducked under the water, coming up just as he entered the bathing chamber.

'Washing again?' he asked, then his expression grew hungry as he took in her wet, rosy skin. 'There's something to be said for bathing.'

He dropped his breeches, climbed into the tub and reached for her.

Her mind went away as she planned how to escape. She had to reach Sorne and warn him that Aingeru was going to betray him.

If Eskarnor was leaving tomorrow then she would be left here with Pataxo and his men in the palace. They could not watch her all the time.

THAT EVENING, RONNYN saw one of the T'En women slide a tray through a flap into the secret chamber, when she thought no one was looking. What kind of life was that? Why would they keep a T'En girl hidden? Why be so cruel when they were so kind to the rest of the children? True, they were all boys. As well as his three brothers, there were another four boys, ranging in age from two to six.

The T'En women sang the boys to sleep and All-mother Reoden fed baby Ashmyr. As she settled him in his cot, her Malaunje servant came over to Ronnyn.

'The healer's going to work on your bad arm,' Meleya said. 'Go wait in the bathing chamber.'

He did as he was told and, a moment later, the healer joined him. She took a seat at the marble table. 'Roll up your sleeve.'

He did this, leaned forward and placed his bad arm on the cool, slick marble. Looking at his forearm, with its misshapen muscle and scar tissue, he felt a pang of shame. It hurt, too. Sometimes, when he moved it without thinking or tried to carry something heavy, bolts of pain would shoot down his arm, making the muscles lock up.

The healer sat opposite him and turned up the lamp. He could feel her gathering her gift. The power was pure and clean, and it made his heart race and his body sing.

'Both arms,' Healer Reoden said. She studied his arms, then placed her hands on his forearms and closed her eyes as her fingers pressed into the muscles down the length of his forearms, driving her gift into his body.

'What are you doing?' he whispered, fascinated.

A smile tugged at her lips. 'I'm working out how your good arm is made and comparing it to how your bad arm has been injured and healed imperfectly. That way I can urge your bad arm to grow in the right direction.'

'Could you have healed it completely, if I'd come to you when it happened?'

'Yes.'

But he'd been living on the island then. His mother and his sister had done the best they could for him. Aravelle had massaged his arm every day, trying to make the knotted, twisted muscles straighten, pulling, twisting, forcing his arm to work.

'Your Malaunje sister did well.'

He stiffened. 'Can you sense my thoughts?'

'With touch, sometimes. It's something we can all do, but it's considered rude and intrusive, if we do it without consent. I wasn't sensing your thoughts. I was focusing on the healing and thinking how much worse this would have been if not for your sister's dedication. Were you thinking of her?'

Only all the time. But he didn't say that.

'Without her massages, your arm would have curled up, pulling tight until it was useless.'

He flushed, remembering how Aravelle would massage his arm and how he had used the opportunity to call his power and try to breach her defences. Back then, his gift had raged to be used.

On board the ship, his gift had not risen once. The way the healer's power pulsed through his body should have roused it.

Now that he thought about it, his power hadn't risen properly since the night the Mieren had raped his mother and sister. He'd been so furious then that his gift had broken free, leaving him exhausted and drained.

He should have protected them...

'You're tensing up. I need you to relax.' Reoden gave a little huff of annoyance. 'It's a pity your gift isn't manifesting. I could have tapped into it, to help the healing.'

'It isn't?'

She shook her head, eyes still closed in concentration. 'I feel no hint of power in you.'

But it had been moving.

His gift's drive to be used had once been so powerful it had shaped the way he thought, making him resent Aravelle because she wouldn't let him test his power on her. Looking back, he found it hard to believe he'd behaved like that.

'What I'm going to do next will hurt. I have to reform some of the worst muscle damage. Try to think of something else. Ready?'

'Ready.'

But he wasn't. His bad arm was his flaw and the pain had worn pathways in his mind and body. Try as he might, he could not recall the happy times back home on the island. All he could do was close his eyes and remember to breathe.

At last, the healer released him. 'There. That's all for tonight.'

He felt dizzy with relief.

'You did well. I've known adults who could not cope with that level of pain.'

He shook his head, drew breath, then hesitated. He had been about to ask the healer about the hidden girl, but didn't want to get her in trouble.

'What troubles you, choice-son?'

Where to start? 'Why must we keep our distance from our Malaunje kin?'

'I know it seems cruel to turn your back on your sisters, but it is for their own safety. You know my Malaunje servant?'

'Meleya?'

Reoden nodded. 'Before I began my initiate training at seventeen there was a terrible accident. My little choice-brother was hurt. Driven by my love for him, my gift broke free of my control. The power healed him, but Meleya was right beside me. It crashed through her defences and imprinted itself on her. She couldn't prevent it and I couldn't help it. I made her my devotee.' The healer shrugged. 'Since then, Meleya has been linked to me, addicted to my power. The gifts are dangerous and we T'En have a responsibility to the Malaunje around us. Meleya and I are lucky, in that we're well-suited.'

Reoden's keen, wine-dark eyes sought his and held them. 'Imagine being tied to someone you despise. Or perhaps you loved them once, and you've grown to hate them. A devotee is for life, Ronnyn. And when we love someone our emotions are harder to control, making our gifts harder to contain. Why do you think the custom of keeping our Malaunje kin at a distance arose? We do it to protect them. The gifts are a great responsibility.'

And he had nearly forced his gift on Aravelle. Shame made him hang his head. He hated himself and his gift. Yet, at the same time, he longed for the power to return. He was as much addicted to it as any devotee.

What if it never came back? What would happen to him, with his crippled arm and crippled gift?

His T'En father would reject him. No other brotherhood would take him. He'd...

'Ronnyn, what is it?'

He couldn't tell her. No one must know.

A pure T'En without a gift. It was too shameful.

'One day you'll learn you can trust me.' The healer squeezed his hand. Coming to her feet, she gestured to his bad arm. 'It may be stiff and feel worse than usual. We'll have another session in a couple of days. Tomorrow I'll see if I can fix your broken nose.'

Chapter Thirteen

ARAVELLE STUMBLED OUT of the foredeck cabins. It was the end of her first day serving the all-father and she was too tired to think. A fog had rolled in. The lantern that hung from the nearest mast formed a dull golden halo. She should have been watching where she was going, but all she could think of was curling up next to her little sister and going to sleep, hopefully with no nightmares of her family being kidnapped, her father murdered, her mother dying of blood loss after giving birth to her little brother.

She rubbed her eyes and took a deep breath, only to sense the abrasive tang of power. Going completely still, she closed her eyes and opened her mouth to taste the chill, foggy air.

This was T'En male power, laced with something terrible. Her stomach knotted with fear.

Heart racing, she looked along the flagship's mid-deck towards the rear-decks, but the mist was so thick she could not see more than a body length in front of her.

There were dangerous men hidden in the fog.

She swallowed and edged slowly along the deck towards the hatch. If she could just slip below...

A muffled curse.

'Catch him!'

A young, wiry T'En man came running out of the fog towards her.

Seeing her, he hesitated.

Someone grabbed him from behind. Another pair of arms joined the first and dragged him back. His boots thumped on the deck as he bucked and writhed, disappearing into the fog. She heard the dull thud and grunt of a struggle.

Then nothing but muffled breathing.

After a moment, a man muttered, 'Who would have thought the beast-lover had so much fight in him?'

His savage satisfaction made her shudder and her frozen muscles unlocked.

She spun on her toes and went to run, only to slam into someone's chest. Strong hands caught her. One arm went around her waist, lifting her off her feet, and a hand covered her mouth.

The Mieren rapist had grabbed her, knocking her to the ground, knocking the air out of her chest. No matter how hard she'd struggled, she could not throw him off.

But the Mieren hadn't smelled like this. This was one of her own people.

Saskar?

She looked into his dark eyes and saw fear as he glanced over her shoulder towards the fog that hid the struggle.

His eyes returned to hers and held her gaze, asking a silent question.

She nodded; she would be quiet.

He let go, took her hand and he drew her back with him.

She expected him to lead her into the passage under the foredeck. Instead, he drew her under the steps. There was just enough room to stand huddled together. In silence, they stared into the fog that hid the mid-deck.

She could still sense aggressive male gift and hear the occasional muffled gasp. 'It's the all-father's duty to protect his people. Shouldn't we tell Hueryx? We –'

'There's nothing we can do for him, Vella. We're only Malaunje.'

'But –'

'Besides, he was one of Kyredeon's T'En and our all-father can't interfere with the way another all-father runs his brotherhood.'

She could feel the tension in Saskar's body as he listened, senses on alert. When the sounds of the struggle faded, he let his breath out slowly and his shoulders relaxed.

She shivered. The night was cold, the fog damp and now that her heart was no longer racing...

'You'll catch a chill.' Saskar rubbed her arms.

It made her feel warm and protected, and she didn't like that. She had to be strong. Stepping out of reach, she came up against the wall. 'Why were you right behind me?'

He gave her an exasperated look. 'I was making sure you reached Charsoria's cabin safely.' He tilted his head to listen. She saw him inhale, weighing the scents and traces of power on the air. 'I think they've gone. Come on.'

He caught her hand and drew her out from under the stairs. They crossed the deck, heading for the fore-hatch.

She could sense residual gift-working, but there was no sign of the struggle or the initiate. That could be Ronnyn in a few years, trying to make his way in the brotherhood. She felt sorry for the young initiate.

'Why were they so cruel to him?'

'Because they could be.' Saskar slowed as they reached the open hatch that led to the Malaunje deck. He sighed. 'They called him beast-lover, Vella. That means he's a bestiare. His gift allows him to commune with animals.'

'So?'

He grimaced. 'T'En prize intellect, culture and control above all things. They look down on us Malaunje because we have no gift, and they regard Mieren as baser creatures, little better than animals. For a T'En's gift to link him to beasts...' Saskar shuddered. 'It demeans him. He has no hope of ever gaining high stature.'

'But it's not like he chose his gift. It was born in him.'

'And it's not like we chose to be born Malaunje. But we were.'

She felt the force of Saskar's anger. It didn't frighten her; she understood it. The same anger burned in her.

He gestured to the hatch. 'Go on.'

She climbed down the ladder into the dimness of the Malaunje deck.

Glancing up, she saw him there in the lantern-lit fog, standing over the open hatch. Saskar... her only friend, making sure she was safely returned to the Malaunje deck. She raised a hand and waved.

He nodded and turned away.

For all that he served the brotherhood's hand-of-force and slept in the all-father's cabin, he was as trapped as she.

As Aravelle returned to Charsoria's cabin her mind was abuzz with the faces and names of Hueryx's inner circle, as well as the tug and pull of the adepts' jostling for stature.

When she opened the door, she found the children were already asleep. The women of Charsoria's inner circle sat together, talking softly. Aravelle counted four young women who wore the warrior temple plaits, as well as the older women. Redravia played a haunting melody on the pipes.

When Aravelle entered, Hariorta whispered to her half-sister and Charsoria's eyes narrowed. Redravia looked up and stopped playing.

Aravelle bowed and would have scurried to her bedroll, but Charsoria greeted her sourly. 'I suppose you think you're favoured now.'

Aravelle knew it was petty, but Charsoria's resentment pleased her. She kept her eyes lowered. 'I live to serve.'

'You might have charmed your way into Hueryx's good graces just like your mother did, but I know you for what you are; a scheming stature-seeker!'

There was nothing Aravelle could say. The all-father's-voice judged everyone by her own standards. Stature-seeker, indeed.

'She thinks she's clever,' Hariorta said. 'But she doesn't realise. If the all-father truly honoured her, he'd keep his distance. Instead he toys with her.'

Charsoria nodded and a malicious smile split her face. 'You'll end up paying for your mother's transgressions,

Vella. How Sasoria would hate it, if she knew you were in his power.'

Aravelle refused to react. She was a personal scribe to the all-father of the one of the great brotherhoods. What could happen to her? She knew the dangers of the gifts.

Charsoria snorted. 'I can sense their power on you from here!'

Aravelle opened her gift awareness. 'I sense nothing.'

'Because you're saturated with it.'

'She needs to learn how to shield herself,' Redravia said.

'Is that so?' Charsoria asked, a nasty gleam in her dark eyes. 'Have you had no training, Vella, none at all?'

Aravelle shook her head.

Hariorta and Charsoria exchanged a glance. Charsoria nodded to Redravia. 'You train her. And do a better job than you did on Sasoria.'

Aravelle wanted to ask what she meant by this, but did not dare. Instead, she retreated to the bedroll she shared with Itania.

As she stroked her little sister's back, she repeated the same thing she'd repeated every night. *Nothing was going to break her. Not the cruel Mieren, not her mother's spiteful half-sister...*

And certainly not her charming T'En father.

IMOSHEN HEARD A clatter and a shriek. That was the problem on the overcrowded ship; there was no privacy. A cry of protest followed. The noise made her children stir in their sleep, and her devotee lifted her head.

'Stay here, Fray. I'll go tell them to be quiet,' Imoshen whispered.

As she entered the passage, the door to the communal bathing chamber swung open. Egrayne spotted her and beckoned. Two bright spots of colour burned in the voice-of-reason's cheeks. Imoshen could sense that she was having trouble controlling her gift, which was unusual.

When Imoshen stepped into the chamber, she found Iraayel on his knees, pinned by the sisterhood's hand-of-force. Fear for her choice-son roused Imoshen's gift and she read everyone in the room, all but Iraayel. She hadn't been able to read him since the day the healer's sacrare daughter was murdered in front of him.

Egrayne was furious, and hurt. Kiane felt vindicated. She believed that all T'En men were dangerous, and whatever had happened here had confirmed this for her. The two shield-sisters, Dretsune and Ysattori, were regretful but determined to see this through. And Egrayne's choice-daughter, Saffazi, was ablaze with righteous anger.

'Let him go.' Saffazi struggled against the two shield-sisters who restrained her. 'We –'

Egrayne slapped her. 'How dare you shame me?'

Shocked, Saffazi stared at her choice-mother. She went absolutely white, and then her gift rose.

'No.' Imoshen held the young initiate's eyes and let her own gift rise in challenge. Saffazi was powerful and inclined to be impatient with anyone not as quick of mind as herself. 'Are you a newly-empowered thirteen-year-old with no control over your gift, or an initiate with half a year's training?'

Saffazi's blazing gaze faltered, then dropped, and the threat of gift power eased. 'Your pardon, all-mother.'

'Now, what's going on here?' Imoshen calmly asked, as though her heart wasn't racing fit to burst. 'Why is my choice-son restrained?'

'They were...' Dretsune, the warrior-turned-scholar, glanced apologetically to Egrayne. 'We came in here and found them trysting.'

'What?'

'It's not true.' Iraayel lifted his head.

'Close enough,' Dretsune said.

Imoshen took a step back.

'So what if we were?' Saffazi demanded. 'We love each –'

'Enough,' Egrayne barked. 'Ysattori, fetch the rest of the inner circle.'

The younger of the two shield-sisters slipped out. With the deaths of the last hand-of-force, her shield-sister, two gift-warriors and the gift-tutor, the sisterhood's inner circle had shrunk and its nature had changed.

When Imoshen was made all-mother instead of Gift-tutor Vittoryxe, she had chosen an inner circle that included some of the gift-tutor's supporters to win them over. These women tended to be traditionalists with closed minds. Hand-of-force Arodyti and her contingent had been Imoshen's supporters and forward thinkers. Now the mix of women veered towards the conservative. This put Imoshen in a difficult position.

Ysattori returned with three T'En women.

'What's going on?' Tiasarone asked. She was one of the conservatives.

Iraayel went to speak, but Imoshen sent him a look.

Saffazi lifted her chin. 'We want to make the deep-bonding –'

'Foolish, foolish girl!' Egrayne was angrier than Imoshen had ever seen her.

'...so that Iraayel can stay with us,' Saffazi finished.

The inner circle shifted, muttering in shock and dismay.

'What makes you think Iraayel won't be going to a brotherhood?' Imoshen asked.

Saffazi glanced to Iraayel.

He lifted his chin.

'Oh, let him up, Kiane,' Imoshen said. 'It's not like he's going to turn on us.'

The hand-of-force released Iraayel and stepped back. She was also one of Vittoryxe's old supporters.

'What makes you think we'd let him stay, Saffazi?' Egrayne asked. 'No one has made the deep-bonding since the covenant, four hundred years ago.'

Saffazi gestured. 'The all-mother –'

'Imoshen was seventeen and a brotherhood captive,' Egrayne snapped. 'She didn't know any better.'

Imoshen flushed and bit her tongue. She wanted to

defend Reothe, her dead bond-partner, but now was not the time. Not when her choice-son's future hung in the balance.

'What makes you think the deep-bonding would mean Iraayel could stay with us, Safi?' Imoshen asked.

'We'd share a link. The sisters wouldn't be afraid of him if they knew I could reach into his mind and cripple his gift at a moment's notice.'

'You'd be just as vulnerable to him,' Egrayne said. 'That's why we don't commit to the deep-bonding anymore.'

'Imoshen did.'

'Her bond-partner was dead when she came to us. If he had been alive, we would never have been able to accept Imoshen. Her loyalty would have been compromised. We would have executed her.' Egrayne had been a gift-warrior before she became the empowerer, and this was evident in the decisive tone of her voice. 'This isn't about Imoshen. It's about you.'

'And Iraayel,' Saffazi insisted. Her chin trembled and tears of fury filled her eyes. 'I won't let you kill him!'

The women gasped.

'You'd put him ahead of your sisterhood?' the warrior-scholar asked.

'Of course she wouldn't.' Egrayne sprang to her choice-daughter's defence. 'She's not thinking clearly.'

'Yes, I am. I know that none of the all-fathers will take Iraayel because they hate Imoshen and, if one of them accepted her choice-son, the other all-fathers would despise him.' Saffazi's beautiful eyes glistened with furious tears and she had trouble controlling her gift. 'Just the other night I was on deck when a brotherhood rowboat went by. I don't think they realised how far their voices carried. They said it would be kinder if...' – her voice caught – 'kinder if the causare's inner circle killed Iraayel themselves, rather than turn him out and let the brotherhoods hunt him for sport, or send him back to Chalcedonia and let the Mieren execute him. It's not fair. I won't let you do it.'

'Is it true?' Iraayel asked Imoshen, eyes glittering with anger. He would be seventeen soon and then she couldn't protect him. 'Have all the brotherhoods rejected me?'

Imoshen flushed. 'All-father Tamaron has not yet returned.'

'And may not,' Saffazi said. 'That's why we tried to set up the deep-bonding.'

'It's not the physical act of trysting,' Imoshen said. 'The mind, body and gift must be in alignment. It's' – her throat closed with emotion – 'it is the greatest joy there is.'

Everyone looked down as though she'd embarrassed herself. Imoshen felt sorry for them because they would never know what she had known.

'The deep-bonding is dangerous,' Egrayne said. 'It's not permitted. It leaves both partners open to attack. No one, other than Imoshen, has –'

'That we know of,' Imoshen corrected.

They all turned to look at her.

She lifted her hands in a shrug. 'How do we know if others have made the deep-bonding? When the sisterhoods and brotherhoods are so paranoid about each other, we are hardly going to admit to loving and trusting –'

'I trust Iraayel,' Saffazi insisted.

'There's no point. The deep-bonding wouldn't save him,' Tiasarone said. 'It would make him more dangerous. He would have intimate knowledge of the workings of the female gift.' She shuddered. 'We could not have him living alongside us.'

'Then what's going to happen to Iraayel?' Saffazi asked.

Imoshen held her tongue, wanting to hear what her inner circle would say. No one spoke for a moment.

Then Egrayne answered. 'This is why, once they are empowered at thirteen, we segregate the lads and begin to distance ourselves from them. We know that when they turn seventeen and go into the brotherhoods, we must declare them dead to us and they are reborn as men of the T'En. Once their gifts have matured, we cannot have them amongst us.'

'It's wrong, cruel and wrong.' Saffazi shook her head. 'What's going to become of Iraayel? You can't turn him out.'

Everyone looked to him and he looked to Imoshen.

If Ardonyx convinced Tobazim to take over Kyredeon's brotherhood and they succeeded, Iraayel would have somewhere to go. But she couldn't reveal her plans before the sisterhood's conservatives without admitting she'd made the deep-bonding with Ardonyx. If she did that, these powerful women would feel justifiably betrayed. They would be so angry... her gift surged and she knew they just might kill her.

'Imoshen?' Egrayne pressed.

'There's still time.' But time was running out for her choice-son.

NOW THAT SHE was alone, Jaraile found the chambers that formed her prison enormous. Eskarnor had left at dawn, boasting he could force-march his men to the port in four days, long before the half-blood could gather an army and be back to defend the king. She'd watched the barons' men pour out of the city, thinking, *good riddance*.

They were all gone by mid-morning and then the city had stood empty – empty boulevards, empty shops, empty balconies. It was a city meant for thousands, and there were two hundred men here now. She heard distant noises, which she took to be Pataxo's men. The sounds seemed to echo up from the courtyard far below, though it was hard to tell just where they came from.

All day she had paced, trying to think of a way out.

How could she escape when two hundred men stood guard between her and the gate and she didn't know her way around?

If she could just make it over the causeway to the town, she could borrow a horse. But first she had to escape these chambers, and she was afraid if she did, she'd blunder into one of her captors.

Her stomach grumbled.

Feeling hungry and impatient, she went into the bathing chamber and stretched out on the tiles to listen at the grate. She'd done this several times already today and each time she did, she'd hoped to learn something useful but all she ever heard was the guards betting on dice.

'...fair gives me the creeps,' one of them was saying.

'Your roll.'

'I mean, think about it. All them Wyrds, living here, doing their foul gift-working year in, year out. It has to sink into a place. I tell you, there's a spot down near the big stairs where I get the shivers.'

'Are you going to roll or not?' There was a pause, rattling, then... 'That's the third time in a row you've rolled a six.'

'Just lucky, I guess. Pay up.'

Another pause.

Then the lucky one said, 'Old Four-fingers says he can feel it when Wyrds use their gifts and he says the whole place stinks of gift power. He says he's been having dreams since the first night here, dreams about a beautiful woman.'

'Old Four-fingers wouldn't know what to do with a woman if he found one in his bedroll. Shut up and roll the dice.'

Jaraile heard distant footsteps, which meant they were bringing her food. She sprang to her feet, hurrying to the reception room.

Since arriving here, she'd pretended to be frightened and spiritless. Now she clutched her shawl around her shoulders as she stood at the balcony doors. She heard the lock turn in the key and the door open. Someone backed in with a tray.

She let them put it on the table before looking around. The two guards stood in the doorway, while the kitchen lad placed a tray of food on the table.

'I thought all the Wyrds had gone?' Jaraile said.

'They'd better be gone,' one of the guards muttered. She

recognised his voice. He was the one who just wanted to play dice, despite his bad luck.

'Then why was a woman walking on the rooftop garden over there?'

'Where?' The lucky guard came over to peer through the balcony door with her.

'Over there.' She pointed. 'It's too dark to see her now, but she was there twice today.'

'What did she look like?'

'Silver hair, beautiful.'

The two guards exchanged a look. Even the lad, removing her lunch tray, looked over. He was about twelve and had a black eye.

'No Wyrds left in the city,' the unlucky guard said. 'You must have been dreaming.'

'If you say so.' She rubbed her arms. 'Could you bring me more firewood? It's gotten very cold this afternoon.'

Again the two guards glanced to each other.

Jaraile decided to leave it at that for today. She wanted them scared of their own shadows. She wasn't sure exactly how this would benefit her, but she might be able to convince them to leave the sisterhood palace and go down to the brotherhood palace. Then she stood a better chance of getting out the gate.

PART TWO

Chapter Fourteen

SORNE RODE INTO Shifting-sands Bay, and was struck by its beauty. The surrounding hills were steep, and as his party rode along the path to the stronghold they looked down on the sparkling waters. Inside the narrow headlands, the bay spread out, dotted with islands. Around each island and along the shore were the sand bars that moved with every tide, giving the bay its name. Between the deep blue water where the Wyrd ships lay moored and the bands of glittering azure over the shallow sand bars, the bay rippled and shone like a gleaming jewel.

Shifting-sands Bay was the closest deep harbour to Navarone, but it was not popular with captains: the sea built up in the narrow entrance to the headlands with each tide, then poured through with devastating force, changing the floor of the bay every time. Entry to the bay had to be timed between the tide's ebb and flow, and the force of the tide varied with the movements of the two moons. Only those familiar with the bay risked it. All this he had learned from Nitzane, who had grown up here and loved the place.

The baron's stronghold stood on the tallest of the sandstone headlands, and was made of the same golden stone. While the castle wasn't large, it was secure. This was where Nitzane had taken Marantza when they married and ran from King Charald. The baron had confessed he could not bring himself to return since his wife's death.

When Sorne rode through the archway into the first courtyard, men and boys came running, but they'd expected Baron Nitzane and stood about uncertainly at the sight of him, the king's guard, the baroness, her children, the two nursemaids and half a dozen men-at-arms. Despite the party's number, they'd made good time, after sending the injured king's guard to the Mother's abbey near Riverbend Stronghold.

Sorne swung his leg over the horse and dropped to the ground. 'Where's the castle-keep?'

She bustled out, and bobbed her head. 'Warrior's-voice.'

'King's agent Sorne, now. Or more correctly, the queen's agent. Baron Nitzane sent this for you,' Sorne said. He pulled a message from his vest. It gave him authority to use Nitzane's stronghold, servants and ships as he wished. There was another message for the leader of the stronghold's men-at-arms. He was to deliver them to Riverbend Stronghold as soon as possible. 'And the baron asked if your cat had had any more kittens with folded ears.'

'Why, bless him for remembering.'

'Are there kittens, Ma?' Aingeru's little girl asked.

'Kittens? There's always kittens, my pretty.' The castle-keep beamed. 'My princess is famous in these parts for producing kittens with folded ears. Most sought after, they are.'

She made them all welcome, bustling inside. In no time at all, the horses had been led away and the children had been sent to the kitchens to see the princess of cats with her latest litter. Bed chambers were allocated and aired, and the castle-keep led Sorne to a chamber overlooking the bay.

'This will be yours. It's the master's when he comes, which is not often enough, if you don't mind my saying so.'

'He was heartbroken when his wife died.'

She nodded. 'He came to the docks after her death, whisked his boy onto a ship and hasn't been to visit us. When you consider he spent his childhood here, you'd think he'd come back to see us.'

Sorne had been afraid the castle's retainers would resent being asked to serve a half-blood, but his part in helping

Nitzane and his wife escape King Charald's wrath was remembered.

'More of the barons' families will come,' Sorne said.

'How long will they stay?' the castle-keep asked.

'Not long. They'll sail for the palace. Prince Cedon's been returned, and the Wyrds have healed his club foot. There will be celebrations.' Sorne glanced down through the open balcony doors to the bay below. As he watched, lanterns were lit on several of the ships. It had been ten days since the T'En had fled the port, time for the some of the Wyrd estates to get the messages he'd sent and make the journey. 'Do you know if many of the Wyrds have arrived by land?'

'I did hear of some coming through the town. Now, what would you like for dinner?'

'See to the baroness first. She'll want to settle the children. I must go down to the ships.'

He noted two of Nitzane's merchant vessels at the wharf. Just as well. He would have to commandeer both, one to send the northern harbours to collect the barons' families and one to take the southern families to Port Mirror-on-Sea.

Kerminzto's messenger had ridden hard and caught up with him on the road here. He now knew where Jaraile was being held in the Wyrd city.

But he did not know if Kerminzto had met up with Nitzane in the north. Nitzane should have reached Eskarnor's estate by now, taken his family hostage and be heading back to Port Mirror-on Sea.

'HE'S HERE.'

Imoshen looked up at Frayvia. Her devotee wore that expression for only one person. 'Sorne's back?'

'He's coming aboard right now.'

Imoshen nodded to Tiasarone and left the children to finish their dinner while she went out onto the deck, where the lanterns had been lit. There were more Malaunje on deck than normal. They pretended to work, or stood about, waiting to catch a glimpse of Sorne.

She glanced to the nearest T'Enatuath ships and saw several lowering boats. Sorne's rowboat had been spotted coming out from port. The all-fathers would be here in no time. 'Send a message to all the ships. We'll hold an all-council. Fetch Ree.'

She wondered if the all-fathers realised the honour they did Sorne, coming to hear him speak.

Egrayne caught up with her. 'You've called an all-council?'

Imoshen nodded.

'Then come back to the cabin and let my devotee do your hair.' Egrayne grimaced. 'You look like a Mieren, with it hacked off so short. Roskara has a real flair for dressing hair. She can hide –'

'I'm not hiding my hair. I cut it to mourn our dead and make a point. And every time the other T'Enatuath leaders see it they're reminded of this.'

At that moment, Sorne climbed aboard and Frayvia threw her arms around him. He laughed, and his usually grim expression lightened.

They came over to Imoshen together.

Sorne gave his obeisance. 'Causare.'

'What news do you have of our people?' Imoshen asked.

'Messages were sent to every estate ten days ago. I hoped you had news for me.'

She shook her head. 'A few of the smaller estates have come in, just a handful of people. There's still time.' Albeit not much. 'Would the king –'

'The king is locked away in his palace. Half the time he's raving, and the other half he doesn't remember what he had for breakfast. Guardians have been appointed to guide the prince.'

'At least little Cedon is safe.'

'He's in hiding. Eskarnor will besiege the port any day now. I'm taking the baron's families hostage and gathering an army.'

She heard a deep voice. The first of the brotherhood triumvirates' boats had drawn near. 'Kiane, send them up to the high rear-deck. Frayvia, prepare the spiced wine.'

As Imoshen led Sorne up the steps, she whispered, 'Is there anything else I need to know before the others get here?'

'Baron Eskarnor abducted Queen Jaraile the night before you returned the prince. Cedon still hasn't seen his mother and Jaraile was told that the Wyrds had killed him.'

'She must be heartbroken. Is there any way you can –'

'I've already sent word that he's safe.'

'Good.' Imoshen found that her people had brought up a brazier and the all-council carpet.

Reoden joined them. 'All better, Sorne?'

He gave her a deep obeisance. 'I feel like a new man, thanks to you, the causare and the gift-wright.'

As the rest of the brotherhood and sisterhood leaders took their places around the circle, Imoshen whispered to Sorne, explaining who each person was. Then she introduced him formally. By the time this was done, the spiced wine was ready to serve.

Frayvia offered Imoshen first, and Imoshen deferred to Sorne.

'What?' All-father Dretsun objected. 'That we have a Malaunje speaking at an all-council meeting is bad enough, but to give him precedence in the spiced wine ceremony?'

Sorne refused the spiced wine and indicated Frayvia was to continue around the circle.

'At least he knows his place,' All-father Saskeyne said. 'A Malaunje cannot have the status of a T'En.'

Imoshen felt Sorne's quiet fury and spoke up quickly. 'It's thanks to this Malaunje that we reached port alive. It's thanks to him that we have the opportunity to shelter here and wait for the people from our estates. I think we can share spiced wine with him.'

'And where are the people from our estates?' Kyredeon demanded. 'I'm waiting on a silver mine and two merchant houses. I know my people at the winery were massacred, but I've not had word from the others.'

'That's because they're travelling across Chalcedonia,' Imoshen said. 'Hopefully unmolested.'

'We were promised until winter's cusp. King Charald –'

'King Charald is raving mad.' Imoshen cut him off. 'The prince is in hiding, the queen has been abducted by Baron Eskarnor and Chalcedonia is about to erupt in civil war. Sorne is gathering an army.'

The all-fathers cast him measuring looks.

'Yet you say he's not your devotee?' All-father Egrutz, oldest of the brotherhood leaders, asked.

Clearly, they felt threatened by Sorne, but Imoshen did not understand why they kept coming back to his status within the T'Enatuath. 'Sorne is a free Malaunje, attached to no brotherhood or sisterhood.'

'Then he is not under anyone's protection,' Dretsun said, and Imoshen finally understood. If a brother was turned out of his brotherhood, he was without protection, hunted down and killed. It followed, an unaffiliated Malaunje...

'He is in the causare's service,' Imoshen said. 'And he should have the gratitude of every one of us.'

There was some muttering at this.

'I ride back to lead an army to war,' Sorne announced, without asking permission to speak. 'It would greatly weaken Eskarnor if I were to free the queen. He's holding her captive in the Celestial City.'

There was even more muttering at the thought of the Mieren baron turning their beautiful city into a prison.

'Why should we help free a queen who made war on our people?' Dretsun countered. 'Why should we care who rules Chalcedonia?'

'It was not Queen Jaraile who declared war on the Wyrds,' Sorne said. 'She owes the T'Entuath a debt for healing her son.'

'And we want someone sympathetic to our kind ruling Chalcedonia.' Imoshen gestured to the fleet. 'Here we sit, waiting on people from nearly thirty estates, most of whom still have to cross the kingdom. And Chalcedonia has emerged as the power of the Secluded Sea. If we want to trade with any of the other kingdoms, we need to be on good terms with their ruler.'

'And then there are the Malaunje born to Mieren parents,' Sorne added. 'Charald was going to forbid anyone who produced a half-blood baby from having children, but that kind of law is unenforceable. More of our kind will be born. The *Wyrd Problem* won't go away. Jaraile –'

'Is still King Charald's queen.'

'The king is raving mad. Weren't you listening, Dretsun?' Hueryx snapped.

Sorne nodded. 'Charald is king in name only, and it's not as if Jaraile had any choice in the matter. She was fifteen when he forced her father to hand her over. Now Eskarnor has raped and abducted her, and –'

'Believe me, we don't want Eskarnor crowning himself king,' Imoshen said. 'He cut a T'En boy's throat without compunction. He will not hesitate to destroy our people.'

'I volunteer my warriors,' Kyredeon said, surprising Imoshen. 'My best assassin Graelen will lead a team into the city, free the queen and bring her back –'

'To Riverbend Stronghold,' Sorne said, unaware of the insult he offered by interrupting a T'En, and an all-father at that. She glanced to Sorne. Would he be able to live with the restrictions of T'Enatuath life?

'The causare thanks All-father Kyredeon and acknowledges his brotherhood's stature,' Imoshen said. Then something occurred to her. 'What part of the city is the Queen being held in?'

'She's in the grandest sisterhood palace.'

'Our palace?' Egrayne was disgusted. 'He's turned our palace into a prison?'

'It's not ours anymore,' Imoshen reminded her then looked across to Kyredeon. 'You'll need my sisterhood warriors. They know the palace inside out.'

'No sisterhood warrior will trust a brotherhood warrior at her back,' Imoshen's hand-of-force stated.

'I'll go,' a voice said from above.

To Imoshen's horror, Iraayel climbed down the mast and dropped to the carpet. He sank to his knees, placing his hands in front of him, then pressing his forehead to his hands in the obeisance of deep supplication. 'Forgiveness, Causare Imoshen. I was up on the crow's nest and did not realise an all-council had been called below.' He looked up, desperate determination in his wine-dark eyes. 'I know the sisterhood palaces. I can go with the brotherhood warriors.'

Part of her knew it was a master stroke to win stature. Another part of her was horrified. Her sixteen-year-old choice-son, alone with Kyredeon's warriors...

'It's decided, then,' Sorne said. 'I'll have to go with them. Jaraile trusts me. They can come back with me to the stronghold tonight. We leave at first light.'

And the all-council broke up. Iraayel packed his travelling kit, and there was barely time for Imoshen to bid him goodbye. She caught up with him as he was heading for the deck.

'I know why you do this,' she whispered. 'You hope to win stature.'

'If I'm going to die anyway, I might as well die rescuing an innocent woman.'

Imoshen grabbed his robe. 'Don't do anything stupid. There's still hope, Iraayel.'

He did not look convinced, and it was on the tip of her tongue to reveal her secret bond-partner and the plans they'd made to take over Kyredeon's brotherhood, but this would put Iraayel in danger, and he was in enough danger already.

'If you die,' she told him, 'I will be very angry with you!'

He laughed and hugged her, then looked past her shoulder and she turned to see Saffazi waiting.

'I should be going with you. I'm trained as warrior,' Saffazi said.

'No sisterhood warrior would trust a brotherhood warrior to defend her back,' Imoshen said, to test them.

Saffazi bristled. 'I'd trust Iraayel with my life,'

So perhaps there was hope for this new generation, forced together by exile, growing up free of the artificial constraints of the Celestial City. Imoshen smiled. 'Make your goodbyes quickly.'

Out on deck, she caught Sorne before he climbed over the side and into the waiting rowboat. 'I don't trust All-father Kyredeon. It's not like him to volunteer his warriors. He's up to something. Be wary of this Graelen. He's a trained killer.'

Sorne stiffened. 'I know Graelen. I'd trust him with my life.'

Imoshen had been going to hint at her plans for Ardonyx and Tobazim and her fears for them. But now she hesitated.

'Don't worry, I'll keep an eye on Iraayel.'

'If only you'd had a vision. We'd know if this scheme to rescue the queen was worth the gamble.'

He laughed. 'No more visions for me. I'm not risking the predators of the empyrean plane. The older I get, the more cautious I become.'

It suddenly occurred to her that she might be able to trigger a vision in him. If she took his hand right now and drove enough power through him, it would knock him out and power his latent gift.

'Imoshen?'

But it could be a vision of anything. That was the problem with the male version of the futures gift. Unlike female scryers, seers could not direct their visions.

And he would be imprinted with her gift. Her raedan ability surged, telling her that if she made him her devotee, the service he gave freely now would be resented.

'I felt your gift rise. Is there a threat?'

Yes, me. I could imprint you and use you... But she wouldn't.

Iraayel joined them and there was no more chance for private talk.

Chapter Fifteen

WHEN HE WAS called into the captain's cabin, Tobazim went expecting trouble. He did not expect to meet Graelen at the door. For a moment they stared at each other, and then Tobazim gestured for him to go first. He didn't want the assassin behind him.

Graelen hesitated, then went ahead.

As they made their obeisance to the all-father, light glittered on Kyredeon's silver and glass sculpture of the Celestial City. Made by the all-father and his voice-of-reason, it was a thing of beauty. How could two such heartless men create beauty?

'You have a chance to win stature for your brotherhood,' Kyredeon told them. 'Grae, you will lead a mission to the Celestial City to rescue the kidnapped Mieren queen.' The assassin looked as surprised as Tobazim. 'You will be his second, Tobazim. You leave tomorrow. Go pack your travelling kits.'

As they stood up to leave, Kyredeon added. 'A word, Grae.'

Tobazim walked out, certain he was not meant to return from this mission. Down in his cabin, Ardonyx, Athlyn, Haromyr and the others waited, their expressions worried and grim.

'What's going on?' Ardonyx asked.

'Athlyn, pack a travelling kit for me,' Tobazim said. 'The assassin is leading a party to rescue the Mieren queen.'

'And kill you,' Ardonyx muttered.

'This is it.' Haromyr's features hardened. 'You must kill Graelen.'

'If Tobazim comes back without Graelen, he's as good as challenging Kyredeon,' Ardonyx warned.

'If he dies, we are all lost,' Haromyr countered. 'Kyredeon will pick us off one by one.'

'He won't kill Ardonyx,' Eryx said. 'He needs the sea captain.'

Athlyn handed Tobazim his travelling kit. 'What will you do?'

'Stay alert. Watch Graelen and if... if I have to kill him, I will.'

Ardonyx drew him into the bathing chamber, the only place they could be private, and shut the door on the others. 'Graelen is older than you. He's killed many times and he's a gift-warrior.'

'He has to sleep sometime.'

Ardonyx smiled and shook his head. 'You would never kill a man in his sleep. Do you want to become my shield-brother?'

He wanted it more than anything, but not for this reason. Tobazim's gift surged, and he forced it down. 'There isn't time to do it properly.' It should be a blending of mind, body and gift, offered in joy, not desperation. After all, a shield-brother was for life. And it would reveal to Ardonyx how he really felt. 'Besides, if I died after we became shield-brothers, it would weaken you.'

'You...' Ardonyx caught the back of his neck in his calloused sailor's palm, pulled him close and kissed his forehead. 'You come back alive. You hear me?'

Why? Because he cared, or because he needed Tobazim to defeat Kyredeon?

A knock on the door. 'The hand-of-force is calling for volunteers,' Haromyr said. 'Do you want us to volunteer?'

Ardonyx caught Tobazim's eye as he replied. 'You can volunteer all you like, but you won't be chosen.'

Tobazim grinned as he walked out.

* * *

GRAELEN REMAINED IN the all-father's cabin when the door closed on Tobazim.

'You know what you need to do,' Kyredeon said. 'It will be a dangerous mission. No one will be surprised if Tobazim is killed. And we're in luck, the causare's choice-son has also volunteered. If you can lead him to his death, that would be a blow to her.'

They discussed who should make up the party. They did not want the group too obviously weighted with Kyredeon's supporters, so they decided on young warriors with no obvious allegiance to him.

Oriemn went out to call for volunteers. Everyone would volunteer – it was a chance to win stature – so he could take his pick.

Head reeling, Graelen left. Valendia was waiting; she drew him to the rail overlooking the mid-deck.

'What did he want?' she whispered, as Oriemn selected volunteers.

'I'm leading a mission.'

Below them, Tobazim left the cabin, heading for the side of the ship with a travelling kit over his shoulder.

Her eyes flew to his. 'No, Grae.'

'I have to do this.' To save her.

'No.'

'Sometimes we have to do hard things.'

She brushed past him, running into the passage to their cabin. He followed, but she was not behind the blanket in the corner. Graelen delayed as long as she could, hoping Valendia would come back, but she was avoiding him. She had a good heart and a kind nature, but she was utterly determined.

If he did this, she would despise him.

But if he didn't, Kyredeon would have him killed, which would kill her; and he couldn't bear that.

Better she despised him.

When he climbed down into Sorne's rowboat, as well as the Mieren oarsmen and Sorne, there were five cloaked brotherhood warriors waiting for him. He could feel their roused male gift. If he were Tobazim, he would be feeling very threatened.

And a threatened T'En adept was a dangerous thing.

ARAVELLE FOLDED THE ornate brocade robe Hueryx had worn for the all-council meeting.

'Can you believe the arrogance of that Malaunje?' Dragomyr demanded. 'Speaking at an all-council isn't enough. He has to interrupt an all-father.'

'I know,' Reyne crowed. 'Did you see Kyredeon's face?'

'Perhaps the Malaunje has something to be arrogant about,' Hueryx said. 'He's used his visions to make King Charald dance to his tune for years. Now he's set off to rescue a queen, raise an army and save a kingdom.'

His seconds said nothing.

Hueryx caught Aravelle's eye. She smiled before she could help it.

'When Imoshen's choice-son dropped from the rigging, I thought the all-fathers would punish him for his temerity,' Dragomyr said.

'He volunteered to win stature, a clever move. Everyone is manoeuvring,' Hueryx said. 'Meanwhile, Dretsun keeps picking away at Imoshen, even though she demolished him the last time he tried to undermine her.' Hueryx gestured to Aravelle. 'And what can we learn from this, Vella?'

Startled, she said the first thing that came into her head. 'That an all-father driven by ambition can overstep his reach.'

Hueryx laughed. 'See, Dragomyr? With a little training she will prove a valuable tool.'

But Aravelle wasn't going to be anyone's tool. She went through to the bathing chamber to clean up. They'd left water in the tub, towels on the floor and clothing where it had fallen as they stripped.

She began by sorting their clothing. As she worked, she stubbed her toe on a small chest filled with semi-precious stones, spilling them across the tiles.

Aravelle looked at the jewels winking in the lamplight. Just one of those stones would have kept her family for ten years. When she thought of how hard her mother and father worked to put food on their table...

'Don't even think it,' Saskar said.

She gave a guilty jump as he joined her.

He dropped to his knees to pick up the jewels. 'You're thinking of stealing the stones and running away. The same thing occurred to me. But we'd have nowhere to go. Even if we dyed our hair, our eyes and fingers would give us away. We can never pass for Mieren, and without the T'En, we're powerless to defend ourselves. There's nowhere to run to, Vella.'

'I wasn't thinking of running away,' Aravelle protested, helping him put the gems back. 'Besides, my parents ran, and we were happy!'

'And look at the price they paid. Both dead and their children captives. You were lucky the causare offered a reward for live Malaunje and T'En, or the Mieren would have killed you.'

She bowed her head.

As SORNE CLOSED the door on the Wyrds' chamber, he noticed that one of the warriors was missing and assumed the missing brother had slipped into the town on a private mission for the all-father.

Sorne turned to the castle-keep. 'We leave tomorrow at dawn.'

'Good, because the silverheads make my skin crawl,' she confessed. So she was sensitive to gift power; some True-men were.

Sorne's stomach rumbled.

'Have you eaten?'

'No,' he admitted.

'I'll have something sent up to your room.'

He thanked her and returned to the baron's chamber. As

he entered, a cloaked warrior rose from the chair by the fireplace.

He reached for his sword.

Valendia laughed and threw back the hood. 'I fooled you. I fooled them all.'

He hugged her, his heart light with laughter. 'Grae –'

'Doesn't know I'm here. We're fighting.' Her beautiful wine-dark eyes glittered with tears. 'Oh, Sorne, it's horrible in the brotherhood. The all-father...' She shuddered, reaching for his hands, shaking with emotion. 'He's sent Grae on this mission as an excuse to kill someone.'

So this was what Imoshen had been trying to tell him. But he knew Graelen to be an honourable man. Sorne noticed her chilled, trembling fingers. 'You're freezing. Come over by the fire and tell me what's going on.'

As he built up the fire, she knelt next to him.

'Kyredeon fears Tobazim and Captain Ardonyx will challenge his leadership, so he's told Grae to get rid of Tobazim.'

'I'll warn Tobazim about Kyredeon's plans for him.'

'He knows. Believe me, he knows.'

'Don't worry. Grae is an honourable man, he won't –'

She shook her head. 'Kyredeon threatened me. Grae will kill to protect me.'

'Then Grae needs to unite with Tobazim and Ardonyx against the all-father.'

'They'd lose. Tobazim and Ardonyx only have low-ranking brothers on their side. Kyredeon's got everyone running scared. And besides, according to Grae, they aren't powerful enough yet. If they challenge and lose, Kyredeon will purge the brotherhood, executing all their followers. If Grae dies, I die. That's why he'll kill Tobazim. But it will make him go hard and cold inside, and I'll lose him.'

Sorne held her while she sobbed, rubbing her back, saying the things their mother used to say. All the while, his anger grew.

After a few moments, she pulled away and wiped her face.

'What do you want me to do, Dia?'

'Sweet Sorne.' She kissed his cheek. 'There's nothing you can do. We're only Malaunje, and this is T'En brotherhood business.'

'There is no "only Malaunje."' It infuriated him to hear her say this. 'You could claim sanctuary with the causare. She's more powerful than any man.'

Valendia shook her head. 'No one can interfere with the way an all-father runs his brotherhood. I shouldn't have come to you.'

'Of course you should. I'm your brother.'

There was a knock at the door. 'Wait here.'

He accepted the tray from the servant and shared his meal with Valendia. She said she wasn't hungry, but managed to put away a good portion of his dinner.

'I should go back.' It was clear she didn't want to.

'Stay the night. You can have my bed.'

'I couldn't.'

'I can't sleep on Mieren beds anyway. They're not long enough.'

She managed a tearful smile.

'Stay here for now. You don't have to go back to the brotherhood, not until they sail. Zaria is here with her children. You'll like her. And the cat's had kittens.'

'Sorne!' She shoved him. 'I'm sixteen, not six.'

He grinned.

She yawned. 'Don't know why I'm so tired.'

Sorne led her over to the bed, slipped off her shoes and tucked her in.

'You'll see, Dia. Things will look better in the morning.'

'That's what Ma used to say.' Valendia raised solemn eyes to him. 'But there's no way out of this. I'm going to lose Grae either way, and it will kill me.'

'No.' He was adamant. 'There's always hope.'

She smiled. 'Silly Sorne...' And she drifted off to sleep.

As he stretched out in front of the fire, he wondered if he should tell Graelen that Valendia was safe. If he did, the adept would probably insist she return to the brotherhood. In fact, now that Sorne thought about it, he was stepping on the other man's toes by coming between him and his devotee.

But Sorne didn't care. Valendia was his sister, and he did not see why she should be put in danger because of the rivalry within Graelen's brotherhood.

Fury at the T'En, their arrogance and the way the brotherhoods were organised churned inside him. Before this was over, they'd see what one Malaunje could achieve.

And he realised he was doing it again. He'd spent years trying to prove to True-men that he was as good as them. Now he had to carve a place for himself in T'Enatuath society.

Chapter Sixteen

'SEE FOR YOURSELF.'

Ronnyn peered into the polished silver mirror.

'No more broken nose,' Reoden said.

Since he'd never seen himself before arriving on the ship, and by then his nose was broken, he wasn't used to this new face. But it did feel good to be able to breathe freely again. 'Thank you.'

The healer beamed. How could she be so kind to him, yet lock the girl away? It couldn't simply be because she was a girl. He'd spotted two girls a little older in the causare's sisterhood.

'Coming out on deck?'

'In a moment,' he said.

Five days had passed and he hadn't been able to get near the hidden girl. It was so hard to find a moment when the cabin was empty. There was always someone coming and going. Now that Reoden had left the bathing chamber, he had a chance.

He slipped into the adjoining cabin, grabbed a chair, climbed up and peered through the grille. The girl was writing, bent over her work.

'Don't you get lonely?' he asked.

She jumped, knocked the ink and spilt it. Quick as a cat, she righted the bottle, but ink had already run across the page and discoloured her fingers. 'Look what you made me do!'

'You should wash your hands.'

She glanced up to him. 'Is the cabin empty?'

'Yes.' He jumped down and moved the chair to one side.

She opened the panel cautiously.

'I'll keep watch while you wash your hands.'

She darted past him into the bathing chamber and he stood at the door.

'What were you writing?'

'I'm illuminating manuscript pages.'

'I couldn't sit still and do such fiddly work.'

'I love it. There's something very pleasing in getting the lines just right.'

He slipped into the bathing chamber so he could watch her.

'I'd rather be outside fishing or hunting,' he said. 'I used to do the work of a man back home.'

'I haven't been out in the open since... for a long time.'

'I'll take you outside.'

She shook her head, but her eyes held such longing that Ronnyn's mind raced. He knew he could lower a rowboat. The challenge would be to do it without being caught. 'Would you like to go out on the bay?

'I'm not allowed.'

'When no one's looking. We could slip out, take one of the rowboats, go fishing.'

'I shouldn't –'

Someone entered the all-mother's cabin.

He crept over to the door and peered through the gap. She joined him, face pale with panic.

'It's the scryer and her shield-sister,' he whispered. 'Did you close the panel?'

'Yes.'

They heard footsteps as someone came towards the bathing chamber door.

'Quick.' Ronnyn caught her hand and ran for the door leading out into the passage.

The pair of them darted into the hall, just as one of the sisters entered the bathing chamber.

'Now I'm in trouble,' the girl whispered.

Ronnyn's heart hammered. 'Nonsense. Come with me...' He took her hand and led her towards the mid-deck.

At the door, she resisted. 'What if –'

'This ship is packed with two sisterhoods. We don't know who everyone is. If the causare's people see you, they'll think you're from the healer's sisterhood, and if her people see you –'

'All right. But –'

He pulled her through the door onto the deck, leading her several steps before she stopped.

He turned back to find her staring up at the sky, eyes glistening with tears of joy. 'Is anyone likely to check up on you this afternoon?'

'What? No, they wouldn't expect me to try to escape. I haven't done this since they shut me away, four years ago.'

He wanted to ask why she'd been shut away, but several Malaunje children ran past, playing and laughing, while their elders strung washing on lines across the deck, obscuring the rowboats. It was a perfect moment to carry out his plan. 'Come on, this way.'

He darted between washing lines, making for the nearest rowboat. He reached up and undid the canvas cover. 'Slip in here.'

He cupped his hands. She placed one elegant foot in his hand, another on his shoulders and sprang up, slipping gracefully into the boat.

He glanced both ways. No one was looking. The flapping washing formed the perfect screen. 'Wait there.'

Then he ran inside, grabbed a blanket and some left-overs from lunch, and rolled it into a bundle.

As he shoved the bundle into the boat he noticed two Malaunje lads of about ten watching him.

'Here, you two, work the pulleys.'

Just as he suspected, they were so used to obeying T'En that they didn't question him. Ronnyn slipped beneath the canvas and into the boat as the lads began to lower it.

He looked nervously to the girl. Her eyes glowed with

a mixture of terror and excitement. With every heartbeat, he expected someone to lean over the side and demand to know what they were doing.

The boat's belly kissed the sea. He undid both clamps and waved to the lads, who raised the ropes.

They were free. He had her all to himself for a whole afternoon.

Feeling in control again, Ronnyn threw back the canvas and took the oars. 'Where would you like to go?'

'Teach me how to row.'

He couldn't be happier.

ARAVELLE UNPEGGED THE bedding and went to fold it, only to discover... 'I can still sense the male gift.' She inhaled the spicy, slightly confronting scent, and with it a rush of power ran through her body. 'It's embedded in the weave of the fabric.'

'What did you expect?' Redravia's voice creaked with age. 'The bedrolls belong to the all-father and his inner circle. Their gifts are more powerful than any others. We've only aired their bedding, we won't get rid of the gift tang without soaking and washing.'

Aravelle finished folding the bedroll, then reached for another.

This summer just gone she'd massaged her brother's arm every day. His gift had begun to manifest and the instinct to revel in his power had been almost overwhelming. Now that same seductive gift essence was all around her.

As Redravia folded each bedroll, the old woman inhaled deeply. Already, her gaze was sharper and the stiffness seemed to have gone from her joints.

Aravelle felt a stab of anger. She'd thought Redravia offered to help out of friendship. Instead, the old woman was motivated by hunger for the male gift. On principle, Aravelle averted her face as she folded and tucked the bedding in the basket.

'You are so like your mother.' Redravia's voice held a mixture of exasperation and affection.

Aravelle tensed. She was nothing like her mother. Her mother had lied to her.

'Sasoria never accepted the limitations of being born Malaunje. She was always pushing the boundaries. There is no point fighting your Malaunje nature, Vella. You will become addicted to the male gift. You will become a true brotherhood Malaunje.'

'How is that different from being a sisterhood Malaunje?'

'The female gift is different. You'll see what I mean one day.'

If she became a true brotherhood Malaunje.

But she wouldn't. She would never give up her independence.

'There.' Redravia dropped the last bedroll into the basket.

Aravelle bent down, picked up the basket and balanced it on her hip. Up on the foredeck, she could hear the T'En initiates practising under Hueryx's hand-of-force, wielding their twin long-knives. They began training with wooden blades; as they grew more skilled they moved onto real blades, the patterns becoming more complex and deadly.

Her gaze returned to the mid-deck, which was reserved for Malaunje. Saskar had already finished drilling the fifteen- and sixteen-year-olds.

She paused to admire Saskar's skill as he supervised the elite Malaunje warriors. Forbidden from picking up the T'En blade, their weapons were the bow and the staff. They moved with such precision, it inspired her. Everything Saskar asked of them, he could do himself, and more.

A shout from the other end of the ship made her turn. On the lower rear-deck, a big T'En warrior confronted a young initiate, who was being restrained. The big warrior demanded something. The initiate shook his head and raised his fist.

When an older T'En protested, the big warrior turned on him. 'The big one is Kyredeon's hand-of-force,' Redravia said.

'What's going on?'

The hand-of-force tossed the youth aside and strode to the rail to address the Malaunje on the mid-deck.

'Devotee Valendia has disappeared,' he said. 'If you are hiding her belowdecks, bring her out right now and you will escape punishment. If you fail to bring her out and I find her, it will go hard on you and all those you love.'

Aravelle shuddered. She watched, but no one came forward with the escapee.

'Right. I'm coming down.'

He strode down the steps to the mid-deck with half a dozen warriors. The Malaunje backed away as they approached.

'He's a bully,' Aravelle whispered.

'Don't let him hear you say that.'

Kyredeon's hand-of-force went below deck.

Aravelle hated bullies.

Saskar had finished the training session. She went over to him. Now that she was aware of his high stature, she felt shy about approaching him, but his lop-sided smile was as warm as ever. He wore his hair pulled back in a long plait, revealing the scar where he'd lost an ear.

'Teach me to be a warrior.'

'Patience, Vella. You'll begin lessons when you turn fifteen.'

'I can't wait a year.' She glanced to the four warriors from her choice-mother's inner circle. Like her, they were as tall as the biggest of the Malaunje men, and incredibly fast.

'Ah, it's an elite warrior you want to be, now? I thought you were a scribe?' He grinned. 'The weapons master who trained me used to say deeds save lives, but without words to recall those deeds, who would remember them?'

'Words were no help to me when the Mieren...' She could not go on.

He nodded his understanding. 'I can teach you how to defend yourself against most Mieren. But even though you are tall, you will never be as strong as a man. A woman must use speed and cunning. She must not hesitate to hurt, or she will not escape.'

'I won't hesitate,' Aravelle assured him.

He looked grim and went to say something, but changed his mind. Instead, he asked, 'Have you ever shot a bow?'

She shook her head.

'I'll teach you. I'll –'

'Saskar?' The hand-of-force beckoned from the foredeck. With a nod to Aravelle, Saskar went up the steps.

She returned to the initiate's cabin feeling lighter of heart. As she unpacked the bedding and put the basket away, she vowed to practise her self-defence lessons until there wasn't a man – Mieren, Malaunje or T'En – who would dare touch her against her will.

She touched her mouth. The split lip had almost healed.

'You want to defend yourself?' Hand-of-force Reyne asked, startling her.

She spun to face him.

'Good reflexes.' He smiled as he let the cabin door swing closed. 'Give me your hand.'

Why? She bit back the query just in time. Malaunje didn't question T'En; they obeyed.

'Come, I won't bite.' Reyne offered his hand.

She reinforced her gift defences before approaching him.

He grabbed her forearm. The speed of it frightened her. Instinctively, she pulled away.

'Don't pull against my strength. Pull against the weakest point.' He released her. 'Grab my arm.'

Having seen how fast he could move, she was queasy with fear. Her heart raced and she was having trouble thinking clearly, but she grabbed his arm and, before she knew it, he was free.

'That's because you are so much stronger,' she said, annoyed.

He grinned. 'No. I pulled upwards, past your thumb. That's the weakest point. Grab me again, as hard as you can.'

She did. This time he moved slowly and she saw what he meant. Even though she held on with all her strength, his forearm slid between her thumb and fingers.

'Now, you try.'

She offered her arm. He grabbed. She flicked up and out of his grasp. A smile lit her face.

'Now what?' he asked.

She didn't know what he meant.

'You got away, but he won't like that. He'll do this.' And he grabbed her around the body this time, lifting her off her feet, arms pinned to her side, against his body.

Shock froze her, then panic engulfed all coherent thought.

She writhed, kicking and twisting. Throwing her head back, then forward, she tried to smash the bridge of his nose. He jerked his head sideways, but even so, her forehead connected with his jaw.

It must have hurt, yet he laughed.

'Let her go,' Saskar urged, suddenly by their side. 'For my sake, let her go, Reyne.'

Saskar placed a careful hand on the big warrior's arm, not daring to use force.

Aravelle went still, heart racing, blood roaring in her ears. Every muscle in her body trembled.

A strange, regretful smile illuminated Reyne's face. Aravelle stared as blood seeped from the corner of his mouth.

'I beg you.' Saskar's voice shook. 'Let her go.'

The arms that held her slowly relaxed and Reyne let her slide to the floor.

As the hand-of-force stepped away, the strength went out of Aravelle's legs and she swayed; a roaring filled her ears.

'I'll see to her. Just go,' Saskar ordered.

Surely, he couldn't be telling the third-highest-ranked T'En in the brotherhood what to do? Aravelle wondered, before pitching forward. Saskar caught her and helped her to a chair. She was already pushing his hands away when he sat her down. He leant against the all-father's desk, shaking so badly he could hardly stand.

As he collected himself, she studied him, trying to make sense of what had just happened.

He swallowed. 'How are you feeling, Vella?'

'Fine,' she lied. Her head still spun. 'I'm not weak. It's just... he surprised me.'

Saskar's gaze slid away from hers, as if there was something he wasn't telling her.

Aravelle waited and when he didn't speak, she asked, 'Why did you ask him to let me go for your sake?'

Saskar turned away.

'I don't understand.'

'I know.' He sighed. 'I'm sorry, Vella. He's got his claws into you now, and he won't let go.'

She shook her head. 'I still don't –'

'You radiate determination and anger. His gift is unusual. It feeds on emotions. I could feel his exultation from out on the mid-deck.'

'How? I thought Malaunje...' She ran down, seeing his expression. It was an odd combination of embarrassment and pride.

'I'm his devotee,' Saskar confessed.

A conversation Aravelle had overheard between her parents finally fell into place. Her mother had run away before Hueryx could make a devotee of her.

'We're linked,' Saskar explained. 'I feel what he feels. Surely your mother told you?'

'It seems there was a lot my mother didn't tell me,' Aravelle said.

He went to the cabinet and poured them each a glass of wine. 'Drink this. You need it.' His hands shook only slightly now.

She drained hers in one gulp. So did he.

'How?' she asked, voice rasping. 'How does a Malaunje become a devotee?'

'With Reyne and I, it was an accident... Back when King Charald attacked the city, his men overran our palace. I was fighting at the bottom of the courtyard stairs, trying to protect the Malaunje women and children. It was hand to hand. Finally, there was only Reyne and I holding the stairs, but we'd killed every Mieren.

'Then another dozen charged through the far arch into the courtyard and saw us. Reyne tried to link to the all-father to call for help. It took everything he had. When his gift surged, it breached my defences and tapped into my life force to empower itself. I passed out.

'When I came round, the Mieren were attacking again and Reyne was holding them off. I staggered to my feet, just as Hueryx led a dozen warriors to take the Mieren from behind.' Saskar met her eyes, half defiant, half apologetic. 'I'm Reyne's devotee, Vella. I'm linked to him, imprinted on his gift. My affinity for the gift is enhanced because of the link, my stature as well. This is what your mother gave up when she ran away.'

Aravelle nodded, not at all surprised that her mother would make this choice.

Saskar studied her. 'From what All-father Hueryx let slip, he loved your mother and believed she loved him.'

'She loved her freedom more,' Aravelle said, and found her anger draining away, to be replaced with pride.

'At least she had a choice. If Reyne dies, I die.'

'Oh, Saskar.'

He shrugged. 'Reyne didn't mean for it to happen, but the gifts have a way of looking after themselves. Besides, there are some who would be willing to swap their independence for a devotee's life. There are compensations.' His voice dropped. Then he swallowed as if something tasted bad. 'And there are drawbacks.'

'I don't want to be Hueryx's scribe anymore,' Aravelle decided. 'I'll ask him to send me back to the Malaunje.'

'You can't do that. You'd insult him. He honours you with this position.' Saskar took the cup from her hand, put it aside and clasped both of her hands in his. 'Trust me. I will protect you from Reyne.'

'Why?'

'Because I serve the hand-of-force, and seeing that he does not dishonour himself is part of my duty.'

Her mind reeled with the implications.

'Your gift defences are surprisingly strong, considering you haven't been trained. But you also have a strong affinity for the gifts, Vella. And you feel very intensely. This will entice him. So...'

She caught a glimpse of the scar where his ear had been. 'Did you lose your ear fighting the Mieren?'

'No.' He grinned. 'It was a bet, a silly bet that went wrong.

'It was back in the Celestial City. I was sixteen. Having come into the T'Enatuath as the unwanted child of Mieren parents, I was greedy for stature. I bet that I could steal a rival brotherhood's banner. Some of their warriors caught me and sent me back minus an ear.' He saw her expression. 'They spared my life. Only T'En had ever attempted to steal a banner before. As a Malaunje, I overreached myself. So it was nothing glorious, you see. Just foolish bravado on my part. '

She decided she liked him better for admitting it.

Deep, angry voices made them both look to the mid-deck.

'That's Reyne.' Saskar ran to the door and she followed him out onto the deck to see Kyredeon's hand-of-force and half a dozen of his warriors confronting Reyne. Saskar joined him, and other brotherhood warriors came to his aid.

'Why would we shelter your runaway devotee?' Reyne asked.

'We've searched our side of the ship and she's not there. She must be with your brotherhood.'

'Well, she isn't. You should take better care of your devotees so they don't want to run.'

'You should mind your tongue!' Oriemn reached for his weapon.

'What's this?' Hueryx came down the steps. 'Kyredeon is missing a devotee? What did she look like?'

'She was young and beautiful.'

'Of course she was. If we see her, I'll be sure to send her your way. But I can tell you right now. We are not sheltering her.'

Even from a body-length away, Aravelle could feel the force of Hueryx's gift.

Kyredeon's hand-of-force backed down.

No one moved until the rival brotherhood's warriors had returned to the rear-deck.

Then Hueryx's supporters slapped him on the back and laughed as though they were drunk on power. But Aravelle thought of the poor devotee. There was nowhere she could have run to; if she was not on the ship, she must have thrown herself in the sea. How horrible to feel such desperation.

Chapter Seventeen

RONNYN GUIDED THEM to an island where they pulled the boat onto the hard-packed sand revealed by low tide. He grabbed the bundle, and they climbed up the steep rocks. He'd had his eye on this island for a while, after he'd glimpsed the golden stones of an abandoned building amidst the trees.

'Wait...' the girl gasped.

He turned to find her flushed and breathing hard. It was no wonder she was unfit. 'Why do they shut you up?'

She would not meet his eyes. 'Please don't ask.'

He gathered it was something shameful and blushed for her. 'I'm Ronnyn.'

'My friends call me Sar.' She smiled. 'Thank you, Ronnyn, I didn't know how much I missed the sky.' Tilting her head to the sun, she spread out her arms and breathed deeply.

He watched, happy for her. 'Let's explore and then we can have some lunch.'

They headed for the ruin, glimpsed through the trees.

'Is it Mieren or T'En in origin?' the girl asked.

'I don't know.'

They entered the courtyard where weeds grew thick between the paving stones. Inside the ruins, there were places where the roofs had fallen in, leaving the rooms open to the elements. But in the deepest corners they found colourful frescoes on the walls, depicting people dancing and singing.

'T'En, like us,' she said, eyes glittering with excitement. 'Do you think this could have been abandoned three hundred years ago, during the first war with the Mieren?'

'Possibly.'

'Look.' Sar pointed to a T'En man and woman dancing. 'What if this place predated the covenant that divided brotherhoods from sisterhoods? Maybe they held midsummer trystings here?'

Ronnyn's mother had told him stories, but he hadn't spent years locked up reading books like Sar. She made him feel ignorant.

'I wonder why it was abandoned?' She wandered into another chamber. 'It could be a tainted site.'

'Tainted?'

'In some places, the walls between this plane and the higher plane are thin. We're lucky it's not season cusp. That's when the walls are thinnest. Sometimes predators come through. They crave our power, and gift-warriors have to protect us. I used to hope I'd be a gift-warrior. But...' She turned away.

'I don't think it's a tainted site,' Ronnyn said. 'I can't sense anything.'

'Is your gift manifesting?'

He looked down, avoiding her gaze. 'I'm hungry. Come on.'

They went outside into the courtyard, where he spread the blanket in a patch of sunlight and unpacked the food.

She tucked her legs neatly underneath her. 'This is wonderful.'

He grinned and devoured a chicken leg.

Selecting an apple, Sar nibbled it with delicate, precise bites, studying him. 'I heard the inner circle talking. You're All-father Hueryx's son and your mother ran away so she could keep you. What was it like growing up free? And how did you hurt your arm?'

As Ronnyn answered her questions, he wondered what she had done that was so terrible that All-mother Reoden would keep her in seclusion.

* * *

'WHAT'S WRONG, REE?' Imoshen put her notes aside. It was late afternoon and Frayvia was teaching Deyne to speak T'En language, while Umaleni joined in. Baby Aro slept in her cradle at Imoshen's feet.

The healer glanced around the crowded cabin and gestured for Imoshen to follow her to the doorway where they could speak privately.

'One of the rowboats is missing,' Reoden revealed, 'along with two children.'

'Which children?'

'Ronnyn, the runaway, and –'

'You think he's run away again?'

'No... he's very protective of his little brothers. But Imoshen, he's taken Sardeon. I kept him in the cloister, and he's gone.'

'Why did you shut him away?'

'For his own protection. His father is a brotherhood leader and for his son to be trapped in the body of a twelve-year-old boy with no gift... the shame!'

'There is no shame, Ree,' Imoshen said. 'If there is any shame, it should be Kyredeon's. He sent the warriors who killed your daughter. Sardeon saw it happen. Even though he had no training, he segued to the higher plane to escort her shade to death's realm. If anything, he should be honoured for his bravery.'

'But he's crippled, Imoshen. He hasn't grown in almost five years. And now he's missing.' Tears filled her eyes. 'He's such a good boy. He never complains. I failed him –'

'Hush.' Imoshen hugged her. 'Ronnyn probably thought he was setting him free.' Imoshen caught her devotee's eye. Frayvia nodded; she would watch the children. 'Ronnyn and Sardeon can't have gone far. We –'

'The tides!'

Imoshen went cold. It was getting close to winter's cusp, when the moons were both full and the tides were higher than usual.

She took Reoden's arm. 'We'll send out Malaunje to look for them. They'll be all right. You'll see.'

But when she went up on deck, the ship's captain was not eager to send the boats out. 'Send them out anyway. Just tell them not to venture near the rocks.'

RONNYN WOKE WITH a start.

He didn't remember falling asleep. It was twilight and he was cold. 'We should be getting back.'

As Sar woke, she frowned and bit her bottom lip, obviously regretting their escapade. But if their absence had been discovered, then so be it. He didn't care what the reason was, it was wrong to keep her shut away.

'Hurry up,' Sar pleaded, as Ronnyn rolled up the bundle.

As soon as he was ready, she darted off, running through the trees to the place where they'd climbed up from the beach.

Sar jumped down to the next rock, before they realised the tide had risen. The swirling water swept her legs out from under her. Terrified, she reached for Ronnyn. He darted forward, grabbed her arm and pulled her up to safety.

The pair of them lay panting for a moment. Then Ronnyn stood, pulling her to her feet. 'That was close. You all right?'

Sar seemed stunned. 'You saved my life.'

'Not really.' But when he studied the way the rising water swirled around the rocks, he shuddered. There was no sign of their boat, not that they could have risked launching it. 'We're trapped.'

'Look.' Sar pointed to spots of light floating in the bay. 'Boats with lanterns. They must be looking for us.'

Ronnyn climbed onto a rock and waved.

After a few moments the nearest boat headed their way. It was clear they'd been seen, but the sea was too dangerous to venture close. Someone signalled with the lantern and the boat went back to the ship.

Ronnyn jumped down from the rock. 'They know we're safe. We can spend the night in the ruins. It'll be fun.'

'It'll be cold.'

'Not if we gather firewood.'

'How can we light...?'

But Ronnyn was already running back to the ruin, grabbing fallen dry branches as he went. He thought he'd spotted a flint in the deserted kitchen.

He had and, by the time, Sar returned with an armful of firewood, Ronnyn had a small flame going.

'We can shelter in here. We'll have a fire. We have a blanket and two more apples. We'll be a bit hungry.' He grinned. 'But it'll be fun!'

'All-mother Reoden –'

'She knows we're safe, and we're already in trouble, so we might as well make the most of it.'

Sar's expression lightened, just as Ronnyn hoped it would, and a mischievous smile lit her face.

'ON THE ISLAND?' Reoden repeated. 'Why didn't your sailors bring them back?'

'The tide made it impossible,' the captain said. 'I could send a boat back later when the currents have settled.'

'No... They've disobeyed me by sneaking off. Let them spend a night in the cold. I take it the island is safe?' The captain nodded. 'Tomorrow morning will be soon enough to bring them back. By then, they should be suitably sorry.'

He nodded and left them.

Reoden turned to stare across at the island. It was only a dark smudge on a sea silvered by the twin moons' light.

As a child, Imoshen had roamed Lighthouse Isle, reporting to no one. 'I imagine Ronnyn is used to coming and going as he pleases. He grew up wild on an island.'

'You won't convince me to forgive them, Imoshen. They could have drowned!'

'Very true.' She took the healer's arm. 'But come inside now. It's growing cold. Perhaps this is all for the best. You can't keep Sardeon locked away forever. His gift will corrupt.'

'It can't corrupt if it isn't manifesting. Ceriane believes his gift has frozen, and that's why he hasn't aged.' She pressed trembling fingers to her mouth. 'Oh, Imoshen, what am I going to do with him?'

'At least your inner circle won't insist you turn him out,' Imoshen said, thinking of her own choice-son, who was even now travelling across Chalcedonia, into the path of Mieren armies, to save a queen.

RONNYN LOOKED AWAY from the fire and waited for his eyes to adjust, before making his way to the edge of the ruins to relieve himself.

'Did you go camping on your island?' Sar asked, coming up behind him and making him jump.

Sar unlaced her breeches and...

Ronnyn glanced down. She was a *he*.

He felt like an idiot. 'You're...' he was going to say *a boy*, then he remembered the odd creature the women referred to as a 'geldr.' Did geldrs have any genitals? Perhaps Sar was a geldr and that was why... But then he remembered the causare's sisterhood didn't lock up their geldr.

Even more confused, Ronnyn laced up and went back to the fire. As he stared into the flames, Sar joined him and they shared the blanket.

After a while, Ronnyn couldn't bear it any longer. 'Can I ask you a question?'

'Perhaps.'

'What's your full name?'

'Sardeon Choice-son Reoden, son of All-father Paragian. We're choice-brothers, you and I.'

Ronnyn frowned. 'Why –'

'We share the same choice-mother.'

'No. Why do they keep you in seclusion?'

The silence stretched and it seemed Sardeon would not answer, then he took a deep breath and began. 'Five years ago come spring, several brotherhood warriors murdered the all-mother's sacrare daughter.' His voice caught but he forged on. 'A sacrare is a T'En born of two T'En parents. They're very rare and have the potential for great gifts. She was my choice-sister. I saw it all. I couldn't save her and I... I haven't been the same since.'

That explained his sadness.

'The Mieren raped my mother and my sister. And there wasn't a thing I could do to stop them. It made me so angry –'

'No one would talk about what happened that day. It was like they wanted me to forget it ever happened. But I'll never forget her.'

'Of course not.' Ronnyn understood. He would never forget his Malaunje kin.

'I'm glad we became stranded,' Sardeon said, and his stomach rumbled.

'Even if we have to go to bed hungry?'

He gave an elegant shrug. 'What's a little hunger?'

Chapter Eighteen

IMOSHEN CLEARED THE mid-deck of Malaunje, while Reoden lined up all the T'En children from both sisterhoods. Saffazi had wanted to be here, but she was an initiate now. Only the children, the two all-mothers and their voices-of-reason were present.

'These two boys could have drowned,' Reoden told the children, who watched her solemnly. 'They were lucky they only had to spend a cold, miserable night on the island.'

'Let this be a lesson to you, not to disobey your choice-mothers,' Egrayne added.

Both of them came back to stand beside Imoshen.

'I'll have to punish them,' Reoden muttered. 'But how?'

'You could send them with the Malaunje to find the missing rowboat,' Egrayne suggested. 'They'd have to endure the insult of doing work beneath their stature.'

A moment later Ronnyn and Sardeon climbed over the ship's side and jumped down to the deck. They didn't look miserable. Instead, they looked rather pleased with themselves.

Ronnyn's two younger brothers would have run to him, but Nerazime restrained them.

As the two boys took in the children before them and the sisterhood leaders, Imoshen studied Sardeon. He was the same as he'd been the day Lyronyxe was murdered – a boy so beautiful he could pass for a girl.

According to his birth date, he would turn seventeen three days before her choice-son, but there was no hint of the man in him. All-father Paragian would be expecting the delivery of his son, ready to take his place in the brotherhood.

They would have to speak with Paragian.

Ronnyn marched straight over to All-mother Reoden and dropped to one knee. 'I beg your forgiveness, choice-mother. It is all my fault. I teased Sardeon until he came out with me. I lured him into the rowboat and –'

'Not true,' Sardeon insisted. He knelt gracefully next to Ronnyn. 'I went willingly. I went because I needed to see the sky and feel the wind on my face. I needed to be free.' He looked up at Reoden. 'I am sorry I went without permission, choice-mother, but I am not sorry I went.'

Reoden looked down at Sardeon, and Imoshen read her. The healer struggled with the realisation that she had done wrong by Sardeon when she had shut him away.

'You boys must have had a cold night,' Imoshen said.

'Oh, we had the blanket,' Ronnyn said. 'And a fire.'

'And we explored the ruin. It was fascinating. We discovered frescoes!' Sardeon announced. Imoshen glanced to Reoden, who was trying not to smile. The boy rushed on. 'It used to belong to the T'En, and by their clothing, I'd say it predated the schism of the covenant. Do you think we could go back? I'd love to make drawings of the frescoes. I'm sure our sisterhood's historian will want to study it.'

'I'll send Alynar,' Reoden said, then added sternly, 'But you will have to be punished.'

'Of course, choice-mother,' Sardeon said.

Ronnyn echoed him.

'You can go with the Malaunje to look for the missing rowboat. When you find it, you will have to row it all the way back on your own.'

'Really?' Ronnyn sprang to his feet, face bright and eager.

'Today?' Sardeon asked.

Egrayne muttered in surprise. Imoshen had to turn away to hide her laughter.

'I think the tide will be safe by mid-afternoon,' Reoden said. 'The ship's master will tell you.'

'Can I go, too?' Vittor asked. 'Please?'

As boys from both sisterhoods clamoured to go with them, Imoshen caught Reoden's eye and they shared a smile.

Egrayne gestured to Ronnyn and Sardeon. 'Your hand-of-force should be drilling these two every day with the older lads. Then they won't have any energy left to get into trouble.'

'Could we?' Ronnyn pleaded.

Sardeon glanced from Ronnyn to his choice-mother, almost as if he couldn't bring himself to hope.

'I'm used to working hard all day,' Ronnyn said. 'We'll both work hard. I promise you won't regret it.'

'Very well.' Reoden smiled. 'Nerazime, time for the boys' lessons. As for you two, I imagine you're starving. Go have some breakfast, then report to the ship's master.'

Ronnyn grinned but Sardeon hesitated.

'Does this mean I don't have to be shut away anymore, choice-mother?' he asked.

Reoden nodded.

He hugged her. 'Thank you!'

As he walked off with Ronnyn, the healer wiped her cheeks.

Ronnyn said something, and Sardeon laughed. Ronnyn slung an arm around his shoulder. Vittor and Tamaron ran back to hug their brother and ask about their adventure. And they were not the only ones. A sea of small boys surrounded Ronnyn and Sardeon. Imoshen's gift surged. Ronnyn, the son of runaways, was a natural leader.

'I think you have a potential all-father in Ronnyn,' Imoshen said.

Reoden nodded. 'I had one in Sardeon, too. Now what will become of him?'

'Paragian needs to know. You can't hide his son's state any longer.'

'You're right.' The healer turned to Imoshen. 'I'm not looking forward to it.'

* * *

THE NEXT DAY the sisterhood's hand-of-force stood Ronnyn and Sardeon in front of the empowered lads. The smallest was taller than them and the biggest was a head taller than her. 'From now on, these two will be joining you for armed and unarmed combat practice.'

'But they're not empowered,' a lad with a gap between his front teeth protested.

'Are you telling a hand-of-force how to run her training sessions, Toryx?' Cerafeoni asked. 'Perhaps you'd like to run today's class?'

The rest of the lads laughed and he glowered.

She clapped her hands. 'Now line up.'

The empowered lads fell into position, laughing and jostling, the hum of the male gift a constant undertone like distant music that could, at any moment, surge up to drown all sound.

'We're going to start with the warrior's exercises to promote balance in mind, gift and body,' Cerafeoni told Ronnyn and Sardeon. 'Stand at the back, follow the moves. We begin with the same basic moves every time, so that when you are attacked, you won't have to think. Your body will take over without conscious thought.'

Ronnyn worked with total concentration, committing every move to memory. He looked over at Sardeon and saw him working with the same intensity.

The elegance that had made him think Sar was a girl expressed itself in the precise, fluid way he performed the exercises. Ronnyn realised he would have to work hard to keep up with his new choice-brother.

Cerafeoni kept them at it until they were sweating and trembling from exertion. Then she called them up in pairs, matching them by size and skill. Under her watchful eye, the lads went through sparring sequences, pulling their punches and kicks.

By the time the hand-of-force dismissed them, Ronnyn was happy, but exhausted. In the jostle to return to the cabin and use the bathing chamber, he and Sardeon held back.

'You might have gained stature by discovering the ruin,' Toryx said as he came up behind them. 'You might be the all-mother's choice-sons and her favourites, but once you're in with the empowered lads, you have to earn your stature among us.' He let his gift rise with a hint of violence. 'So watch out.'

IMOSHEN WATCHED THE sun set beyond the headlands, thinking that Sorne and Iraayel would be camped near the Celestial City soon: tonight or tomorrow at the latest. She understood why Iraayel had volunteered, even admired him for it, but she just wished he was not with Kyredeon's warriors. Almost any other brotherhood would have been preferable.

Yet if Tobazim were to become all-father, as she so fervently hoped, then he was the one her choice-son had to impress.

Her sisterhood's historian passed by, debating hotly with the Mieren scholar Sorne had brought aboard. Igotzon was just as fascinated by the ruin's frescoes as the two sisterhood historians.

Someone hailed the ship and Imoshen went to the side to see several rowboats drawing near, filled with bedraggled Malaunje.

'Is this the causare's ship?' an old Malaunje woman asked.

'Yes,' Imoshen called down. 'Who are you?'

'Survivors from All-mother Parazime's party.'

'Survivors?' Imoshen's heart sank.

'We were attacked on the road...' The old woman broke off as a rope ladder was unrolled and they began the climb aboard.

'So Parazime's dead,' Egrayne said, surprising Imoshen, who hadn't heard her approach. 'I remember when she won the sisterhood... This is not good. That means one less sisterhood vote.'

'And half a sisterhood lost.' Imoshen had given the rest of the sisterhood shelter on her ship.

Egrayne watched the survivors climb aboard searching for someone. 'Parazime's daughter's not amongst them. Such a waste.'

As news of their arrival spread, the other half of Parazime's sisterhood came running. There was weeping for those lost, but also joy over those who had survived.

Egrayne frowned. 'Looks like there won't be enough high-ranking T'En to reform the sisterhood. Hers was always the smallest.'

'Athazi or Melisarone will have to take in her people,' Imoshen said.

'Make it Mel, she needs some new blood. Most of her T'En are over eighty.'

'I'll call an all-mother council.'

Imoshen headed down the steps to the mid-deck, where she sent messages to the other ships. Then she found the old Malaunje woman and drew her aside. 'What happened?'

'The all-mother waited until we'd brought the harvest in, and we loaded up the wagons. The roads were bad, little more than churned mud for the most part. I don't know what it's been like here, but up north we've had nothing but rain. We'd been travelling for eight days in the rain and everyone and everything was wet. The first fine day the all-mother said we should try to get our clothing and blankets dry before the little ones took a chill. I had my people strip the carts and lay everything out to dry.

'That night, a dozen armed men attacked. Parazime and her inner circle fought them off, but they paid a heavy price. Her hand-of-force died in the attack. Parazime was injured. When she learned her daughter was missing, she segued to the higher plane. I think she went looking for her. Our voice-of-reason only lived for another day. After that we abandoned everything heavy, and travelled as fast as we could. We would have been here sooner, but we had to detour around the army besieging Port Mirror-on-Sea.'

'The port is besieged?'

The old woman nodded. 'There's a sea of tents surrounding it. What will happen to us?'

The same question was echoed by the eldest of the T'En survivors. That night All-mother Melisarone welcomed them onto her ship and, the very next day, Imoshen sent a message to Riverbend Stronghold, telling Sorne that King Charald was under siege.

ARAVELLE BRUSHED HER little sister's hair then separated it into lengths and wound the sections around her finger to form ringlets.

Asher, the man she'd thought was her father, had such a head of curls they'd been near impossible to tame. Thinking of him made her chest ache and her eyes blur with tears.

'Vella sad?' Itania's bottom lip trembled.

Aravelle summoned a smile and kissed her nose. 'All done.'

'Where's the tortoise-shell hair comb?' Hariorta demanded. Itania flinched.

'It was right there in the chest.' Charsoria pointed. 'Nariska, did you take it?'

'No, no I never.' The girl ducked her head, shoulders hunched as if she expected a blow.

'Well, don't just stand there, you stupid girl. Find it,' Hariorta snapped. 'Charsoria makes her report to All-father Hueryx tonight. She needs to look her best.'

While Nariska darted about the cabin frantically searching, Aravelle unrolled Itania's bed-mat.

'Hurry, girl. I'm nearly ready for it!' Hariorta's hands flew, as she pulled and twisted long strands of Charsoria's hair to create an ornate style.

'I'm done,' Hariorta announced. 'Now, where is that comb, Nariska?'

Charsoria studied herself in a polished silver mirror. She had painted her face to accentuate her eyes, reddened her lips and powdered her cheeks until they were pale as the moon. Aravelle didn't consider the all-father's-voice to be as pretty as her mother, who had never worn face paint. Taken individually, there was nothing wrong with Charsoria's features. It was her expression... the line of her mouth expressed displeasure and her eyebrows drew together in a habitual frown.

Why did she have to find fault with everything?

As Aravelle knelt next to Itania to sing her to sleep, she noticed the tortoise-shell comb in the corner. And she remembered how Charsoria had been in a temper that morning and had sent the chest flying, scattering clasps and necklaces across the floor.

Before anyone could notice, Aravelle picked up the comb. Keeping it hidden in her hand, she edged over to Nariska, and slipped it into the girl's hand.

The girl looked down, then up into Aravelle's eyes in amazement. Aravelle gave her a nod of encouragement.

'Here it is,' Nariska said, hurrying over to Hariorta.

'Finally.' The woman snatched it from her and went to use it, only to discover that one of the teeth was broken.

'You stupid girl, I can't use this.' She flung it across the room. 'Fetch me the mother-of-pearl clasp, instead.'

As Nariska hastened to obey, Aravelle had to bite her tongue. If Charsoria hadn't been in a temper and knocked the chest to the floor, the comb would not have been broken. And Hariorta was just as bad, always looking for an excuse to take offence.

According to Redravia, if Aravelle's mother hadn't run away, she would have been the next all-father's-voice, and Aravelle was sure her mother would never have ruled with spite and sly pinches. She would have organised things efficiently, with a laugh and a smile, and everyone would have run to do her bidding to please her, not because they feared her.

Hariorta stepped back to survey her sister, putting her heel on a dinner tray. In a flash of temper, she kicked the tray aside, shattering the bowls.

'Now look what you've done!' Hariorta pointed. 'You should have taken this back to the kitchen, Nariska.'

She should have, but she hadn't been able to, because she'd been running around the cabin looking for the tortoise-shell comb.

Hariorta snapped her fingers at Aravelle and Nariska. 'You two, clean up now.'

They gathered the broken crockery, stacked it on the tray and went down to the galley, where the cook's army of helpers were cleaning up after dinner.

On the way back, Nariska turned to Aravelle. 'Why did you give me the comb?'

Aravelle didn't know what to say. 'Why wouldn't I?'

'You could have pointed out my fault and won favour with them.'

Aravelle stiffened. 'I don't want anything from them.'

Nariska nodded. 'Charsoria says you're proud, too proud.' The girl glanced up and down the passage. 'She told Redravia to teach you how to block the brothers' gifts, but once you were out of the room, she told Redravia not to show you the best techniques. She wants you to suffer.'

Aravelle was not in the least surprised. 'Charsoria is petty and mean-spirited. She's nothing like my mother.'

'Don't talk about your mother. Both the sisters hated her.' She glanced down the passage to make sure they were alone. 'Charsoria should protect us, but she only looks out for herself and her sister. You must be careful of them.'

'Don't worry.' Aravelle was not going to drop her guard. 'But thank you.'

Nariska smiled, and for a heartbeat, she was beautiful. Then the pinched, frightened look returned. 'We should hurry back.'

Chapter Nineteen

JARAILE LISTENED AT the air vent. The same two guards were on duty again, and their talk made her smile.

'...searched the city and we're the only ones here,' the unlucky guard said. 'Your roll.'

'I heard a woman weeping. And I'm not the only one.'

'If there was a silverhead hiding in this palace, we'd have found her.'

'We won't find her because she's the shade of someone killed in the battle for the city. I bet she's a beautiful young virgin.'

'A virgin? Amongst the Wyrds?'

Jaraile marvelled. Several nights ago, she'd claimed she'd heard a woman weeping. Now they'd embroidered the story further. Her father had once told her that fighting men were simple, superstitious creatures. This was not surprising when an arrow could pass over one man and kill the man behind him. It was no wonder they clung to their talismans and lucky rituals.

'There had to be virgins amongst the silverheads,' the lucky one said. 'The sisterhood leaders kept the young ones locked up, separate from the brotherhoods.'

'Yeah? Just think of all those women, locked up together. What did they get up to?'

'I tell you, her shade's going to haunt this palace until she finds the man who killed her. Then she's going to drag him into death's realm with her.'

'And if she can't find him?'

Footsteps echoed up the long passage. One of the men

swore. The other one laughed softly. 'It's just the kitchen lad with the queen's evening meal.'

Jaraile sprang to her feet and put the next stage of her plan into action. She hid in a corner of the bedchamber. Heart racing, she unravelled her hair and ran her hands through it. Then she deliberately raked her cheeks with her nails, so that she appeared crazed and terrified. The pain made her eyes fill with tears. Sinking to crouch in a corner, she covered her head with her arms.

As the door to the reception chamber opened, she discovered she was shaking with excitement. Hopefully, they'd take it for fear.

'Queen Jaraile? Your dinner's here,' the lucky guard called.

She heard his footsteps as he came to the open door.

'Queen Jaraile?'

She lifted her head.

He gasped and behind him the unlucky guard swore.

'Is she gone?' Jaraile whispered.

They assured her there was no one else there, as they came over and helped her to her feet.

'The weeping woman was here again, I tell you. Why won't you believe me?' Jaraile drew them to the doorway, peered into the reception room and pointed to the balcony doors, which were hidden behind drapes. 'She was out there, on the balcony. Trying to get in.'

The lad ran over to them, clearly terrified.

The two guards exchanged looks.

Jaraile shuddered. 'I'm not coming out until I know she's gone.'

The guards looked grim as they edged towards the balcony doors. Jaraile clung to them and the lad clung to her. She laughed inside, exulting in her power over them.

The the unlucky one drew his sword.

'What good's a sword against a spirit?'

The unlucky guard gestured to the drapes. 'Open them.'

His companion dragged the curtains back.

'There's no one there.' The unlucky guard sounded relieved.

'Take the lamp out there,' Jaraile urged. 'I have to be sure.'

As soon as they took the lamp and stepped through the doors it was clear the balcony was empty, but they went up and down its length to be sure.

'There now, you're safe,' the lucky guard told Jaraile, while his companion closed the doors and pulled the drapes.

'Thank you,' she said. 'You'll be just outside, won't you?'

'Just outside.'

'Good. Her shade won't hurt me, will it? After all, I'm just a woman. I've never raised a weapon against her kind.'

The unlucky guard swallowed audibly.

Satisfied she had them sufficiently unnerved, Jaraile let them leave the chamber. Tomorrow morning, she would send for Captain Pataxo, weep on his shoulder and insist she could not stay another night in the sisterhood palace. By then, news of what had happened would be right through his company. If she was lucky, they'd move down to the brotherhood palace near the wall and she'd be one step closer to escaping.

GRAELEN HAD THOUGHT he would never see the Celestial City again, but there it stood, a pale shape on the dark water. Last night, the white stone of city had glowed in the moons' light, reflecting in the lake, and his heart had ached to think of his home in the hands of the barbarian Mieren.

But he could not afford the luxury of emotion. Instead, he retreated to the cold distant place inside himself, where he had lived for so long before he found Valendia. Everything he did, he did for her.

He'd been on edge since they left the fleet. It made his gift hard to control. The journey had given Graelen a chance to observe the men under his command. Sorne had seemed reserved and preoccupied, while Tobazim was contained and wary, as well he should be.

As for the causare's choice-son, Iraayel was nothing like he had been at the same age. Before Graelen joined the brotherhood, he'd been full of hubris and eager to prove himself. Iraayel had already killed in defence of the sisterhood, and it showed in his eyes. The lad was no innocent, yet Graelen refused to kill Iraayel just so Kyredeon could strike a blow against the causare. So maybe there was still a shred of the decent man Valendia loved.

That left the three initiates, hand-picked by Oriemn. These three laughed too easily, agreed too readily and were so eager to win stature they would obey him if he told them to leave the others to die.

Graelen despised them.

There had been another cloaked figure on the boat back in Shifting-sands Bay, but he'd disappeared the first night, so Graelen assumed he had been on a private mission for Kyredeon.

In the past, Graelen had always worked alone, or with Paryx. Now he led these men to save King Charald's queen, something he had never imagined himself doing in his wildest dreams.

'The cloud cover is patchy,' Sorne whispered. 'But I can't delay, waiting for a better night.'

'We go in tonight,' Graelen confirmed.

'When Eskarnor marched for Port Mirror-on-Sea, he left a company of men to hold the city and protect the queen,' Sorne said. 'They've closed the gates and manned the wall-walks.'

'We'll need a diversion while we climb the walls,' Graelen said.

'We don't need to go over the walls,' Tobazim said. 'I can get us in through the ruined palace boat-house.'

'Good,' Sorne said. 'I know where we can steal a boat.'

Graelen smiled grimly. Either of them could have led this mission, but he was in charge. They weren't far from the lakeside town. 'We'll set fire to the tavern stable. The stable lads will rush to save the horses, and the commotion and the flames will distract the guards on the city wall-walk. Fires are common enough – it shouldn't make them suspicious – but someone will need to stay behind to set the fire.'

Graelen left one of the initiates to guard the horses. The other two, he sent to set the fire. He would not go into danger with men he did not trust. Tobazim wouldn't stab him in the back. He'd kill him in a fair fight.

Graelen signalled Sorne. 'Lead us to the boat.'

The besieging army had cut down trees, torn up bushes and scavenged every scrap of firewood on the slope down to the lake.

Sorne led them, picking his way along the shore, until he came to a small Mieren house. No light gleamed through the cracks in the shutters.

'Here it is,' Sorne said.

Graelen could make out the dark shape of a boat amidst the reeds.

They climbed in and waited in silence until they heard the shouts of 'fire.'

Then Graelen took the oars, careful to cut the water with the minimum of noise. They were in luck: the cloud cover held, and the commotion of the tavern fire at the end of the causeway distracted the city's defenders.

TOBAZIM REMEMBERED THIS section of wall. He'd spent many a night on the wall-walk, watching the Mieren army on the lake's shore.

It was so dark that even when he gift-enhanced his night vision, Tobazim could only just make out the arch of the ruined palace's boat-house gate.

He nudged Graelen's foot, and the big adept shipped the oars. The boat glided in until it came to rest against the wall. Tobazim's gift surged, gauging the weights and stresses of the defensive wall, gauging the stresses and alliances of those in the boat with him. They were all focused on the task at hand, but their motivations were so different they were like threads threatening to unravel.

Sorne was focused on saving Queen Jaraile and saving the kingdom for Prince Cedon. Tobazim didn't entirely understand why the queen and prince had Sorne's loyalty, but he respected loyalty.

Iraayel was keen to prove himself worthy of a place in the brotherhood.

And Graelen was utterly determined.

Tobazim suspected Kyredeon held Valendia's life as surety of Graelen's cooperation. Somehow, he needed to convince Graelen to change sides and support him and Ardonyx. But Graelen would only do this if he was certain they could defeat Kyredeon.

And even Tobazim was not sure of this.

Coming to his knees, Tobazim felt along the wall until he came to the gate, then gingerly climbed onto the narrow stone ledge next to it.

He reached through the gate to the hinges and worked the pins loose. Once both pins were removed, the gate hung from the catch and lock on the other side. He wriggled through, stepped inside and opened the gate.

They guided the boat into the boat-house.

Tobazim led them out through the ruined palace to the street.

Here, Graelen took the lead and Tobazim was happy to let him. He preferred not to have the adept at his back.

No lights gleamed in the brotherhood palaces. It felt strange. This had been his home, yet if they were spotted they'd be killed.

When they left the brotherhood quarter, they were not far from the causeway gate. Tobazim could see a dozen men in the gate-house, drinking and dicing by the light of a lamp.

The gate guards were engrossed in their game and the wall-walk guards would be watching the fire across the shore. Even so, Graelen kept to the shadows as they made their way up the causeway road.

They were about level with the dome of empowerment when Iraayel signalled for him to stop. He pointed to the tallest sisterhood palace, to a light moving on a verandah. As far as they could see, the rest of the palace was in darkness.

'That's our palace and that's the initiates' verandah. That'll be where they're keeping the queen.'

Even as he spoke, the light disappeared and Graelen led them on. When they reached the sisterhood quarter, the adept stepped back. 'Take the lead, Iraayel.'

It was an honour for a lad who was not yet seventeen. He led them through the sisterhood quarter to what had been the causare's palace, and around the side into a courtyard. In the distance they heard faint music.

'Sounds like the men-at-arms have made their home in the Malaunje chambers near the kitchen,' Iraayel whispered, then went across the courtyard and into the palace.

He led them down several corridors, before coming to a halt. At the far end of a hall, they could hear voices and music. The smell of onions and bacon lingered on the air.

They retreated to the nearest empty chamber.

'The bulk of the men-at-arms are a long way from where they're keeping the queen,' Sorne said. 'There'll be guards on her door, but –'

'They'll be able to signal the others,' Iraayel said. 'Each chamber has a bell-pull, which connects to the Malaunje servants' wing. All they have to do is ring that bell and we'll never get the queen out of the palace, let alone the city.'

'Then we'll have to surprise them,' Graelen said and signalled Iraayel. 'Take us to the queen.'

The sisterhood palace was a rabbit warren of wings, courtyards, stairs and balconies, but the lad had grown up here, and he found his way without difficulty.

At last they came to a point where several passages met. Iraayel gestured down one of them.

First Graelen, then each of them peered down the long corridor. At the far end, a lamp glowed and two men sat playing dice. It was impossible to approach without being seen.

They went a little way down the corridor.

'Is there no other way into the initiates' wing?' Graelen whispered.

'I could go across the roof and drop onto the balcony,' Iraayel said.

'Yes, but can we get the queen out that way?'

'We could try.'

'I'll go with Iraayel,' Sorne said. 'You two stay here.'

Tobazim watched them go, then turned to Graelen. 'So, are you going to kill me now, or after we get the queen out of the city?'

Chapter Twenty

SORNE HAD NO trouble following Iraayel out a high window onto the roof. He had no trouble crawling across the roof's terracotta tiles, despite the steep pitch and the terrifying drop. It wasn't until he realised that the roof projected well beyond the balcony and Iraayel meant to hang off the guttering, five floors above the courtyard, then swing his legs, let go and trust to luck to land on the balcony below that he baulked.

It was a long time since Sorne had swung from the branches of the maple tree back at the retreat, and the drop had not been a tenth as high.

'Wait. You might not swing wide enough to carry you onto the balcony. Have you done this before?'

'No,' he said. 'The overhang looked smaller from below.'

Sorne let his breath out slowly. They lay side by side with their heads lower than their feet. He could feel the youth's gift like the heat of a forge on a cold day. The longer he spent in the company of adult T'En men, the more their gifts called to him, wearing down his self-control.

'I can do it,' Iraayel insisted. 'I know I can.'

'You might be able to, and there's a chance I might. But we'll never get Jaraile out this way. Even if she has a head for heights, she's small for a Mieren woman.'

Iraayel considered this. 'She can call the guards into the chamber and I can take them out.'

Sorne nodded as the lad began to lower himelf.

Iraayel swung his legs once, twice... on the third swing, he let go and dropped to the balcony.

Sorne breathed a sigh of relief.

* * *

JARAILE HEARD A soft *thump*. She pushed her plate away and wondered if the men-at-arms were playing a prank on her. It sounded like something had landed on the balcony. Nothing could have dropped down from above, the roof jutted out too far. And the courtyard was five floors below.

Yet... she heard a soft tapping at the glass doors.

She came to her feet, heart racing. She did not believe in the weeping woman. It had to be a prank, but she didn't see how...

More tapping.

Heart in her mouth, Jaraile watched the door handle turn. Locked... thank goodness.

And a shade did not need to come through doors.

Still, every sense was on alert as she strode to the balcony doors and thrust back the curtains.

A beautiful T'En stood there. For a heartbeat, she thought it *was* the weeping woman; then she realised it was a youth, and he wanted her to let him in.

Fighting a dreamlike sense of unreality, she opened the balcony door.

Instead of stepping into the chamber, the warrior caught her arm and tried to draw her out onto the balcony. She resisted until she heard Sorne's voice.

'Jaraile, it's all right. He's a friend.'

She looked around, until she spotted Sorne's head hanging over the roof above her. 'For goodness sake, get down from there. You'll fall to your death.'

He laughed, softly. 'We've come to save you. This is Iraayel.'

She put her hands on her hips. 'If you think I'm climbing up there –'

'No. We wouldn't dream of it,' Sorne said. 'Jaraile, the Wyrds didn't hurt Cedon. He's –'

'I know. I overheard Eskarnor speaking with one of his men. You've seen Cedon?'

'I held him in my arms and he asked after you.'

Her chest ached; she had to swallow before she could speak. 'Where is he? Is he safe?'

'As safe as any of us. I have him hidden, and you'll see him soon. Just do as Iraayel says. I'm going back to the others.'

Then he disappeared.

'Where are the others?' She turned to the youth.

'At the end of the corridor. They can't get close to the guards without them sounding the alarm,' he said. 'If you call the guards in, I'll deal with them.'

Her mind raced. Now that she was up close, she could see he was just a boy. The guards were veterans, and the hallway was so long they'd cut Iraayel to shreds before the rest of his party could come to his aid. Then the commotion would alert her captors. Somehow she had to distract the guards, and had to buy enough time for Sorne and the others to reach the chamber and overcome them...

'I have a better idea.'

She led him into her bedchamber, opened a chest and piled armfuls of beautiful silken pants, satin vests and brocade robes on the bed, speaking all the while. 'The men-at-arms think there's a T'En ghost, a beautiful young woman. If they think you're the ghost, it will give Sorne and the others time to come up behind them and kill them silently.'

For a moment she thought he would object. A True-man would consider dressing up as a woman demeaning. But Iraayel gave this some consideration, then nodded. 'They'll be watching the guards. They should be here in no time.'

He began stripping.

Jaraile blushed and looked away.

'What happened to your face?' he asked. 'Did the Mieren hurt –'

'No, I scratched myself to convince them I was half-crazed with fear of the ghost.'

He smiled. 'My choice-mother would like you.'

She blushed and helped him dress, finding ways to

disguise his broad shoulders. Unravelling his long silver braid, she threaded jewels through his hair. Then she painted his lips and eyes, and stood back. 'There. I know women who would envy you.'

'What does this ghostly woman do?'

'She weeps and searches for the man who murdered her, the night King Charald attacked the city.'

'So, ARE YOU going to kill me now, or after we get the queen out of the city?' Tobazim asked, his heart racing, gift on edge. Graelen blinked. 'Because I think it makes more sense to combine forces and defeat Kyredeon.'

'You can't beat Kyredeon. His gift is more powerful than yours and yours is not a martial gift. You and Ardonyx are not shield-brothers, like –'

'We could be. You can't tell me you give Kyredeon your loyalty because you admire him.' Tobazim took a step closer, feigning a confidence he did not feel.

Graelen could easily snatch his essence, drag him to the empyrean plane, wound him and leave him for the predators. But he didn't. He listened, even as his gift readiness pounded on Tobazim's senses.

'Do you really want to spend the rest of your life serving Kyredeon? He's half crazed with fear now. It's only a matter of time before his gift corrupts.' He saw Graelen's eyes widen and knew he'd hit a nerve. 'The brotherhood will rise up against him. They'll kill all of his supporters. They'll kill Valendia.'

'Leave her out of this.'

'I will. But Kyredeon won't. He's holding her life as surety of your cooperation, isn't he?'

'Yes. But you can't win a challenge.'

'We won't know unless I challenge. When I get back –'

'*If* you get back.'

'I will have to challenge Kyredeon, because you will either be dead, which means that I know he sent you to kill me, or you'll be by my side, which means he'll know you've sworn to support our faction.'

'There's a third alternative. I go back without you and everything returns to normal.'

A cry for help made them turn.

Sorne came running down the corridor towards them. He skidded to the corner, glanced up the passage and swore. 'Quick. Iraayel needs help.'

JARAILE PUT THE lamp on the floor behind the table and positioned Iraayel so that the light illuminated him from below, glinting on the jewels in his hair.

'You ready?' she whispered.

He nodded.

She ran to the door, thumping on the panels. 'She's here! She's come for me! Let me out!'

The guards opened the door and she tried to get past them, but they blocked the doorway, standing slack-jawed in awe.

She glanced over her shoulder. A glowing radiance clung to Iraayel's skin. He lifted his hands beseechingly, eyes shimmering with tears. He really was very good.

Jaraile peered down the hall, but didn't see the others coming. They were supposed to be watching. She raised her voice. 'Help!'

The unlucky guard's eyes narrowed and he drew his sword. 'Let's see if she'll bleed.'

Iraayel grinned as he drew his knife.

The other guard swore and charged. Jaraile snatched a statuette and swung it with all her strength as he went past. But he turned at the last moment and the statuette only caught him a glancing blow on the shoulder.

Cursing, he back-handed her. She went flying into the wall and the air was knocked out of her. She could only stare, gasping for breath as both guards attacked Iraayel. He blocked and backed away.

Two adult T'En warriors ran into the room, followed by Sorne. The first one one caught the unlucky guard from behind and snapped his neck. It happened so fast she barely had time to blink. As the second one reached for the other guard, Sorne appeared in front of her.

'Jaraile, are you all right?' He helped her to her feet.

She heard a scuffle, then nothing.

'Don't look.' He led her into the bedchamber. 'Grab some clothes suitable for travel.'

While she did this, he fetched a washcloth and wiped the blood from her face. He was just finishing when Iraayel came in. He stripped, dressed and bound his hair, while she rolled up her few things in a blanket. Sorne took her bundle. 'Come, Jaraile.'

When they entered the main chamber, she glanced over at the dead guards. There was no sign of blood. 'Throw them off the balcony.'

'Why?'

'The fall will disguise their injuries. Captain Pataxo's men think a vengeful female shade haunts this palace. If I disappear from a locked room and it looks like the guards jumped off the balcony –'

'It will confuse them, even if they don't believe in the ghost,' Sorne said.

GRAELEN WAS PLEASED with the way the rescue had gone – none of his people had been hurt, and they'd confounded the Mieren.

They made it out of the palace and down through the free quarter without any trouble. But as they stepped into the brotherhood quarter, they came face to face with a man holding a hooded lantern. He was accompanied by seven or eight Mieren, laden with chests and sacks. It was clear they had been looting the palaces.

Graelen's gift surged. The Mieren stared in shock.

'Tobazim, get the queen to the boat,' Graelen ordered.

Stepping forward, he slammed the heads of two Mieren together and kicked the legs out from under another. As Iraayel took down a man, Graelen was aware of Tobazim running towards the ruined palace, with Sorne and the queen.

The fight was strangely quiet. The stunned Mieren hadn't had time to react, and already several of their number were down. Graelen caught a man by the shoulders and used him as a shield, feeling the man jerk as his companion's knife drove up under his ribs.

The others made no outcry. The penalty for looting must be steep.

A man grunted in pain as Iraayel elbowed him in the stomach. Someone collided with Graelen and he tripped, falling to his knees. A boot caught him in the head.

As Iraayel struggled with several assailants, the first two Mieren recovered and scrambled to their feet.

'Grab the big Wyrd. Don't let him get up,' one of them said. Two men pinned Graelen, one on each arm. A third came in, knife drawn. He wasn't going to get out of this.

Then one of the men holding Iraayel dropped. As he fell aside, Tobazim caught the other and spun him around, driving him head first into the wall and cracking his skull.

The men restraining Graelen turned to meet the new threat.

Soon all eight Mieren were dead.

Graelen cleaned his knife. 'The queen?'

'Sorne's taken her in the boat,' Tobazim said. 'But I saw another one we can use.'

Iraayel was bent double. Graelen helped him up. 'Can you walk?'

'I... I think so.'

They returned to the boat-house, piled into a rowboat and closed the gate. By now it had begun to rain. A downpour drowned all sound and made the night dark as pitch, cloaking them as they rowed across the lake.

Wet through from the rain, they dragged the boat onto the bank.

'I killed tonight. Their shades will come after me.' Iraayel had to raise his voice to be heard above the drumming of the rain. 'I don't have the training –'

'I'll shield you,' Tobazim said.

And Graelen knew Tobazim saw the lad as one of his brothers, his to protect. Just as an all-father should.

In that moment, he knew that he wasn't going to kill Tobazim.

'Come on.' Graelen led them up the slope, heading for the horses.

SORNE COULDN'T SEE his hand in front of his face. He followed the slope of the land and the faint smell of horses. A soft whicker greeted them as they drew close. He could sense roused male gift, laced with aggression, and that worried him. The three initiates had been back with the horses for a while now. Their gifts should be settled.

'Where are the others, half-blood?' It was one of the initiates and, clearly, he could see enough to make out that there were only two of them.

'We were attacked. They sent us on ahead.'

The initiates let them pass. Sorne helped Jaraile onto her mount and tied her bundle onto the saddle, then mounted up and waited. He thought he caught whispering and had the feeling these three were up to something.

Then the gift aggression faded and he sensed he and the queen were alone with the horses.

Jaraile urged her mount close to his. 'Are they going to be all right?'

Just then the rain started, drumming down around them and drowning all noise. Sorne felt uncomfortable. The longer he sat here, the more vulnerable they were. He had the queen, he should just go.

Instead he took the reins of Jaraile's horse, turned his mount and went along the ridge a little, then downhill.

* * *

GRAELEN WAS TIRED. Every bone in his body ached. As he walked uphill in the cold rain, he felt every blow he'd taken tonight. He thought that one of his ribs was cracked and several teeth were certainly loose.

Only years of training helped him avoid the knife that came out of the dark. He blocked, sidestepped and caught his attacker's arm. Skin on skin, he felt T'En power and knew the three initiates had been told to kill him. His instinct was to segue to the higher plane, but that would leave his body vulnerable here.

Someone collided with his back and he heard Tobazim curse as he struggled against an assailant.

He had no more time for thought as he fought in the rain, in the dark. He slipped in the mud and a blow went over his head. As he lurched to his feet, he shouldered his attacker in the stomach.

Someone kicked his knees from behind, and he went down. They caught his head by the hair.

A horse whinnied. Hooves flashed, thudding into his attacker, who grunted and collapsed.

He looked up to see someone dismount.

'Grae, is that you?' Sorne asked.

'Quiet. There were three of them,' Graelen warned. 'I think we've only accounted for two.'

'The third won't be giving any trouble,' Tobazim said.

'Iraayel?' Sorne called.

No answer.

Graelen spotted a pale face and felt it. Stubble on the jaw. Not Iraayel, then. Just as well, this one was dead. He found Iraayel next. The lad was unconscious, but breathing. They lifted him across Sorne's horse.

Then they took the initiates' arm-torcs and knives, and dragged their bodies to the lake, where they weighed them down and left them to sink. In the east, the sky was pale with the promise of dawn.

Now that the rain had ceased, it was fearfully cold. As Graelen waded back to the shore, there was just enough light to see the queen, huddled on her mount. Sorne had led their horses down to the shore; he handed them their reins.

Tobazim mounted up, then turned to Graelen. 'You realise this means Kyredeon meant for us both to die.'

'That, or Oriemn took it upon himself to make sure I didn't get back. I hate to think what may happen to Valendia.'

'Dia's safe,' Sorne said.

'What?'

'The night we left the ship, she came to me in tears.' Sorne shrugged. 'I didn't tell you because I thought you'd say it was none of my business, but I couldn't have my sister in danger. She's in Shifting-sands Stronghold. So you don't need to worry.'

'You should have told me,' Graelen said.

'I'm telling you now.'

'No, you should have told us right away,' Tobazim said. 'This changes everything. If Valendia's missing, Kyredeon will take it to mean Graelen has changed allegiances and has hidden her, to protect her until after we challenge him. Kyredeon might have already moved against our supporters.'

'I'm sorry. I didn't realise,' Sorne said. 'But I don't have time for brotherhood politics. I have a queen to protect and a kingdom to save. I'm riding for Riverbend Stronghold –'

'Riverbend?' Jaraile sat up. 'You can't go there. Baron Aingeru betrayed you to Eskarnor. He and Baron Ikor rode for Riverbend Stronghold days ago. They were going to pretend to change sides, then turn on you.'

Sorne cursed. 'Forewarned is forearmed. We ride for Riverbend.'

He took the lead with the queen right behind him.

Graelen realised Valendia must have been the extra person in the rowboat the night they left the brotherhood ship. Kyredeon had not known she was missing when he told the three initiates to make sure neither Graelen nor Tobazim returned from this mission.

As they rode uphill, Tobazim turned to him. 'Sorne has no idea how his actions have complicated things. He's forced you to side with us.'

'I always wanted to side with you. Valendia was the only reason I agreed to serve Kyredeon, but he never meant me to return alive. He meant to keep her for himself.'

'I thought she'd die, if you died.'

'If a powerful T'En was there, ready to link to her when she lost me, she might survive.'

'Kyredeon.' Tobazim sounded disgusted. He stopped his horse and turned to face Graelen. 'If we come through this alive, I would be proud to have you as my hand-of-force.'

It was everything Graelen had wanted at sixteen, a brotherhood leader he admired and the stature of his hand-of-force. But an all-father would go through several hands-of-force, and he had Valendia to think of.

'I offer my loyalty without the reward of stature. I offer it because Kyredeon must be removed, before his gift corrupts and the contagion infects our whole brotherhood.'

'You're right.' Tobazim said. 'I only hope...'

'You're strong enough.' Graelen didn't think Tobazim was, but he had no choice now. And he had no intention of fighting fair, not against Kyredeon, who had lied and manipulated his way to power.

Chapter Twenty-One

SORNE APPROACHED RIVERBEND Stronghold by crawling on his belly through the thigh-high bushes. These were covered in white winter-bell flowers, which grew so thickly they looked like early snowdrifts in places. He'd left his horse and the rest of his party down in the hollow behind him.

Sixteen days ago, he'd sent the king's guards to the barons' estates. Since Dekaitz, Rantzo and Dittor had been killed by Eskarnor's men, their sons or younger brothers would take their places. Ikor had changed sides, but the men on his estate wouldn't have known this when the king's palace guard arrived and ordered them to ride to Riverbend Stronghold, and they were Chalcedonians born and bred. They would not be eager to serve a jumped-up southern baron who meant to usurp their rightful king. By Sorne's calculation, the men-at-arms from Shifting-sands Stronghold should also be here, which meant there should be an army waiting for him.

But when he reached the crest of the hill, pushed the sprigs of winter-bell flowers aside and looked down on the valley with its winding river, he had no way of knowing if Riverbend Stronghold held the remains of south Chalcedonia's army, because there was no way he could get near it.

The stronghold was built on a small hill, at a bend in the river. A town had sat around the base of the hill, but the inhabitants had withdrawn and the town had been burned to the ground. Camped on the winter-bare fields were several hundred men. Smoke from their fires drifted straight up on the late afternoon air.

'What's going on?' Tobazim whispered, joining him.

Sorne pointed to the two banners propped below. 'Aingeru and Ikor have besieged the stronghold.'

'Two barons? Surely there are enough men in the stronghold to deal with them?'

'You'd think so,' Sorne said, 'but the besieging men are battle-seasoned troops. Meanwhile, Captain Ballendin and Nitzane are both in port, leaving the stronghold's men leaderless. Most of the mustered troops are farmers, and they'll be led by the barons' younger brothers or inexperienced sons. Dekaitz, Rantzo and Dittor would have kept their best men with them to maintain the seige of the Wyrd city. Those men will have been killed defending their barons the night Eskarnor made his move. As for the king's guard, they're used to strutting about the port in fine uniforms taking orders from Commander Halargon. And...' Sorne grimaced. 'I told them to wait for me here. So they could be waiting for me to bring help.'

'I thought Baron Aingeru's plan was to appear to go over to your side, then kill you when your guard was down?'

'Plans are written on the shifting sands of battle.' Frustration churned in Sorne's stomach. 'There's a small army in that stronghold, in need of a leader, and I can't get to them.'

Graelen crept up the rise to join them. 'We've got company. A column of men approach from the western road.'

Sorne glanced to their camp.

Iraayel had spent two days groggy from the blow to his head, but seemed back to normal today. He was on his feet, inspecting the bushes for something. Meanwhile, Jaraile huddled miserably in her cloak. Sorne had promised her a warm bed and dry clothes for the first time in three days. No chance of that now, and soon they would be trapped between two of Eskarnor's barons and... 'Did you see what banner these men flew?'

'It was white, with a black bear.'

'Dekaitz,' Sorne said, relieved. He headed down the hill.

As he approached Jaraile, he was in time to see Iraayel present her a bunch of winter-bell flowers. 'To brighten your day, Queen Jaraile. You said they reminded you of where you grew up.'

Tears filled her eyes and slid down her cheeks.

'They were supposed to make you smile.' Iraayel looked over to Sorne. 'I didn't mean –'

'It's all right. Give us a moment,' Sorne said, kneeling in front of Jaraile.

The bedraggled queen held the flowers in both hands. She raised tear-filled eyes to Sorne. 'I did say they reminded me of where I grew up. That was a chance remark yesterday.'

He squeezed her hand. 'I need you to be strong now. Can you play the queen?'

'Yes, of course I can.'

'Good. Come with me.'

When he helped her remount, she kept the flowers.

Graelen came up behind him. 'What are you going to do, Sorne?'

He swung into his saddle and turned his horse towards the western road. 'Charald always said war is won in men's minds.'

The three T'En looked bemused as he rode off with the queen.

'What *are* you doing, Sorne?' Jaraile whispered.

They climbed over the rise and saw the column of men coming towards them. Only two were on horseback; the rest marched, and there could not have been more than fifty. Sorne's heart sank.

'Play along,' he said as he rode down to meet them.

Seeing him approach, the riders called a halt. One was nearly seventy and the other was no more than fourteen.

'Who's in charge here?' Sorne asked.

The grizzled old man spoke. 'I am. I'm Dekornz's tutor. This is Baron Dekornz of Black-bear Stronghold.'

'Where are the rest of your men? Where is the king's guard I sent to your estate?'

'He's riding east to deliver the baron's mother and the rest of the children to Shifting-sand Bay.'

'What delayed you?'

'My lady had just given birth. She would not have left at all, except the king's guard insisted. He's escorting her, but I sent twenty of our men with him, because I didn't like his manner.'

Sorne rubbed his mouth to hide his smile. 'What did he tell you?'

'That the king was celebrating the return of his son and young Dekornz here is now the baron, since Eskarnor betrayed the king. He said nothing about Queen Jaraile being on the road.'

Sorne glanced to Jaraile.

'Hello, Scholar Mozteben,' Jaraile said. 'It's been a long time. What are you doing, riding to war?'

'Trying to save a baron who's still wet behind the ears.'

'Please accept my sympathy on your loss, Baron Dekornz,' Sorne told the lad. 'Scholar, does the young baron have a set of plate armour?'

'A fine set, newly made for him.'

'Good. We'll need to borrow it.' As Sorne led Mozteben and young Baron Dekornz off the road, he told them his idea.

It was full dark by the time Sorne rode towards the besieging barons' camp with Jaraile in the armour. She'd tucked a sprig of winter-bell flowers in her breastplate for luck. Seven of the burliest of the farmers pretended to be their honour guard. The torches fizzed as a few drops of rain fell. Sorne hoped the rain would hold off for now. It was essential to his plan.

Sentries ran to fetch the barons. Ikor approached first. He took in Sorne and the queen in full armour and went pale. Aingeru was next. He glanced to Jaraile once, then to Sorne. About a dozen men-at-arms stood with their hands on their weapons as Aingeru and Ikor strode out to meet Sorne and the queen.

'You picked the wrong side this time, half-blood,' Ikor gloated. 'Eskarnor has Charald surrounded in Port Mirror-on-Sea. Once the port falls, the kingdom will be his!'

'Port Mirror-on-Sea's defences are strong and Eskarnor has no fleet to blockade her harbour. After we mop up your men, we'll ride there and crush his army.'

Ikor snorted. 'How will you do that? Putting a queen in plate armour doesn't grow her a pair of balls. You need men.'

'Sometimes brains are more important than balls,' Sorne said. 'You have made the mistake of besieging Nitzane's stronghold. Queen Jaraile has graciously granted you this opportunity to surrender.'

Ikor laughed. 'To her?'

'To the queen and her army,' Sorne said. 'She has five hundred men camped over the rise.'

'Impossible!' Ikor protested.

'Go look if you don't believe me.'

Ikor called for a horse.

While they waited for it to be saddled, Sorne raised his eyes and saw the men clustered on the castle wall-walk. They'd recognise him, but not Jaraile in her armour. 'Take off your helmet, my queen.'

'I bring Queen Jaraile and an army to break the siege,' Sorne yelled. The men on the wall cheered.

A horse was delivered to Ikor, who jumped astride it and rode to the crest of the hill. As the horse's galloping hooves faded, Sorne turned to Aingeru. 'Zaria sends her love.'

'I know you have her.' Aingeru glanced to Jaraile. 'Last time I saw you, you were keeping Eskarnor's bed warm.'

'Not by choice,' Jaraile said. 'Next time I see Eskarnor, he's going to beg my forgiveness as he bleeds to death at my feet.'

Sorne turned in the saddle, surprised by her vehemence.

'He means to kill my son,' Jaraile said, eyes glittering in her sweet face. 'He has to die.'

'Fair enough.' Sorne turned back to Aingeru.

By now, Ikor would have reached the top of that hill.

What he'd see was a dark valley dotted with many camp fires around which clustered huddled shapes. Around the closest fires were the fifty men. Towards the middle of the camp was the royal tent, its banner in silhouette against the torches. At a quick glance, it would look like a camp of five hundred men. And the sentries had been told to challenge Ikor, allowing him no closer. Sorne's bluff relied on the baron's nerve failing and Aingeru changing sides.

'Zaria was convinced you'd support King Charald.'

'I have no love for Charald.'

'The king is dying,' Jaraile said. 'The reign of King Charald the Tyrant is over. My son will be a very different kind of ruler.'

Sorne could hear Ikor's horse returning; time was running out. He urged his mount forward. 'If you meant to swear allegiance to King Charald, then betray me, why are you besieging Nitzane's stronghold?'

Aingeru lowered his voice. 'I never meant to betray you. I revealed Zaria's message as a ruse to escape Eskarnor. He'd have taken my head if he guessed my true intentions. But he was too clever for me. He sent Ikor along to make sure I didn't switch allegiance. Ikor's keen to prove his loyalty to Eskarnor. When we arrived here, he got into a pissing match with one of the king's guard, and before I could do anything, it escalated and...'

Aingeru stepped back as the baron thundered in on his horse, and jumped down from it to confer with Aingeru, who glanced to Sorne.

'Ikor tells me you have five hundred men in the next valley,' Aingeru said.

Sorne nodded. 'Tomorrow morning, I'll march them over the hill. The stronghold will open its gates and your men will be crushed between the hammer and the anvil. But, if you reconsider your allegiance to Eskarnor the Usurper, you can surrender tonight. I understand it was a matter of die or change allegiance the night Eskarnor returned to the Wyrd city.'

'For me, yes,' Ikor said. He was young and ambitious, and had come to his title after King Charald returned from the Secluded Sea campaign, so there had been little opportunity for advancement until now. 'On the other hand, Aingeru has always been one of Eskarnor's supporters.'

'Are you surrendering to Queen Jaraile?' Sorne asked Ikor.

'Gladly.' He gestured to the other baron. 'But you can't trust him.'

'Baron?' Sorne met the other's eyes.

'My wife and children will be unharmed.'

'As far as it is in my power to ensure this,' Sorne said, noting that Ikor had not asked after his family.

'Then yes, I surrender.'

'We'll go into the stronghold to accept your formal surrender.' Before they learned his army consisted of fifty farmers and fifty empty fire circles.

A worm of impatience gnawed at Tobazim. He should be back with his brotherhood. He feared what Kyredeon would do while he was away. It had been nine days, time enough for the all-father to manipulate Haromyr into doing something stupid, time enough for naive but loyal Athlyn to follow him into danger. But mostly he feared for Ardonyx. There weren't many T'En survivors from the captain's old brotherhood, which left him in a very vulnerable position.

Or perhaps Kyredeon thought that once Tobazim was removed, the others were harmless. At any rate, he should be back with his brotherhood, not here in Baron Nitzane's great hall.

It was a surreal experience to find himself standing on the high dais with Kyredeon's best assassin and the causare's choice-son, behind the king's disinherited half-blood son.

Queen Jaraile sat on the baron's chair nearby. She still clutched the bunch of winter-bell flowers Iraayel had given her. Eight of the king's guard stood behind her, along with other high-ranking Mieren, though they were a motley lot; boys and old men, mostly. One belligerent lout, who was no more than twenty, glared at Tobazim and his companions, and tried to tell Sorne how to run things.

Ikor and Aingeru had brought their men into the stronghold and were now camped in the main courtyard. Sorne had posted archers along the walls; if the men revolted, he was ready.

As barons Aingeru and Ikor approached to formally surrender and swear fealty to Prince Cedon, Sorne turned to the three T'En behind him. 'I'm going to call on one of you soon, so play along. But first...'

Before they could ask for more information, he began proceedings.

'Queen Jaraile has graciously granted Barons Aingeru and Ikor and their men their lives, but before we proceed, we must acknowledge the queen's saviours. While King Charald lay ill in his bed, Baron Eskarnor, his invited guest, kidnapped the queen and locked her in the Celestial City. It is only thanks to these three T'En warriors that she is here with us today.'

Jaraile came to her feet. 'Step forward, T'En warriors.'

So Tobazim found himself kneeling in front of the Mieren queen, who thanked them and handed them each a sprig of winter-bell flowers as a sign of her favour. The men showed their approval with a cheer, but Tobazim suspected it was directed more at the queen than at himself and his two companions.

As the T'En retreated to stand behind Sorne, both barons came forward.

Ikor and Aingeru knelt, placed their swords on the dais and said the words of surrender.

The queen accepted their surrender and came to her feet, but before they could swear fealty, Sorne spoke up.

'I do not trust men who turn their coats so easily. I have a suggestion, my queen. Ask the T'En to discover if these barons bear treasonous thoughts towards Prince Cedon.'

Everyone turned to the three T'En warriors and Sorne came over.

'None of us can trawl for the truth without destroying a man's mind,' Tobazim whispered. 'We'd have to crush their natural defences and –'

'They don't know that.'

Graelen chuckled, but it was Iraayel who stepped forward.

Aingeru was closest, and the lad stood behind the baron, put his fingers on the man's temples and called his gift. Tobazim could feel it from here. What was the lad doing? He didn't need to actually gift-work for the ruse to succeed.

'Say the words of fealty,' Sorne ordered.

Aingeru placed his hands between the queen's and said the oath, then everyone looked to Iraayel.

'I saw a beautiful, black-haired woman with dark laughing eyes.'

'My wife, Zaria,' Aingeru said.

'Was there any deceit in the baron's heart?' Sorne asked.

'His words tasted of the truth,' Iraayel said.

Tobazim glanced to Graelen. Among their kind, there were some rare T'En who had the ability to taste the truth. Could this lad be one of them, or was it just chance that he chose exactly those words?

The queen removed a sprig of winter-bell and presented it to Baron Aingeru. 'I accept your fealty and hope that my son will grow up to call your sons his friends.'

Then she moved to stand in front of Ikor and offered her hands as Iraayel shifted to stand behind him. Tobazim could not see the baron's face, but something about the set of his shoulders warned him. As Iraayel reached for the baron's head, Ikor grabbed his sword and leapt to his feet, aiming the tip of the blade for Jaraile's throat.

Sorne dived towards her.

The same instant, Iraayel caught the baron's sword-arm and swung him around, straight into Graelen, who had covered a body length in the blink of an eye. Catching the man's head in both hands, Graelen snapped his neck.

There was utter silence as the dead baron dropped to the floor.

Tobazim saw that Sorne had thrown himself over Jaraile, protecting her with his own body. Looking shaken, he helped her to her feet.

Graelen stepped away from the body of the dead Mieren and bowed. 'Queen Jaraile.'

As he went to stand beside Tobazim, the hall erupted.

JARAILE GASPED, HEAD ringing with the impact of the fall. The big T'En warrior had moved so fast and killed so efficiently that her heart quailed, even though he'd been protecting her.

The great hall had been absolutely silent.

Then everyone seemed to draw breath and shout at once. Baron Rantzo's younger brother, now Baron Ramanol, was amongst the loudest. How dare a silverhead kill a True-man!

The Wyrds had rescued her from Eskarnor. They had uncovered Ikor's treason and saved her life. But the fact remained that a silverhead had killed a True-man. Fearful, angry eyes were directed to Sorne and his honour guard.

Jaraile glanced to Sorne. He was about to speak.

Quickly, she lifted her arms, drawing all eyes to her. 'Take this traitor's body away and let the feasting begin!'

The servants carried out great platters of food and the men took their places on the benches. Jaraile made it to her seat at the high table before her legs gave way.

Sorne came over and leant close to whisper. 'I'll see to Ikor's men. You did well, my queen.'

And he left with his three T'En warriors.

'Just as well,' Baron Ramanol said. Somehow he had claimed the seat beside her. 'You can't have that half-blood at your table, not after what happened tonight.'

'You mean them saving my life?' she asked sweetly and saw his eyes widen.

'Be careful what you say in jest, my queen. There are some who might take it the wrong way and think you a Wyrd-lover.'

She wanted to pick up her knife and stab him through the hand, but she gritted her teeth, smiled and listened to the boasts of men who had yet to prove themselves on the battlefield.

SORNE APPROACHED THE queen's bedchamber early the next day. It was not long after dawn, but decisions had to be made and orders given. When he tapped on the door, a maid answered it, a forbidding expression on her face.

She shook her head. 'The queen –'

'Needs to see me.' He pushed her aside and strode in.

Jaraile was kneeling over a bowl, throwing up.

'I tried to stop him,' the maid cried.

Sorne ignored her, knelt next to Jaraile and held her hair out of the way. After a moment she lifted her head, tears streaming down her face.

'I should never have had the cream with the dessert last night,' she confessed. 'I love it, but I can't have it when...'

'When you're pregnant. Kerminzto told me about the baby.'

Jaraile wiped her cheeks. 'Why are you so good to me?'

'My mother was fifteen when she married Charald. Fifteen when she had me, and fifteen when he had her murdered. No one stood up for her.'

'Oh, Sorne.'

He helped her to her feet. She asked the maid to clean up and stepped behind the screen to dress.

'I'm sending the three T'En back to Shifting-sands Bay today,' Sorne said. 'You can travel with them. From there you can take one of Nitzane's ships up the coast to

Port Mirror-on-Sea. It would inspire the people to have their queen returned when the port is under siege.'

Jaraile came out from behind the screen dressed in a vest, robe and borrowed breeches with the cuffs rolled up. Sorne suspected she'd raided Nitzane's wardrobe.

'You're not wearing your palace clothes.'

'That's because I'm not going back. I'm staying with the army. This is where I'm needed. You said yourself, Port Mirror-on-Sea is safe behind its walls.'

'As long as the defenders don't open the gates and ride out to meet their besiegers. Jaraile, we're going to war. You can't ride into battle, even if you wear plate armour.'

She took his hand. 'Sorne, I know you are King Charald's firstborn son. You are kind and clever, and loyal. I think you would make a wonderful king.' He stared at her, throat tight. No one had ever said this to him before.

'But the fact remains, you are a half-blood.' She squeezed his six-fingered hand and released it. 'And after the way Graelen killed Baron Ikor last night –'

'He saved your life.'

'He killed a True-man in front of hundreds of True-men. The only reason he's still alive is because he saved their queen's life. Baron Ramanol made that clear.'

'What are you saying, Jaraile?'

'That you cannot lead the army when we attack Eskarnor. I must lead it, and you must ride behind me and tell me what to do, because I've no idea what I'm doing.'

He smiled. 'Don't sell yourself short.'

'It's not false modesty, Sorne. We both face limitations imposed on us by the True-men of Chalcedonia, me because I'm a woman and you because of your tainted blood. But together, we can lead this army of left-overs against Baron Eskarnor and his men. Will you do it? Will you serve a woman?'

'You know I will.'

Jaraile smiled in relief and plucked a sprig of winter-bells from the vase. Coming back to Sorne, she tucked it in the pin that fastened his winter cloak at his shoulder. 'Then wear this and know I have faith in you.'

'Thank you. We must march as soon as possible. You need the barons to get their men organised.'

'I'll call them to the great hall. While they're assembling, you can send the T'En back to their people.'

There was a knock at the door and the maid answered it. She came over with a message for Sorne.

He accepted it. 'Your kinsman, Baron Kerminzto, writes that he has returned to Port Mirror-on-Sea to find the city besieged. He doesn't have the men to attack Eskarnor, so he needs me to hurry with the men from south Chalcedonia. But there is good news. Kerminzto met up with Baron Nitzane in the north. Nitzane took the barons' families, including Eskarnor's wife and daughter, and sailed south with them. He reached port safely and spoke to Eskarnor from the gate tower on...' He did the mental calculations. 'It must have been the day we rode for Riverbend Stronghold. Nitzane told Eskarnor he's holding the barons' families hostage.'

Jaraile looked up at Sorne. 'But it won't matter to Eskarnor. He told me if Nitzane killed his wife, it would leave him free to marry me.'

Sorne didn't tell her that Charald had said that if Eskarnor killed Queen Jaraile, the baron would be doing him a favour. 'He also writes that Charald has signed the decree appointing you and the other guardians to rule until Prince Cedon comes of age.'

She looked relieved then frowned. 'Eskarnor said decrees are only good if you have the power to back them up.'

Sorne passed her the letter. 'Don't worry. This is all exactly what I planned with Kerminzto.'

'Where is my son, Sorne? You said you had him safe. Eskarnor may be able to sneak assassins into the port. What if he sends someone to kill Cedon?'

'He won't be able to find him. Only the commander of the king's guard knows where he is. High Priest Faryx has the boy hidden in the secret apartment above his private chambers in the Father's church.'

'I didn't know there was a secret apartment.'

'Exactly. We'll need to be on the road by tomorrow at the latest.'

When they rode out the next morning, every man, boy and horse sported a sprig of winter-bells.

Chapter Twenty-Two

'PUT IT HERE.'

Imoshen had the Malaunje servants place the low table on the centre of the carpet. They'd erected a tent on the foredeck for the meeting with All-father Paragian. Tomorrow Sardeon would be seventeen and, had everything been normal, he would have been handed over to Paragian's brotherhood.

In three days time, her choice-son, Iraayel, would be seventeen, and two days after that it would be winter's cusp. As she'd made preparations for the meeting, more people had come in from the estates. But there was bad news with the good. This morning, she'd had word that All-father Tamaron's party had been massacred, which meant his brotherhood survivors would have to be accepted by another all-father. If they joined one of the lesser brotherhoods, it could upset the balance of power. She hadn't made an official announcement about Tamaron's death, yet but she would have to soon; word was bound to get out eventually.

Reoden came up the steps. The healer's gift was running so high that Imoshen could sense her coming across the deck.

'He'll be here any moment,' Imoshen said, taking her hand and siphoning off a little of Reoden's power. 'Are the boys ready?'

'Yes.'

They'd decided it would be easier on Sardeon if he didn't know he was being inspected. So they'd told Reoden's hand-of-force, as soon as Paragian arrived, to give the empowered lads a training session on the mid-deck. Ronnyn and Sardeon would be training with them.

Hand-of-force Kiane came running up the steps. 'The all-father's here. But he's come with his devotee.' Her tone conveyed her disapproval.

Imoshen glanced to Reoden for an explanation.

'She's the boy's mother. Paragian is devoted to Sardoria.'

'Then by all means, bring them up.'

They waited at the entrance to the tent. As soon as Imoshen saw the devotee, she knew where Sardeon got his looks.

'All-father Paragian, Devotee Sardoria.' Imoshen gave an obeisance of welcome. 'I am here today to mediate. Please come in.'

As they entered the tent, Imoshen felt the force of Paragian's gift.

Paragian took one look at the kneeling cushions and table and turned to Reoden. 'What's wrong with my son? You haven't let me see him since the day your daughter was empowered. I know he was with her the day she was murdered. I know he was carried up to the sisterhood palace right afterwards. You sent me a message to say he had recovered, but...' He gestured abruptly to Imoshen. 'Now you bring the causare in to mediate. What's going on?'

Reoden went very pale.

Paragian and Sardoria reached for each other. Imoshen's gift surged as she read both of them. They expected the worst.

'He's alive and his wits are unharmed,' Imoshen said quickly. The devotee swayed with relief. 'But he was injured, the day Reoden's daughter was murdered.'

'Injured?' Paragian turned to Reoden. 'You're the greatest healer of our time. Why –'

'The injury was to his gift,' the devotee guessed, her eyes going to Imoshen, who nodded.

Paragian's shoulders sagged.

'Sit down.' Imoshen gestured to the cushions and began to prepare the spiced wine. This was normally a Malaunje task; both the all-father and his devotee looked surprised.

'Reoden has done everything she possibly could for your son,' Imoshen said as she prepared the wine. 'I saved your son's life, the day Reoden's daughter died. He went onto the empyrean plane to try to escort her to death's realm.'

'But he had no training,' Paragian protested.

'His gift was beginning to manifest. The shock of seeing his choice-sister murdered triggered a surge in power. It was very brave to go after her as he did. I found him and brought him back, but since then...' Imoshen glanced to the healer.

'Since then, his gift has been entirely dormant,' Reoden said, her voice low and hoarse.

The devotee leant forward. 'But surely the gift-wright –'

'Has worked with him,' Reoden said. 'Believe me, she's done everything she can. But what's happened to Sardeon... well, there's nothing like it in the records.'

Paragian looked grim. 'You're telling me my son is crippled and will not be able to defend himself when he enters the brotherhood?'

'He will not be able to enter the brotherhood,' Imoshen said. 'He may never be able to. When his gift went dormant, it somehow halted his growth. For all that he is technically seventeen, he is physically twelve years old.'

The devotee gasped.

'There's nothing else wrong with him,' Imoshen assured them. 'Come see.'

They went to the foredeck railing, where they could look down onto the mid-deck and see Ronnyn and Sardeon training with the youths.

'He really hasn't grown,' Paragian whispered. 'I know you told me, but... He's exactly the same. How can this be?'

'The mystery of the gifts is still being unravelled,' Reoden said and she led him and his devotee back to the tent.

Imoshen watched as Sardeon finished his exercises. The boy turned and looked up to her, meeting her eyes. Her gift surged.

He knew. He was sharp.

Cerafeoni called the next set of moves. Sardeon's natural elegance made every kick and strike a thing of beauty and precision. Meanwhile, Ronnyn moved with the grace of a born dancer. They were well suited. And they had become fast friends, but with every passing year the age difference would pull them further apart...

Imoshen went back to the tent, where they were sipping their spiced wine. She knelt next to Reoden.

'...so you see,' the healer was saying, 'even though he is seventeen tomorrow, I cannot return him to the brotherhood. He's welcome to stay with me for...'

'Forever?' Paragian sounded devastated. 'Will he be like this forever?'

'We don't know,' Reoden admitted. 'We just don't know.'

JARAILE WAS DETERMINED not to slow down the army, so she rode without complaint all through that first long day. Sorne kept them marching from dawn until well after dark when the men ate a cold meal and slept on the ground. But he insisted on erecting a tent for her comfort.

'Jaraile, you are their queen. Let them treat you like a queen,' he told her.

So he set up a brazier to keep her warm and a hot meal was prepared for her and her barons. Dekornz was the youngest at fourteen; Dittor's brother had joined the church and never expected to be leading men. Baron Ramanol was the most experienced of the lot of them, and the closest he'd come to war was keeping his brother company during the siege of the Wyrd city. Then there was Aingeru, who listened and said little. Also present were the king's guard and Dekornz's tutor. The only person not at the table was Sorne, and it was his opinion she most wanted to hear.

As the men talked, Jaraile gathered the barons who supported Eskarnor each had a core following of ruthless ex-mercenaries. The old Chalcedonian aristocracy despised the southern barons and feared their men. They talked of how Eskarnor's army would be camped in the fields outside the port. Baron Ramanol did not like their chances without superior numbers. When they all retired for the night, Sorne slipped out of the private chamber at the back of the tent to join her.

'You heard them?' she asked. 'They're saying it will be pure butchery if we go up against Eskarnor's men. They're saying there is no way we can use the lie of the land to our advantage, because there's hardly a hill within sight of the port.'

'Then we will have to use guile and lead Eskarnor into making an error. In the early days of his campaign, after half his barons deserted him and he'd invaded Maygharia, I once saw Charald lure a larger army into a devious pincer manoeuvre.'

'Show me what you mean.'

Sorne demonstrated with the remains of someone's meal, moving the food around the plate. 'The ground was flat and the opposing armies lined up like so, facing each other. Charald put his best men in the centre, with instructions to retreat on his signal. When they did, the opposing army gave chase, pouring into the gap created by their retreat and the two sides of Charald's men closed around them in a pincer attack.'

'So simple.'

'Not easy to do. Pick the wrong moment and you'll be routed. If the men commanding the arms of the pincer don't close in quickly enough, your army will be divided.'

'Still, could we do that?'

'This battle happened before Eskarnor joined our army. But he's cunning. He may not fall for the ruse.'

She nodded. She knew how smart the baron was.

Just then a messenger arrived, looking for Sorne.

Jaraile watched as Sorne unfolded the message and read it.

He lifted his head, his expression solemn. He turned to the messenger. 'I'll write a reply. Take it straight to Baron Kerminzto, and I'll thank you not to speak a word of this on your way out.'

The man nodded.

Sorne handed Jaraile the message and sat down to write. Nitzane was injured, half his men were lost, half of her kinsman's men were also dead and the port blockaded.

Her heart raced. She felt sick with shock and horror. 'How could everything go so wrong?'

'Wait.' Sorne held up his hand as he finished writing. 'I've told Kerminzto we'll be there within a couple of days and to do nothing until we arrive.'

He sealed the message and handed it to the man who left.

'Give me that.' Sorne held out his hand and Jaraile passed him the original message. He burned it.

'Now, how will we –'

'Remember how I told you sometimes the battle is won in the minds of men before one blow falls?'

She nodded and watched the flames until the message was reduced to ash.

'Our men don't need to know this.'

'What possessed Nitzane?'

'He has always been impulsive. I was hoping Captain Ballendin would be able to advise him, but I imagine Eskarnor manipulated him. Nitzane rode out in challenge with his men. Eskarnor surrounded them, cut them off; this forced Kerminzto to attack, which allowed the remnants of Nitzane's men to get back inside the gate with the injured baron. But Kerminzto lost of a lot of good men. How Eskarnor must be laughing.' Sorne ground his teeth.

'And the port's under blockade? You said he had no ships.'

'Eskarnor sent a company of men to steal five ships. The headlands are narrow. They're not letting anyone in or out.'

'Aren't you glad now that I refused to sail back to port?'

He grinned, despite the grim news. 'Jaraile... King Charald did not appreciate you as he should have.'

She blushed, then held his eyes. 'Are we riding to our deaths? With the loss of Nitzane and my kinsman's men, Eskarnor has the larger army. According to Ramanol –'

'Who's twenty-two and has never been to war. Numbers are not the only things that win battles. War is not like the counting of tithes.'

She liked the way Sorne talked to her, as if he expected her to understand and valued her judgement. She would never have let Eskarnor manipulate her into riding out from behind perfectly defensible walls. She wanted to grab Nitzane and shake him. Come to think of it, the baron had often made her feel that way.

Sorne poured them both a glass of wine. 'Eskarnor has more men and they are battle-hardened, while the majority of our men are reluctant warriors. But I've been battling against the odds since I was seventeen, and you know what that's like. We'll have to be cunning. We'll have to lure Eskarnor into making a mistake.'

Jaraile went to bed lighter of heart. Until she remembered it was only five days until winter's cusp. What was she going to do without Sorne?

Chapter Twenty-Three

TOBAZIM WAS SURPRISED when the castle-keep at Shifting-sands Stronghold welcomed them back. Then he realised she wanted them to take Valendia with them when they left.

'Not that she isn't a sweet girl,' the woman said, as she led them up to the baron's best bedchamber. 'But she belongs with her own kind, and it's only three days to winter cusp.'

The castle-keep stopped in front of the chamber door. 'I'll send up a meal. I expect you'll be famished.' And she bustled off.

Tobazim could feel Graelen's roused gift as the warrior knocked on the door.

It flew open. 'Grae?' Valendia's brilliant smile faltered as she took in Tobazim and Iraayel. 'Where's Sorne? Is he all right?'

'Sorne's fine,' Graelen said.

As they followed Graelen into the chamber, his devotee sent Tobazim a wary look.

'We've formed an alliance,' Graelen said.

'You did?' She threw her arms around him, kissing him. 'I'm so glad.'

Laughing, he picked her up and kissed her with great tenderness. It was a side of Graelen that Tobazim had never seen, or imagined existed.

The big adept led his devotee over to the chairs by the fireplace. 'I'm glad you approve, Dia, but our troubles are not over. When we go back to the ship, Tobazim will have to challenge Kyredeon.'

'Do you want me to leave?' Iraayel offered.

'Why?' Valendia asked.

'He's not one of our brotherhood, and we're discussing brotherhood business,' Graelen explained.

'He is brotherhood,' Tobazim said. 'If I survive the challenge, he'll be welcomed as one of us.'

Iraayel flushed and dropped to his knees. 'Thank you, all-father.'

Tobazim took him by the shoulders and drew him to his feet with a laugh. 'Let's not rush things. First we have to deal with Kyredeon.'

They had been gone thirteen days. Tobazim dreaded to think what might have happened in that time. Just then, the servants arrived with their meals. They ate by the fire as they discussed who in the brotherhood would come over to support Tobazim. If enough of them severed their brotherhood links to the all-father, they would weaken Kyredeon. But would it weaken him enough for Tobazim to defeat him? The problem was that the brothers knew if Kyredeon won, he would execute everyone of high rank who had stood against him, and those he let live would have a miserable existence under his rule.

Iraayel listened to all of this, his eyes following them as they spoke. It was the sort of thing most brotherhood warriors weren't privy to, let alone a lad of sixteen who had not yet given his vows.

When they had argued themselves back to the start again, Iraayel said, 'If it's power you need, why not ask my choice-mother to gift-infuse you?'

Tobazim's heart leapt and his gift surged at the thought. An infusion of her power could give him the edge he needed.

Valendia turned to Graelen. 'I thought you said the causare could not interfere in brotherhood business?'

'She shouldn't. If the other brotherhoods knew...' Graelen did not need to spell it out.

'She won't be interfering,' Iraayel said. 'She will gift-infuse you both as a reward for saving my life. It's no lie.

You did save me at least twice, after all.' He grinned and shrugged. 'You can't help it if by chance she gift-infuses you on the very night you offer challenge to Kyredeon. Coincidence, nothing more.'

'I like him,' Graelen told Tobazim. 'He has a devious mind. But seriously, Tobazim, what he says makes sense. You can't survive tonight without the causare's gift-infusion. And you should take Ardonyx as your shield-brother.'

It was everything Tobazim wanted, and it was right there for the taking. But he would find it doubly hard to resist the lure of Imoshen's gift if he...

'You wouldn't be indebted to her, as she'd be rewarding you for saving my life,' Iraayel said, misinterpreting his hesitation.

'It's decided then.' Graelen stood and went to the balcony, opening the doors to look down on the T'Enatuath's fleet. 'We're in luck. There's a fog tonight. Kyredeon won't see us coming. You'll have time to find Ardonyx and form the shield-brother bond, Tobazim.' He returned to stand over them. 'There are too many people relying on you to hesitate now.'

A HAND TOUCHED Imoshen's shoulder. She looked up to see her hand-of-force standing over her. 'Yes?'

Kiane signalled for silence and led Imoshen across the packed cabin, stepping over sleeping children and inner circle sisters to the passage, where she turned to face her. 'Iraayel is here –'

'Where?' Imoshen glanced past Kiane's shoulder to the door at the end of the passage. 'Why didn't you bring him in?'

'He's with two brotherhood warriors. Tobazim and –'

Ardonyx, of course. Imoshen darted around her and ran down the passage. She had not had a private moment alone with Ardonyx since midsummer, when they had slipped away to tryst. Back then they'd planned for him to win Tobazim's trust and support the young adept so he could take over the brotherhood. Now they'd come to her with Iraayel.

She threw open the door. The fog was so thick she could barely make out Iraayel standing in a halo of lamplight.

'You're back safe!' She threw her arms around him. Skin to skin, she sensed his gift and knew it was riding him tonight.

'I'm not alone,' he warned and beckoned the others.

As a hard-faced gift-warrior stepped out of the fog, Imoshen took a step back.

'It's all right,' Iraayel assured her. 'This is Graelen. He saved my life, twice. So did Tobazim. You need to gift-infuse them as a reward.'

'Iraayel...' Tobazim muttered. He gave the formal obeisance. 'Causare Imoshen. Apologies for the lad, he's over-excited.'

Imoshen blinked. Since when did Tobazim assume responsibility for her choice-son? She glanced from one to the other and read a bond, forged by danger and cemented by mutual respect. The same thing united them to Graelen.

'And this is Dia,' Iraayel added, drawing a beautiful young Malaunje woman forward. 'She's Sorne's sister.'

'I'm so glad you're safe, Valendia.' As Imoshen took her hands, she read a rich joy in her and identified its source. 'You are with child, congratulations. If there is ever anything I can do for you, just ask. I owe Sorne more than I can say.'

Valendia blushed and stepped back to join Graelen.

Imoshen turned to Iraayel. 'Speaking of Sorne, where is he? Did you save the Mieren queen?'

'Sorne is marching for port with Queen Jaraile at this moment,' Iraayel said. 'You need to gift-infuse Tobazim and Graelen tonight, or they'll be killed and I won't have a brotherhood to go to.'

'Manners!' Kiane muttered, coming up behind Imoshen. 'Your choice-mother raised you better than this, lad.'

'We don't have time to stand on ceremony. It has to happen now,' Iraayel said.

'It's all right,' Imoshen told her hand-of-force. As far as Tobazim knew, she had gotten to know him and Ardonyx while they served on the exile-council. So it wouldn't be strange if she asked after the sea captain. 'Does Ardonyx know your plans for tonight?'

'Not yet,' Tobazim admitted. 'We came to your ship first. As soon as Kyredeon knows we're aboard the brotherhood ship, he'll order his hand-of-force to execute us. The warriors he sent on the mission with us had orders to ensure we did not return.'

'I suspected as much.'

'They had orders to kill Iraayel, too,' Graelen said. 'And they nearly succeeded.'

Imoshen bristled, her gift gathering force. She gestured to Graelen and Tobazim. 'Kneel. The rest of you, stand back.'

She would rather gift-infuse Ardonyx and Tobazim, but this would have to do.

When it was done, Kiane escorted them off the ship and Imoshen turned to her choice-son. 'So you have a brotherhood willing to take you, and all you had to do was rescue the Mieren queen?'

He laughed.

'Iraayel?' Saffazi appeared at the passage door, face alight with joy.

He opened his arms. She went to him and threw her arms around him, kissed him, then pulled back and thumped his chest hard. 'You should have taken me with you. I hated the waiting. It was unbearable!'

He grinned, too happy to argue.

'Kiane will be back in a moment,' Imoshen said. 'Come inside.'

When they slipped into the bathing chamber and bolted the door, she did not protest.

* * *

TOBAZIM GAMBLED THAT the brotherhood's hand-of-force had placed Haromyr and the others on watch again. And this was confirmed when Eryx peered over the side in answer to his soft call.

'Tobazim, is that you?'

'Quiet, lower the rope ladder.'

Valendia went first, followed by Graelen, then Tobazim. As he climbed aboard, he heard Imoshen's oarsman row away.

Haromyr, Athlyn and Eryx grabbed him, hugging him one after the other. They whispered excitedly, their gifts barely contained and, as they responded to the residue of Imoshen's gift, their power rose along with their voices.

'Quiet,' Tobazim warned. Graelen and Valendia stood to one side, for the moment ignored. His gift surged and he saw how they had to be incorporated into his power structure if the challenge was to succeed.

'You're drenched in female power again,' Haromyr whispered. 'What happened?'

'We saved the life of the causare's choice-son.' Tobazim reached out to Graelen, caught the adept's forearm and raised it between them. 'We have formed an alliance.' And to be sure they knew he meant it, he let his gift defences down just enough to form a shallow link with Graelen, who recognised what he was doing and responded in kind.

'Harm Grae and you harm me.' Tobazim said. 'All of us live or die tonight based on the strength of our trust in each other.'

'You're going to challenge Kyredeon?' Haromyr said. 'I knew it!'

Tobazim nodded. 'Now go back to your posts and wait for my signal. Where's Ardonyx?'

Haromyr glanced up to the high rear-deck.

Relief flooded Tobazim.

The fog was so thick the lights in the rear cabins were just a hazy glow. Tobazim ran across the mid-deck and up the steps to the lower rear-deck, where he parted from Graelen and Valendia with a nod.

Heart racing, he ran up the steps to the high rear-deck.

As Ardonyx turned to face him, Tobazim was shocked to see that he had been beaten. Furious, he crossed the deck, took Ardonyx's shoulders in his hands and drew him closer to the light. The captain's features were a mask of bruising and swelling. 'What did they do to you?'

'They said you weren't coming back and tried to break my spirit. But' – tears blazed in Ardonyx's eyes – 'you proved them wrong.'

Tobazim hugged him. 'When Oriemn's men tried to kill me, I thought I'd come back to find you dead.'

Ardonyx pulled away, inhaling sharply. 'You're radiating Imoshen's power.'

'She gift-infused us. Grae and I have formed an alliance –'

'You and Graelen are shield-brothers?' Ardonyx took a step back.

'No.' Tobazim rolled up his sleeve, aware that before he left, he would never have dared to say this. 'No. I want *you* for my shield-brother.'

Ardonyx didn't say anything.

'I can't do this without you,' Tobazim told him.

'You do realise that this bond will be for life?'

'If I cannot have you, I don't want anyone. I need you at my side, as my voice-of-reason, to lead this brotherhood into a new age.'

'And what kind of new age will that be?'

'I grew up and trained under the values of the Golden Age: honour, duty and service. But...' Tobazim hesitated as his mind raced. 'I don't believe in blind service. I think we need to open the T'Enatuath to new ways.'

'An age of enlightenment?'

'Yes.' Fresh conviction rose in Tobazim. Ardonyx saw further than he did, and this was why he needed him. 'Will you accept?'

For answer, Ardonyx took Tobazim's left hand. Bypassing the formal wrist-to-elbow touch to establish gift awareness, he opened his knitted vest and placed Tobazim's left hand over his own racing heart. 'Lower your defences.'

Tobazim did not hesitate. He felt Ardonyx's excitement pour directly into him as his heart kept time with Ardonyx's.

'Are you afraid, Tobazim?'

'Yes. If we fail, we'll both be dead before dawn. But I would rather die with you at my side tonight than live a lifetime under Kyredeon's rule.'

Ardonyx swallowed. Holding Tobazim's eyes, he placed his left hand over Tobazim's heart and lowered his own defences. 'I swear to be your shield when you are threatened.'

'And in return, I will shield you with my body and my gift,' Tobazim whispered, and he led Ardonyx through the complex maze of shields he had erected to defend his gift's source. He revealed his gift so that its nature would be evident to Ardonyx, letting him savour its flavour.

Ardonyx gasped and responded with an intimate glimpse of his own gift. It was completely alien to Tobazim's experience. He'd known that Ardonyx's gift wasn't martial like his choice-brother Learon's gift, but he did not recognise the nature of his power.

Before he could make sense of what he had seen, Ardonyx severed the connection and they both swayed, falling to their knees.

Tobazim had never felt so powerful, or so humbled.

GRAELEN SLIPPED INTO the infirmary, where a lamp burned low. Patients slept, but the saw-bones was still awake, making notes at his desk. He looked up, saw them both and went white as a sheet.

Graelen felt like laughing as Ceyne drew them into the bathing chamber, shot the bolt and hugged them both, then hugged them again.

'They told me you were dead, Grae.' With tears in his eyes, he cupped Valendia's cheek. 'And I thought you'd thrown yourself overboard. I blamed myself for not...' Overcome, he covered his face and wept.

Valendia hugged him, whispering soft words.

After a moment, he pulled away. 'Where were you, Dia? We searched the ship. Oriemn almost caused an incident with All-father Hueryx.'

'I went to see Sorne in the stronghold.'

'Enough of this.' Impatience drove Graelen. 'The causare has gift-infused Tobazim and me as a reward for saving her choice-son's life. Tobazim and Ardonyx are going to challenge Kyredeon tonight.'

Ceyne went pale. He felt behind him for the edge of the bath and sat down. 'It had to happen.'

Graelen nodded. 'This is my chance to serve an all-father I admire. Are you with us? If you come over, with your stature, others will be sure to follow.'

IN THE FOG, all Imoshen could see of Ardonyx's ship was the glow of the lanterns on the masts. She wondered whether Tobazim had reached him in time to form the shield-brother bond.

'Dead by dawn or triumphant!'

She spun around. 'Tancred?'

The geldr danced in front of her, watching her with a sly grin. Seeing that he had her attention, he performed a kick, leaping and pivoting light as a cat.

Signalling for silence, Imoshen led the geldr back to the stern rail of the rear-deck.

Had he been hiding in the fog, listening when Iraayel had returned?

'You should go to bed, Tancred,' Imoshen told him. Most of the time he was like a five–year-old child and, like a child, he often responded to a firm voice.

The geldr laughed and turned on one heel in mockery of the spring dances the men performed.

'They all dance for you. Clever Imoshen, cunning Imoshen.' Tancred waved a finger in front of her nose like a choice-mother admonishing a child. 'The lad whispers of love with the girl, while the one who would die for you faces death.'

Tancred knew about Ardonyx? Back in the Celestial City, the geldr had often been in her chambers, playing with Umaleni while Imoshen spoke with Egrayne or her devotee. She'd never told Egrayne about her secret bond-partner and, although her devotee knew about Ardonyx, Imoshen didn't think she'd discussed him with Frayvia in front of Tancred.

He must be thinking of Graelen or Tobazim, who she had gift-infused tonight. He'd mistaken that ceremony for something deeper, but he was so close...

If it was revealed that Ardonyx was her secret bond-partner it could cost him his life. Kyredeon might be dead by dawn, but there were other brothers who would kill Ardonyx to cripple her. Why, her own inner circle would be horrified if they knew she'd made the deep-bonding with one of the brotherhood men.

Which brought her back to the geldr. She studied him.

Falling to his knees, Tancred peeped up at her from between his fingers.

Would he remain silent?

Did it matter if he didn't? No one would believe him, after all; they all thought him mad.

The geldr lifted his head with a shaky laugh. 'Tancred lives another day.'

Imoshen shivered. She was the only raedan in the T'Enatuath.

But the geldr had just read her.

Tancred rocked his weight onto his heels and performed a backward shoulder roll before coming to his feet.

He gave a shallow obeisance. It was the bow of equals.

Startled, Imoshen hesitated. She not sure if she was dealing with the simple child or the sly geldr. Some people were opaque to her raedan skill – not that she let anyone know this – and Tancred was one of those.

She swallowed and reached out to the geldr.

'It hurts to touch the causare.' Tancred flinched. 'The causare has killed, and the shades she banished stole a little from her when she sent them into...' He shuddered. 'Tancred doesn't like that place. Afraid of it. One day, Tancred won't find the way back.'

'The higher plane,' Imoshen whispered. She hadn't realised Tancred could slip onto the empyrean plane. It was a wonder the predators hadn't hunted him down and devoured him. 'You poor thing. I can help. I can come and find you if you get lost there. All you have to do is let me link with you.'

He backed off. 'No, no, no.' The words stopped but his mouth kept working, eyes wide with fear.

'It's all right, Tancred. I won't force a link on you.'

But the geldr wouldn't listen. He scurried away, clambering over the rail and jumping to the lower rear-deck.

Talk of the empyrean plane reminded Imoshen of the risk Ardonyx took tonight. Her gaze was drawn back across to his ship, an insubstantial glow in the fog.

It was time to go to the bathing chamber and prepare. If Ardonyx needed her, she would help him.

But she must keep her identity hidden from Tobazim. He had accepted her gift-infusion because he had earned it, but the causare could not interfere with a brotherhood challenge.

Chapter Twenty-Four

TOBAZIM RAN LIGHTLY down the steps to the rear-deck, where he met Graelen coming out of the passage leading to the cabins.

'Ceyne is with us.' Graelen reported. He closed his eyes and concentrated, a slight frown puckering his brows. Tobazim realised he'd opened his empyrean sight to see them on the higher plane. 'You've formed the bond. It's deep and it's made you both much stronger. You'll make good brotherhood leaders.'

Tobazim glanced to Ardonyx, who nodded once. 'We want you for our hand-of-force.'

Graelen gestured to the mid-deck where the others were on watch. 'You have other gift-warriors.'

'We want you.'

'Your hand-of-force must be ready to die in your defence. I have Valendia to consider.'

'I'm not going to lead through fear and intimidation,' Tobazim said. 'Think about it.'

And they went down to the mid-deck, where the others joined them to congratulate Tobazim and Ardonyx. Only Haromyr hung back. He regarded Graelen with mistrust, and Tobazim knew the impetuous young gift-warrior had wanted to be hand-of-force.

'Wait here, I'll fetch the initiates and young adepts,' Ardonyx said.

This was where they would get most of their supporters from. At least Tobazim hoped so.

Ardonyx disappeared into the passage to the rear-deck

cabins and, after a few moments, the initiates and young adepts poured out. They'd come from their beds and still wore their sleeping wraps, or were dressed only in their breeches. They shivered in the chill, fog-laden air as they whispered amongst themselves. Some looked relieved, but more looked worried. Did they fear Kyredeon so much?

Ardonyx signalled for silence. 'Tobazim has something to tell you.'

'Ardonyx and I are shield-brothers,' he said. 'By dawn, Kyredeon will be dead and I will be all-father. I promise to lead our brotherhood with honour. When you give your vow to serve me, my vow to serve you will be equally binding.'

They murmured in approval.

'Are you with me?' Tobazim asked.

Ionnyn and the remainder of Chariode's decimated brotherhood crossed the deck, but there were only seven of them in all. The young adepts and initiates who had accompanied Tobazim and Ardonyx to the port also crossed the deck. But that still left a large number who were too fearful of Kyredeon to risk supporting him.

'I've only ever read about brotherhood challenges,' Athlyn admitted. He was nervous, yet determined. 'What do you want of us, Tobazim?'

'When the time comes, Kyredeon will try to draw on your strength to defeat us. Block your brotherhood link to him.'

Ardonyx put a hand on Tobazim's shoulder. 'Ready, shield-brother?'

'Ready.'

As Ardonyx climbed the steps to the rear-deck Tobazim watched him go with a mix of trepidation, fear and excitement.

When Ardonyx entered the passage to the captain's cabin, Tobazim tried not to think of all the things that could go wrong. Instead, he concentrated on mentally preparing himself.

Ardonyx was sure to sense the force of his gift through their link, just as he sensed the steady pulse of his shield-brother's power.

Tobazim drew a long, slow breath.

Leadership challenges were meant to take place in the privacy of the brotherhood's palace. Strange to think that his future would be decided on the deck of a ship just a few days before they left their homeland for ever.

At the other end of the ship, in the foredeck cabins, All-father Hueryx and his inner circle would be aware that something was happening.

Tobazim smiled grimly when he heard Kyredeon's raised voice. He was furious.

Ardonyx returned, moving swiftly down the steps to join Tobazim on the mid-deck.

First out the door was Kyredeon's hand-of-force, followed by the voice-of-reason. They both descended to the mid-deck and stalked towards Tobazim, radiating barely-contained fury.

Strangely enough, it was not Oriemn who confronted Tobazim first, but the voice-of-reason.

Farodytor's top lip lifted in a sneer. 'So this is who challenges my all-father's rule? An adept still wet behind the ears, stinking of female gift power. What have you been up to tonight? Unsanctioned trysting?'

This explanation had not occurred to Tobazim, and he laughed.

It unsettled Farodytor, who deliberately turned his back and returned to the ranks of the high-stature initiates who had come down to the mid-deck. Their gifts were on alert, and their bodies radiated energy.

Kyredeon took his time coming down the steps. He had dressed in breeches and boots, nothing more. His chest bore the scars of past battles, and he exuded power as he prowled towards them.

He was everything Tobazim was not, an all-father of many years' experience, empowered by a martial gift, unhampered by the limitations of conscience and honour. Why had Tobazim ever imagined he could beat Kyredeon?

Ardonyx leant close. 'Let me have the honour of trading insults on your behalf.'

Tobazim nodded, mouth too dry to speak.

Folding his arms, Tobazim spread his feet and projected a confidence he did not feel as he waited. This was all part of it: the baiting, the testing of resolve – it offered those supporters whose loyalty wavered a chance to make their final decisions.

And it could be very final.

'What is this?' Kyredeon asked his high-ranking adepts, gesturing to Tobazim. 'He is barely two years an adept, yet he thinks he can challenge an all-father. I'm insulted!'

'Challenge has been given and accepted by your voice-of-reason,' Ardonyx said. 'All that remains is to meet on the empyrean plane. Or are you afraid of what you will discover there?'

Kyredeon's eyes narrowed, the scars of long-ago challenges pale against the flush of anger staining his skin. 'You. You sweet-talked your way into my brotherhood and this is how you repay me?'

'I've served two all-fathers, but I believe the third will be the greatest,' Ardonyx said.

There was a murmur of approval.

Kyredeon laughed. 'I don't see any high-ranking adepts crossing the deck to support you and your shield-brother, sweet-tongue. What makes you think this pup can best me?'

'I have the best interests of the brotherhood at heart,' Tobazim said. 'I'll ban duels to the death. I'll ban forcing the young initiates to fight for the entertainment of the higher ranks. And I'll ban the usage of initiates by adepts unless they are willing to tryst.'

Kyredeon laughed. 'That will not win the high-ranking adepts to your side.'

'Maybe not. But it is fair.'

Kyredeon gave bark of laughter. It was clear what he

thought of 'fair.' Eyes on Tobazim, he waited to see if any initiates crossed the deck.

'I will serve an all-father who is fair,' Ceyne said and crossed the deck, followed closely by Deimosh, the gift-tutor. Both were from Kyredeon's inner circle, and both were indispensible to the smooth running of the brotherhood.

In a rush, other adepts joined Tobazim and Ardonyx, all mid-ranking.

This left a core of the most vicious gift-warriors in Oriemn's service, and high-ranking adepts whose stature depended on serving Kyredeon.

Deimosh slipped through the crowd until he stood at Tobazim's side. 'You're not a gift-warrior and neither is Ardonyx. How –'

'No,' Tobazim admitted. 'But I fought alongside my choice-brother Learon when we were dragged onto the higher plane by the shades of the dead we'd killed. I have some experience of the empyrean plane.'

Deimosh looked as if he'd hoped for more than this. 'As the challenged party, Kyredeon will impose form on the empyrean plane. He'll try to make you bleed. Any shedding of your physical essence will drain you. He'll try to prolong the battle and use his greater experience to hold his essence together while you lose power. If enough empyrean beasts are attracted to the battle, he will leave you at their mercy.'

Ardonyx nodded.

'What do you advise?' Tobazim asked.

'Try to get in and out, quickly,' Deimosh said. 'I sense you two are shield-brothers now.'

Tobazim nodded.

'Stay close,' Deimosh said. 'This will help you sustain your essence on the higher plane.'

Ceyne joined them. 'Kill his voice-of-reason first. It will weaken Kyredeon to lose his shield-brother. Then go after his hand-of-force. Who is your hand-of-force?'

'We don't have one yet,' Tobazim said. Learon should have been here beside him, tonight. He would have made the perfect hand-of-force; this was why Kyredeon had driven Tobazim's choice-brother to suicide.

'I offer myself,' Haromyr said.

'You're too inexperienced, lad,' Deimosh said. 'You'd be more of a liability than an asset.'

'I offer myself,' Ionnyn said.

Ceyne shook his head. 'It won't do. Both of Tobazim's seconds can't come from Chariode's brotherhood. It must be someone from our brotherhood, someone of high rank, with experience.' And he was looking at Graelen as he spoke.

The hard-faced adept folded his arms. 'There are others more worthy.'

'But not as deadly,' Ceyne countered. 'Grae, we need –'

Before he could finish, a single chime rang out. The pure note cut the air, cutting through all conversation.

'Enough preparation,' Kyredeon said.

'To win the bout, you must kill Kyredeon and both his seconds, then return and ring that chime,' Deimosh told Ardonyx. 'It is how we do it, in this brotherhood.'

'Stay near me,' Ardonyx whispered as they both stepped forward into the clear space between the two factions. 'I'll watch your back, you watch mine.'

Tobazim nodded. Even without looking, he could feel Ardonyx's presence at his side; could feel the way their gifts responded to each other.

Kyredeon and his voice-of-reason clasped arms, wrist to forearm, letting down their gift defences as they prepared for battle. Oriemn ripped off his shirt, throwing it on the deck and baring his forearms. He stepped in close, touching skin to skin, forming the triumvirate, strongest of the gift-working forms.

Tobazim and Ardonyx only had each other.

He could feel his gift straining to break free, engorged by the causare's power.

'With the greatest risk comes the greatest gain.' Ardonyx offered his arm.

Elbow to wrist, their hands met.

'Then let it be all!' Tobazim linked fingers and dropped his defences.

Ardonyx's gift welled up through him, empowering his own, tempering it with a different kind of strength.

The single chime rung out, severing their connection with the earthly plane.

IMOSHEN FELT THE tug on their link as her bond-partner segued to the empyrean plane. A glance to the bathing chamber door told her it was secure.

She could have closed down the link with Ardonyx and left him to do battle without her, but she had asked this of him. He deserved her support. And she gave it willingly, knowing that if he failed and died on the empyrean plane, then she would die too.

She must not fail, and she would not fail, because she would not follow the rules of engagement.

Imoshen was prepared to risk all for Ardonyx.

TOBAZIM STOOD IN a hall of mirrors. A blue-white light bathed him and his breath misted with each exhalation, although in truth, he had no body and no breath. The only substance he had was that which his will gave him.

He looked down and found he was dressed in an ornate robe, reminiscent of the fashion in the Celestial City during the Golden Age of the T'En. Loss pierced him as he mourned the T'Enatuath's home, with its grand palaces, manicured gardens and brilliant works of art.

There was no sign of Kyredeon, or Ardonyx for that matter. Why was his shield-brother not by his side?

Stay close, Deimosh had advised, and already they were apart.

Footsteps sounded behind him and he turned to see a young T'En girl approaching. He blinked and found himself looking at his own reflection.

Dismissing the child as a product of his mind, he crept down the corridor, seeing himself reflected endlessly. At the end of the passage, he opened a silver-plated door, only to find another mirrored hallway.

A cold chill settled on him as he realised that this was not a representation of one the Celestial City's palaces, as he had first assumed. This thing of silver and icy glass was an embodiment of the sculpture Kyredeon had made with Voice-of-Reason Farodytor: all silver and blown glass. Only those two knew what traps lay within its exquisite, tortured walls.

From a great distance, Tobazim heard running boots. The tinkling of falling glass echoed from metal walls. His heart raced.

He spun around, trying to make sense of endless reflections.

Oriemn appeared behind him, armed with two long-knives. Tobazim reached for his own knives, focusing his will and power. Bringing them up, he took a step back, tripped and fell backwards through a mirror. Shards of icy glass rained down around him. One dagger-like shard pierced his side. He felt the cold in the marrow of his bones and looked up, fully expecting to see the hand-of-force about to finish him. As Oriemn went to strike, Ardonyx approached from behind, knives raised.

The hand-of-force turned and the knives melted, reforming into a spear as he lunged.

Ardonyx ducked and ran, drawing Oriemn away.

Tobazim stumbled to his feet, pulled the glass shard from his side and tried to heal the wound. Here his body was a product of his mind. If he could concentrate... The wound closed more easily than he'd expected, thanks to the causare's gift-infusion.

He took off after Oriemn and Ardonyx, but as soon

as he turned the first corner, he knew he'd lost them. So many reflections. Yet, he could hear footfalls and harsh breathing.

And where were the all-father and his voice-of-reason in all this? Were they observing, testing the skill and power of their challengers?

Tobazim opened his senses to the shield-brother link he shared with Ardonyx, and turned one corner after another until he found him.

Oriemn had trapped Ardonyx in a dead end. The sea captain turned to face Oriemn, who lunged with the spear. Ardonyx sidestepped, but he was not fast enough; the tip of the spear gouged into his thigh.

The same little child Tobazim had seen earlier stepped out of a mirror behind Kyredeon's hand-of-force. She looked no more than six and, when she laughed, the sound stung like breaking glass.

Oriemn spun around.

Tobazim was close enough to see his confusion.

A vicious spasm of hatred crossed his face. He raised the spear and lunged at the girl, who caught the blade. The moment she touched it, she changed form, growing as she absorbed his power.

Was this a fiant, most dangerous of the empyrean plane's predators?

Tobazim could feel his own form wavering, as the creature sucked Oriemn's power from him. Truly, there were things on the higher plane that no one should have to face.

Edging past them, he slid his arm around Ardonyx's shoulder, and urged him to run. Each time his bad leg struck the ground, Ardonyx lurched with pain. He was leaving a trail of blood. Little drops of power that would lure the fiant after them.

Tobazim stopped, pressed Ardonyx's shoulders against a mirror and covered his thigh wound. Feeling Ardonyx's life force and power pulsing under his hand, he sealed the injury.

Ardonyx lifted his head, face free of pain. To Tobazim's horror, glistening hands reached through the mirror behind, closed around Ardonyx's chest and dragged him through the glass.

Furious, Tobazim plunged his hands into the glass, reaching for Ardonyx. This was the all-father's illusion, not his. But once before, when he and Learon were in danger, he'd been able to manipulate the higher plane.

Kyredeon struggled to keep him out of the mirror. He could taste the all-father's gift and his fury. The battle of wills cost them both dearly in power.

At last the mirror shattered, but there was no sign of Ardonyx. Tobazim stepped through to look for him. He opened his link and followed it until he came to the silver-plated door again. His own reflection appeared dull and distorted in the metal. The door shivered.

Tobazim had to concentrate to prevent his form wavering in sympathy.

The reflection hardened, reforming into Farodytor. As Kyredeon's voice-of-reason stepped through the door, the silver coated him in brilliant living armour, turning his face into a terrifying blank mask.

Farodytor's left hand whipped out and Tobazim pulled back, but not fast enough. Talons slashed across his face, slicing through his mouth and the tip of his nose. Blood blinded him and he stumbled, falling to the ground.

Farodytor's hand slashed out again.

This time, Tobazim was ready. He blocked with his knife, severing the silver talons. They fell to the floor, forming puddles of shining silver that were quickly absorbed by the higher plane.

Stunned, Farodytor backed off.

Tobazim sprang to his feet. He could sense Ardonyx was in trouble, and he ran towards the threat, turning corners until he found his shield-brother on his knees, head bowed. Kyredeon stood over him, holding a mirror like a blade, about to sever his head.

They were too far away.

Tobazim focused his gift on reforming the mirror, which turned into a sheet of silk in Kyredeon's hand. He dropped it in surprise and it settled over Ardonyx like a cloak.

Kyredeon looked shocked, then stepped through a mirror.

Tobazim hauled Ardonyx to his feet. They had to get out of here.

Reaching out, Tobazim tried to form a handle in the nearest mirror. It resisted as Kyredeon's will battled his. The easy energy of before was gone now. He'd used up the causare's gift-infusion and everything was an effort. Tobazim gritted his teeth as he focused and, finally, the handle formed.

He opened the door and stumbled onto a formless plain.

Ardonyx pressed his forehead to Tobazim's. Via their link, Tobazim saw the snow-covered ground of the free quarter park.

Raising his head, he saw they were in the park. Fanciful topiary trees wore mantles of winter snow. Tobazim's breath steamed and he felt the chill rise up through his feet.

Ardonyx drew him across the snowy park, towards a frozen pool. In the centre was a statue erected to honour the fallen. It was a massive winged horse made of white marble, rearing on its hind legs with its wings extended.

Tobazim glanced behind them, expecting to see the three-storey building where the sisterhoods had their trysting bowers. Instead, he saw Kyredeon and Farodytor's sculpture of the Celestial City realised on a vast scale. It loomed over them and from its balconies hung fingers of ice, or perhaps glass; he could not tell.

When they reached the edge of the pool, he and Ardonyx turned to face their enemies. The park was their creation. If Kyredeon and Farodytor wanted to attack them, they had to risk venturing into the park, which Tobazim and Ardonyx controlled.

A shape jumped down from the nearest balcony. Tobazim saw footprints appear in the snow as an indistinct form approached them. With a start he realised that it was Kyredeon, wearing armour made of mirrors. Farodytor dropped from a balcony and joined him. His silver armour reflected the white snow, making him hard to see.

On the higher plane, the T'En gifts sometimes revealed their owner's true essence. Both Kyredeon and Farodytor were the embodiment of slippery deceit. It made him wonder how he appeared to them.

A strange whistle cut the air. Before Tobazim could comprehend the threat, a spear of shining glass ploughed into the snow next to his feet. Then there was a chorus of mournful whistles as the air was filled with a hail of icicles.

Ardonyx produced a shield and Tobazim created one for himself, raising it in defence. His arm and shoulder shook with the repeated impact of the ice spears.

With every strike, Tobazim felt his life force flicker and it was harder to regroup his essence under the assault. Ardonyx gave a grunt of pain and Tobazim knew he also suffered. A spike skidded over Tobazim's shield, narrowly missing his head.

Ardonyx staggered. A silver icicle pierced his thigh; his leg gave out and he went down on one knee.

SHOULDER TO SHOULDER with Ionnyn and Haromyr, Graelen formed part of the ceremonial guard while Tobazim and Ardonyx battled on the empyrean plane.

'How are they doing?' Haromyr whispered.

Graelen opened his empyrean sight to study the bodies of the challengers. No life force pulsed in Oriemn. 'Oriemn's dead.'

'Tobazim's face is bleeding.'

Twice he'd seen wounds appear on Tobazim and Ardonyx, and twice they'd healed. But the new wound on Tobazim's face dripped blood; it would be leaking power on the higher plane. A wound suddenly opened on Ardonyx's thigh.

Frustration gripped Graelen. He should be on the empyrean plane fighting by their side. He was a coward to let his love for Valendia prevent him from protecting Tobazim and Ardonyx.

'Watch out!' Valendia called.

He looked up to see her on the rear-deck, trying to stop one of Oriemn's supporters, who was about to throw a knife at Tobazim and Ardonyx. Graelen could not believe it. The challenge for leadership was sacrosanct.

Graelen darted around the challengers, making for the steps and the knot of gift-warriors.

As if this was a signal, the deck erupted in battle. Kyredeon's supporters tried to reach Tobazim and Ardonyx's vulnerable bodies, and the rebel brothers fought back.

By the time Graelen reached the deck, it was too late. The gift-warrior let Valendia fall to her knees on the planks, clutching her belly as blood leaked between her fingers.

'Grae...' She raised frightened eyes to him.

The five gift-warriors laughed.

He went utterly still and silent inside. He did not remember drawing his knives, did not remember attacking. But suddenly he was amongst them. He stabbed one, gutted another and caught a third around the chest, using him as a shield and allowing his companion to stab him.

Three rapid blows struck Graelen's back, one high, one low and one to the side. He dropped the dead warrior, drove the next man over the balcony and kicked the legs out from under the last one, pinning him to the deck with a knife through his chest.

Then he crawled to Valendia, pulling her into his arms. He would not let her die. His back and side felt hot and sticky. Below, on the mid-deck, he could hear the battle raging on.

IN THE FOREDECK cabins, Aravelle huddled on her bedroll with her little sister in her arms as Kyredeon's brotherhood erupted in violence.

'This is why we should be grateful for our all-father,' Charsoria said, and her inner circle nodded. A single lamp burned, illuminating their faces. 'Hueryx maintains the peace. He keeps the arrogant young warriors in line. He protects us Malaunje from the T'En warriors of our own brotherhood.'

After a few more moments, the shouts grew fainter and the screams eased.

'Sounds like it's nearly over,' old Redravia whispered.

'But not before they've torn the heart out of their own brotherhood,' Charsoria said.

Aravelle rubbed Itania's back. She was grateful for All-father Hueryx, and grateful her brothers were protected by the sisterhoods.

Chapter Twenty-Five

As TOBAZIM SLID an arm under Ardonyx and hauled him upright, a shaft of silvery winter sunlight illuminated the frozen pool and statue. He'd heard that only the most powerful of T'En could produce sunlight on the empyrean plane. But there was no time to wonder as he felt for the broad stone seat around the rim of the pool. They climbed onto it and edged backwards, retreating across the frozen pool's surface.

Farodytor moved around one side of the fountain and Kyredeon the other. He could not keep his eye on both of them.

Ardonyx's shield had evaporated and the icicle protruded grotesquely from his thigh. With painful clarity, Tobazim understood they were in danger of bleeding to death here, shedding gift force on this plane while their life force seeped from their torn bodies on the earthly plane.

It could not end like this.

Tobazim felt the winged-horse statue at their backs. They could go no further.

As Farodytor stepped up onto the fountain's rim, a long silver scythe appeared in his hands. The scythe cut the air, whistling towards Ardonyx. There was a screech as the scythe connected with the horse's white marble wing. That wing had not been lowered before. Tobazim had not moved it; it must have been Ardonyx.

He smelled burning metal.

Kyredeon took on more solid form as he stepped onto the seat around the rim of the pool. His lips pursed in a soundless whistle. Glass icicles tinkled on the balcony behind him. One snapped off with a musical chink and speared straight for Tobazim's heart. The horse's wing swept down between them, shielding him.

Since Ardonyx was using the horse to protect them, Tobazim lowered Ardonyx and took the opportunity to try to heal him. Ardonyx gasped and grasped his injured leg. Tobazim knelt beside him, closed his hands on the ice spear and dissolved it, then covered the wound and sealed it shut. But it took everything he had. Exhausted, he huddled on the statue's plinth next to Ardonyx.

Kyredeon and Farodytor stepped off the broad stone rim and onto the ice, closing in for the kill.

Ardonyx grabbed Tobazim, and shielded him with his body. Looking up, Tobazim saw the winged horse rear, its hooves pawing the air.

As it landed, those hooves struck sparks from the ice, and the ice screamed like an injured animal. The marble horse reared and struck the ice again. Tobazim could see dozens of crazed cracks racing across the pool's frozen surface. Kyredeon tried to spring back, but the ice parted under him. The all-father writhed, slipping ever deeper with each desperate attempt to free himself.

Tobazim glanced to Farodytor, who was in the same predicament. His body steamed as his gift was leached from him, stolen by the greedy higher plane.

Chest-deep now, the glass surface of Kyredeon's body grew opaque, his struggles weakening with every heartbeat.

Tobazim came to his knees to watch the empyrean plane devour them. The ice closed over Kyredeon's body. Farodytor was also trapped below a sheet of ice. He beat at the underside of the frozen pool, his blows growing weaker and weaker. The end was inevitable. Even as Tobazim watched, Farodytor's form lost solidity as his life essence and gift were absorbed into the higher plane.

Tobazim glanced back to Kyredeon, but he could hardly make out where the ice ended and Kyredeon began; there was only a faint man-shaped form, which even now dissipated.

They had won.

His head reeled.

Looking up, he saw the statue had resumed its usual pose of a rearing horse, wings outstretched. The shaft of sunlight flickered as several dark, broad-winged creatures circled, coming lower with each spiral. Harrowravens... The predators had found them.

They had to flee.

Tobazim lifted his hand to his face and ran his fingers over the open cuts, urging them to heal. It took such effort that he knew he would be scarred for life. Very well. He was content to wear those scars as a tribute to this night.

Ardonyx offered his hand. Tobazim took it and tried to leave the empyrean plane, but he was too exhausted. Then he felt Ardonyx latch onto something and they returned to the ship.

IMOSHEN RETURNED TO the earthly plane, shuddering with the effort, her mind a confusion of images: death, ice and silver. At least she had managed to disguise her intervention. Tobazim would assume that Ardonyx had been controlling the winged-horse.

When she stood, her right leg gave out and the thigh muscle ached around a phantom wound. But Ardonyx was safe and, unless something went drastically wrong between now and tomorrow, her choice-son's future was secure.

But she felt no triumph, only relief.

It would be interesting to see how the two non-martially-gifted men chose to run the brotherhood. Could they hold onto the leadership against the threat of the more aggressive gift-warriors in their own brotherhood? Could a peaceful brotherhood survive the other brotherhoods?

Only time would tell, but it gave her hope for the future of her people.

She had drained and killed Oriemn, mimicking a fiant, one of the most feared empyrean predators. Now nausea filled her, as her gift processed the nature of the man and his gift.

Revolted, Imoshen staggered to the privy and emptied her stomach, tears streaming down her cheeks.

TOBAZIM RETURNED TO his body with a lurch that made his heart race and the gorge rise in his throat. He swayed and had to remember to breathe. He would not disgrace himself and empty his stomach before the whole brotherhood.

He fought the nausea.

Ardonyx staggered as his leg was still weak. Tobazim steadied him, and the pair of them almost fell to their knees on the planks.

Tobazim was disoriented, but the thing that hurt most was the three slashes across his face. They burned in the still, damp air. The fog was so heavy he could barely see his hand in front of his face.

Perhaps this was why their supporters weren't cheering.

He could not believe they'd survived. Ardonyx's eyes held the same mixture of amazement and relief.

'Trust you.' Ardonyx gestured to his face. 'Your challenge scars will be the envy of the other all-fathers.'

Tobazim laughed and it stung, bringing tears to his eyes.

They were free of Kyredeon.

He hugged Ardonyx, fighting the urge to weep with relief.

'Sound the end of the challenge,' Ardonyx urged.

It was only as he released Ardonyx and set off for the chime that Tobazim realised how exhausted he was. Everything looked flat and dull. Sounds echoed in his head, and his gift...

His gift was drained, leaving him with an empty ache; an absence that begged to be filled.

He felt disgustingly vulnerable.

Until his gift revived, he was helpless. All a mid-rank initiate had to do to steal the leadership was strike him down and claim victory.

No one must suspect.

Bluff was all he had left.

His knees wavered as he headed over to sound the chime. The deck seemed to rise and fall with each step.

His foot caught on something and he tripped, falling on a body. The man groaned.

'Eryx?'

The other's eyes flickered open. 'You won? You're safe?'

'What happened?'

'One of Oriemn's men went to throw a knife at you during the challenge. Valendia tried to stop him and Graelen went to her aid. Kyredeon's people attacked us, but we held them off.'

Now that he was on his hands and knees, Tobazim could see other bodies in the mist. Horror gripped him. Was everyone dead? He felt Ardonyx's shock as he made the same discovery.

Tobazim staggered to his feet, picked his way through the bodies and, lifting impossibly heavy arms, struck the chime. A single clear note sliced the air, signifying the end of the leadership challenge.

It should have been a moment of triumph. The cheering should have rung out from the ship, letting all the other brotherhoods know that there was a new all-father.

Instead he heard moaning and pleas for help.

'Tobazim?'

'Here, Ardonyx. Can you find Ceyne? We're going to need him.'

'I'm here. And I'm glad it's your voices I'm hearing. I sent Haromyr to get my bag.'

Other voices spoke up now, as the scholarly initiates and adepts gravitated towards Tobazim. A large figure loomed out of the mist and, for a moment, Tobazim almost thought it was his choice-brother Learon.

'Ionnyn!' He caught the sailor and hugged him.

The warrior bled from a number of small wounds, but he was on his feet and able to function.

'Find all those who can still stand,' Tobazim told him. 'Help Ceyne treat the wounded.'

He nodded and moved off, taking the others with him. Ardonyx reached Tobazim, limping through the fog. Tobazim swung his arm around Ardonyx's shoulders and together they made their way across the deck to the bodies of the old brotherhood leaders and the inner circle. Oriemn, Farodytor and Kyredeon lay together.

Tobazim knelt to study them. A sheen of white hoar frost covered all three. Oriemn had shrunk and curled in on himself until he was no bigger than a child, his gift and life force sucked from him by that empyrean predator. When Tobazim touched him, he crumbled to dust.

Kyredeon and Farodytor were frozen solid. From their contorted poses, it was clear that they had fought to the very end. At his touch, they shattered and melted clean away.

The rest of the inner circle lay nearby; they had been drained while trying to sustain their all-father and his seconds. Their bodies were cold and lifeless, but had not been devoured by the higher plane.

'They should be honoured with a proper burial, but we have no crypts and we cannot burn them,' Ardonyx said. 'Their bodies will have to be weighted and dropped into the sea.'

Satisfied that none of Kyredeon's inner circle presented a threat, Tobazim concentrated on his supporters. He and Ardonyx went from group to group, speaking to the injured as they waited for treatment, and calling for help if their wounds were life-threatening. Meanwhile, Ionnyn and the others collected the dead and laid them out, dividing them into his supporters and Kyredeon's supporters.

So many dead.

Tears burned Tobazim's eyes. 'If Kyredeon were alive, I would kill him all over again. He's decimated our brotherhood. How can an all-father do that to his own brotherhood?'

Ardonyx hugged him. 'You'll restore us.'

He nodded and struggled to compose himself.

They moved on, coming across Ceyne, who was packing and binding a gift-warrior's wound. When he tied off the bandage and came to his feet, he swayed.

Tobazim steadied him. 'Are you all right?'

'Kyredeon's supporters came for Deimosh and me,' Ceyne said. 'He was always a vindictive fiant!'

What would the brotherhood do without a gift-tutor? 'Is Deimosh –'

'Alive. He took a blow to his head, but he'll recover. What do you want me to do with Kyredeon's injured supporters?'

Tobazim glanced to Ardonyx.

'They attacked us, breaking the sacred trust of the challenge, but it could be argued they were only following Kyredeon's orders,' Ardonyx said, fulfilling his role as the voice-of-reason.

'In my brotherhood there is no place for men who follow those kind of orders,' Tobazim said. He wanted to cut out the rot and throw them overboard, but something Ceyne had said came back to him. 'This brotherhood has been ruled by fear for over forty years. I'm not going to be that kind of all-father. Treat them. Give them a second chance.'

Ceyne surprised him by dropping to his knees and kissing the sixth finger of his left hand. 'All-father.'

Touched and disconcerted, Tobazim drew him to his feet.

As Ceyne went back to work, Haromyr came out of the fog and threw his arms around Tobazim and Ardonyx.

Tobazim pulled back. 'Do you know where Athlyn is?'

'I think he went to help Graelen.' Haromyr grimaced. 'It was a close thing. Without Valendia's warning...' He shook his head, suddenly sober.

'Valendia...' Tobazim crossed the deck at a clumsy half run; everything ached. Ardonyx limped along behind him.

Up on the rear-deck, he found Athlyn crouched next to Graelen, who held Valendia in his arms. Blood covered her stomach and thighs. Her lips were colourless and she was barely breathing.

Tobazim dropped to his knees beside them.

'You're here.' Pale and shaken, Athlyn was relieved to see them. 'I've been trying to help him. He's holding onto her life force with his gift.'

Tobazim reached out to Graelen, but he had no power left to give; all he could offer was the comfort of touch.

The man who had been Kyredeon's greatest assassin opened his eyes. 'Send for the causare. She promised. She'll bring the healer.'

'I'll go,' Ardonyx offered, slipping away.

Tobazim watched Valendia, willing her to hold on.

EXHAUSTED, IMOSHEN WAS about to climb into her bunk when Kiane came to her.

'Ardonyx is here to speak with you,' she whispered. 'I don't know why these brothers think they can come to you at all hours of the night.'

'If I'm their causare, they can call on me whenever they need me.' Her hand-of-force still saw the T'En divided into brotherhood and sisterhood.

As Imoshen threw on her cloak and boots, she projected a calm she did not feel. She hurried out to the deck. 'Ardonyx?'

'Causare.' Ardonyx gave the obeisance of supplication. He was pale and he moved with a limp.

'Valendia needs a healer, desperately. Can you –'

'Of course.' Imoshen gestured to Kiane. 'Run down to All-mother Reoden. Tell her I need her help urgently.'

As soon as Kiane left them, Imoshen reached out to Ardonyx. Trusting to the fog to hide them, she cupped his face in her hands, kissing his bruised cheek and split lip. She could tell both of them had drained their gifts, but it was a relief to hold him.

'What happened?'

'Kyredeon's supporters broke the sanctity of the challenge.' Ardonyx's voice caught and she could feel his whole body trembling. 'Half the brotherhood is dead. It was carnage.'

Imoshen's mind raced. 'If the T'En contingent of your brotherhood has been halved, it throws out the balance between the all-fathers. Dretsun is already too cocky and Saskeyne burns with ambition.' Her mind raced. 'You sheltered All-father Tamaron's people on your ship?'

'Yes. Kyredeon cursed us for burdening him with more mouths to feed.'

'Tamaron is dead. You've housed his people, fed them and protected them. They're yours. Have Tobazim take their vows of fealty.'

'Imoshen...' He shook his head, a rueful smile on his lips. Her heart turned over. She loved him so much, yet she hardly ever saw him. 'This is internal brotherhood business. The decision should go to an all-father-council.'

'So they can argue over who gets the survivors and stir up dissent?' She shook her head. 'If Tobazim swears them in, your brotherhood remains in the ranks of the great brotherhoods. The balance is preserved. Paragian and Hueryx are not fools. They'll see the benefit of keeping Dretsun's wings clipped.' She tilted her head. 'That's Ree's voice. Come on.'

By the time they reached the brotherhood ship, the fog was beginning to lift. When Imoshen climbed aboard, she'd thought she was prepared, but the sight of Malaunje mopping the blood from the deck and the T'En bodies laid out in rows still shocked her.

Kiane shook her head. 'This is why you needed an escort.'

Her hand-of-force had insisted that she and two gift-warriors accompany the causare and the healer. They followed Reoden and Ardonyx up the steps to the rear-deck, where Tobazim knelt next to Graelen and his devotee, holding a blood-soaked cloth over Valendia's wound. A young initiate supported Graelen.

The brotherhood's saw-bones met Imoshen and the healer. 'Tobazim's gift is drained from the challenge.' He gestured to the young initiate. 'Athlyn's been sustaining Graelen and Valendia. Grae can't hold on much longer. The moment he dies, Valendia will die with him unless a powerful T'En can impose their gift on her.'

'And she's pregnant?' Reoden asked.

'Not for long, with a wound like that.'

'We'll see.' Reoden bustled forward. 'I'll need someone to sustain Grae.'

'Athlyn's already doing it,' Ceyne said. 'We can't risk changing over.'

Imoshen knelt next to Tobazim. There was nothing she could do. Reoden rubbed her hands together; focusing her gift, she nodded to Tobazim. 'Take the cloth away.'

As he did, he told Valendia. 'Don't leave us, you hear me?'

Imoshen opened up her empyrean sight. Despite Athlyn's best efforts, Imoshen could see Graelen slipping away. 'Are you nearly ready, Ree? He won't last much longer.'

'Nearly. I just need to –'

Too late. Imoshen saw Graelen's life force flicker and fade. As the breath left his body, Valendia's back arched.

Reoden swore. 'She'll tear the wound open.'

Athlyn threw himself across her upper body. Between them, he and Reoden restrained the girl until the spasms passed.

Then she lay still.

'Dia?' Athlyn clasped her hand to his chest and sobbed.

Ceyne dropped to his knees weeping. Tobazim sank his head into his hands and Ardonyx slid an arm around his shoulders.

Imoshen looked up to see about a dozen T'En watching them, some weeping, others beyond tears.

Reoden felt Valendia's throat. 'Wait...'

The silence stretched.

'She lives.'

'How is that possible?' Tobazim whispered, then looked to Reoden. 'Did you imprint your gift on her?'

'No,' Reoden said. 'But...' She looked to Imoshen, who shook her head. Her gaze went to Athlyn.

'Me?'

'You.'

'Athlyn?' Tobazim shook his head.

'He linked with Graelen to sustain him, and when Grae died the link went through to Valendia.'

Athlyn looked stunned.

'Eryx, help Athlyn carry Valendia into the infirmary,' Ceyne said. He caught the young initiate's arm. 'You'll need to stay near her, lad. Skin on skin, until she's stable.'

He nodded and, between them, they carried Valendia inside.

Ceyne closed Graelen's eyes. 'Ah, lad...' Tears slid down his cheeks.

'He died in defence of the brotherhood,' Haromyr said.

'He died because Kyredeon was bloody-minded,' Ceyne ground out. 'No one will mourn the all-father's passing.'

Tobazim said nothing as he helped straighten Graelen's limbs.

Reoden stood, swayed, then collapsed. Imoshen tried to support her.

Ardonyx came to her aid. 'What's wrong?'

'She's drained her gift to save Valendia and the baby,' Imoshen said. She brushed Reoden's hair from her face and kissed her cheek. 'Typical Ree.'

'We'll look after her.' Kiane directed the two gift-warriors to take Reoden from Ardonyx and carry her down to the mid-deck.

Ardonyx followed and told his sailors to set up the sling to lower the unconscious healer into the rowboat.

'If there is ever anything I can do...' Tobazim said to Imoshen, bowing low in obeisance.

Her gift surged and she read him. She'd first read him

when she'd gift-infused him. He was still pure of heart, but his gift was different now. Of course, he'd formed the shield-brother bond with Ardonyx.

A spasm of jealousy ripped through her. The bond of shield-brothers was almost as profound as the deep-bonding she shared with Ardonyx. From now on, Ardonyx's life would be entwined with Tobazim's. They would spend every day together, while she...

She gave herself a mental shake. She'd known this was necessary if they were to win the brotherhood. Tobazim would make a good all-father, and he would take her choice-son into his brotherhood.

'Imoshen?' Tobazim was concerned.

She shook her head as Ardonyx joined them, going to Tobazim's side.

He could never stand at her side, not unless she eradicated the brotherhood-sisterhood divide. But how could she overcome a distrust that went back beyond recorded history? It always came back to this...

'Imoshen?' Ardonyx sensed her distress.

Before Imoshen could speak, Gift-tutor Deimosh came over to Tobazim. 'Forgive the interruption, all-father, but those who killed their own brothers this night fear being dragged onto the higher plane.'

'You're busy. I should go,' Imoshen said and slipped away.

Ardonyx escorted her to the mid-deck.

'He's a good man,' she said.

'He's also smart. We'll have to be careful, or he'll realise what you and I share. He once likened the deep-bonding to betraying the brotherhood, and now that he's the all-father, his instinct will be to protect the brotherhood at all cost.'

Chapter Twenty-Six

THE MORE JARAILE observed her tired army, the more she worried they would crumple when confronted with Eskarnor's forces.

Her army would reach port by dusk tomorrow night. They'd had little rest, eaten cold meals, and were wary of Sorne. They'd been uneasy ever since the T'En warriors had killed Baron Ikor in her defence. It didn't matter that Sorne had sent the three T'En warriors away. She'd seen the looks they cast him and heard them muttering about half-bloods belonging with their own kind. Baron Ramonal took every opportunity to lecture her.

Fools, didn't they realise she needed him to plan the attack? How Eskarnor would laugh, if he knew.

And something the baron had once said came back to her.

She edged her tired mount closer to Sorne. 'I've been thinking. It was a mistake bringing you along. I should send you back to the Wyrds.'

She saw his face grow guarded, and realised she'd phrased this badly.

'As a ploy. You said we need to convince Eskarnor to send his army into a trap. Now that Charald is in his dotage, Eskarnor believes you're the only man in Chalcedonia who can outwit him on the battlefield. He thinks the rest are fools. If he hears I've sent you into exile, he'll be much more likely to believe my army is retreating and fall for the pincer move you showed me.'

'Jaraile...' A slow smile split Sorne's face.

It made her stomach feel funny.

'Do it,' Sorne urged. 'Banish me tonight, in front of all your barons and captains. I'll ride off as if I'm heading for Shifting-sands Bay, then double back and ride for port, slip in and seek out Kerminzto. I'll tell him what you're planning. He can slip out of port to meet you and you can claim the pair of you came up with the battle strategy together. Ramanol and the rest are more likely to accept the plan if they think I had nothing to do with it.'

'You don't mind?'

He shrugged. 'Give Aingeru command of your centre. It will infuriate Eskarnor and entice his men to follow them when they retreat.'

She nodded.

'I ask only one thing. I want to be in the middle of the front ranks, disguised as a common man-at-arms. I want to judge when the centre should crumple and signal Aingeru.'

'You could be killed.'

'That's always true in battle.' He laughed softly. 'But I plan to live.'

They rode on in silence for a while.

'The shift happened the moment Graelen killed Baron Ikor,' Sorne said. 'Before that, they didn't like me, but they tolerated me.'

'Yes. I'm sorry.'

He shrugged again.

'You could use me as bait,' she suggested. 'Eskarnor needs me to legitimise his claim to the throne. If I were in the centre –'

'Not on your life, Jaraile.'

If she was honest, she felt relieved.

'Although we may be able to use you to raise the stakes, so he fully commits his men.'

'Wouldn't he fully commit them?'

'Charald would hold men in reserve and send them to where his lines faltered.'

That evening, Jaraile banished Sorne, and he rode out of the camp to the jeers and taunts of her men-at-arms. It made her face burn with shame, but she knew she'd done the right thing when Baron Ramanol congratulated her on 'getting rid of that arrogant half-blood.'

Four years of marriage to King Charald had taught her to hide her true feelings. She smiled sweetly and nodded.

ARAVELLE WATCHED THE healer's ship, hoping to spot her brothers. Earlier, she'd seen Ronnyn set off for the isle of ruins with the sisterhood leaders, but her little brothers might come out on deck. Meanwhile, Saskar leaned against the rail, facing towards the mast.

'So this new all-father, Tobazim, sent his voice-of-reason to invite us to his cabin tonight, to renew the vow Kyredeon made, giving us safe passage on this ship.' Saskar had a habit of speaking about the brotherhood leadership as if he was one of them. Since he accompanied them to all-council meetings, it was almost as if he was. 'Hueryx doesn't know what to make of Tobazim. How could such a young adept win the brotherhood from Kyredeon? Not that we aren't relieved. Anyone would be better than Kyredeon. The causare has called an all-council for later this afternoon. She'll have him give his covenant vow then. But what our all-father wants to know is why the causare came to this ship after the challenge last night.'

'She was here?'

Saskar nodded. 'Along with the sisterhood healer. They were spotted leaving when the fog started to lift.'

'Lots of warriors were injured. The healer –'

'Her gift is not all-powerful. We have to petition her to heal one of our people. And if she does, it makes our all-father beholden to her. If Imoshen and the healer came aboard in answer to Tobazim's petition, then he must be beholden to her. And no all-father wants to start his leadership beholden to two of the most powerful sisterhood leaders.'

'Perhaps he thinks it's worth it, to save his brothers' lives?'

'And perhaps he cheated.'

Aravelle was shocked.

Saskar laughed.

She blushed and turned away. A boat was leaving the *Perseverance*. 'Are you sure the all-council meeting is later?'

'Why?'

She pointed. 'Isn't that All-father Dretsun and his two seconds rowing towards the island?'

'Yes, but –'

'The causare, the healer and their seconds are on the island. I saw them row over with some others a little while ago.'

Saskar cursed softly. 'Come on.'

He darted over to Hand-of-force Reyne, and by the time Aravelle reached the all-father's cabin, the three brotherhood leaders had stripped down to their breeches, to don their torcs of office and formal brocade robes.

Reyne knelt, releasing his long hair. 'Do something formal. Be quick, Saskar.'

The voice-of-reason followed suit. Saskar indicated that Aravelle was to do Dragomyr's hair, while he did Reyne's. She mimicked Saskar, as he plaited and pinned with speed and precision.

'See, there is an advantage to short hair,' Hueryx said, binding his back in a simple knot at the base of his skull.

'You look like a barbarian Mieren,' Dragomyr said.

Aravelle gave his hair a sharp tug.

'Ow... take care, clumsy girl.'

She apologised, but Hueryx knew she didn't mean it. He caught her eye, a smile tugging at his lips. It infuriated her; she hated him.

He laughed, selected a silver skull cap and settled it on his head. 'How's that? Will I pass?'

Aravelle finished plaiting Dragomyr's hair and came over to study the all-father. The skull cap looked severe, but strangely enough... 'It suits you. It emphasises your cheekbones.'

Hueryx blinked.

Reyne laughed. 'A compliment!'

'The best kind.' Hueryx's forehead crinkled, reminding her of Ronnyn. 'Because it was given freely, by one who does not like me.'

Fearing she would get a clip around the ear, Aravelle backed up a step. But the all-father was not Charsoria.

Hueryx turned to the others, radiating energy. 'Ready to confront the causare and this new all-father?'

As the three of them walked out, Aravelle felt a wave of male gift roll off them, full of aggression.

She wondered what the causare had been doing on this ship after the challenge, and what would happen to All-father Tobazim, if it turned out he had cheated to win the brotherhood.

IMOSHEN SMILED AS the two lads ran on ahead. They'd come back to the island to view the T'En ruin and hear what the historians had deduced. Sketches had been made of the frescoes and saved for posterity. Imoshen's sisterhood historian had a different theory about the ruin's origin from Reoden's, and the two were arguing spiritedly, while Scholar Igotzon looked on.

Now that they'd seen the ruins and heard the theories, they were going to have a picnic, debate alternate views and hear a poem composed to commemorate the discovery.

The party headed through the trees towards the clearing, where Iraayel and Saffazi were setting up the meal. It was Iraayel's last day with the sisterhood. Later this afternoon, Imoshen would declare him dead to her and he would be given into his brotherhood, but she would never turn her back on her choice-son.

Before that meeting, she needed to call an all-mother-council. They could not afford the divide between brotherhood and sisterhood. It was time to amend the covenant vow, time to foster better relations with the brotherhoods.

Ronnyn and Sardeon darted between the trees.

Reoden leant closer to Imoshen. 'I swear Sar is more like a normal boy every day. I'm hopeful his gift will finally manifest and he will begin to grow again. If not, Ronnyn is very protective of his little brothers. I'm sure he will stand by Sar anyway.'

'Does he know the truth about Sardeon?'

'No. I've left it up to Sar to tell him.'

Behind them, Imoshen could hear their seconds discussing the passing of Kyredeon and what it would mean for the balance of power between the brotherhoods.

'Sar told me he'd like to be a scholar,' Imoshen said. 'He's amazingly well-read.'

'That's what happens when you spend four years in seclusion.'

'You said his gift was just starting to manifest before...' Imoshen did not want to mention the day Reoden's daughter died. 'Did you get a hint of its nature?'

'No...' Reoden paused. 'What are those two up to?'

Both lads had stopped at the edge of the clearing.

Imoshen and Reoden came up to stand behind them, only to find Dretsun and his two seconds confronting Iraayel and Saffazi. The seventeen-year-olds were unarmed and, on Imoshen's arrival, they edged around to join her, never turning their backs on the brotherhood leaders.

'What are you doing here, all-father?' Imoshen stepped into the clearing, placing herself between Dretsun and her companions. Autumn leaves swirled down, carried on an errant breeze. Her gift reacted to the acrid tang of aggressive male power.

'You called an all-council,' Dretsun said.

'For later.' Imoshen's voice hardened. Had Dretsun brought more warriors to flank her party? She glanced over her shoulder to see Kiane and Cerafeoni slip quietly away. 'I ask again. Why are you here?'

'There is a rumour that All-father Tamaron will not be coming into exile. I want to know what's happening to the remains of his brotherhood.'

'That's brotherhood business. The causare doesn't interfere in the internal running of the brotherhoods.'

'Yet you and the healer were on the *Victorious* last night.' Dretsun's eyes gleamed with triumph and Imoshen felt his gift surge. 'All-father Tamaron's survivors have been given shelter there and Kyredeon's brotherhood has new leadership.'

'It wasn't brotherhood business that took us to the *Victorious*,' Imoshen said. Behind the belligerent all-father and his seconds, she saw her hand-of-force hurrying down the path and raised her voice. 'What is it, Kiane?'

'The rest of the all-fathers are on their way here with their seconds, and Cerafeoni is escorting the all-mothers up from the beach.'

'It seems we are about to hold the all-council here,' Imoshen said.

'You haven't answered my question, all-mother,' Dretsun said.

'Since this is now an all-council, you'll address me as *Causare* Imoshen,' she corrected.

Just then the all-mothers and their seconds arrived. As they took up their places on Imoshen's side of the clearing, she beckoned Iraayel and Saffazi. 'Take the lads and the historians into the trees. Stay within hearing distance, but keep Igotzon out of sight. If the brotherhood leaders see a Mieren near the all-council, they'll take it as an insult.'

'Wait,' Egrayne said. 'Since we are all gathered here, Imoshen, you can hand Iraayel over to the new all-father. I'll prepare him.'

Saffazi made a sound of pain in her throat.

'You knew this day would come, choice-daughter.' Egrayne's voice was cold and hard. 'Don't shame me. Do as the causare told you and stay back.'

Imoshen's heart raced and she drew a deep breath. At seventeen, Iraayel was no longer a child; his gift could protect him. As Egrayne said, she'd always known this day would come, and Tobazim's brotherhood was the best possible option for Iraayel. But that didn't stop the pain.

Before she led Iraayel away, Egrayne added, 'While I'm preparing him, you can take the new all-father's covenant vow.'

Imoshen found the idea of forcing a gift-empowered vow on Tobazim repugnant. The covenant vow and the way it took their children from them was the core reason the brotherhoods feared and resented the sisterhoods. The all-fathers hated knowing the vow gave the all-mothers the ability to reach into their gifts and cripple them.

As long as one group had power over another, the T'Enatuath could never be united.

And she believed removing the T'En children from the brotherhoods only exacerbated their violent nature. After her daughter had been born, she had seen how being around small T'En children had a calming effect on the male gift.

Last night, Kyredeon had not counted the cost to his brotherhood. This had convinced her, while individual men might be ready, the brotherhoods as a whole were not ready for the responsibility of rearing rare T'En children.

They had to earn that right.

For a heartbeat, she toyed with the idea of amending the vow, but the other all-mothers would be horrified. They were products of the Celestial City, and weren't ready for change.

Once they sailed into exile, her people would be forced to adapt to survive, and those brotherhood and sisterhood leaders who couldn't adapt would be replaced.

As the rest of the all-fathers entered the clearing, more autumn leaves drifted down. It pleased Imoshen to see Ardonyx take his place on the all-council. He had been known as 'Captain Ardonyx the explorer,' but no one else still lived who knew that he was also 'Rutz the playwright.' Back in the Celestial City, the T'En had flocked to see his plays, which exposed the absurdities and flaws of their society. This was how Imoshen had first realised that someone else questioned the very basis of the T'Enatuath. Not that everyone had understood Rutz's message.

The T'En whispered that Rutz's gift was not just that of a word-smith, that he had the rare ability to imbue words with power to sway the listener.

When Imoshen had asked Ardonyx about this, he'd denied it, saying he wouldn't want that poisoned gift, since his friends and lovers would never be able to trust him.

She trusted him. She'd had to, or the deep-bond wouldn't have allowed their gifts to mesh.

Now that he had a place on the all-council, she hoped his voice would be the voice of reason for the brotherhoods.

As she watched Tobazim's triumvirate take their place, she realised the new all-father had appointed as his hand-of-force a gift-warrior from Tamaron's brotherhood. How diplomatic of him, to blend the three brotherhoods in his triumvirate. But this meant his adoption of Tamaron's survivors was there for all to see.

'Well, causare?' Dretsun prodded. 'Now that we are all here, what were you and the healer doing on the *Victorious* last night when the new all-father made his challenge?'

The brotherhood leaders cast dark looks from her to Tobazim, and muttered about his lack of martial gifts.

'Reoden and I did go to the *Victorious* last night, but it was after the challenge,' Imoshen said. 'I am beholden to Sorne, and his sister needed healing.'

Time to start proceedings. She moved into the centre of the clearing, fallen leaves stirring under her feet.

'Wait,' Dretsun said, and Imoshen felt the rise of his gift. 'Is that Norsasno from Tamaron's brotherhood, acting as your hand-of-force, Tobazim? Since when do you acquire the survivors of another brotherhood without bringing it to an all-father-council?'

The question had been addressed to Tobazim, but he signalled Ardonyx to answer.

'We paid the brigands who delivered Tamaron's people to the wharf and, that night, we saved their lives when the same cutthroats returned. We gave Tamaron's survivors shelter on my ship and fed them. When Imokara needed a gift-benediction to keep her child, the product of Mieren rape, we performed the ritual. And, last night, when I went to the high-ranking survivors of Tamaron's brotherhood and offered them the sanctuary of our brotherhood, they accepted.'

There was a moment's silence.

'You gave them a choice?' Hueryx asked.

'Our brotherhood vow is for life. I didn't choose to serve Kyredeon, yet I was trapped serving him,' Tobazim said. 'Does anyone object?'

Imoshen hid a smile. His calm manner, when combined with the fresh wounds on his face, was much more threatening than bluster.

No one spoke up.

She lifted her hands. 'Then let me welcome you to the last all-council in our homeland. Step forward, All-father Tobazim, give your covenant vow and be acknowledged by the sisterhoods.'

The brotherhood leaders tensed, muttering resentfully as their gifts rose. The power felt oppressive, and she had to fight the instinct to protect herself.

Almost thirteen years ago, she had seen the previous all-mother of her sisterhood force the covenant vow on a new all-father. It had struck her as wrong then.

When she had become the all-mother, the all-fathers already bound to her sisterhood had renewed their vows in a private ceremony. Because the vow had already been made, she had only needed to imprint her power on their covenant scars. Like a crack in a wall, the scar on their gift defences created a point of weakness, through which the all-mother could break their shields and cripple them.

Now she would have to sear her power into Tobazim's gift, scarring his defences.

His jaw clenched as he stepped forward and knelt.

Lifting her left hand, Imoshen touched his forehead with her little finger. Her gift surged and she read the rest of the brotherhood leaders. They could barely contain their anger. They'd always hated the vow, but now they had to watch Imoshen the All-father-killer inflict it on one of their own. But if she didn't, the sisterhood leaders would think she'd betrayed them. Thirteen years ago, they'd made her prove her loyalty was not to the brotherhoods, by forcing her to execute her own father.

'Four hundred years ago, the all-father of your brotherhood gave his vow to the all-mother of our sisterhood. Now you renew this vow.' Imoshen did not command him to drop his defences. That was just insulting.

She remembered meeting her father's gaze that day. She'd had no choice. The sisterhood leaders had made sanctuary for herself, her devotee and little Iraayel conditional on his execution.

Rohaayel had been an all-father of vision. He had risked and lost everything in his attempt to change the T'Enatuath; even his brotherhood had not survived.

The power in the clearing intensified, making it hard to breathe, making her aware of every tiny detail. Something moved above her and she looked up to see dozens of leaves hovering in the air. Sunlight glowed through their delicate viens, enriching the vivid colours.

Twice she'd gift-infused Tobazim, which meant imprinting the covenant vow should be relatively easy. But...

She could not bring herself to do it.

Luckily, with the amount of power in the clearing, no one would be able to tell; so she dropped her hand without taking the final step.

Tobazim looked up, surprised.

The gift tension between them dropped and brilliant leaves swirled down around them as she offered Tobazim her hand, drawing him to his feet.

'The covenant vow is over four hundred years old and what served us in the past does not necessarily serve us in the future. I believe it is time to amend the vow.'

There was muttering at this.

Before anyone could protest, Imoshen plunged on. 'Back in the Celestial City, T'En fathers counted themselves lucky if they saw their sons once a year before the lads joined the brotherhood, and some never saw their children at all. This is wrong and cruel.'

There was more muttering from both the brotherhoods and sisterhoods.

'The T'Enatuath sail into exile, into a world where the Mieren fear and despise us. We cannot afford division. There needs to be a strong bond between brotherhoods and sisterhoods. When we have a new home, my sisterhood will invite the fathers of your brotherhood's T'En children' – she recalled Paragian bringing his devotee to the meeting about his son – 'and their devotee mothers to our feast day celebrations. There are eight feast days a year; they can spend those days with their children.'

There was stunned silence.

It was such a small step, but it would be too much for some. She could already hear Egrayne's voice in her head, warning her that the brotherhood leaders would see this as a weakness. Maybe some of them would, but for others it would bring hope.

Imoshen squeezed Tobazim's hands and sealed the amended covenant vow with a slight gift-infusion.

As Tobazim returned to the brotherhoods, Ardonyx caught her eye and jerked his head towards All-father Hueryx. If she gave this concession to Tobazim's brotherhood, she had to give it to the other brotherhood that was bound by the same gift-enforced vow to her sisterhood.

She turned towards Hueryx to find he was already stepping forward to meet her in the centre of the sunlit clearing. Meanwhile, the sisterhood leaders whispered. Imoshen had not discussed this with them. They would not be happy. She could have handled this better, but Dretsun had forced the all-council meeting before she'd had time to prepare the sisterhood leaders. Sometimes she wished she had the gift to imbue words with power. Perhaps it was just as well she didn't. The temptation to use that power would be overwhelming.

Hueryx held her gaze, anger gleaming in his wine-dark eyes.

He accepted her outstretched hand, but before she could speak, he whispered, 'Why is it that Imoshen the All-father-killer, executioner of covenant breakers, offers this amendment to the covenant?'

'I had no choice the day Rohaayel was executed,' she said softly. 'You're smart. You figure it out.'

His eyes widened and she amended the vow, sealing it with a slight gift-infusion.

Before Hueryx could step back, Reoden spoke up.

'Wait.' The healer came to Imoshen's side and took the all-father's hand. 'Your brotherhood is also vow-bound to my sisterhood. You should be very proud of your son, Ronnyn. He discovered the ruins, which have so delighted our historians.' And she also amended the vow.

Imoshen watched as Reoden offered the same concession to Paragian, whose brotherhood was also vow-bound to hers. Then the healer beckoned Tobazim. Imoshen realised he had formed a bond with Reoden's sisterhood by taking in Tamaron's survivors. Reoden's sisters were already rearing some of All-father Tamaron's T'En children. Once there had been more brotherhoods, but they'd been absorbed, and now a single brotherhood might be gift-bound to three sisterhoods.

As Reoden took Tobazim's hand, Imoshen realised the healer was about to discover Tobazim's covenant vow had been a sham, but Reoden did not seek to imprint her power on top of Imoshen's gift-enforced vow. She merely repeated the promise.

All-mothers Melisarone and Ceriane made the same amendment with their vow-bound all-fathers. Athazi was last to step forward. She was furious, but had to present a united front before the brotherhoods.

As the sisterhood leaders made these promises to their vow-bound brotherhoods, Imoshen read the two groups. This had eased the brotherhoods' anger. She had done the right thing, despite Athazi's misgivings.

Across the clearing, she met Ardonyx's eyes. He sent her a single nod, and it warmed her heart. He had once accused her of being a coward because she saw the flaws in their society and did not seek to change things. She had countered that she was only one person. How could she effect change?

Today, she had taken the first step towards a more enlightened T'Enatuath, such as she and Ardonyx had discussed back when they were both taking lessons in the Sagorese language. Then it had seemed an impossible dream, but now that she was causare and now that Ardonyx advised All-father Tobazim, they had a chance to change things for the better.

The brotherhoods and sisterhoods parted, returning to their sides of the all-council.

'There should be trysting to celebrate,' Saskeyne declared, his eager gift barely under control. The rest of the brotherhood leaders were quick to agree.

Imoshen laughed.

'The causare has taken a vow of celibacy until the T'Enatuath are safely at sea,' Egrayne said. 'You would do well to honour her vow with one of your own.'

They didn't like that idea at all.

Imoshen hid her smile. 'I fear we will all be too busy for celebrating. We sail into exile the day after tomorrow.'

'But now we must hand over the causare's choice-son to his brotherhood,' Egrayne announced.

As Imoshen turned to see Iraayel, her heart swelled with a mixture of pride and sorrow. He stood barefoot and naked under his knee-length robe. He would leave the sisterhood as he came into this world.

Normally, the brotherhoods did not see this part of the ceremony. It was performed inside the sisterhood quarter, and the lad was handed over at his brotherhood gate.

Imoshen led Iraayel into the centre of the clearing. Egrayne had already plaited his hair in one long braid and tied a leather strip around it at the base of his neck.

Tears blurred Imoshen's vision, as she took his plait in her hand. She had been braiding his hair since it was first long enough. Now it was thick and strong in her hand, filled with the residue of his gift.

She drew her ceremonial dagger and began to cut through the plait. This was symbolic of cutting the link that all T'En mothers shared with their children.

After what they'd been through, Imoshen's link with Iraayel was far deeper than normal. She should have been severing this gift link as she cut his hair. But she didn't. Let Iraayel sever it if he wanted to. His plait came away neatly in her hand.

His hair settled around his shoulders as he turned to face her.

Lifting the severed braid to show the sisterhood, Imoshen said the words to complete the ritual. 'My choice-son, Iraayel, is dead. This is all I have to remember him by.'

But she would never close her heart against him. She felt this so strongly, her gift tried to break free of her control.

The sisterhood leaders moaned in sympathy as they responded to the surging of her gift.

She hung Iraayel's plait over her arm and lifted her hands to his neck to slide the robe off his shoulders.

Then she stepped away.

There he stood, naked – perfect. Definitely an adult male, for all that he would not attain his full growth until he was about twenty-five.

Tobazim stepped forward. 'Iraayel, formerly choice-son of Imoshen, you proved your worth when we rescued the Mieren queen. You will be an asset to our brotherhood. Come, give your brotherhood vow.'

Iraayel knelt, graceful as always.

Imoshen felt a hand on her arm, and Egrayne drew her back to stand with her sisterhood. As Iraayel gave the brotherhood oath, she could hear nothing for the roaring in her ears.

Tobazim raised his left hand, pressed the tip of the sixth

finger to Iraayel's forehead and created the link which could be used to save him if he ever got into trouble on the higher plane. It could also be used to breach his defences and drain him of his gift, if his all-father ever had cause to discipline him.

As Iraayel rose, Tobazim pulled the robe off his own shoulders and settled it around Iraayel's. Then Tobazim's hand-of-force drew her choice-son to stand behind his new brotherhood leaders.

Imoshen had to clear her throat before she could speak. 'The day after tomorrow, we set sail. Prepare your ships to cross the Secluded Sea.' Now she could legitimately meet Ardonyx's eyes and call on him. 'The renowned explorer, Captain Ardonyx, will explain what we face.'

The leaders of the T'Enatuath had all led such insular lives, some had never left the Celestial City. A few had journeyed to outlying estates, but none had sailed as far as the Lagoons of Perpetual Summer like Ardonyx.

'We sail into winter,' he said. 'Although it is called the Secluded Sea, the winter storms can be vicious. Captains will only cross it at this time of year if there is great gain for them. Most would prefer to hug the coast of the mainland before crossing the southern channel to Ivernia. But this would leave us open to attack by any of the Mieren kingdoms still loyal to Chalcedonia.' He cast Dretsun a look. 'This is why we rescued Queen Jaraile. If we can't trade with the kingdoms of the Secluded Sea, we can't prosper. But until she retakes the throne and opens the ports to us, we can't take the safest course. We'll follow the mainland coast south, as far as mid-Navarone, before striking out south-south-west for Ivernia.'

'Wouldn't it be faster to sail through the islands?' All-father Saskeyne asked. 'I was looking at a map, and that's certainly the shortest path.'

'True, but those islands are a maze of perilous channels, home to sea-vermin, ruthless pirates who prey on the shipping lanes. There are passages through the maze that would shorten the voyage to Ivernia, but the fleet would sail in single file as we followed the deep channel, leaving us vulnerable.'

'Surely they would not attack ships packed with warriors?' Saskeyne said.

'You think they wouldn't risk their lives for ships packed with all the wealth of the Wyrds?' Ardonyx countered. 'Everyone knows we've been exiled. Down south they believe the palaces of the Celestial City are sheathed in gold. They know we must sail by winter's cusp, and they know we sail south because there is nothing north of Chalcedonia but the ice-floes. Our fleet is enough to tempt even the sell-sword ships the great merchant houses hire to protect their trading vessels from sea-vermin.'

At this, there was muttering from the T'Enatuath leaders.

'Saskeyne is right. Our ships are packed with warriors, but the children, old folks and nursing mothers outnumber the warriors four to one.'

'Then we must make the journey as quickly as possible,' Paragian said and others agreed.

'We will, but we can only go at the pace of the smallest ships, so the greatest ships will reduce their sails.'

'How long will it take?' All-father Abeliode asked. Like Melisarone, he sailed a small three-masted vessel.

'That depends on the winds. It can take twelve days, it can take twenty. Some ships never reach Ivernia.'

'And the Sagoras have offered us sanctuary?' Paragian asked Imoshen.

'Yes.' She lied; she had no other choice. Either her message hadn't reached them, or their reply hadn't reached her. Either way, her people had no choice but to set sail.

After that the all-council ended and the brotherhood leaders returned to their ships. Imoshen chose to escort them off the island. All-father Egrutz hung back. He was accompanied by his two seconds, his devotee and the younger T'En warrior he was training to replace him. It was an unusual arrangement for a brotherhood. When he sent the others down to the rowboat and turned to Imoshen, she was a little surprised. When he led her away from her two seconds, she was even more surprised.

He clasped one of her hands in both his. Though she was somewhat taken aback, she did not object to this familiarity.

'I am old and no longer ambitious, so I can say what I like. I knew and respected your father. Rohaayel's mind was sharp as a blade. It is rare for one of us to father a female child, but he had you and was inspired to break the covenant. He had a vision for the T'Enatuath, to unite the brotherhoods –'

'He was ambitious and he used me.' But he had loved her in the end, and she had never stopped loving him.

'He did use you. The irony of it is that you have fulfilled his vision and more, Imoshen. He thought only of the brotherhoods. With the amendment to the covenant today, you have taken the first step to truly unite the T'Enatuath. As long as we bicker amongst ourselves we are weak.' He sighed and shook his head. 'I've lived long enough to see these problems coming, but I couldn't see how to avert them, or how to save our people.' He squeezed her hand. 'You have done Rohaayel proud, T'Imoshen.'

Releasing her hand, he shuffled over to his devotee, who helped him make the climb down to his rowboat.

A great weight lifted from Imoshen, and tears stung her eyes.

Egrayne came over to join her. 'Are you all right?'

'Yes.' Imoshen wiped her cheeks and turned to face her voice-of-reason.

'What did he want?'

'To tell me that I've done well.'

Egrayne snorted softly. 'By the brotherhoods, perhaps.'

'And he called me T'Imoshen.'

'When no other brotherhood leader could hear him do it,' Egrayne muttered. 'But it's a start. Now you'd better come back and smoothe some ruffled feathers. Athazi is not pleased.'

Chapter Twenty-Seven

JARAILE LIFTED HER arm so the servant could adjust the strap securing her chestplate. She felt excited and slightly nauseous, but then she always felt sick in the first stages of pregnancy. Every day she checked for blood, hoping to lose the child Eskarnor had forced on her, but other than the nausea, she was doing well. Every time she thought of Eskarnor's smug smile, she wanted to throttle him.

The servant made one last adjustment so the plate wouldn't chafe, then Jaraile dismissed him, picked up her helmet and turned to face her commanders.

They were so different: her dour kinsman, Baron Kerminzto; Baron Aingeru who had placed his faith in her for a better future for his family; and Baron Ramanol, who was fast becoming her least favourite person after Eskarnor and Charald.

Kerminzto and Ramanol would lead the two arms of the pincer movement. Aingeru would take the centre to lure Eskarnor's men into the trap.

The three barons went down on one knee. The rest of her army were already lined up in the chill predawn. Last night, she had looked out across the fields towards the walls of Port Mirror-on-Sea and her heart had sunk at the sight of so many campfires. Then she'd remembered Sorne saying that battle was not like counting tithes.

Last night, when she rode through the camp, her followers had seemed determined, but they were armed with old, stolen or makeshift weapons and apart from the king's guard and the barons, the mounted riders were an odd assortment of farmers and labourers mounted on borrowed horses. Not really what you could describe as elite cavalry. They did, however, have excellent archers. Chalcedonia was renowned for the quality of her archers.

Jaraile's tent had been pitched on a small rise overlooking the fields and the port. She hadn't seen Sorne since he rode off two nights ago, and wished he was here now.

'You will do me proud this day,' she told the barons.

Kerminzto came to his feet. 'You'll stay on your horse, Jaraile. You carry your helmet, so the men can see your face, and ride up and down on the crest of this hill in front of the royal banner.'

She'd been up half the night sewing the makeshift banner. She knew what she had to do.

'I'll be in the centre of our line, with my men,' Aingeru said. 'Young Baron Dekornz will play a Chalcedonian martial air to inspire our troops and irritate Eskarnor. He'll want to capture you. I know his style of leadership. He'll lead an assault on you, and that's when my men will retreat and draw him in.'

Kerminzto nodded to Ramanol. 'And we'll close around his army.'

'You can rely on us, my queen,' Ramanol said.

She nodded and the three of them strode out of the tent. No, Ramanol hesitated. She prayed for patience.

'Don't worry, Queen Jaraile, this will all be over soon. Once you're in the palace with your servants, life will return to normal,' he assured her, then left.

The thought horrified her. Other than seeing her son, she had no reason to want to return to the palace. She'd never felt more alive since Eskarnor kidnapped her. No, since King Charald came back from besieging the Wyrd city.

Since Sorne came back.

The thought shocked her.

'Jaraile?'

She turned to see him slip out of the private chamber of her tent. 'Where's your armour?'

'This is what your average man-at-arms wears: leather vest, breeches and boots. I do have a helmet.' He set it on the table, then adjusted her cloak on her shoulders, checking that the sprig of winter-bells was secure. 'If this succeeds, you should add those flowers to your coat of arms.'

A surprised laugh escaped her.

Sorne sobered. 'If it fails, be assured Eskarnor will not find your son. I told High Priest Faryx to change his name and rear him as a priest. So if our army loses, you ride and don't look back. First chance you get, ditch the armour and change into the farmer's garments I've hidden in your saddlebags.'

She was touched, but... 'You don't think I should raise another army and regain the throne for Cedon?'

He sighed. 'If you lose this battle, Eskarnor will execute every high-ranking man who supported you. You'd have to go south to raise an army, and make promises you might not want to keep. For what? King Charald has spent his life defending his crown, constant battles and political manouvering. There is so much more to life.'

'But your plan will work?'

'Once the battle starts, plans have a way of going awry, so keep your wits about you.'

SORNE HAD SPENT eight years travelling with King Charald on the Secluded Sea campaign, and a year quelling the rebels after the first Maygharian revolt, but he had never once been in a shield-wall.

You stood your ground, you hacked, you slashed and, if you were lucky, you survived.

He stood in the front ranks with Aingeru's men. Behind him, the baron rode and up and down with his banner-men and honour guard. The warriors in the front ranks were hand-picked by Aingeru, men who could keep their heads and obey orders under pressure.

Sorne stamped his feet and waited, shoulder to shoulder

with the True-men his life depended on. Down here, the battlefield looked vast. They'd spread themselves thin. It was that or be surrounded.

Down here in the centre of Queen Jaraile's army, it was impossible to tell where everyone was. Sorne was used to standing on a hill, watching the ebb and flow, while Charald sent messengers with directions to send in the reserves or retreat. Often a whole battle rested on the charge of the cavalry, or the appearance of reserves when the enemy's troops wavered. Charald had been a master at timing these things. Sorne missed him now: the father who had disowned him, then made use of him as a servant.

He glanced over his shoulder, catching a glimpse of the rise where Jaraile's tent was pitched. Their small body of mounted men lay in wait behind the hill. Scholar Mozteben would signal if the cavalry were needed.

As the sun rose behind them, long shafts of light speared across the fields into the eyes of Eskarnor's men. They'd been lined up to mirror Queen Jaraile's army, but their numbers were split so as to guard their backs against Commander Halargon opening the gates and making a surprise attack.

All Sorne could see of the enemy was the men directly opposite, just outside bowshot range. The sun glinted on their shields and helmets. Then he heard the pipes, as behind him, on the rise, young Baron Dekornz played a martial air. The music carried on the still dawn and Queen Jaraile's warriors began to sing. Their deep voices filled Sorne with a sense of solidarity and safety, even though he knew it was an illusion.

Eskarnor's own pipers started up and his men began shuffling forwards. Sorne felt the ripple of readiness as the men to each side of him shifted, adjusting their feet and their grip on their swords and shields. But they did not advance or give ground. Eskarnor's men were going to have to come to them.

Each of Eskarnor's barons rode with his foot soldiers, his

banner and honour guard riding beside him. Sorne could see where the ground dipped by the way the line moved as the army advanced. Behind the front ranks, archers let loose a volley. Aingeru's disciplined men raised their shields. Sorne heard the arrows strike. Very few men dropped.

Directly in front of him, he heard a thundering and felt the ground shake, as Eskarnor's men-at-arms parted for the mounted warriors. They rode through, aiming straight for Aingeru's forces. The cavalry were elite troops, riding armoured horses trained to bite and kick.

Sorne and the men in the front row dropped to their knees, locking shields, and the men behind them stepped up and did likewise, while the soldiers behind them tilted their lances forward, projecting a good body length beyond Sorne.

And then they waited.

He could feel the thunder of the horses' hooves through his knees. It was the task of the first row to spring to their feet when the horses became entangled with the lances. They would gut the poor beasts and pull the riders off their saddles.

Sorne clenched his teeth and prayed he would not disgrace himself. Waiting for those flying hooves was the hardest thing he had ever done.

And then the cavalry collided with the line. The broad armoured chest of a war horse barrelled into Sorne, and he was knocked off his feet. The rider plunged through as far as the second row, driving the standing men apart and hacking at the lancers.

Sorne rolled to his feet and hamstrung the horse. It screamed, collapsing. He felt sorry for it, even as Aingeru's men pulled the rider from his mount, driving their swords through the joints in his armour.

Another horse shouldered Sorne aside. He fell to his knees and covered his head as a mounted rider leapt over him. Springing to his feet, he glanced around, saw some of Aingeru's men dragging riders from their mounts, while a core of mounted men slashed and hacked from their superior height. He pulled one of Aingeru's lancers out from under the hooves of a circling horse, then caught the rider, unseating him. The horse reared up and took off, running back the way it had come through the ranks of men-at-arms about to pour through Aingeru's crippled centre.

It was almost time to start to the retreat.

A fallen rider tried to slash Sorne's thigh. He diverted the blow and cut the man down before he could get to his feet.

Someone collided with him. He turned, ready to strike, only to find it was one of Aingeru's men and steadied the fellow instead.

Over the heads of the men struggling around him, he saw the knot of riders had made it through Aingeru's men-at-arms and were battling the baron's honour guard. Sorne tried to spot Aingeru to give the signal to fall back, but the baron was nowhere in sight.

On the hill, he saw Jaraile astride a horse in front of the banner. Sorne was shocked to see that several of Eskarnor's elite mounted men had made it that far and were riding for her. Mozteben would surely call up the cavalry to protect her.

'Fall back,' Sorne cried. 'Fall back.'

No one heard him amidst the yelling, the crashing of metal on metal and the screaming of the wounded.

He grabbed the man he'd steadied. 'Fall back, tell them.'

He shoved the man in one direction and Sorne went the other way along the line. 'Fall back. Steady now, fall back.'

They started to back up.

Seeing this, Eskarnor's men charged.

Quicker than Sorne would have thought possible, Aingeru's men fell back, some tripping over fallen horses and men. Sorne spotted Aingeru's horse and found the baron pinned under the fallen mount. He hauled him out, slung an arm around his shoulders and staggered with him.

Behind them, Eskarnor's men cheered. Sorne spared a glance and saw them pouring into the opening left by the retreating centre. He realised he stood a very real chance of being cut down as he tried to lead the retreat.

Ahead of him, Sorne looked up to see the knot of mounted men battling at the base of the hill. The cavalry were finally protecting the queen's position. Unfortunately three riders had already made the crest and were battling with the banner-men, Dekornz and his tutor. Jaraile struck right and left as a man tried to pull her off her horse.

'Leave me,' Aingeru shouted, shoving him away.

Sorne grabbed a nearby riderless mount, leapt astride it and turned the horse towards the hill.

Sorne glanced behind him. Eskarnor's army cheered as the centre bulged forward.

He skirted the mounted men skirmishing at the base of the hill, and rode for the crest. Grabbing the queen's standard, he waved it to signal Barons Kerminzto and Ramanol were to close the trap.

As the two arms of the queen's army closed in on Eskarnor and his barons, the rest of Aingeru's men poured out from behind the hill to cut off any who had made it through the broken centre.

Seeing that the pincer movement was working, Sorne dropped the banner and turned to defend the queen.

Young Dekornz and his tutor had dealt with one of the riders and were struggling with the second, but the third had hauled Jaraile off her horse and was about to ride off with her across his saddle.

Sorne rode his mount straight at the man, whose horse reared. The rider tumbled backwards and the horse took off with Jaraile hanging across the saddle. She fell before Sorne could reach her.

He jumped down and went to help her up, but the unseated rider staggered towards him, sword drawn. Sorne had to duck and weave as his sword clanged on armour and skipped over the rider's helmet.

Jaraile struggled to her feet, picked up a shield and slammed it into the rider's back. He barrelled forward, falling on Sorne's sword, which punched through a joint in his armour.

As Jaraile stared, stunned, Sorne grabbed the reins of the horse and hoisted her into the saddle. 'Sit there, so your army can see what they're fighting for.'

Dekornz was on his knees, bent over the body of his old tutor, weeping, but there were no more of Eskarnor's men on the hill top. Sorne studied the flow of the fighting below. As he watched, the first hornets' nest of arrows streamed into the air, falling into the tightly packed ranks of Eskarnor's army, which had now been surrounded. Some men raised their shields in time, but many fell to the deadly hail.

Sorne grabbed Dekornz. 'Help me raise the queen's banner.'

They secured it and Sorne found the lad's pipes.

'Play for the queen. Make your tutor proud.'

Sorne returned to Jaraile's side.

'It's working,' she cried.

'There's still Eskarnor's reserves to consider.' Sorne pointed to the men manning the first row of defences around the port's walls. 'If they come in from behind before Kerminzto and Halargon attack, they'll cut our men down and Eskarnor's warriors will –'

'The gates are opening.' Jaraile kicked the horse in her excitement and it protested, sidling sideways.

Sorne caught the bridle and soothed the beast as he studied the port gate. For a moment, all he could see was the darkness within the gate tunnel before the mounted men poured out. They rode hard for Eskarnor's defenders. For a moment it looked like the men would hold. Then they turned and ran.

The moment they did, it became a rout. Commander Halargon, leading the remains of Nitzane's men and the palace guard, dealt with the fleeing reserves.

The surrounded army had contracted into a tight knot of men, who threw down their swords and surrendered.

'It's over, my queen,' Sorne said. 'And it isn't even lunch time.'

She started to laugh, which turned into sobbing as exhaustion took over.

He helped her dismount, carried her into the tent, sat her down and poured her a glass of wine. 'Here, drink this.'

She gulped a mouthful, hiccupped and wiped her chin. 'Make sure Eskarnor doesn't get away.'

'Yes, Queen Jaraile.'

He walked outside.

IMOSHEN STOOD ON the high rear-deck as the T'Enatuath fleet sailed out of Shifting-sands Bay. It was mid-morning, the first day of winter – the first official day of exile.

About half of their estates had made it to Shifting-sands Bay. So many had been lost, and the worst of it was the children, both Malaunje and T'En. She felt as if she had personally failed them.

She did not know where Sorne was, or even if he lived, but he knew she planned to go to Ivernia and approach the Sagoras. He would make his way there when he could.

The only problem was that she had not heard back from the Sagoras and she had no idea what awaited them in Ivernia.

IT WAS LATE, and Tobazim was tired. They had dropped anchor for the night, but it seemed brotherhood business did not stop. Tonight he had the cabin to himself. Deimosh was still recovering, Ceyne was down in sick bay and Ardonyx and the hand-of-force were patrolling the ship.

Tobazim dismissed the all-father's-voice with instructions, and turned to the cabin boy. 'Toresel, see if there's any dinner left over. I'm starving.'

The lad ran off and Tobazim cleaned his pen nib, remembering the silver nib his choice-mother had given him. As he'd neared his seventeenth birthday, he'd feared going into the brotherhood with his non-martial gift. She'd told him it was easy to kill and destroy, but much harder to build and grow. He wished she could see him now, but everyone who lived on the sisterhood estate where he'd grown up had been massacred.

When he'd heard, he'd had to carry on as though her death meant nothing to him. Once their choice-mothers declared them dead and they joined the brotherhood, T'En men were never supposed to acknowledge the women who raised them.

Tears burned his eyes. He rubbed his face, stood, stretched and went to the windows across the stern of the ship.

Someone knocked on the cabin door.

He turned. 'Come in.'

'Ceyne sent me to fetch you,' Iraayel said. 'Valendia won't wake up.'

Tobazim's heart sank. He gestured for Iraayel to lead the way.

The young initiate paused at the infirmary door to whisper, 'Athlyn hasn't left her side for days. We've dribbled water into her mouth and she swallows on reflex, but....'

Tobazim prepared himself for the worst.

The infirmary was packed, but Ceyne had rigged a curtain across one corner to give Valendia some privacy. Lamplight glowed through the muslin, silhouetting two figures.

When Iraayel held the cloth aside for him, Athlyn looked up. He clasped Valendia's left hand in both of his, as if he was afraid to let her go. Now he looked to his all-father with hope.

Tobazim knelt next to Ceyne and asked, 'What can I do?'

'At first I thought she was in a deep healing sleep,' Ceyne said softly. 'And perhaps she was, but this is no longer normal sleep. If I didn't know better, I'd say she had segued to the higher plane to search for Grae, but...' He took her hand. If she'd been on the higher plane, he would have been drawn through to join her.

'Besides, Malaunje can't take themselves to the empyrean plane.' Gently, he placed her hand on her chest, which rose and fell with each breath. 'She hasn't eaten or taken more than a few sips of water for three days now.'

'Has Athlyn tried to reach into her mind?'

Ceyne gestured to the young initiate who said, 'Her mind is full of long dark tunnels, which she seems to be searching, but I can never quite catch up with her. And when I call to her, she can't see or hear me.'

'He lacks the skill to pierce her preoccupation,' Ceyne said.

Tobazim was not sure he had the skill, but he had to try.

'Take his hand,' Ceyne advised, moving aside so Tobazim could kneel opposite Athlyn. 'Use Athlyn's link to her, to find her.'

Tobazim grasped Athlyn's other hand and prepared to...

He found himself in a long tunnel, following a figure who held a guttering candle. And he remembered how Valendia had saved Graelen, when he'd been chained in the crypts far below the Father's Church.

Tobazim took off after her. At first, no matter how fast he ran, he couldn't catch up with her, but – driven by Athlyn's determination – he gradually closed the distance.

Then she turned the corner, taking the light with her and leaving him in darkness. He sprinted around the corner only to find her further away again.

In desperation, Tobazim called out to her.

She stopped and turned to him, her face full of hope. The distance between them contracted until he stood next to her and he sensed Athlyn's relief.

'Grae?' Her face fell. 'Oh, it's you, Athlyn.'

Tobazim realised she saw him this way because he was using Athlyn's link to reach her.

'You have to help me,' she pleaded. 'I can't find Grae. I know he's down here somewhere. He needs me.'

Tobazim sensed Athlyn was at a loss.

He took her hand. It felt solid in his, if a little chilled. 'You already found Grae, Dia. You saved him. He told me the time he had with you was the happiest of his life. Remember?'

Her gaze became distant as she looked inward.

He lifted her hand to his mouth and breathed warm air on her skin, imbuing it with his gift. The candle flame grew brighter.

She smiled. 'Yes, I remember.' Then she frowned. 'Why I can't find him this time?'

'He had to go. He asked Athlyn to look after you until you could be together again.'

She started to shake her head.

Tobazim stepped closer and put his hand on her belly. 'He said you had to come back to the brotherhood so that his child could grow up under our protection.'

'There is the child... But I can't leave Grae.'

At this, a small True-woman appeared beside Valendia. Her red-gold hair shone in the candle light.

'Of course you can leave him. Your child needs you, Dia,' she said in a kind, but firm voice. 'Didn't I choose you over your father?'

'Ma?' Incandescent joy lit Valendia's face. 'Oh, Ma, I've missed you so much.' She hugged the woman, then pulled back. 'But you can't be here, you're dead.'

Her mother laughed fondly, cupping her cheek. 'Silly Dia. I'll always be with you. I'll be there in the way you love your child. And that child needs you now.'

Just like that, they were back in the infirmary. Valendia woke with a gasp. For a moment, she looked stunned, and then she sobbed as if her heart would break. Athlyn took her in his arms, weeping with her.

Tears burned Tobazim's eyes, because he'd felt his own choice-mother's hand on his cheek. He looked to Ceyne, who held his hand to his face, eyes full of wonder.

'What was that? I... I heard my choice-mother's voice, and I haven't seen her since she declared me dead almost seventy years ago.'

'That was Valendia, choosing to live,' Tobazim said and came to his feet.

Ceyne walked him through the infirmary, past the injured initiates and adepts, who whispered in wonder. They'd felt it too.

When Tobazim came to the door, the saw-bones caught his arm. 'Kyredeon couldn't have done what you just did. I'm proud of you, lad.'

Chapter Twenty-Eight

JARAILE WAS TIRED and slightly shaky. The euphoria of battle had drained away, leaving her glad to be alive, but utterly exhausted. She was sure by tomorrow she would ache all over. Right now, she had to be strong; they were bringing Eskarnor to her.

She stood on the rise outside her tent, impatient to be done with this so she could ride into port and see her son. She hadn't seen Cedon since spring cusp, when the Wyrds had abducted him. Did her little boy think she had abandoned him? Sorne said Cedon had asked after her...

'What's the half-blood doing here?' Baron Ramanol asked.

'It was Sorne who suggested the manoeuvre that won us the battle, so you can keep a civil tongue in your head,' Jaraile told him. She was tired of being sweet.

Ramanol drew back and Kerminzto's mouth thinned. She knew her kinsman thought women should be sweet and biddable, like his wife and three daughters; as long as she did what she was told, he would approve of her. But she was fed up with being pushed around by men who thought they knew better.

Commander Halargon strode up the slope ahead of Sorne and the king's guards escorting Eskarnor. The commander of the guards dropped to one knee.

'I bring bad news, my queen.'

'Not my little Cedon?'

'No, my queen. This morning Baron Nitzane died of his injuries.'

Poor Nitzane. He'd been kind to her when King Charald

was still well enough to bully her, and she remembered how much he'd been looking forward to seeing his son, who was being fostered with his brother in Navarone.

'See to it that his son is returned to Chalcedonia. He'll be raised alongside Prince Cedon.'

'You are very kind.'

No, she wasn't. She wanted to know where her son's heir was at all times. She wanted the two boys to grow up as brothers. Hopefully, Nitzane's son wouldn't betray hers.

'Here comes the traitor, Queen Jaraile,' Commander Halgaron said.

Eskarnor had raped her, abducted her, told her Prince Cedon was dead, planted his own child in her belly and boasted that he'd be sitting on Charald's throne by summer.

She'd proven him wrong, and after what she'd been through today, she fully expected to lose the child, although there was no sign of this as yet.

Jaraile lifted her chin to meet Eskarnor's eyes. He'd lost his bid for the throne, his army was decimated and the barons who had followed him had died on the battlefield.

Despite this, he returned her gaze with arrogance.

One of the king's guards kicked the back of his knees and he fell to the ground in front of her. With his hands bound behind his back, it took him a moment to come to his knees.

'King Charald should have him executed,' someone muttered from behind her.

But Charald had signed the decree, and since Nitzane was dead, that meant she ruled, with Baron Kerminzto, High Priest Faryx and the commander as her advisors; the traitor's fate was in her hands.

Jaraile remembered feeling helpless. She remembered the fury and frustration of being held prisoner, of being forced to accept him into her bed and into her body. She never wanted to be helpless again. 'I sentence him to death. And I'll be the one to carry out his execution.'

'What?' Ramanol protested. 'That's not –'

'I'm the one he wronged,' Jaraile said.

'Hold the prisoner,' Sorne ordered. He stood directly behind Eskarnor. 'Halargon, give the queen your knife.'

Jaraile accepted the knife. She had often fantasised about killing Eskarnor, but now she held a blade, he was just so alive...

'Go on,' Eskarnor said. 'Or can't you do it, Raila.'

She hated his pet name for her. Hated him.

'Cut his throat or drive the knife up under the ribs,' Sorne said. 'That'll be quickest.'

Eskarnor laughed. 'They all think you're so sweet. Now they'll see the real Queen Jaraile. They'll see the Raila I know. I bet I was the only lover man enough to make you...'

Hands snapped his neck, cutting him off. He toppled sideways and Jaraile looked up to Sorne, who'd killed him.

Heat raced up her cheeks.

'Take the traitor away. Put his head on a gate spike,' Sorne said. He dropped to his knees where Eskarnor had been. 'Forgive me, my queen. He had a poisonous tongue and I thought he'd made you suffer enough. You shouldn't have his death on your conscience.'

She burned with embarrassment. Had anyone other than Sorne guessed what Eskarnor had been about to say?

Sorne came to his feet. 'Commander, the queen needs an honour guard to escort her into port.'

The men bustled about, calling for their horses and arguing over their exact position in the royal party. Baron Ramanol was insisting that he should ride beside the queen, since he was one of her three commanders.

Meanwhile, she retreated to her tent, where Sorne found her. He took her hand. 'I'm sorry for your loss. Nitzane was a good man.'

'He was. But the kingdom did not need a good man. It needed you. I wish more men were like you.' She eyed Baron Ramanol, who strode past the tent opening, ordering people about. 'I've discovered I like being a queen when a king is not telling me what to do.'

'Then the longer King Charald lives, the longer you'll have your freedom. That pup, Ramanol, has plans to be your next husband.'

He was right. She'd have to tell Charald's manservant not to dose him with the arsenic medicine anymore.

'Go back to the palace, Jaraile. I'll bring Cedon to you.'

'Here, off you go, half-blood,' Ramanol said, striding into the tent. 'We don't want your kind in the official party.'

Jaraile went to protest, but Sorne had already disappeared. She consoled herself with the thought that she would see him later.

SORNE CARRIED THE prince down the corridor to the queen's chamber. He was followed by the queen's nurse, who had cared for Cedon since Jaraile had been abducted, and High Priest Faryx, who had hidden him.

'We go to see Mama?' Cedon asked at the door to her chamber.

Kerminzto opened the door and took the prince from Sorne. The moment he put the boy down, Cedon ran to his mother, who sat up in bed and opened her arms to him.

Jaraile's joy was all Sorne had hoped it would be.

'Come this way,' Kerminzto said, drawing him along the corridor. 'There's a ship waiting to take you anywhere you wish to go.'

'I had hoped to have time to say goodbye to Jaraile.'

'You've done enough damage where she's concerned.'

Sorne stared at him, stunned.

Kerminzto turned to him. 'The queen's in love with you, Sorne. Women are foolish creatures. They let their hearts rule their heads. We can't have a half-blood on the throne, or in the queen's bed as her lover. When she marries, it will be to a worthy baron, who will help her hold the kingdom.'

Sorne thought Jaraile might have something to say to that. As for her being in love with him... 'I'm sure you're mistaken. The queen –'

'You rescued her, saved her life and restored the kingdom to her. Now you are going to get on a ship and sail away.'

Kerminzto's meaning was clear. If Sorne did not, there were a dozen True-men who would make sure he did.

Sorne felt his face grow hot. 'If it's all the same to you, I'd like to say goodbye to King Charald.'

As Kerminzto escorted him to the king's chamber, he called for the king's guard, so there could be no mistaking his intent.

When Sorne reached the door, Kerminzto asked, 'Do you have any belongings that I can send for?'

'No. Everything I value is already with the Wyrds.'

Sorne shut the door after him.

King Charald sat in front of the fire, with a blanket over his legs. His head had sunk into his shoulders and he was snoring softly, mouth agape.

His manservant saw who it was and hurried over to greet Sorne.

'No one comes to see him now. No one cares,' Bidern said.

'How has he been?'

'He has his good days and his bad days. He's a bit vague today.'

Sorne knelt next to the chair and took the king's hand.

Charald woke with a start, looked frightened then pleased to see him. 'Bidern, what did I tell you? It's the Warrior god himself, come to reward me.'

And Sorne accepted that he would never win his father's love. Charald could not see him for who he was.

He sailed with the tide.

PART THREE

PART THREE

Chapter Twenty-Nine

NORMALLY, SORNE GOT his sea-legs within a day, but the captain insisted he keep to his cabin and it was stuffy below deck. That second evening, when the cook's boy brought him food, he asked to go up on deck, and the boy said he'd check with the captain.

Sorne paced the narrow cabin. Three strides to the wall, three strides back.

Saying goodbye to King Charald had convinced him of one thing: if he was lucky, he would live to grow old. Already he had wasted thirty years chasing his father's love and the respect of True-men, only to be unceremoniously bundled onto a ship and banished on the day of his greatest victory.

If he was lucky, he had another sixty years in him, and he wasn't going to waste it. He'd find his people, offer his service to Imoshen and share his life with Frayvia. Maybe they would have children.

With his people exiled, it was madness to contemplate having a baby, but if he waited until they were settled, he might never have the chance.

The cabin door opened. 'Cap'n says you can come up for a bit, but you're not to talk to the crew and you're to wear the hooded cloak.'

Sorne pulled on his cloak and raised the hood. He had done this so many times, resenting the fact that True-men did not want to see the evidence of his tainted blood. Now, he no longer cared. The problem was in their perception, not in him and he had accepted he could not change that.

It was strangely liberating.

At least amongst his own people, he would be welcome. But he would never be more than a servant, because of his birth. And there would be the constant tug of the T'En gifts. He should offer to work amongst the Malaunje to avoid the temptation.

Climbing out onto deck, he strode to the ship's side and watched the mainland roll by. Wait... That wasn't the mainland. They were sailing west into the setting sun, not south. Even as he thought this, they passed the headland of an island.

Sorne went cold as he realised the ship was threading its way through islands notorious for sea-vermin. The riff-raff of the Secluded Sea congregated here: outlaws, brigands and men who were foresworn. They made their way to the maze of islands, where they hid and came out to prey on the shipping lanes.

As Sorne headed up the steps to the rear-deck, he spotted the captain, who eyed his approach with misgiving.

Since he was no longer the king's agent in command of the king's ship, Sorne moderated his tone. 'Wouldn't we be safer sailing south along the coast?'

'Aye, but it would make the journey twice as long.'

'It would be safer. The sea-vermin –'

'I know these channels. I've done this before, slipped through without them noticing. Besides, we have the advantage of more canvas.'

But the sea-vermin were notoriously good sailors, and their craft were small, shallow skiffs that skimmed across the surface of the sea like dragon flies. The merchant ship would be forced to follow the channels between the sand bars, rock shoals and the islands. 'I don't –'

'You don't have a say. Get below. If you start talking about sea-vermin and frighten my crew, I'll be forced to lock you in your cabin.'

Sorne recognised his type. The captain was a bully, who led through bluster and intimidation. It wouldn't serve any purpose to get on the wrong side of this man. He decided to keep his head down, cause no trouble and be grateful to reach Ivernia in one piece.

IMOSHEN SHADED HER eyes and studied the horizon. The setting sun was slightly behind them as they sailed south-east, following the coast as it curved inwards. The wind had been patchy and they'd made poor progress. At times, she could see islands to the west. They were part of the archipelago that lay off the coast of Chalcedonia. At times she could see sails keeping pace with theirs, skimming across the azure sea like fire flies on a mill pond. The vessels had come close enough to count the number of ships in her fleet, then retreated.

She joined the ship's master. 'Any more sails sighted?'

'Not since this morning.'

'Are they sea-vermin?'

'Could be.'

'Should we be worried?'

He grimaced. 'Always wise to worry at sea.'

Imoshen hid a smile. The ship's master reminded her of one of the fishermen back on Lighthouse Isle. He had been able to read the sea like a book, but getting information from him was like getting blood from a stone. 'If they were sea-vermin, will they attack?'

'Only if there's profit in it.'

She left him, heading for Saffazi, who stood at the rail on the high rear-deck.

The young initiate barely glanced at Imoshen. Instead she watched the ship's passage through the sea. White foam rode on the bow wake, forming intricate lace-like patterns. Paragian's flagship brought up the rear of their fleet and her segmented sails looked misleadingly fragile, illuminated by the setting sun.

Normally Saffazi's gift buzzed just below the surface, as unruly and lively as she was. Today Imoshen sensed nothing. Five days had passed since Iraayel joined

Tobazim's brotherhood. Imoshen missed him, and she knew Saffazi did too.

When Imoshen had lost her first bond-partner and her newborn son, she'd felt there was no point in going on, but little Iraayel and her newly-made devotee had depended on her. She had not had the luxury of abandoning herself to grief.

No one depended on Saffazi.

'Safi.' Imoshen placed her hand on the young woman's arm and tried to draw off a little of her sorrow. But Saffazi's defences were too strong. That only left Imoshen with the spoken word.

And to her horror, she heard herself echoing Egrayne. 'We all knew this day would come.'

Saffazi spun to face her. 'How can you say that? Dividing into brotherhoods and sisterhoods is wrong. I don't want to live like this. The covenant –'

'I've amended the covenant vow.'

'Eight days a year with their children? You think that's going to reconcile the brotherhoods to giving up their sons?'

'It's a step in the right direction.'

'It's not enough. They've taken Iraayel from me. We should abandon the covenant, and abandon brotherhoods and sisterhoods. We should all live together as Mieren do.'

'Because that works so well for them? Grow up, Safi. You can't throw everything away, unless you have something to replace it with.'

Saffazi flushed and bit her bottom lip.

Imoshen regretted her harsh words. 'These things take time –'

'I can't wait. And I don't see why I should.'

Imoshen turned away to hide her smile. To be so young...

You could not force change on people who were not ready. There were some in positions of power would resist change because they feared it, and others would resist it because they did not want to give up power. Just as the sisterhoods had not hesitated to tell her to execute her father for daring to break the covenant, there were T'Enatuath leaders who would not hesitate to kill to protect their stature.

Imoshen might agree with Saffazi, but she did not trust the young initiate's discretion. 'Exile will bring change. For now, don't make waves –'

'I can't believe you're saying this. Iraayel says you hate it too.' Her pretty mouth twisted in a grimace of angry frustration. 'How can you be so hypocritical?'

Saffazi went to walk off, and Imoshen caught her arm. She had been about to warn the girl to hold her tongue, but she could sense the young initiate's gift wound tight inside her and her own gift surged. What it revealed frightened Imoshen.

'Safi, the gift is tied to you. If you feed this anger it will corrupt your gift. Even the gift-wright can't help you if you aren't willing to let her.'

'So I should just make the best of it?' Saffazi gave a bitter laugh. 'You might, but I am never going to give up what I believe in.'

Which stung, but Imoshen let it pass as the seventeen-year-old stormed off.

SORNE WOKE WITH the sense that the ship was at anchor. For a moment he didn't understand why this was significant. Then he recalled they were making their way through the islands. Perhaps the next section was tricky and could only be navigated in daylight.

He thought it was dusk. Why had he fallen asleep during the day? He rolled off the too-short bunk and came to his feet, feeling dizzy and nauseous. Was he sickening with something?

Fresh air would help.

Opening the cabin door, he stumbled up the passage to the ladder. He just wanted to get up on deck, where he could think straight. As he climbed out and staggered to the side of the ship, he was aware of the ship's crew watching him warily. The horizon kept moving, yet they were at anchor in still water.

Out of the corner of his eye, he saw someone run up the steps to the rear-deck.

If they thought he was sick with some contagion, they might dump him on one of the islands, for fear he'd infect the rest of the ship.

Sorne straightened up and turned around... Only to see several skiffs at anchor and, beyond them, a small jumble of dwellings gathered around an inlet. Lights glowed in ramshackle buildings, and smoke drifted from chimneys.

This wasn't Ivernia.

Sorne set off to confront the captain, only to find him coming across the deck.

'You don't look well. You should go back to your cabin,' the captain said, but his gaze flicked to something over Sorne's shoulder.

He started to turn.

Too late, someone grabbed him from behind, pinning his arms as a hessian sack descended on him.

'Bind his arms good and tight. He's a big one,' the captain shouted as several men struggled to contain him.

Onions... the sack had contained onion. His stomach heaved. He was not going to throw up inside a sack. But it was a near thing.

They tied the sack around his waist, then they knocked his legs out from under him and he fell heavily.

'Don't get up,' the captain said, delivering a kick to his ribs for emphasis. 'Tell cook, next time he needs to double the dose. When I saw the half-blood on his feet, my heart nearly gave out.'

Sorne took shallow, onion-tainted breaths; each gulp of air sent a jolt of pain through his ribs, but he didn't think anything was broken.

'Just in time,' the captain said. 'Here comes the Maygharian. You know he calls himself a sea-king? Even has his own banner!'

They were selling him to the Maygharians? That was both good and bad – bad, because he was hated in Maygharia, after he'd helped put down their revolt, and good because the queen owed him a favour, having set her on the course to depose Norholtz and reclaim her kingdom. But only he and the queen knew this.

Sorne managed to sit up as the Maygharian and his men came aboard.

'So, what have you got for us this time, captain?' The Maygharian spoke Chalcedonian with only the slightest of accents. 'More pretty little exotics?'

'Not so little and certainly not pretty, but this one will fetch a good price.' The captain's voice came closer as lantern light seeped through the hessian weave. 'It's the Warrior's-voice, the Butcher of Maygharia.'

'You don't say? Well, you'll forgive me if I make sure.'

'Go ahead, take a look.'

Someone grabbed the top of the sack and a sharp blade sliced clean through the material, just missing Sorne's throat. He blinked in the sudden light.

The Maygharian swore in three languages, caught Sorne by his hair and tilted his head this way and that. Then let him go with a vicious twist that brought tears to Sorne's remaining eye.

'Hard to fake a face like that,' the Maygharian said. 'That bald patch over his left temple, half the ear missing and smooth skin where the left eye should have been.'

'He'll fetch a good price.'

'That he will.' The Maygharian hesitated. 'I don't have that much coin with me. Come ashore, take a drink with my men.'

'You'll forgive me if I turn down your invitation. You'll wait out here with me, until your men bring me my coin.'

'Fair enough. Take the butcher to the boat, boys.'

Hands grabbed Sorne, hauled him to his feet and drove him towards the side. His head spun. He took one look at the rope ladder and shook his head. 'I can't climb down with my arms –'

Someone clipped him over the head. While his wits were still reeling, they lowered him over the side into the ten-man rowboat.

The waiting man shoved him into the boat's belly and the rest climbed down. As they rowed back to the sea-vermin's nest, Sorne thought it best to cooperate for now. When they neared the kingdom of Maygharia, he would ask to speak to the sea-king. He'd convince the man that the queen would pay a better price for him than anyone wanting revenge. At least he hoped she would.

They hauled him out of the boat, drove him up the beach above the high tide line, towards a lop-sided tavern built of driftwood and wreck salvage. As they drove him up the steps, he spotted cellar doors, which opened at ground level, and then he was inside the one-room tavern. He spotted about two dozen disreputable-looking True-men and a sprinkling of women. A sea-eagle banner hung over the fireplace. Then they shoved him down a ladder into the darkness of the cellar. The stairs went down further than he anticipated and he tripped on the final step, sprawling onto the sandy floor.

The light disappeared as they slammed the door. All he could smell was onions, but he'd caught a glimpse of ale barrels.

It could be worse.

After a moment, he heard soft scrabbling. Rats. He hated rats.

Sibilant whispers. Indistinct words.

'Who's there?'

No one answered.

Glimmers of light came through the cracks in the cellar doors and under the tavern door at the top of the stairs. The floorboards themselves were ill-fitting, letting in shafts of pale light. His sight gradually adjusted, and he spotted pale faces and dark eyes, watching him from the corners of the cellar, peering around barrels and sacks – children.

'It's all right. I won't hurt you,' Sorne told them. Then he wondered if they'd hurt him.

Why would sea-vermin lock up children? He suspected they were unfortunate captives who were destined to become indentured servants, or perhaps they were to be sold to brothels down south.

Up in the tavern above, he heard shouting, laughter and frenetic pipes. The floorboards shook. Dust drifted down on slivers of light. Someone was exhorting the others to join them.

Sorne sat on the second step and shrugged his shoulders to ease the tension. 'How about one of you release my arms before my fingers go numb?'

He might be able to steal a boat. He knew how to raise and lower a sail, and how to handle a rudder, and he knew Ivernia lay to the south-west.

One of the children ventured closer. Sorne could make out a pale face, fair hair, dark eyes. Judging by his size, he was no more than seven or eight.

'That's right.' Sorne tried to sound friendly and hoped they wouldn't be frightened of his missing eye.

Another child grabbed the boy's arm. 'Don't, Orza.'

They'd spoken T'En. Sorne went cold with shock, and a sick feeling settled in his stomach.

'How did T'Enatuath children end up in the cellar of sea-vermin?' he asked in their language.

And he was inundated by children of all ages and sizes. There had to be over twenty of them, mostly Malaunje, but he spotted a few fair-headed T'En, like Orza. The smallest were no bigger than two, while the eldest would have been around thirteen.

They all spoke at once, in intense whispers, as they told him their stories. And they pawed him, seeking the reassurance of his gift. He realised they'd mistaken his white hair for silver in the dimness.

'You came to save us,' Orza said and burst into tears.

A nimble-fingered T'En girl undid Sorne's bindings. He pulled the remains of the hessian sack over his head and tossed it aside with relief. As if this was a signal, the littlest ones climbed into his lap, while several children climbed up the steps behind him. He could feel them hugging his back, patting his head.

'Where's your gift? Why don't you share?' little voices pleaded.

'I'm Malaunje,' Sorne said.

They told him their stories, and by the time he had settled them down, he'd worked out who they were. Not everyone on the estates had been massacred. Some children had escaped, been captured and passed on from Mieren to Mieren. Others had been on their way to port with the people from their estates when they'd been attacked. Again, they'd been captured and passed on.

And they had ended up here.

'But why?' Sorne asked.

They didn't seem to know.

'I think they mean to sell us,' said the T'En girl who had freed him from the ropes. 'The one with the strange way of speaking –'

'The Maygharian,' Sorne inserted.

'He called us "exotics."' She pronounced the Chalcedonian word as if it didn't make sense. 'He said wealthy southerners would pay top price for us. I don't trust him, but when the dirty men tried to take Tiasely away, he wouldn't let them.'

The other children gestured to a beautiful Malaunje girl, who was as big as an adult Mieren woman, for all that she was probably only thirteen.

'I think he's going to sell us as slaves,' the T'En girl said. 'I didn't know the Mieren kept slaves.'

They didn't, strictly speaking, but these children would have ended up in high-class brothels or in the private collection of wealthy men.

'Now that you're here, we don't need to worry,' Orza said, wrapping his arms around Sorne.

The little ones believed him and many wept with relief. Sorne soothed them, but his heart sank; he could not desert them, yet he did not see how he could save them all.

'Quiet, everyone,' Tiasely said.

They obeyed her and tilted their heads, listening. The music had stopped, and there was only one pair of footsteps shuffling across the floor above.

'Everyone's gone,' Orza said.

Several children ran up the stairs to peer into the tavern through the cracks in the door and confirmed this. Others ran over to the cellar doors, climbed onto barrels and peered through the gaps.

'There's a couple of rowboats on the beach. Everyone's getting into them,' one reported.

Sorne slid two small children off his lap and went over to the cellar doors. From this angle he could see the slope down to the beach, the inlet and the different vessels.

'No lanterns,' a boy said. 'They're being sneaky.'

He was right. The rowboats glided from the shore, making their way across the silvery sea of the inlet towards the merchant vessel.

'They're attacking the ship that delivered me,' Sorne said.

'Why would they do that?' someone asked.

'Because then they don't have to pay for me.' Yet he'd gained the impression they'd paid for 'exotics' in the past.

'The ship's crew have spotted them,' one of the boys reported. He kept up a running commentary for the rest of the children, as the sea-vermin boarded the ship. The crew fought valiantly, but they were overrun. Before long, bodies tumbled into the sea and there was celebrating on the ship.

Sorne climbed down. Perhaps he could escape, but in good conscience, he could not leave these children behind.

What was he going to do?

Chapter Thirty

TOBAZIM LOOKED UP from his book, not sure what had disturbed him. Then he heard it again.

The thump of bodies hitting a wall.

'Fighting in the cabin below,' Hand-of-force Norsasno said, coming to his feet. 'That's the initiates' cabin. They're not known for thinking before they act. I'd better –'

'Wait...' Ceyne held up a hand. 'There's bound to be some rivalry between the survivors of Chariode and Tamaron's brotherhoods and ours. Let them work it out.'

An even louder thump was followed by the sound of breaking glass.

Ceyne snorted and reached for his bag.

Tobazim almost got up, but his gift rose and he sensed the forces at play in his brotherhood. If he went with the saw-bones and Norsasno it would make it seem he did not have faith in his hand-of-force. He waved them off.

This left him alone with the brotherhood's gift-tutor. It was the perfect opportunity to broach something that had been bothering him.

He joined Deimosh at the desk. 'What I am about to ask must go no further.'

The gift-tutor nodded.

'The night we fled the wharf, the causare gift-infused me. Since then...' He swallowed. 'The nature of my gift has changed. I used to be able to sense the stresses and weights of a building. I can still do this, but I can also sense the stresses on the brotherhood now, as if it was a building constructed of people.'

'That's... interesting.'

'Have you come across anything like it before?'

He shook his head. 'Your gift-defences were down, thanks to the concussion you'd received that night. You were vulnerable. The causare's gift is the ability to read people. It sounds like she has triggered a new facet of your gift, one that combines her ability with yours. I wonder –'

'If it can be repeated?' Tobazim had been wondering the same thing. He rubbed his head and grimaced. 'I wouldn't recommend trying it.'

Deimosh grinned. 'If I were you, I'd call it a lucky accident and be grateful.'

Tobazim came to his feet. 'Think I'll stretch my legs.'

As he went to open the door, the gift-tutor added, 'No more problems with craving her gift?'

Tobazim turned around. 'You noticed? Did anyone –'

'No. If they wondered why you were pushing yourself so hard, they put it down to the tension with Kyredeon. But I would be wary of her in future. Any taste of her gift could trigger the craving. Now that I think of it, you're lucky you didn't have a bad reaction when she used her gift to enforce the covenant vow.'

Tobazim nodded. He'd told no one, not even Ardonyx, that the causare hadn't enforced the covenant vow. He was grateful, but he didn't understand why she had broken four hundred years of custom.

Still wondering, he went along the passage and out onto the rear-deck. The ships were at anchor tonight, shrouded in fog. He climbed the stairs to the high rear-deck where he found Ardonyx on watch, wrapped in a cloak. His shield-brother smiled when he saw Tobazim, but the smile didn't reach his eyes.

'What is it?' Tobazim asked.

'This fog. We're becalmed until it lifts, and it provides perfect cover for any sea-vermin in the area.'

'We should warn –'

'Don't worry, any sea captain worth his salt will be on alert tonight. If trouble comes, we'll be ready for it.'

RONNYN CURLED UP with his brothers, part of the huddle of T'En boys in the sisterhood's cabin. The ships were at anchor until the fog lifted. The all-mother and her inner circle were on the deck above. He could hear the murmur of their voices and soft music. He wasn't sure why he had woken. Beside him, Vittor shifted restlessly.

'I miss Vella,' his six-year-old brother whispered.

'Tani...' Tamaron muttered in his sleep and rolled over.

Baby Ashmyr stirred, working himself up to a cry. Ronnyn rolled to his feet before Ashmyr could wake the children. When he took the baby outside, he found that the fog had grown even thicker. The lanterns cast pools of golden light, making the air almost tangible.

Ashmyr was crying in earnest by the time Ronnyn climbed up to the foredeck. The women laughed and All-mother Reoden glided over, taking the baby to feed him. When Ashmyr latched on, Ronnyn could hear him gulping.

'He'll get wind.'

'So wise for one so young.'

A cry came from the nearest ship. Through the fog, Ronnyn could just make out the lanterns on the ship's five masts.

Another cry followed.

'Ree, what is it?' Nerazime came running over. 'Not more brotherhood feuding? They swore a vow.'

'That's the *Endurance*, Ceriane and Athazi's ship. I wonder –'

A scream cut her short. Flames leapt up from the ship's deck, glowing in the fog.

'Fire,' Reoden said. 'Send help, Nerazime.'

Her voice-of-reason ran down the steps to the mid-deck.

Ronnyn went to the rail to watch them lower the boats. There was shouting as they organised buckets and volunteers. The empowered lads surged out of the cabin below, jostling and teasing, eager to help.

Through their excited talk, the roar of the fire and desperate shouts of those on the *Endurance*, Ronnyn made out the clang of metal on metal. His stomach clenched.

'Did you hear that?' he asked the all-mother. 'Their ship's under attack.'

Reoden thrust baby Ashmyr into his arms and ran down the steps onto the mid-deck, calling to her hand-of-force. 'Athazi and Ceriane are under attack. Cerafeoni, hand out weapons and go to their aid. Nerazime, secure our ship.'

The mid-deck erupted in a flurry of activity as the hand-of-force from the causare's sisterhood came out with their warriors. Cerafeoni shouted, and the empowered lads poured over the ship's side. Ronnyn shivered, impressed and a little terrified by their eagerness to wade into battle.

He watched the rowboats pull away. Soon the first was swallowed by the fog, and only a dim pool of light told him of its progress. A second followed.

Shouting came from another ship, and more ringing of metal. If he was right, it came from a brotherhood vessel.

Fear chilled him. What if his sisters' ship was under attack? Even as he thought this, Vittor came running out on deck, calling for him. By the time Ronnyn reached the steps, Tamaron was there too, frightened and bewildered.

They both threw their arms around him. He could feel Vittor shaking. How could he protect them all with the baby in his arms?

'Not so tight, you'll squash Ashmyr.' Ronnyn tried to reassure them. It's all right. It's –'

'No, it isn't!' Vittor cried. 'You said we'd be safe with our people, and we're not!'

ARAVELLE SURFACED FROM the sleep of exhaustion. She surfaced with her heart pounding so hard it seemed to shake her whole body. For an instant she didn't know what was wrong. Then the slippery sound of steel-on-steel set her teeth on edge. She sprang into a crouch, ready to run with Itania. Her little sister clutched her, trembling.

In the dimness of Charsoria's cabin, the women woke and whispered fearfully.

Nariska lit a lamp, turning it down low. Children whimpered. The women soothed them, but Charsoria ignored Aravelle and Itania.

Aravelle opened a window. The harsh sound of the fighting increased as tendrils of fog reached into the cabin. 'It's coming from the ship next to us.'

'We should go help,' one of the young warriors said.

'You stay,' Charsoria snapped. 'They'll send for you if they need you.'

The four warriors pulled on their breeches, leather jerkins and boots. They'd just finished dressing when the cabin door swung open. A Malaunje youth gasped for breath. 'Hand-of-Force Reyne calls on all warriors to help fight the sea-vermin.'

'Is our ship under attack?' Charsoria demanded.

'No. It's the *Perseverance*. And I heard that one of the sisterhood ships is on fire.'

'Which one?' Aravelle asked, thinking of Ronnyn and her brothers.

'Don't know.' He dashed off, accompanied by the four warriors.

Aravelle backed up, felt a bunk behind her knees and sat down abruptly. Itania gave a little squeak of fright and her fingers worked on Aravelle's shoulder, seeking reassurance.

Thrusting Itania into Redravia's arms, Aravelle made for the door. 'I must –'

Charsoria grabbed her as she passed, swinging her around. 'Where do you think you're going?'

'To the deck, to find out which sisterhood ship –'

'You'll stay right here.'

'But my brothers –'

'You think they're thinking of you right now? You're nothing to them.'

'Ronnyn will never –'

Charsoria slapped her hard enough to make her stagger.

'Arrogant brat!' Charsoria was so angry she quivered. 'Never make claim on your T'En kin. Do you hear me?'

Aravelle blinked tears of pain from her eyes. 'I just need to know if they are all right.'

'You think you're the only one with T'En kin? I have a son on All-mother Melisarone's ship. He's only two. Do you think I don't worry about him?' Her voice had grown shrill and she made a visible effort to regain control. 'The sisterhoods have sworn to protect the T'En children with their lives. There's nothing we can do, so you can just sit down and keep your mouth shut.'

Charsoria turned away and Hariorta consoled her.

As much as Aravelle hated Charsoria, in that moment she also felt sorry for her. For all of them.

She retreated to her bedroll, where Itania crept into her arms.

After a while, the fighting died down. But now she could smell smoke and hear a dim roaring.

Charsoria told Redravia to prepare a soothing hot milk posset to settle the children. When the old woman brought Aravelle a mug for Itania, it smelt of almonds, lemons and brandy, just like her mother's posset.

'Don't fret,' Redravia whispered. 'Your brothers will be safe. They're on the causare's ship with Healer Reoden.' She squeezed Aravelle's hand. 'You need to accept it, Vella. By the time your brothers take their place as initiates, they won't acknowledge you. If you try to reach out to them, you'll only embarrass yourself and them.'

Rebellion burned in Aravelle's heart. She told herself Ronnyn would never abandon her. But she found Redravia's sympathetic warning much harder to ignore.

* * *

'COME WITH ME.'

Ronnyn led his brothers back to the cabin. He found two empowered lads at the door, armed with long-knives. He knew the lads from weapons practice and had admired their skill. Both were head and shoulders taller than him, and both looked determined. Violence-tinged gift readiness radiated from them, making his heart race.

Inside the cabin all the children and the three old T'En women were clustered at the windows. They'd doused the cabin lamp so that Ronnyn had to pick his way across the floor, which was littered with bedding.

'Over here.' Sardeon made room for them.

Ronnyn let his little brothers climb up to peer out the windows, while he looked over Sardeon's shoulder. All he could make out through the fog was leaping flames and the shadows of people fighting.

'Ronnyn?' Reoden's devotee tapped his shoulder. She held out her arms, dark eyes gleaming with fierce determination. 'Let me take Ashmyr. I can protect him if there's trouble.'

He did not doubt she meant it, and if the sea-vermin attacked, he would have enough to do watching out for Vittor and Tamaron. He handed baby Ashmyr over to her.

And a weight lifted from him. Ever since his father had been gored by the sea-boar, he'd shouldered the load of protecting his family. At least now he didn't have to do it all on his own.

'With that fire we've so much lost,' old Alynar muttered, shaking her head. 'The paintings, the treatises –'

'Just like a historian to value the past over people,' Gift-tutor Sarodyti said, sharing a smile with her scarred shield-sister.

'The fighting's died down,' Sardeon said.

Sarodyti took the old, scarred woman's arm. 'Come, Lysi.'

They lit the lamp and mixed up a warm posset to settle the children. Ronnyn tucked his little brothers into bed. All the while, he watched the other ship.

At last, they heard the sounds of oars breaking water and the rowboats approached the ships.

Ronnyn and Sardeon tried to slip out of the cabin, but Sarodyti spotted them.

'Where are you two off to?'

'They're coming back,' Ronnyn said.

They all went outside then, leaving the devotees to watch over the sleeping children.

The mid-deck was full of Malaunje helping as the empowered lads, Malaunje warriors and T'En sisters from both Reoden and the causare's sisterhoods returned.

'What happened?' Sarodyti asked their hand-of-force.

Cerafeoni was sooty and bloody, but she seemed unharmed. 'Sea-vermin attacked, using the fog as cover. Ceriane's dead, her voice-of-reason and hand-of-force, too, but we saved the T'En children and none of the Malaunje children were lost.'

'How could this happen?' The historian turned on Sarodyti's scarred shield-sister. 'You should have foreseen it, Lysi. You should have warned us.'

'Don't,' Sarodyti warned.

'Don't what? Don't say what everyone's thinking? What good is a scryer, if she won't scry?'

Ronnyn glanced to the scarred woman. She lifted one trembling hand to her mouth, her lips working as if she was trying to hold something back. Her left eye just above the scar twitched and the scar climbed further up her cheek.

He blinked. Surely that scar had not advanced? And, if this sister could see the future, why hadn't she warned them?

With a strangled moan, the scryer turned and ran down the passage towards the cabin.

'Now, look what you've done,' Sarodyti muttered, going to follow her.

The historian caught her arm. 'It's about time someone said it. She might be your shield-sister, but you're not doing her any favours. She has to face this or –'

'Saro, we're going over to the *Endurance* to help treat the injured. You're in charge,' Nerazime announced as she delivered an empowered lad, who was clasping an injured arm to his chest. Blood poured from between his fingers. 'This is one of Ceriane's lads. He fought well. Have Ree's devotee see to him.'

When Nerazime left him, the big lad swayed and almost fell.

Sarodyti beckoned Ronnyn and Sardeon. 'Help him into the cabin before he passes out. Get Meleya to sew him up.'

They guided the injured lad, stumbling and groggy from blood-loss, down the hall. Just inside the cabin, his knees gave out.

Between them, they lowered him to the floor and called for the healer's devotee.

Meleya rolled him over, clucking her tongue as she inspected the wound in his forearm. 'This is deep. It'll need stitching. Fetch the bag, Sardeon.'

The devotee wrapped a cloth around the lad's forearm. 'Ronnyn, I need you to hold this tight as you can and keep his arm raised. We must stop the bleeding.'

Sardeon returned with the bag and she unrolled it, selecting powder, thread and needle. 'This will hurt, lad.'

'You think it doesn't hurt now?' he muttered.

Ronnyn met Sardeon's eyes with a smile.

Meleya threaded the needle. 'Do you want something to bite on... What's your name?'

'Vittor. And I don't want anything to bite on. I want to go back and help.'

'Good lad,' the devotee smiled.

'My brother's called Vittor, too,' Ronnyn said, trying to distract him.

'I'm ready.' The devotee nodded to Ronnyn. 'Release his arm.' He removed the cloth to reveal a long jagged wound in his forearm. 'Nasty. The blade's gone through the muscle.'

Blood pumped from the wound.

Without a sound, Sardeon pitched forward in a dead faint, right across the big lad's legs. It was so unexpected that Ronnyn laughed.

'I should have known,' Meleya muttered. 'His heart's in the right place, but he hasn't got the stomach for it. Get him out of here, Ronnyn.'

He caught Sardeon under the arms, lifted him off the injured lad's legs and dragged him towards the cabin door. By the time they'd reached it, Sardeon had shrugged off his hands and staggered to his feet.

Ronnyn tried to draw him into the hall.

Sardeon brushed him aside. 'I'm all right. I'm not afraid.'

'I didn't say you were.'

'It's just... I hate the sight of blood.'

Ronnyn wondered what Sardeon would do if he had a martial gift.

SORNE HEARD VOICES coming back up the beach towards the tavern. He crept over the sleeping children to peer through the gap in the cellar doors. From the shape of the bodies silhouetted against the silver sea, it was the Maygharian and two of his men. The celebrations on the captured ship had died down; it was late.

'...this ship has fallen into our laps at just the right time,' the Maygharian was saying as they entered the tavern.

Sorne crept through the sleeping children to the steps and positioned himself at the tavern door. Peering through a crack in the wood, he could make out the edge of a table and something on the floor.

The Maygharian lit a lamp, revealing an old woman asleep under the table. He gave her a shove with his boot. 'Get us some food and ale, Loris.'

She scurried off, while the three men sat down. Sorne could only see the edge of a shoulder and the side of someone's face. From their talk, he gathered they were planning a big raid. He'd heard of sea-vermin uniting to attack port towns.

'I don't like it,' one of the men muttered. 'The Marlin sea-king claims he has a power-worker. They're almost as bad as Wyrds.'

'It might be handy to have a power-worker,' the Maygharian said, 'as long as he knows his place.'

'The prize is big,' the other man said, 'but it could be a trick to lure us away so they can steal our exotics. I'm not sure we should trust the other sea-kings.'

'Of course I don't trust them. I don't trust anyone. But only our people know we have a cellar full of exotics. And this is too good an opportunity to miss. The spoils will be divided according to the number and size of the ships we bring. That fat merchant ship means all the more for us.'

'What about the exotics?'

'They'll keep.'

The woman returned with plates of onions and beans. Sorne's stomach rumbled.

The rest of the conversation was about who they'd take and who would remain behind. He gathered the more fighters the better. All of which pleased him.

If everyone who could swing a sword went on the raid, it would be easier to escape with the children. But if the sea-vermin took all of their boats, there was no point escaping the cellar.

Chapter Thirty-One

IMOSHEN WATCHED AS All-mother Ceriane's body slid over the ship's side into the water. It made one small splash as the sea swallowed her body. Ripples spread across the incoming swells. They'd held the farewell ceremony on the deck of the burned ship.

Imoshen was surrounded by the other all-mothers, and their sorrow felt like needle-sharp rain, drumming on her senses.

The scent of burned wood still clung to everything and everyone. The fire had left its mark here on the scorched planks, but it was worse on the foredeck, where Ceriane's cabins had been gutted.

A rope fell down to coil on the deck. A Malaunje sailor hastily retrieved it and scrambled back up the mast. Working silently, out of respect for the dead, the sailors clung to three of the five masts, rigging spare sails. As it turned out, Athazi's ship was well named – the *Endurance* – and Imoshen suspected it was a quality they would all need.

'Poor Ceriane.' Melisarone wiped her cheeks. 'Our only gift-wright, too.'

'What will we do?' Athazi asked. She was barely sixty, yet her face had settled into a perpetual scowl. 'The ability to repair damaged gifts does not arise in every generation. We'll...' She looked up at the healer. 'I'm sorry.'

Imoshen met Reoden's eyes. Her dear friend's sacrare daughter had been identified as a gift-wright when she had been empowered. But thanks to Kyredeon, Lyronyxe hadn't lived to grow into her power.

'Yes, we lost more than a beloved girl-child that day,' Imoshen said. 'But we can be thankful at least half of All-mother Ceriane's people survived, and we didn't lose any of the Malaunje or T'En children.'

Deep, mournful singing carried across the sea to them.

'Over on the *Perseverance*, the brotherhoods are bidding their dead farewell. Both All-fathers Egrutz and Dretsun survived, although I hear Egrutz lost a lot of warriors,' Imoshen said. 'Unfortunately, not enough of Ceriane's high-ranking sisters lived to reform the sisterhood. We'll have to –'

'I'd take her people in,' Athazi said. 'But you can see the state of my ship, half-gutted by fire. Ceriane's sisterhood will have to be split up and spread around the other ships. The most I could take would be the two T'En girls and perhaps some of her Malaunje.'

Imoshen's gift surged and she read satisfaction underneath the offer. Athazi had always envied and resented the gift-wright. Now she would add two girl-children to her sisterhood, while her rival's sisterhood was disbanded.

Imoshen wished her gift left her with some illusions.

'I can take some Malaunje, but my three-masted ship is already too small,' Melisarone said, with genuine regret. 'Ceriane's choice-sons will have to go another all-mother. I'm too old to take on more children, especially boys.'

'I'll take the T'En boys,' Reoden said, prompted by generosity of spirit. Imoshen could have kissed her.

As they organised the details of breaking up Ceriane's sisterhood, Imoshen realised only four all-mothers remained, while there were seven all-fathers. If the brotherhoods put the causareship to the vote, she would be hard-pressed to retain it.

Later, as they were rowing back to the *Resolute*, Reoden said, 'I should have thought before I spoke. Taking in more boys means there's no room for Ronnyn and Sardeon in my cabin, and I don't want to put them in with the empowered lads. It would be cruel when their gifts haven't manifested.'

'You said Sar has been improving since Ronnyn became his choice-brother. I think it might help bring on Sardeon's power if you put them in with the empowered lads.'

'You're not a gift-wright, Imoshen, what makes –'

'We know our gifts react to each other. What if shutting Sardeon away from the other youths on the cusp of –'

'I kept him in seclusion because his gift had gone dormant and he'd stopped growing. I shut him away to protect him.'

'As I recall, before this happened his gift had begun to manifest and he was on the cusp. Maybe he's ready now. Try it and see. What have you got to lose?'

TOBAZIM HAD ALWAYS loved the brotherhood songs. The martial songs, the love songs and the dirges, like this one. It called to something deep inside him as the men sang to farewell those lost on the *Endurance*. The all-fathers and their seconds stood on the high-rear deck, while the Malaunje filled the mid-deck.

As the singing ceased, Ardonyx slipped away to speak with the ship's master.

Meanwhile, the rest of the all-fathers offered their sympathy to Dretsun and Egrutz. The old all-father looked exhausted. His brotherhood had borne the brunt of the attack.

'I hear the adept Egrutz was grooming to replace him was killed last night,' Norsasno whispered. 'Egrutz's brotherhood has been stable for thirty years. But now I fear –'

'Tobazim, it was your voice-of-reason who chose where we anchored last night.' Dretsun stepped up to them. The other brotherhood leaders fell silent, and all turned to watch the confrontation. Tobazim could sense Dretsun's gift, laced with challenge. The all-father gestured to the gathered mourners. 'And look what happened.'

'The wind dropped. That's why we anchored where we did,' Tobazim said. 'We couldn't go anywhere while becalmed.' He felt Norsasno behind him, felt the build-up of gifts feeding off Dretsun's aggression. 'I suppose you're going to blame us for the fog as well.'

'He's got you there,' Paragian said.

'This morning the sea-vermin's sails were still hugging the horizon,' Dretsun said. 'They're waiting for another opportunity to attack us.'

'Depending on the wind, we'll pass the last of the islands sometime today.' Tobazim was glad Ardonyx had shown him the course he'd plotted. 'Then we'll head south by south-west. Our course takes us straight across the Secluded Sea, if the winds favour us. If not, we'll have to tack.' He saw Dretsun did not understand, and gestured. 'Weave back and forth.'

'Why waste time?' Dretsun snapped. 'Why not sail straight?'

'If the wind is blowing from the west and we want to sail into the west, we –'

'What landsmen we all are!' Hueryx mocked. He'd been leaning against the mast, now he straightened up. 'He's saying we have to cut across the wind to fill the sails.'

The all-fathers turned to Hueryx with a certain wariness and Tobazim got the impression they'd felt the sharp edge of his tongue in the past.

Hueryx gestured impatiently. 'Not one of us knows the sea as well as Tobazim's voice-of-reason. Leave it up to him, unless one of the brotherhoods is hiding a weather-worker?'

Had anyone else said this, there would have been laughter. As it was, they broke up and returned to their ships.

'I spoke with Egrutz,' Ardonyx said, as they climbed down to the rowboat. 'He's shattered.'

Tobazim felt his gift rise to incorporate all the other brotherhoods, in a structure that protected but could also threaten his own brotherhood.

When they reached the *Victorious*, Tobazim found the adepts cheering from the rear-deck as they watched a fight on the mid-deck. The brotherhood's initiates crowded around the participants, but they were strangely silent.

He pushed through them to find Iraayel and a skinny youth in his mid-twenties circling each other. Both were bleeding. Up on the mid-deck, Karozar took bets. This was just the sort of thing Tobazim wanted to eradicate.

Furious, he was about to plunge in and pull the two combatants apart, when Ardonyx took his arm and Norsasno broke it up.

Iraayel fell to his knees, holding his side.

'Get him up to the infirmary,' Norsasno ordered.

No one came forward to help Iraayel. As he struggled to his feet, Tobazim's gift told him that although he had accepted the causare's choice-son, his brotherhood hadn't. Even Haromyr and Eryx stood with their arms folded, faces grim.

'This must be a personal grudge match, because when I became all-father I said the initiates would not have to fight for the entertainment of the adepts,' Tobazim said. He rounded on Iraayel. 'Did you offer this initiate insult?'

Iraayel looked offended.

Tobazim turned to the other combatant. 'You...'

'Oteon.'

'Did you offer him insult?'

As Oteon glanced up to the adepts on the rear-deck, Tobazim noticed faded bruising on his ribs. Old habits died hard; his warriors were used to winning stature through force and violence.

Oteon swallowed and grimaced. 'Yes, I insulted him.'

Iraayel blinked in surprise.

Tobazim hadn't expected Oteon to lie. It put him off his stride.

Luckily, Ardonyx stepped in. 'In that case, you are appointed Iraayel's carer until he is healed. Take him up to the infirmary.'

Oteon offered Iraayel his arm. The seventeen-year-old refused it and limped off, holding his side. Oteon followed. The initiates parted for them.

Tobazim looked up at the adepts along the rear-deck rail. Most would not meet his eye, while a few stared down with barely concealed contempt. From the age of seventeen they'd lived under Kyredeon's rule, bowing to fear and intimidation. It was all they understood. Did they think that because he was fair, he was weak?

'Karozar, come down here.'

'What are you going to do?' Ardonyx whispered. 'Reasoning won't convince them.'

'Let me discipline him,' Norsasno offered. 'A certain type only understand violence.'

Tobazim didn't know what he was going to do.

Karozar reported to him, eyes dutifully lowered, but Tobazim noticed the twist to his top lip.

'You were taking bets,' Tobazim said.

Karozar shrugged.

'Do you want to go back to Kyredeon's rule?'

He looked up at that, surprised.

'Because you can,' Tobazim said. He gestured to the side of the ship. 'You can go join him, right now. Him and his inner circle.'

Karozar's eyes widened as he realised what Tobazim meant. He shook his head.

'No?' Tobazim asked. He looked up at the others. 'Anyone else nostalgic for Kyredeon's ways?'

They shook their heads.

'Good. Because this is my brotherhood and we do things my way. Initiates don't fight for the entertainment of adepts.' And he walked off.

'RONNYN, SARDEON?'

They left the ship's side as the last of All-mother Ceriane's people and stores arrived, and reported to the hand-of-force.

Cerafeoni led them to the empowered lads' cabin and stood in the doorway. 'We're moving Ronnyn and Sardeon into this cabin.'

'But neither of them are empowered,' Toryx objected.

'The all-mother's cabin is overcrowded. I want everyone out on deck, now. Time for unarmed combat.'

Having spent all morning moving belongings and stores, the lads groaned, but spilled out onto the mid-deck nonetheless.

Cerafeoni turned to Ronnyn and Sardeon. 'Go get your bedrolls, then join the class.'

Behind her back, Toryx held Ronnyn's eyes and made an obscene gesture.

As they headed down the passage to the all-mother's cabin, Ronnyn felt sheer terror. He'd been able to ignore it up until now, but what if his gift never came back? He grabbed Sardeon. Since the only place they could be private was the bathing chamber, he pulled him in there and shut the door.

It was on the tip of his tongue to confess everything.

'What is it?' Sardeon asked. He looked pale and slightly ill.

'I'll make a pact with you. I'll watch your back, if you watch mine. Like shield-brothers.'

'We can't be shield-brothers,' Sardeon said. 'You'll be joining Hueryx's brotherhood and I'll –'

'Shield-brothers until we leave the sisterhood?' Ronnyn rolled his sleeve, baring his arm from the wrist to the elbow. 'I swear on my honour to protect you.'

Sardeon hesitated for so long Ronnyn thought he would refuse, then he pulled up his sleeve, clasped Ronnyn's hand, and entwined their fingers. 'I swear to protect you.' He released Ronnyn's hand. 'Did you see Toryx?'

'Yes. If we were empowered, they'd accept us.'

'We'd still have to prove ourselves, but yes, they'd be more accepting.'

'Has your gift manifested yet?'

Sardeon went very still. 'Has yours?'

'Yes.' It had, but not since he reached port. 'It was...' Ronnyn recalled the intense rush of power. He missed this. 'It was driving me crazy back on the island, always demanding to be used. I spent all my time trying to hide it or guide it. Back then there was no one to show me what to do. My mother told me to beware the higher plane. But I had no idea what she meant. How about you?'

Sardeon looked away. 'I...'

Ronnyn waited.

'I think we should get our bedrolls. Cerafeoni will be waiting.'

In the all-mother's cabin, the sisters were fussing over three little T'En boys from Ceriane's sisterhood. The boys were uninjured, but they looked stunned by what they'd been through. Ronnyn remembered that feeling.

Vittor spotted Ronnyn rolling up his bedding and hurried over with Tamaron at his heels. 'What's going on?'

'We've been sent to the cabin with the big lads,' Ronnyn told him.

Tamaron's chin trembled.

Ronnyn knelt, taking his little brother's shoulders in his hands. 'You have to be brave. Vittor will be here to look after you, and I'll be coming back to check on the three of you.'

Tamaron nodded, but tears slipped down his cheeks.

'I'm only going up the hall to the next cabin,' Ronnyn said, but they all knew the move was much more significant. He glanced over to the three little boys. 'I want you to do something for me. See those three new boys? Their mother died last night, fighting to save their lives. We know what it's like to lose our mother. I want you to look after them. Can you do that?'

They both nodded and Vittor put his arm around Tamaron. 'We'll be good to them.'

Tamaron nodded.

'I know you will.' Ronnyn kissed his brothers. 'I'm so proud of you.'

When he came to his feet, Sardeon was watching him. 'What?'

'I'm glad you became my choice-brother.'

Ronnyn shrugged, but he was touched. He slung his bedroll over his shoulder and wrapped his arm around

Sardeon's shoulder. 'Me too. I'd hate to move into the empowered lads' cabin without you.'

As soon as it was light enough, Sorne inspected their prison. The cellar was dug into the earth and lined with scavenged boards. The low side, facing the beach, was half exposed. He thought that with a bit of effort he could force the cellar doors, but he would have to choose the right moment. He was not leaving the children behind, and there was no point escaping if they could not get them all off the island.

The tavern door at the top of the stairs could also be forced, but when he peered through a knot-hole in the wood, he saw several people snoring under the tables.

After the capture of the merchant ship and subsequent celebrations, their captors were late waking up. The Maygharian had to bellow to get them moving, but before long, they were packing supplies onto the three skiffs. The Maygharian's banner now hung from the tallest mast of the merchant ship. They appeared to be stocking all their sailing vessels, which did not fill him with hope.

It was not like he could put to sea with twenty children in an open rowboat. That morning, no one remembered to feed them, and the children resorted to eating raw potatoes and carrots, and chewing on grain. Since they'd run out of water, Sorne gave them ale. It was mild, but it made them sleepy. And then, of course, they had to pee and filled the buckets.

It was almost mid-afternoon by the time the tavern door opened and a shaft of light came down the cellar steps.

The Maygharian entered, carrying a lantern. One of his men followed, his hand on his sword hilt, and the old woman carried a pot and a basket of bread scraps. The two biggest boys, brothers Vivore and Vivane, were sent to take the buckets away and bring down fresh ones. Meanwhile, the Maygharian hung the lantern and beckoned Sorne.

As he ducked his head to step under a beam, the swordsman kicked him in the back of the knee and he fell at the Maygharian's feet.

'No, don't get up,' he told Sorne, then gestured to the swordsman. 'Pass me one of those brats. The little one over there will do.'

The swordsman picked her up by the back of her shirt like a kitten and tossed her to the Maygharian. She flew through the air with a shriek.

The Maygharian caught her and held her in front of Sorne. 'I've got plenty of exotics, but only one Warrior's-voice. If you give me trouble, I'll kill this one, or another one. I don't mind which. If you give me trouble a second time, I'll kill two of them. You get my drift?'

Sorne nodded, keeping his head lowered.

'Good.' He tossed the child aside.

She rolled and came to her knees sobbing. The rest of the children crowded around her, consoling her. Then they drew her over to Tiasely, who was doling out the scraps. There was no fighting; they waited patiently.

'I'm going away for a few days,' the Maygharian said. 'But I'm taking the skiffs and the merchant vessel. Don't you even think of escaping. I know this island like the back of my hand, so there's no point running off.' He gestured to the old woman. 'This is Loris. If I come back and find you've hurt her, I'll let my men take the pretty girl and do what they've been wanting to do all along.'

Sorne nodded again.

After they'd gone, he sat on the steps and rubbed his face, feeling overwhelmed. He couldn't take twenty-two children out on the open sea in a ten-man rowboat. It would be suicidal. And running away was pointless. What he really needed was one of the skiffs the Maygharian was taking with them.

Tiasely brought him a crust of bread.

'Thank you,' he said. 'Tell the oldest and most sensible of the children to come over here.'

She returned with seven youngsters who looked to be ten years of age or older. Apart from the T'En girl, they were all Malaunje. 'Can any of you sail a boat?'

'He's taking all the ships,' the T'En girl said.

'But he isn't taking the rowboat.'

'You'd put twenty-two children in a rowboat? That'd be awfully crowded.'

'It would,' Sorne agreed. 'What's your name?'

'Yosune.'

'Well, Yosune, I'd put twenty-two children in a rowboat and take you all to the nearest uninhabited island to make him think we've sailed off. Then, when they came back, I'd steal the smallest skiff. Does anyone here know how to handle a boat?'

They all looked at each other.

'We're from a winery,' Vivane said, gesturing to himself and his brother, 'but we used to fish on the river.'

'That's a start,' Sorne said. 'Anyone else?'

They shook their heads.

'When would we go?' Tiasely asked.

'We'd have to escape just before they returned from the raid,' Sorne said. 'Then I'd come back here. If last night is anything to go by, they'll celebrate and get drunk. That'll be the best time to steal the skiff.'

'But how do we know when they're due to come back?' Yosune asked.

'We'll watch the old woman. She'll know.'

'They're leaving,' one of the smaller boys said.

All the children ran to the cellar doors. The tallest climbed up to peer through the gaps in the panels.

Sorne watched the Maygharian put to sea with his fleet of the skiffs and his merchant vessel flagship. Half a dozen children, a very pregnant woman, three old men, the tavern keeper Loris and a girl of about fourteen waved them off. Every able-bodied man and woman had gone on the raid.

As though released from work, those left behind spent the afternoon frolicking on the beach. The children played, while the old folk and pregnant woman watched. They all went to bed early.

It was the perfect opportunity, but Sorne had to time their escape. Too soon and the children would be left exposed on an uninhabited island. Too late and the Maygharian and his cut-throats would return.

And even if he timed it perfectly, slipped back and stole a small skiff... Sorne had a theoretical knowledge of the sea. He'd watched captains plot courses. He'd watched first mates bellow orders to sailors, to lower or raise sails. He knew how to tack before the wind. He knew Ivernia lay to the south-west and the port of Sorvernia, which was home to the Sagoras, lay halfway down the southern island.

If he put to sea in a skiff with these children they could all die.

But if he didn't...

KNOWING THEY WEREN'T welcome, Ronnyn and Sardeon had slipped into the empowered lads' cabin late when everyone had already spread out their bed-mats. As soon as Ronnyn opened the cabin door, the feel of so many gifts packed into one chamber hit him.

It was powerful and raw, and it should have triggered his own gift, but nothing happened. It frustrated him, but more than that it frightened him. He felt robbed, as if he'd lost the ability to speak; he could still hear and understand, just not communicate.

Several of the lads were still awake, playing cards. Vittor nodded to them, then laid down his cards one-handed. 'I claim the sisterhood. I have the all-mother, both seconds and a gift-tutor.'

The others laughed and threw in their cards.

In another corner, two lads arm-wrestled. Toryx spoke to his friends and they all cast Ronnyn and Sardeon filthy looks.

There was not a lot of floor space left. Ronnyn chose a spot against the wall, near the door to the bathing chamber, and they unrolled their bed-mats.

The laughter and talk went on for a long time. Ronnyn lay still and pretended to sleep. He didn't think Sardeon was asleep either. At one point he woke because the tang of gift was so strong on the air. He heard muttering and realised one of the lads was having a bad dream and his gift had surged in response to his nightmare.

Ronnyn put his arm over his head but he couldn't escape the pall of power that surrounded him.

Chapter Thirty-Two

THAT NIGHT, WHEN Sorne lay down to sleep, the little ones wanted to be next to him. The ones furthest from him would wake, climb over the sleeping bodies and wriggle in beside him. After a while, the child who had been shoved to the edge would wake and the process would be replayed. It happened over and over. He didn't mind. It meant he slept lightly and was awake when the raiders arrived.

The Maygharian's second had been wise to suspect trickery. The first Sorne knew of it was when he heard a shriek from above. It cut off abruptly, followed by a thump and heavy footsteps.

Deep voices spoke, their words indistinct.

Sorne slipped from the tangle of children and climbed the steps to peer into the tavern. Someone had lit a lamp. He saw the old woman, Loris, sitting on a chair, her face obscured by a man's broad shoulders.

'Tell us,' the man ordered. When he didn't like her response, he slapped her and stepped back.

Blood covered her mouth, chin and chest, but anger burned in her pale blue eyes as another raider stepped into view.

'It's really simple,' the second man said. 'We know the Maygharian sea-king has been successful. We want to know where he keeps his spoils. You'll tell us before we're finished, so save yourself the pain and tell us now.'

'And then you'll kill me. Why should I tell you a thing?' She spat a gob of bloody phlegm at him.

He swore and back-handed her, knocking her off the chair.

Sorne heard whimpers behind him and hurried down the steps. He gathered Tiasely, Yosune and the two big boys. 'Take the children into the shadows. Hide. Bad men have come.'

Then he returned to the top of the stairs to peer through the crack. He spotted four raiders and the old woman. Of the three old men who usually slept on the tavern floor, only one was present. He lay in an ever-widening puddle of blood.

Hopefully, the other two had slipped out to warn the women and children.

Even as Sorne thought this, a fifth man returned. 'They got away, but there's cunny here. I found this.' He held up a pale night gown and sniffed it. 'Still warm, smells of –' He broke off as two of the raiders launched themselves out the back steps, and he followed, yelling that he wanted his share. Sorne could hear their taunts as they searched the nearby buildings.

This left the leader and his brute.

The leader cursed and turned.

Loris had grabbed a knife from somewhere. She sprang for him, slashing his chest.

Sorne threw his shoulder at the door, felt it give. Slammed into it again and stumbled into the tavern.

The leader grappled with Loris, his chest bleeding freely. The brute turned to Sorne. Seeing a white-haired, one-eyed half-blood come out of nowhere, he stood stunned for a heartbeat.

Sorne charged him, took him in the belly and drove him into the bar. He heard the man's spine crack. Stepping back, Sorne pulled the long knife from the raider's belt and the sword from his sheath, then let him fall.

As he turned, he looked through the open tavern door and saw a small, single-sailed fishing boat anchored in the shallows.

The sound of smashing glass made him spin around to find the leader throttling Loris. She'd just broken a bottle over his head, but she was failing.

Sorne rushed the raider.

Thrusting Loris aside, the man drew his sword and swung at Sorne, who deflected the blade, catching it on his sword hilt, and stabbed him under the ribs with the knife.

The leader of the raiders fell to his knees, then pitched forward.

Loris lay on her back panting, amidst spilled alcohol and the toppled lantern. As Sorne went to her, she lifted a hand to protect herself.

He knelt. 'Are you all right?'

She nodded.

'I'm going, and I'm taking the children in the skiff.'

She didn't argue.

He sprang to his feet and turned towards the dark cellar steps, where he saw the eldest two boys watching.

A scream reached them through the tavern's open back door, followed by desperate shrieks. The other three sea-vermin had found the women and children.

'Stay here. There's more of them,' Sorne told the boys. 'I'll be back.'

And he ran out the rear door. He hadn't been outside the tavern, and he'd only ever seen the settlement at night. There was a jumble of buildings, but light only spilled from one open door and he ran towards it.

The single room was a shambles. Bedding lay strewn across the planks, and an old man lay in a puddle of blood, gasping. He pointed out the back door as someone shrieked again.

Sorne ran through the room to a back verandah. Here the earth fell away and he could see bushes silhouetted against the starry sky. Right below him the three raiders had the fourteen-year-old girl on her knees, by her hair.

One of them looked up, saw Sorne and went to warn his companions.

Sorne jumped the railing. Thumping into their backs feet first, he drove two of them to the ground. The third released the girl, who scrambled away as Sorne rolled to his knees.

The two he'd knocked to the ground were still down, but the third drew his blade and tried to run Sorne through before he could rise.

Sorne ducked lower and deflected the sword stroke. His blade snapped off not far from the hilt, but he was already driving the knife up into the man's groin. His attacker screamed and crumpled.

Before Sorne could rise, he was tackled from behind. He fell forward and rolled out of the way as a sword buried itself in the dirt near his face. A man stood over him, pulled the sword free and went to strike again.

Sorne lifted his broken sword to deflect the blow.

A skinny arm snaked around the man's head as the girl cut his throat. He toppled and she spat on him.

Sorne snatched the raider's fallen sword and came to his feet. When he looked around, he saw Loris had come to the girl's aid. The old woman clutched her stomach and collapsed as the third man pulled his sword free.

The attacker turned to confront Sorne, who moved into position, sword tip raised, knife arm behind him. The girl backed off.

They circled each other on the uneven slope. When the light from the open backdoor was in Sorne's eyes, the man struck, swinging his sword in an arc that would have taken off Sorne's head.

He dropped, stepped in and under, and gutted the man with the knife.

The man fell to one side, and Sorne leaned forward on one arm, gasping for breath.

After a moment, the dizziness passed and he lifted his head to see a dozen small faces watching him from underneath the verandah: the sea-vermin's children.

The fourteen-year-old girl eyed Sorne. He struggled to his feet, feeling light-headed and shaky. The very pregnant woman came running through the shack, one hand under her belly, a meat cleaver in the other.

She looked at Sorne, then to the fourteen-year-old.

'It's all right,' the girl said. She beckoned the children. 'You can come out now.'

Sorne ran around the building and up the lane between the two shacks. Something moved in the shadows behind a water barrel.

Sorne reached in and hauled out a third old man, who whimpered and lifted his hands.

Letting him go, Sorne ran out onto the street to find the tavern well alight. Flames poured into the dark night. The roar of the fire drowned all other sounds.

Horror gripped him. He'd told the children to stay in the cellar.

Sorne ran towards the rear door, but flames beat him back. Desperate, he ran around the front of the tavern, took in the empty beach, the skiff at anchor and the overturned rowboat.

He made for the cellar doors. The heat was incredible, singeing his face, searing his throat with each breath.

He kicked the cellar doors, pulling burning timber apart to reach the children. Before he could get to them, the roof of the tavern fell in with a terrible crash. Flaming cinders swirled around him, landing on his shoulders. The tavern was nothing but a raging inferno.

Someone grabbed him, dragged him back and rolled him on the sand, beating at his head. He tried to fight them until he realised his hair was alight.

A bucket of water was dashed across his head and shoulders.

He gasped, tasting salt on his tongue.

The fourteen-year-old girl backed off with the empty bucket and the old man watched him, wiping his sooty hands on his stomach.

Sorne struggled to his knees in the sand and stared at the tavern. Only the shell remained. Most of the building had fallen into the cellar, where flames still burned fiercely, crackling and roaring. Smaller flames licked the remaining upright beams.

Tears streamed down his wet face.

He lifted his hands to wipe the tears away, only to discover his palms and fingers were blistered.

Someone tapped him on the shoulder.

He shrugged them off. Why had he left the children?

The hand persisted, tugging at his singed shirt.

He glanced at them.

Tiasely?

Seeing his stunned expression, she smiled and led him over to the rowboat. When she knocked on the boat's belly, one side of the boat rose and the children crawled out. All of them.

Sorne fell to his knees, stunned with relief and joy as they swamped him.

A few moments later, he lifted his head to see the girl and the old man watching them. There was no sign of the pregnant woman and the other children.

Sorne stood. Finding he still had the knife tucked in his waistband, he drew it and backed off towards the skiff.

'I'm going and I'm taking the children,' Sorne told them. 'Tiasely, get the little ones in the boat. Vivane, pull up the anchor.'

Behind him, he could hear splashing and soft voices as the bigger children waded out to the skiff with the little ones in their arms.

The old man said something to the girl. She ran back to one of the buildings.

Sorne didn't wait to find out what she was up to. He waded through the shallows until he felt the boat at his back. He passed the knife over to Yosune and pulled himself into the vessel.

Twenty-two small faces looked up hopefully at him. From the size of the small cabin, he guessed it would have two bunks. There was only one sail. That would make it easier for him to manage.

The sound of splashing made him turn.

The girl reached the boat and thrust an armful of blankets and supplies at him. He accepted them automatically.

'Wait,' she told him. 'You'll need more. Do you have fresh water?'

'I don't know.' He beckoned the nearest boy. 'Put this in the cabin. Check what food and water is aboard.'

When he turned around, the girl had gone again, but the old man had come down to stand on the hard sand revealed by the retreating tide. If Sorne wasn't careful, the skiff would be stranded here.

He grabbed the oar and went to the prow, pushing off the sand to free the boat's nose. The old man grabbed the rope to prevent it drifting out further. In all, the girl made four trips, supplying them with water, blankets and food.

As she handed over the final bundle, she told him, 'This is one of the last habitable western islands. You'll need to be careful picking your way through the channels back to the coast.'

'We're not going back. We're going to Ivernia,' Sorne said, then cursed his too-ready tongue.

'Then sail south-west and you'll hit the northern island. If you want the south island, make your way down the coast. Less time in the open sea.'

He thanked her. 'What will you tell the Maygharian?'

'The raiders came. They took you all and burned the tavern.'

He nodded and waved goodbye.

Then he unfurled the sail, but there was no breeze and dawn was still a little time off. He let the ebbing tide draw them out of the bay into the channel, where the current took them and, by the time the sun rose, bringing with it a light wind, they were already out of sight of the island.

As long as he kept the rising sun behind him and the wind proved fair, they would be all right. It was just a matter of holding to their course.

He hoped.

At least he didn't have to worry about sea-vermin any more.

In this craft, he would be mistaken for one of their own.

Chapter Thirty-Three

RONNYN KICKED, REMEMBERING to keep his toes curled back so that the ball of his foot struck the padded target. He enjoyed martial training. It felt good to push his body, feeling it grow stronger every day. Even his bad arm was improving, although it would never be perfect.

'Come on, you can kick harder than that,' Toryx teased.

Ronnyn ignored him. He wasn't sure why Reoden's hand-of-force had put the trouble-maker with him and Sardeon. If she hoped Toryx would get over his dislike of them, it wasn't working.

Adjusting his stance, Ronnyn wiped sweat from his top lip and kicked again.

'Good,' Cerafeoni said as she came up behind him. 'You and Sardeon are quick learners. When you've mastered the basics, I'll teach you the first pattern. They're all based on the goal of disarming an armed opponent. When King Charald the Peacemaker forbade us carrying any blade larger than our hunting knives, he didn't realise what he'd unleashed. And we've had three hundred years to perfect the techniques.' She grinned, mischief clear in her one good eye. 'And one day I'll show you how much damage a long-knife can do.'

With a nod of approval, she indicated that it was Sardeon's turn.

Ronnyn watched his choice-brother concentrate, trying to impress Cerafeoni. Sardeon tried so hard, he tensed up too much and made a poor job of it.

'Keep trying,' she said as she moved on.

Sardeon would be furious with himself. To give his new

choice-brother privacy, Ronnyn turned to watch the older empowered lads, admiring their flexibility and skill.

Glancing back, Ronnyn was just in time to see Toryx move the target as Sardeon struck. Then the older lad stepped through, knocking Sardeon off his feet before he could recover his balance.

'Hey!' Ronnyn protested.

Sardeon sprang to his feet, fast as a cat. Despite being a head shorter and slender, he confronted Toryx. Ronnyn tensed. This was going to end badly; maybe not today, but one day soon. Toryx had almost three years' training in gift-working and martial techniques.

Toryx smirked. 'Try me, pretty boy.'

Cheeks red with fury, Sardeon trembled with anger.

Toryx smiled and took a step forward, eager for confrontation. 'Come on. Give me a reason to lay a hand on you!'

'Leave them alone,' Vittor warned.

Toryx turned.

The injured lad from the gift-wright's sisterhood pushed away from the rail where he had been leaning. With his arm stitched and strapped to his chest, he could do little to back up his threat. Even so, Vittor's eyes glittered with gift immanence. Ronnyn's heart raced.

Toryx backed down, slipping away.

Ronnyn watched him go. 'Why does he hate us? Why goad Sardeon?'

'To establish his dominance over him.'

'Toryx has been training since he was thirteen. Now he's almost sixteen. He should be teaching us, not trying to belittle us.'

Vittor rolled his eyes. 'I know you're sharing our cabin because we've run out of room, but why are you practising martial training with us?'

'Cerafeoni said we were the same size so we'd make good training partners.' Ronnyn felt defensive. 'She says we're doing well.'

'You're going to have to do better than that. Lads who are prettier than most girls have a hard time in the brotherhood.'

'I'm not pretty,' Ronnyn objected.

'No, but there's something appealing about you. It'll have the sisters requesting you for trysts.' He gestured. 'As for you, Sardeon, your face is going to get you in trouble. You'll need backup.'

At that moment, Cerafeoni ended the training session.

Vittor gestured to her. 'Ask your hand-of-force. It's her job to prepare you for the brotherhood.' And he strode off.

Ronnyn watched Vittor go, thinking there were so many things he didn't understand. 'You'll be sent to your father's brotherhood and I'll be sent to mine, Sar. Let's make a pact. If we both become all-fathers, we'll form an alliance.'

No answer.

'Sar?'

His choice-brother had walked off.

Had he said something to offend him?

'Ronnyn?' Their choice-mother had been watching from the foredeck. She beckoned him.

By the time he'd climbed up there, the scryer and Sarodyti were with her. Scryer Lysitzi barely glanced at Ronnyn, her expression dismissive. Or perhaps it was just the way the scar turned down the corner of her mouth.

'So, Ronnyn,' Reoden turned to him after the old scryer and Sarodyti left. 'How are you and Sardeon settling into the empowered lads' cabin?'

'They're not so bad. I like Vittor,' Ronnyn said, then dared to ask, 'Why didn't you heal the scryer's scar?'

The healer cast him a sharp look and seemed to consider before answering. 'That wound will not heal until she forgives herself. She failed to foresee my sacrare daughter's murder. She hasn't been able to scry since. Her gift eats away at her, just as the scar eats away at her face. Did you notice how it grew the night of the sea-raiders' attack?'

He nodded, dry mouthed. 'I was wondering if I'd imagined it.'

'The gifts are dangerous, Ronnyn. They exact a price. Lysi's gift will consume her if she does not forgive herself. I've forgiven her. I've even forgiven the warriors who killed my little girl.'

'I don't understand how you could,' he confessed. He'd want revenge. 'And I don't see how you can rear us boys, knowing we are promised to the brotherhoods.'

Reoden was half a head taller than him. She leaned closer so that she looked deep into his eyes. He saw her sadness, and beneath it a compassion that had no end.

'I do it because I'm rearing all-fathers who will be able to see beyond their own brotherhood. These all-fathers will serve the whole T'Enatuath.' She gestured to the upper rear-deck cabins. 'We elected Imoshen to be our causare to save us from the King Charald the Oath-breaker, but I believe the role of causare will live on. I'm rearing all-fathers who will be worthy of becoming causare or, if the causare is an all-mother, they will be her trusted commanders. Then, instead of tearing ourselves apart, the T'Enatuath will grow in strength!'

Inspired by her vision, Ronnyn's heart soared.

IMOSHEN LIFTED THE spy-glass to her eye to study the sea-vermin's sails. Like a wolf pack following a herd, the raiders had been trailing them, even three days out from the coast.

'Here.' She handed the spy-glass to Saffazi.

'There's more than yesterday.' The initiate lowered the glass and returned it to Imoshen. 'I thought they wouldn't follow us into the Secluded Sea in winter.'

'Usually sea-vermin stay close to the islands, where they can hide or escape over shoals the deeper-keeled ships cannot cross. But they are notoriously good sailors.'

'Their ships are so much smaller than ours. Surely they can't mean to make a frontal assault?'

'Their vessels might be small, but each one is packed

with warriors eager for gold. Our ships are packed with old folk, nursing mothers, babies and children.'

Imoshen beckoned the ship's master.

The veteran Malaunje sailor strode over to them.

'What do you think?' She passed him the spy-glass. 'Will they attack?'

He planted his legs and studied the sails, which had kept their distance, sometimes drifting back until only the tips of the tallest masts could be seen above the horizon.

Just then Egrayne joined them on deck. She stared towards the horizon, a frown drawing her dark brows together. 'We've already beaten them back once, and their losses were terrible. Surely they won't attack again?'

Imoshen waited, but the ship's master didn't speak. 'Each ship is a little kingdom, and they prize their freedom too much to form a fleet under one leader.'

'Usually. But...' The ship's master lowered the spy-glass, speaking up at last. 'There's twice as many sails as this time yesterday.'

'Then they are massing to attack?' Imoshen asked.

'They've known all summer that we were to be banished. They've had time to plan.'

They all stared at the distant sails.

'The threat of our gifts used to keep our enemies at bay,' Egrayne said.

'I've heard...' the ship's master began, then hesitated. Imoshen gestured for him to go on. He shrugged. 'I've heard Mieren captains claim that there's a sea-vermin power-worker who speaks directly to the sea god. They say he can call the wind.'

Egrayne snorted. 'Save me from Mieren captains and their sea god!'

'But Mieren don't have innate power,' Saffazi objected. 'How could –'

'He would have to draw power from the empyrean plane,' Egrayne said. 'If he can summon the wind, he's using stolen power to do it.'

'If he can summon the wind, then his prey would benefit from the wind just as much as the sea-vermin,' Imoshen said. 'Unless he could make the wind blow only over his own sails!'

The ship's master chuckled.

'Do they or don't they have a power-worker?' Egrayne asked.

He shrugged. 'You hear things...'

Egrayne sent Imoshen a look of exasperation, but underneath it there was fear. Back in the Celestial City, her voice-of-reason's insights had been invaluable navigating the shoals of brotherhood and sisterhood rivalry, but out here, Egrayne was out of her depth. She knew it and she didn't like it.

Out here, there was only one T'En whose knowledge of the sea Imoshen trusted, and Ardonyx would take precautions if he thought the fleet was in danger.

RONNYN RAN OVER the dunes, searching for his sister. Aravelle was here somewhere, lost and alone, needing him. He just knew it.

The axe felt good in his hand; felt right, like an extension of himself.

He looked down – his bad arm was perfect – and knew this was a dream. Yet it felt so real.

The sense that Aravelle was in danger returned, stronger this time. He recognised where he was. It was the last dune before the beach; the dune they'd rounded to find a Mieren fisherman washed up on the shore, so long ago. It was the day they saw their gentle father strangle a defenceless man to protect their family.

It was the end of their childhood, although he hadn't realised it then. He'd felt safe on their island. Now nothing was safe and he had to save Aravelle.

When he reached the crest of the dune, he saw her on the beach, silhouetted against the sparkling water, looking into the setting sun.

'Vella!'

She turned. But it wasn't his sister.

This girl had the silver hair of the T'En, and he didn't recognise her. Now he felt something else on the beach with them, something big and dangerous and not civilised.

Raw and powerful, it surged between him and the girl. Terror filled his chest.

He woke with a start and sat bolt upright. Silver moonlight came in through the windows, illuminating the empowered lads' cabin.

'Lyxie...' Sardeon moaned.

A wave of gift immanence rolled off him, engulfing Ronnyn, prickling across his skin. It seemed his choice-brother's power had manifested but it didn't trigger his own gift.

Sardeon's breathing grew short and tight. He frowned and muttered under his breath. 'Watch out. It's coming. Watch –'

'You're having a nightmare, Sar,' Ronnyn whispered, shaking his shoulder gently. 'Wake up.'

But Sardeon didn't wake.

Ronnyn cupped his cheek. Immediately, Sardeon's nightmare engulfed Ronnyn. They were back on that beach. No, the beach dissolved into a formless plain of shadows, hillocks and prowling, sentient danger.

Terror engulfed Ronnyn. So cold...

He spun around.

Saw Sardeon. Really *saw* him for the first time. Without the distraction of his beauty, Ronnyn saw that his choice-brother was a blade: keen, sharp, driven and determined. He was so surprised that he forgot his fear.

Then he sensed something stalking them, creeping closer and preparing to pounce.

He ran, tackled Sardeon and...

They both woke, gasping with terror.

For a heartbeat, Sardeon stared at Ronnyn as though he was a stranger. Then recognition hit him and he shuddered so badly his teeth chattered.

'You were having a bad dream,' Ronnyn told him, rubbing Sardeon's chest, over his racing heart, like his mother used to do. 'Your gift dragged me into your dream.'

'My gift?' Sardeon brushed off his hand. 'Don't be cruel.'

Cruel? Ronnyn frowned. 'I felt your gift, Sar. I would never lie to you.'

Still, his choice-brother didn't believe him.

He caught Sardeon's wrist, brought the tender skin to his face and opened his senses. 'There... It's still on your skin. See.'

For a moment it seemed his choice-brother would refuse to open his gift awareness; then he closed his eyes, and when he opened them, they blazed with hope.

Ronnyn nodded, happy for him, despite his own disappointment. 'You dragged me into your nightmare. In the first dream, I saw a T'En girl on the beach. She was in danger. Was it Lyronyxe? You called her Lyxie.'

'I was dreaming of her,' he admitted. 'I'll try to...' He hugged his knees, then closed his eyes.

Ronnyn watched, and waited. He wanted Sardeon to reach for his gift and find it. He wanted it so badly...

He realised it was his own gift that he wanted to find.

Sardeon frowned in concentration and his knuckles went white. If sheer force of will could have made his gift rise, then it would have.

But Ronnyn could sense nothing. His heart sank.

Sardeon let his breath out in a long sign of resignation. 'It won't come when I summon it. I'm still useless.'

'Don't say that. It's normal for the gift to rise and fall.' Or it had been in his experience. Sardeon shook his head with such certainty that Ronnyn asked, 'What aren't you telling me?'

His choice-brother looked down.

'There should be no secrets between shield-brothers.'

'You're right.' Sardeon drew him out of the cabin and into the passage, where he turned to face him, his beautiful face stark with determination. 'You need to know the truth if we are to be true friends. I've been lying to you since we first met.'

Ronnyn tensed. Some he knew what was coming.

'It's all very well for you,' Sardeon told him. 'Your gift was manifesting, back on the island, but I...' He looked down and his perfect features became a mask.

'You lost your gift,' Ronnyn said.

'Yes. How did you know?' Sardeon asked, then didn't wait for an answer. 'The day Lyronyxe was killed, my gift suffered a flare-out when I followed her onto the higher plane. I haven't felt even the smallest glimmer of power for nearly five years. When my gift went dormant, I stopped growing. I'm not turning thirteen like you. I'm already seventeen. I should be with my brotherhood.'

Ronnyn stared at him, stunned. To be trapped in the body of a twelve-year-old. He shuddered.

'I sicken you,' Sardeon whispered. 'I don't blame you. I sicken me. There have been times when I thought of taking the honourable –'

'You don't sicken me. Your predicament frightens me,' Ronnyn admitted, 'but tonight I felt your gift manifest, so –'

'Then why can't I call it? Our gift-tutor once praised my control. She was preparing me for empowerment. Now...'

'Ask our choice-mother's advice. Tell her tomorrow.'

'Tell her that I'm a liability who can't control his gift? What if it wasn't a dream? What if I'd dragged you onto the higher plane? What –' Sardeon broke off. 'You said there were two dreams?'

Ronnyn nodded. 'In the first one I was on the beach and I saw Lyronyxe. Then I woke up and you were having a nightmare. I touched your cheek to wake you, but your dream swamped me. We were –'

'On a formless plane. I remember now. You came after me, Ronnyn...' He raised shocked eyes. 'We were on the empyrean plane.'

Ronnyn's mouth went dry. 'Are you sure? I thought you had to be empowered and trained to segue to the higher plane.'

'With control, yes. But it can happen by accident. All it takes is a gift surge and you don't need training. The day Lyronyxe died, I followed her, looking for her shade. Tonight...' Sardeon clutched his arm. 'I could have gotten us both killed.'

Ronnyn squeezed his hand. 'But you didn't. We came back safe and your gift has manifested.'

'When I'm asleep and unable to control it. What good is a gift I can't harness? It's worse than no gift at all. At least if my gift was dead, I couldn't be dragged onto the empyrean plane.'

'You must tell our choice-mother.'

Sardeon pulled away from him.

'Why not? She'll be pleased.'

'I have no control. She'll be disappointed in me. I'll tell her when I can...' He succumbed to a jaw-cracking yawn and frowned. 'Why am I so tired? I can hardly think.'

Ronnyn wasn't surprised. The first few times his gift had surged beyond his control, he'd been exhausted afterwards. Come to think of it, he was tired now. That last dream had really taken it out of him. 'Go to sleep. Things will look better in the morning.'

'I've had nearly five years of mornings, and it hasn't improved.' But even as he said this, Sardeon yawned again. Somehow, he even managed to yawn elegantly.

Ronnyn slid an arm around his choice-brother and led him back to their bedrolls. 'Go to sleep. I'll wake you if you have a nightmare.'

'Thank you.' Sardeon tried to keep his eyes open. He frowned. 'I don't know why you're such a good friend to me.'

'You think too much.'

A weary smile tugged at Sardeon's lips. His eyes shut and stayed that way, but he still fought sleep. 'You're a true friend. I tried to be a true friend to Lyronyxe, but I failed. Sometimes I dream that I saved her and we're together, and I'm so happy. Then I wake up and it's like I've lost her all over again. I don't think I can live with the pain.'

'Sleep,' Ronnyn whispered, tears stinging his eyes.

'I shouldn't let you talk about your Malaunje sisters, but...' – Sardeon's voice was the merest thread – 'at least you can still see them.'

Ronnyn lay beside his choice-brother, fighting the weariness until he was sure Sardeon slept. In time, he believed that Sardeon's gift would rise to his conscious control. But a gift out of control was a dangerous thing.

He decided he would tell their choice-mother. At that moment, the exhaustion won and he let it.

Chapter Thirty-Four

DAWN FOUND TOBAZIM studying the sea-vermin sails. There were more of them. 'But you said they rarely attack en-masse.'

'That's right.' Ardonyx accepted the spy-glass as Tobazim returned it. 'And they prey on each other when pickings are slim. Why, there must be seven or eight who call themselves sea-kings. They don't trust each other but...'

'But?' Tobazim prompted.

'Every now and then they unite under a charismatic leader to claim a prize worthy of cooperation.'

'And we're that prize?'

Ardonyx nodded. 'With their numbers, they'll overrun us like a plague of rats.'

It was what Tobazim had feared. 'Then they'll attack before we can make Ivernia. What can we do?'

'We're already doing everything we can.' Ardonyx gestured to the fleet. 'Sailing in tight formation with the ships lit up at night and the decks patrolled by armed warriors.' He lifted the spy-glass to study the sails, then lowered it, looking grim. 'They've gained on us overnight.'

'Can we outrun them?'

'We can't abandon the slow merchant ships, and sea-vermin ships are built for speed. Also' – he gestured to the slack sails – 'we've been plagued with poor winds since we set sail.'

* * *

As soon as breakfast arrived, Ronnyn slipped out of the empowered lads' cabin into the all-mother's chamber. There he found the children eating their porridge. Vittor and Tamaron were delighted to see him and, after a moment, he wandered over to his choice-mother, who was feeding his baby brother.

She patted the bunk. 'Come to make sure I'm looking after your brothers properly?

He flushed as he sat down. 'I've come because I'm troubled. There's something I should tell you, but it means betraying a confidence.'

When she met his eyes, he glanced to the hidden chamber, where they used to keep Sardeon.

The healer nodded her understanding. 'You may speak freely. I won't reveal it was you who told me.'

Sardeon would know it was him, but he had to betray Sardeon's confidence, or betray his own judgement. 'Last night, Sardeon's gift manifested while he was asleep.'

'Really?' Delight illuminated her face. Then she sobered. 'He told you everything?'

Ronnyn nodded, then frowned. 'How can I know if he told me everything?'

'Oh, Ronnyn...' Reoden laughed softly, and kissed his forehead. 'I'm so pleased. He trusts you. The causare brought him back from the higher plane, but you've brought him back to life.'

Ronnyn shrugged this aside. 'Afterwards, he tried to call his gift, but he couldn't. He said he didn't want to tell you until he could control it. But I'm telling you now, because he drew us both onto the empyrean plane.'

'Are you sure it wasn't a dream?'

'I was awake when it happened. We escaped this time, but what if...' Ronnyn broke off as Sardeon opened the cabin door and spotted him with their choice-mother.

Furious, Sardeon picked his way through the children.

Heart pounding, Ronnyn came to his feet and waited for his choice-brother to join them.

Despite his anger, Sardeon gave his obeisance before speaking. Ronnyn found his control more unnerving than any outburst.

'Choice-mother, I –'

'Before you tear strips off Ronnyn, let me say this, Sardeon,' Reoden said. 'You should have come to me yourself. Gift-wright Ceriane spoke of just this possibility.'

'She did?'

Their choice-mother nodded, then raised her voice. 'Sarodyti, come here.'

The sisterhood's gift-tutor picked her way through the children, who chattered on oblivious.

'Sar's gift has regenerated, but he can't call it,' Reoden said. 'What do you think?'

'He always had exceptional control,' Sarodyti said. 'That could be the problem.'

'I'm not trying to stop myself calling my gift,' Sardeon said. 'I want it back.'

'I'm sure you do,' the gift-tutor agreed. 'But until you forgive yourself for Lyronyxe's death...'

Sardeon flinched.

Ronnyn saw the two adults share a look.

'Don't worry.' The healer reached out to take Sardeon's hand. 'This is the first step in a long road. You were lucky to survive the empyrean plane that first time. You were only twelve, with no training.'

Sardeon shook his head, refusing to accept excuses. Ronnyn felt the force of his choice-brother's will. The gift-tutor was right; Sardeon's own will was what was stopping him.

'Ronnyn tells me you segued to the higher plane in your sleep,' Reoden said. 'That's dangerous, Sar. You must resume your lessons with Sarodyti.'

Reoden finished feeding baby Ashmyr and passed him to her devotee. After fastening her bodice, the healer came to her feet and bestowed a kiss on Sardeon's forehead, then Ronnyn's. 'Now, you two go eat before the empowered lads clean up everything. With any luck, we'll be holding a double empowerment, soon.'

Sardeon glanced to Ronnyn, who knew this was his chance to reveal the truth about his gift, but fear froze him. What if it had burned out?

He gave his obeisance. 'Thank you, choice-mother.'

'So formal, Ronnyn?' Reoden laughed. 'Sardeon must be rubbing off on you.'

His choice-brother closed his mouth and said nothing.

As they headed for the door, Ronnyn's face burned. He hated lying, even if it was a lie of omission. He was almost at the door when Sarodyti called him, dismissing Sardeon.

Ronnyn worked his way back through the chattering children to rejoin the gift-tutor.

'You're a good boy, Ronnyn. Watch over Sardeon. He's like a bow that's been strung too tight. He could snap.'

Ronnyn nodded. 'Can the gift die?'

'We'll cover gift lore when you begin training.' Seeing his expression, she sighed. 'If the T'En's mind or heart becomes corrupted, the gift can corrupt.'

'Can it wear out?'

'With age.' One of the children tripped and began to cry. Sarodyti made as if to go to him, but her shield-sister picked him up and consoled him.

'Can it burn out?' Ronnyn asked. 'Like a fire?'

'You're describing a flare-out. That's when the gift flares up and consumes itself. Sometimes the spark is entirely extinguished, and sometimes it regenerates.' She sighed. 'I suppose the empowered lads have told you that all-fathers sometimes punish a follower by draining his gift, then handing him over to his brothers for their use? Without his gift, he can't resist theirs.'

He schooled his face to hide his surprise.

'Don't worry. These are extreme cases. We're a civilised people, who live by a code of conduct. We aren't beasts!'

The more she said, the more he worried. Without his gift, he'd be a victim.

'We'll cover all this and more when your gift manifests and you're empowered. Off you go.'

He stumbled to the door, consumed with worry.

The night Aravelle and his mother were raped, he'd felt his power move across his skin like a thousand stinging ants. His gift had suffered a flare-out. He was useless. Crippled arm. Crippled gift.

'Ronnyn?' Sardeon's hand settled on his shoulder.

He found himself standing in the passage.

'What's wrong?' Sardeon asked.

'Leave me alone.' Ronnyn brushed past.

Sardeon came after him. 'What's going on? Why didn't you tell our choice-mother about your gift?'

Frustration burned in Ronnyn. Back when he didn't want his gift, it had surfaced and caused him no end of trouble.

Now...

Now he felt as if something precious had been stolen, before he could begin to truly explore it.

'Tell me,' Sardeon ordered. 'I told you about Lyronyxe. I loved her, and seeing her die nearly killed me.'

Ronnyn swallowed and met his eyes. 'My gift's gone dormant. It hasn't manifested since the night my sister and mother were raped and I couldn't save them.'

Sardeon went pale. 'Your gift will regenerate. Mine did.'

'After nearly five years!'

'I was dragged onto the higher plane.' Sardeon shuddered. 'You'll come good. Your gift will regenerate much sooner than mine.'

'And if it doesn't?' Ronnyn lifted his scarred arm between them. 'I'll be a cripple twice over!'

Sardeon's mouth fell open.

Ronnyn turned and left, and this time it was a while before his choice-brother followed.

SORNE CAST A look over his shoulder, marking the position of the sun. He adjusted the rudder, feeling the blisters on his palms burst. The pain brought tears to his eyes. He'd been awake for three days with hardly any rest. Soon, he would have to sleep, but first, he wanted to put as much distance between himself and the Maygharian as possible.

He was never bored, never alone. The children took turns sitting with him. Two or three would keep him company, talking of their homes and how they looked forward to seeing their families again. Sometimes they just chattered, as children will, of small concerns, and he caught a glimpse of their world, where everything they had ever known had ended; yet they still looked forward, undaunted.

Tiasely sent Orza to him with a mug of hot water in which floated chunks of salted fish and carrot. They had plenty of carrots. He'd eaten them raw, over-cooked and under-cooked. Turned out Tiasely had been an apprentice seamstress. She had no idea how to cook.

The children were just happy to be free and eating something warm.

He thanked Orza and tucked the rudder under his arm, taking the mug in both hands. The bandages gave him some protection, but they were seeping. He should wash the burns before they turned bad. He should rest.

Later.

Right now he drank the lumpy soup – or runny stew, depending on which way you looked at it – and resumed his task, watching the sail, the direction of the wind, the state of the clouds, the size of the swells and the arc of the sun as it travelled through the sky.

A little later, Tiasely came out on deck, beaming. 'Look what I found.'

'Scissors?'

'I've sharpened them as best I can.' She saw he did not understand. 'You look a fright. Your hair is all singed and you have no eyebrows left.'

He didn't object as she set to work. Bits of singed white hair blew about the deck.

'I'm going to have to make it really short to even it up,' she warned.

'I'm not worried.'

'You're not like any other Malaunje I've ever met.'

And he realised the children had no idea of his past. All the mistakes he'd made, the time he'd wasted... none of it mattered to them.

It was liberating.

She climbed down and studied him critically.

'Do I pass muster?' Sorne asked, amused by her serious expression.

'No,' she said with a twinkle in her eye. 'But it's the best I can do. You look tired. You should sleep.'

'I'll sleep, soon.'

A little later Yosune came out with the two biggest boys to keep him company and he had the impression Tiasely had sent them.

Chapter Thirty-Five

IMOSHEN LOWERED THE spy-glass. They'd been fleeing before the sea-vermin since dawn. 'They're gaining on us.'

'Can't we raise more sail?' Egrayne asked the ship's master.

'We can, but then we'd leave our slower ships behind.'

Imoshen studied the sky. 'If a fog rolled in, we might manage to slip away.'

'Oh, for a weather-worker...' Egrayne muttered.

'How long do we have?' Imoshen asked the ship's master as she returned the spy-glass.

'At this rate, they'll run us down by evening.'

'Surely there's something we can do?' Egrayne insisted.

'We're doing it. If a storm blows up, it might scatter their fleet, but it could also break up ours. Other than that...' He looked grim. 'When the time's right, we'll prepare to repel them.'

The ship's master returned to his duties and Egrayne returned to pacing. She'd been trained as a gift-warrior and she wanted to take action. Imoshen could sympathise.

Egrayne gestured to the sea-vermin sails. 'If only we could get close enough to touch the leader of the sea-vermin, we could plant fear and doubt in their mind.'

Imoshen didn't need physical contact to influence someone's mind. All she needed was something intimately connected with a person: an item of clothing, or even better, hair or blood.

But she had no way of getting what she needed.

Frustration made her grip the rail and look up. Far above, she noticed a sea-eagle riding the air currents. Its lazy loops quartered the sky as it searched for prey.

Excitement bubbled through her as she felt things slot into place. A bestiare could command that bird, identify the leader of the sea-vermin and make the bird bring back what she needed.

It just might work.

'Whatever happened to that bestiare you empowered?' she asked Egrayne.

'You remember that?'

She remembered not understanding why the T'En despised his gift. But then she hadn't grown up in the rarefied atmosphere of the Celestial City. She'd grown up surrounded by Malaunje, and had worked alongside them. She'd known the rhythm of the seasons in the land and in the sea.

Egrayne frowned. 'It was a year or two after you came to us. He must have gone into his brotherhood around seven years ago.'

'Does he still live?'

'I don't know. It's a rare and repugnant gift. I can't remember his name, but I do recall his disappointed face, the day I uncovered the nature of his power.' Egrayne grimaced. 'Why?'

Imoshen pointed to the sea-eagle circling far above. 'If that bird could bring me a piece of cloth worn close to the skin, a drop of blood or a single hair from the leader of the sea-vermin, I could cast an illusion into his mind –'

'You could plant an illusion in their leader's mind?'

Imoshen nodded, well aware of how her voice-of-reason would react. 'Blood would be best to overcome his natural defences.'

Egrayne's eyes narrowed. 'Illusion is a male gift.'

'My first bond-partner taught me the technique,' Imoshen said, then realised what she'd said and hurried on before Egrayne could wonder why she'd described Reothe as her 'first' bond-partner. 'It was a game we used to play.'

'Why didn't you tell us?'

'If I'd told you, when I first came to claim sanctuary, none of you would have trusted me. As it was, you all thought I was corrupted, addicted to the male gift.'

Egrayne did not deny this. 'And have you always been able to influence someone's mind from a distance?'

Imoshen shook her head. 'When our city was besieged, I was looking for a way to influence King Charald, so I researched gifts that worked without touch. I'm no expert, but I figure the sea-vermin will be paranoid of each other. It shouldn't take much to set them off.'

Egrayne gave her a thoughtful look, but all she said was, 'I'll need to consult the lineage book and go through empowerments of eleven years ago. I can't remember which brotherhood the bestiare belongs to.'

As soon as they entered the cabin the children's game stopped. Tancred gave a guilty yelp and crawled behind the desk. At the sight of the big geldr hiding under the desk, the children went into hysterics.

Egrayne rolled her eyes. She would have ordered him out, but Imoshen caught her arm. 'Let him stay. The empowered lads tease him. He's happier with the little children.'

Umaleni and Deyne ran to Imoshen, wanting her attention. Hearing Imoshen's voice, baby Arodyti demanded a feed. Imoshen laughed, as her devotee brought the infant over.

Umaleni looked resentful, which only confirmed Imoshen's decision to take the baby girl for her choice-daughter. Having a younger sister would be the making of her sacrare child.

Imoshen knelt. 'Look at baby Aro, Uma. What a grumpy little thing!'

Umaleni's expression cleared and she smiled. Without prompting, her daughter started to sing. It was only a string of soothing sounds, but it was high and sweet and the intent was clear. Given the chance, she would love her little choice-sister.

'Look, Uma,' Deyne cried. He held a glass prism in the shaft of sunlight that came in through the row of windows across the rear of the cabin. Rainbows danced across the floor. Umaleni laughed with delight. She chased the rainbow across the polished wood.

Forgetting that he was not supposed to be in the cabin, Tancred crawled out from behind the desk to join in.

Imoshen smiled. She had done the right thing, bringing Deyne into her small choice-family. When she'd read him, she had remembered the draught horse back on the lighthouse farm. How she loved that huge, patient intelligent beast.

That reminded her. She came to her feet, returned Arodyti to her devotee and looked over Egrayne's shoulder. 'Have you found the bestiare yet?'

Egrayne ran her finger down a list of empowerments dating back years.

'So many dead,' Egrayne whispered, voice thick with emotion. 'Each name triggers the memory of an eager child on the day of his or her empowerment. So many lives wasted, so many gifts lost to the T'Enatuath.'

'We're free of the Mieren, at least.' Imoshen squeezed Egrayne's arm. 'Or we will be, if we can escape these sea-vermin.'

'Ahh, there he is: Oteon.' Egrayne said. 'He's twenty-four now, still a youth with another nine years of training to become an adept.'

'He's old enough to know the risks.' Imoshen sat down at her desk to write a carefully-worded message to All-father Tobazim. She needed Oteon's agreement, and it had to be his decision. No pressure from the causare.

Her pen poised over the page. Why fool herself?

Oteon was a bestiare; he would agree to anything to win stature.

Imoshen knew there was a good chance he might die. But if it came to a choice between this unknown young man and the T'Enatuath, she had no hesitation.

* * *

TOBAZIM WATCHED THE message stone with its trail of ribbon wing its way from ship to ship. The presence of the sea-vermin had made his brotherhood restless. To occupy them, he'd told his hand-of-force to train them all especially hard today. The initiates were practising on the mid-deck now. The tang of aggressive male gift made his own gift surge.

A sailor caught the message stone and ran to Tobazim to deliver it. 'It's from the causare.'

Tobazim stretched out the ribbon and ran his eye down its length.

'She wants our bestiare, Oteon,' Tobazim said as he handed the message to his voice-of-reason. 'See what you think.'

While Ardonyx read, Tobazim shaded his eyes, studying the initiates on the mid-deck. It was crowded but, as usual, there was a space around Iraayel. This annoyed him. He knew Iraayel's worth. He also knew most of his brothers did not understand why Tobazim had accepted him.

Either they resented the fact that Iraayel had been audacious enough to volunteer for the mission to save the Mieren queen, or they thought the causare had slipped him into the mission to give him an easy way to enter their brotherhood. Since Tobazim hadn't been the all-father then, this wasn't even logical, but that didn't seem to worry them.

Thirteen years of hatred for the causare could not be overcome by Tobazim vouching for Iraayel. The seventeen-year-old would have to win them over.

'That she's asked for the bestiare specifically raises both his stature and our brotherhood's,' Ardonyx said.

'But it doesn't change the nature of his gift.' Tobazim felt an instinctive repugnance for anything associated with the baser instincts and lack of control. 'Now we know why the adepts baited Oteon and forced him to fight Iraayel.'

'He's not an adept. He could lose himself in the sea-eagle. You can refuse. You're his all-father.'

This much was true. But... 'He's the T'Enatuath's only bestiare.'

'At least give him the choice,' Ardonyx urged, returning the message stone.

'You know he has no choice. As a bestiare his stature can never be great. If he succeeds, he serves the T'Enatuath and overcomes the stigma of his gift. No, he has no choice and Imoshen knows this, which means I have no choice, either.'. Tobazim cupped his mouth. 'Oteon?'

The initiate looked up, surprise evident in the way he held his body. Tobazim beckoned.

Ardonyx took Tobazim by the shoulders. 'Tell me you don't mean to ride the beast with him?'

'I'm his all-father. I've sworn to protect him. I'll have to anchor him in case he loses himself in the beast.'

'Then I'll anchor you.'

Ardonyx's offer made the heat race up Tobazim's cheeks.

'You thought I wouldn't?' Ardonyx was affronted. 'You're my shield-brother.'

'Of eleven days. It's not like we've shared a lifetime and our gifts are so deeply linked that my death would kill you. The T'Enatuath need you.' He shrugged 'I'm –'

'Tobazim, I –'

'You wanted to see me, all-father?' Oteon sprang up the steps, then gave the correct obeisance.

Tobazim handed him the message ribbon. 'You don't have to accept. But if you do, I'll be your anchor.'

For a heartbeat Oteon read the delicate script, then shaded his eyes and looked up into the sky until he spotted the sea-eagle. He returned the message. 'I volunteer.'

'In that case, we'll need to deepen our link. Ardonyx, let the causare know. Tell Deimosh and Ceyne to meet us in the cabin.'

Tobazim and Oteon went to the captain's cabin, where they removed their shoes before bathing their faces, hands and feet, to purify their minds and bodies.

By the time Ardonyx returned with Ceyne and Deimosh, Norsasno had joined them. The hand-of-force spread the circular, ceremonial rug on the cabin floor.

Clearly nervous, Oteon knelt on the rug. He wore only the breeches he'd been training in; his hard, muscled chest bare, his toes curled neatly under him.

Tobazim knelt facing him, his left knee beside Oteon's. Tobazim raised his left arm, palm out, revealing the fine skin of his inner wrist where the blood moved close to the surface. This was going to be a deeper link than the average all-father-to-brother link, but not as deep as that of shield-brothers. If Oteon failed, Tobazim did not want to perish with him.

Even so, he would do everything he could to save the youth.

Oteon held up his left arm, but hesitated.

Tobazim clasped his hand so that their forearms touched, elbow to hand, fingers entwined. 'I am your all-father. You can trust me to guide and lead you in this gift-working.'

'You are my all-father. I trust you.' An old ritual, the words repeated often in training, it opened gift defences.

A rush of awareness swamped Tobazim. He shared Oteon's excitement and fear and, underneath it, he experienced the youth's reluctance to reveal his sordid gift before the all-father and his inner circle; indeed, before the whole T'Enatuath.

Reasserting control, Tobazim cleared his mind and focused. 'You do this for the T'Enatuath. We are relying on you.'

Oteon nodded.

Tobazim let his arm drop. Now that the link was established, he could sustain it without contact for a short while. He sent Ardonyx a nod. They were ready.

The others had knelt, forming a circle around them. It was a sparse circle. He needed another three or four high-ranking initiates to fill out his inner circle. But he was holding off until he was sure of his brothers.

That was a problem for another day.

Tobazim returned his attention to the initiate. 'Call your gift, Oteon. I'll anchor you.'

The youth cleared his mind and Tobazim went with him, preparing to segue to the empyrean plane. But this was not your standard gift-working. Instead of that familiar, if dangerous plane, Oteon remained in the earthly plane.

With what could only be described as joy, the youth shed his body as if it was a useless husk and leapt for the sea-eagle, settling into the bird like a second skin.

The transition was so abrupt that Tobazim felt nauseous. Instinctively, he detached a little so that he was not as immersed in the beast as Oteon. But he still experienced the seductive power of the eagle's broad wings and savoured the incredible detail of its sight, as it soared high over the T'Enatuath's fleet.

When Oteon tried to influence the sea-eagle's will, Tobazim sensed conflict. The great predator did not want to be ridden.

Even so, it tilted its broad wings and sailed the air currents in a wide arc that carried it over the sea-vermin.

There were many different vessels scattered across the sparkling sea, and each boat was crowded with desperate, hungry Mieren...

So many that Tobazim despaired for his people.

Oteon had to look for the biggest ship and, once he'd found it, to seek the Mieren with the aura of authority to locate the leader of the sea-vermin.

As the sea-eagle circled lower and lower, Tobazim spotted a merchant ship, bigger than the rest. The three-masted vessel flew a banner depicting a stylised sea-eagle.

The crew saw the sea-eagle and pointed, cheering. Oteon urged the bird towards them.

One of the Mieren on the rear deck had the look of a southerner, and he strode to meet the gliding sea-eagle as though it was his destiny. As he passed, he snatched a shinbone from a companion and offered this along with his arm, encased in worn leather.

The sea-eagle alighted on the captain's arm.

Tobazim felt Oteon fight to control the bird's instinct to feed. Finally, the bestiare won, driving the sea-eagle to strike the captain's face.

The Mieren screamed and covered his eye.

Tobazim experienced Oteon's triumph as the sea-eagle rose above the deck with an eye dangling from its beak.

As the sea-eagle beat its wings to gain height, the bestiare fought the bird's instinct to toss its head back and gulp down the tasty morsel.

Without warning, something hit the sea-eagle's body, striking so hard the bird was driven sideways through the air. As it stuggled to gain height a crossbow bolt hissed past. Another struck and the bird spiralled down.

Tobazim tried to drag the youth back, but Oteon fought him, fought to save the bird.

One of the sea-eagle's wingtips brushed a wave. It floundered, struggling on the surface of the sea. And Tobazim struggled with Oteon. The bird's great talons seemed to tear at him.

Something pulled on them. In the midst of the struggle, Tobazim was aware of a net, and of shouting from the ship as the wounded bird was hauled aboard.

Still Oteon would not let go. Tobazim had promised to anchor him. He tried to save the youth, but... Oteon snapped at him, in pain and rage. A familiar essence enfolded Tobazim and he recognised Ardonyx. In that instant, he lost his hold on Oteon and he was drawn back to his body.

Tobazim opened his eyes to find himself lying on the rug in Ardonyx's arms. His skin was wet with sweat. Long welts crossed his chest and forearms. They stung where sweat mingled with blood.

'I thought I'd lost you,' Ardonyx whispered.

Tobazim rolled to his knees. 'Oteon?'

His heart sank as he looked over at the youth, who was frozen in a seemingly impossible position of contorted pain. He still breathed, but his open eyes were glazed and he did not react when Tobazim tried to rouse him. 'Oteon...'

'You did all you could,' Ardonyx said.

'Ceyne, can you do something?' Tobazim asked.

The saw-bones crouched over the youth, but did not touch him. He shook his head. 'I can set a broken bone. This is gift-working gone awry.'

Tobazim looked to Deimosh.

'I train the gifts. I can't repair them, only Ceriane can...' Deimosh ran down, as they all remembered she was dead.

'We have to do something,' Tobazim insisted. 'What about Reoden?'

'She's a healer of flesh,' Ardonyx said.

'The causare, then?'

'She's a raedan.'

'We have to do something! We cannot leave him like this.' Tobazim leapt to his feet, swayed and almost fell. As Ardonyx steadied him, Tobazim remembered Sorne saying that between them, Ceriane, Imoshen and Reoden had healed his empyrean wound. 'Maybe together the causare and healer can do something.'

Chapter Thirty-Six

RONNYN STOOD AT the side of the ship to watch them winch the unconscious brother aboard. 'Doesn't each brotherhood have its own saw-bones and herbalists, Sar?'

'Yes, but sometimes they petition our choice-mother –'

Cerafeoni strode past, shouting commands and ordering the Malaunje below deck.

Nerazime noticed the boys. 'Go to the cabin, now.'

Ronnyn and Sardeon backed off.

But the moment she was distracted, Ronnyn circled around the T'En women until he found a spot behind Sarodyti, her shield-sister and the historian, Alynar, who were watching the proceedings intently. After a moment, Sardeon joined him.

Meanwhile, the all-father and his voice-of-reason had climbed aboard and waited as their companion was lowered to the deck.

Tobazim wore only his breeches. He seemed unaware that he bled from several long, shallow cuts across his chest and upper arms.

'If this is the result of some stupid brotherhood duel, they deserve everything they get,' Alynar muttered. 'I don't see why our all-mother should help them.'

'What is it, Ree?' the causare asked, as she came across the mid-deck to join the healer.

The sling fell open to reveal a T'En initiate, frozen in a position of contorted pain. Everyone gasped and drew back instinctively. The sudden rise in their gifts heightened Ronnyn's hearing and made everything more intense.

Alynar shuddered. 'That has to be gift-working.'

'All-mother Reoden, we call on your healing gift,' the all-father said. 'Oteon the Bestiare has been injured in the causare's service.'

Reoden glanced to Imoshen, who confirmed this with a nod.

'I'll help if I can,' the healer said. 'Tell me what happened.'

'Oteon was sent to find the leader of the sea-vermin. To do this, he immersed himself in a sea-eagle. But he became trapped in the bird when it was injured.'

'That's the risk a bestiare runs,' Sarodyti said softly.

'Filthy gift,' Alynar muttered.

'This is gift-working,' the healer said. 'I don't –'

'Gift-wright Ceriane is dead. You're all we have.' The all-father knelt beside his injured brother and lifted both his hands, palm-up, in the obeisance of supplication. 'Please, the bird is going to die. Can't you do something for him?'

Reoden looked to Imoshen, who shook her head, at a loss.

The healer seemed both reluctant and sad as she sank to her knees beside the injured brotherhood initiate. Very carefully, she ran her hands over his contorted limbs.

After a moment, she looked across his body to Tobazim. 'I can't reach him. You are his all-father, you have a link with him?' He nodded. 'Then you are the best one to call him back.'

'I tried, but he fought me.' Tobazim indicated his wounds.

'In that case, you've lost him. I'm sorry.'

The all-father turned to Imoshen. 'Surely you can do something, causare? He suffers because of what you asked of him.'

'Impudent all-father,' Alynar whispered.

Just then, the youth's body bucked and thrashed. Cerafeoni darted in, pulled Reoden to her feet and drew her back. At the same time, Tobazim's voice-of-reason dragged him out of the way as the injured initiate's back arched until only back of his head and his heels were in

Rowena Cory Daniells 401

contact with the deck. Even in this extremis, no sound came from him.

Sardeon's fingers dug into Ronnyn's arm. The initiate bucked and writhed one last time, then collapsed.

Ronnyn hoped he was dead. At least then the bestiare's suffering would be over.

Reoden knelt and touched the initiate's neck then his temples. She came to her feet. 'He's gone in both gift and body.'

Sardeon ran to the side of the ship and threw up.

'I'm sorry, Tobazim,' Reoden said. 'At least let me treat you. You're bleeding badly.'

He shook his head, stunned by the loss.

'Our brotherhood thanks you for trying,' Ardonyx said, giving the obeisance of thanks. 'We must take his body back for the farewell ceremony.'

'His gift was torn from his body before he died,' Reoden said. 'I don't know if you'll be able to escort his shade to death's realm.'

There was so much Ronnyn didn't understand. He couldn't get the image of the bestiare's death throes out of his mind.

IMOSHEN SHIVERED. THEY faced death tonight, and she longed for a few moments alone with Ardonyx.

While the dead bestiare's body was being placed in the sling, she drew Tobazim and Ardonyx aside. 'I'm sorry. He died bravely.' And at her bidding.

Tobazim swayed. Ardonyx had to steady him.

'You should let Ree heal you,' Imoshen urged.

Again, he shook his head.

'Your bestiare died in the service of the T'Enatuath, and I'll see that his stature is acknowledged. But now we have to prepare to repel the sea-vermin. They'll be on us by this evening. Ardonyx, there's no time to call an all-coucil. I'm placing you in charge of the fleet.' She smiled at Tobazim's expression. 'What should we do, Commander Ardonyx?'

He did not hesitate. 'The sisterhood ships are already sailing in the centre, with the brotherhood ships forming a protective circle around them. We'll reduce sail and tighten up formation.'

'But the sea-vermin vessels are small enough to get between our ships.'

'We can't prevent that, but we can make it harder for them. The brotherhood ships will bear the brunt of the attack. If the sea-vermin take our ships, they'll throw all the adult T'En and Malaunje men overboard. They'll keep some of the women and children in slavery on their islands, and the prettiest they'll sell to brothels down south. We'll be fighting for our very survival. No quarter given. '

She nodded and swallowed. 'My ship's master says there's rumour of a sea-vermin power-worker.'

Tobazim stiffened. 'Power-worker?'

'I have heard whispers,' Ardonyx admitted. 'The power-worker won't be a problem unless they know how to breach the walls between the planes and bring a predator down on us –'

'Fiant take them!' Tobazim cursed.

'Exactly.' Ardonyx met his eyes. 'If they bring a fiant down on us, or even one of the lesser predators, it will be attracted to our gifts.'

'And there is only one defence,' Imoshen said. 'A costly one, in the case of a fiant.' She saw the same horror in their eyes. A cry from over near the foredeck cabins made Imoshen stiffen. 'Now, if you will excuse me, I must deal with sisterhood business.'

RONNYN JOINED HIS choice-brother at the water barrel. Sardeon gulped a mouthful and wiped his face with trembling fingers.

'What did our choice-mother mean when she said the bestiare was gone in both body and gift?' Ronnyn asked. 'Why won't they be able to escort his shade to –'

'You two.' Nerazime caught up with them. 'I sent you inside. You should not have seen this.'

Ronnyn was about to apologise, when his choice-brother surprised him.

'There are many things we should not see, but we do.'

And Nerazime's reaction surprised Ronnyn even more. Instead of chastising him, she flinched.

Sardeon turned to Ronnyn. 'Our choice-mother means that his gift was torn from him before his body died, so his essential-self will be confused and easy prey for the empyrean predators. He'll never make it to death's realm, never be united with those he loved in life. He'll suffer true death.'

'You've seen too much for someone not yet empowered, Sar,' Nerazime said. She reached out to cup his cheek, but he took a step back. 'You should never have been swept onto the higher plane. It was a terrible accident.'

'It was no accident.' Sardeon's wine-dark eyes burned in his pale cheeks. 'I went looking for Lyronyxe because we shared a link. When we were old enough, we were going to make the deep-bonding. We were in love –'

'Oh, Sar,' Nerazime whispered. 'No one makes the deep-bonding anymore. Your all-father would never have allowed it.'

He ignored her. 'I went in search of Lyronyxe to help her reach death's realm.'

Nerazime looked stunned. 'The causare said she thought that's what you were doing, but I didn't –'

'You never asked. No one would talk to me afterwards. Who was sent to escort Lyxie's shade?'

'Ree was unconscious, so I went.'

'Did you find her?'

Nerazime's mouth worked and tears ran down her cheeks.

'Then she's truly dead, and we can never be together. It's over.' Sardeon brushed blindly past her, pushing through the sisterhood warriors and scholars.

'Go after him,' Nerazime urged.

Ronnyn pursued Sardeon, weaving between the women, and had almost reached him when the three oldest sisters came towards him, blocking his way.

'Filthy bestiare,' Alynar muttered. 'Good riddance, I say.'

'Poor youth, you mean,' Sarodyti corrected. 'What chance did he have?'

'He's better off dead,' the scryer said. Her scar had grown, eating into her bottom lip.

Ronnyn could not tear his eyes away from her ruined face.

'What are you looking at?' Lysitzi glared at him.

Today, he'd seen the bestiare die, killed by gift-working gone wrong, and he'd learned why Sardeon had been devastated by Lyronyxe's death. Who would have thought the link between mind, body and gift could be so powerful?

Ronnyn looked into the scryer's face. Her gift was eating away at her.

Without warning, she slapped him so hard he fell to the deck.

'Lysi!' Sarodyti protested, shocked.

Cerafeoni strode over. 'What's going on?'

Stunned, Ronnyn stared up at the scryer.

Sardeon returned and hauled him to his feet.

'What's going on here?' their choice-mother asked. 'Ronnyn?'

His cheek burned, but he said nothing.

'The lad insulted me,' the scryer said.

'Ronnyn?' Reoden asked, disbelieving.

'He didn't say anything,' Nerazime insisted. 'I was right behind him.'

'It wasn't what he said. It was the way he looked at me,' the scryer insisted. Her mouth twisted, lifting her scar. 'This one's no better than a Mieren!'

The sisters gasped at the insult.

But Ronnyn felt no anger, only pity. He gave the obeisence of apology. 'Your pardon, Scryer Lysitzi.'

'There, he's done the right thing. Be gracious, Lysi,' Reoden urged. 'Forgive him.'

Ronnyn waited.

The old scryer's face worked with emotion, her scar twisting as the muscles in her jaw moved. No, it was her scar that writhed, lifting her mouth and pulling on her left eye.

Quick as a snake, Lysitzi left hand sought Ronnyn's forehead. Before she could touch him, a jolt of power ran through his body. His vision turned white and he was thrown backwards off his feet.

It was only because Sardeon and Nerazime were directly behind him that he didn't hit the deck again. He felt them stagger as they caught him.

A rushing filled his ears and he was momentarily blinded. '...you all right?' Nerazime searched his face.

The buzzing passed. His sight cleared and he made out the old scryer standing rigid, with her eyes rolled back in her head.

'What's going on?' the causare asked, running across the mid-deck to join them.

'Lysi's regained her gift,' Sarodyti announced. 'I felt her gift spike.'

Everyone stared at the old scryer. Her eyes had returned to normal and she focused on Ronnyn.

'You will know great stature, but you will never have what you most want.' She broke into laughter that was almost sobbing. The sound made his skin crawl.

'Make her stop!' Sardeon pleaded.

No one moved.

Darting in front of Ronnyn Sardeon pushed the scryer over. She fell, arms flailing, and hit the deck. The impact drove the breath from her chest, and she dragged in a great gulp of air then curled into a ball, moaning.

At the same moment, Sarodyti passed out. The healer only just managed to catch her. As Reoden struggled with the gift-tutor, who had gone completely limp, the causare rushed to help her.

'Go inside, boys,' Cerafeoni ordered. She beckoned two warriors.

'It's all his fault.' Historian Alynar pointed to Ronnyn. 'I knew no good would come of taking in the children of runaway Malaunje!'

Ronnyn bristled. He wanted to defend his mother, but Vittor came running onto the deck.

'Come quick. The old devotee fell down. There's blood everywhere.'

'That's Sarodyti's devotee,' Nerazime said. 'Of course, she's linked to –'

The hand-of-force took charge, ordering everyone about. Vittor ran over to Ronnyn, who hugged him. Nerazime drew the boys aside as two warriors carried Sarodyti past.

'Will she be all right?' Ronnyn asked.

'She's been Lysi's shield-sister for seventy years,' Nerazime said. 'Sarodyti's strength has helped hold our scryer together since...'

'Since the day she failed to foresee the attack on Lyronyxe,' Sardeon finished for her. 'The scryer never forgave herself. And she never forgave me for surviving, when Lyxie died.'

'That's not true, Sar...' Nerazime whispered.

But Ronnyn could tell it was.

WAVES OF WEARINESS rolled over Sorne, and each time he fought them he felt nauseous with the effort. It was only mid-afternoon, but if he was to sail through another night, he needed to get some sleep.

Earlier today, they had seen the sails of a merchant ship, far to the south. Either the lookout hadn't spotted them or they'd been identified as sea-vermin; the ship had veered away.

He glanced to Vivane and Vivore, the Malaunje brothers. The boys had been taking turns with the rudder for a while now. 'You're doing well. Remember to keep the sun on your right as it sets, and we'll be on course.'

They nodded earnestly.

'Now I'm going to lie down and sleep. Wake me shortly after sunset.'

In the cabin, Tiasely was asleep on the floor, surrounded by small children. Both bunks were full. Sorne grabbed a blanket and curled up in the prow of the boat.

He lay down, feeling consciousness slide from him.

ARAVELLE LOOKED UP as Saskar returned from spying on All-father Tobazim's brotherhood. She sat at a kneeling desk in the corner of the cabin, making a record of the notes Hueryx had made concerning the last thirty years.

Saskar crossed to where Hueryx and his two seconds knelt on the carpet. They'd been talking over events since the all-father had set off with his voice-of-reason and the injured brother. So far they knew only that the causare had requested a service from one of Tobazim's brothers, it had all gone horribly wrong and the brother had been bundled off the ship and taken to the healer. Not long ago, Tobazim and Ardonyx had returned with his body.

'The dead initiate was a bestiare by the name of Oteon,' Saskar reported.

Aravelle remembered returning to her cabin and seeing the initiate run out of the fog, only to be dragged off. She felt for him, whatever his gift.

'All-father Tobazim just held the farewell ceremony,' Saskar said. 'He claimed stature for the initiate and for his brotherhood. The causare has acknowledged the bestiare's sacrifice.'

'Considerate of him to win stature for his brotherhood with his vile gift, then conveniently die,' Hueryx observed. At that moment, Aravelle hated him. 'Did you learn exactly how the causare planned to use the bestiare in the first place?'

'There was whisper of a sea-eagle and spying on the sea-vermin.'

Hueryx shook his head. 'I don't see how that would have helped.'

'Whatever her plan was, it didn't work and he's dead, and just as well.' Dragomyr shuddered. 'No one would want to live out their days with the mind of a beast.'

'There's more,' Saskar said, voice sharp with repressed excitement. 'They expect the sea-vermin to attack this evening, and the causare has named Captain Ardonyx commander of the fleet.'

'What?' Dragomyr was nearly rendered speechless. 'That's...'

'He's not even a hand-of-force!' Reyne sprang to his feet and prowled across the cabin, radiating gift readiness.

'More to the point, he's not an all-father,' Dragomyr said. 'How will the other all-fathers feel taking orders from him?'

'Hue?' Reyne turned to the all-father.

'What will you do about this insult?' Dragomyr pressed.

'What insult?' Hueryx countered, coming to his feet. 'I haven't sailed to the Lagoons of Perpetual Summer and back. This ship doesn't talk to me as it does to him. Ardonyx has been commander of the fleet all along, in fact if not in name. Imoshen has just made it official.' He gestured to his hand-of-force. 'Reyne, go see Tobazim's hand-of-force. I want you to coordinate the ship's defences with him.'

Reyne nodded, beckoned Saskar and left.

'How All-father Tobazim must be gloating,' Dragomyr said. 'His brotherhood's stature just grows and grows.'

'Don't be so sure... Have you seen the number of sea-vermin closing in on us?' Hueryx countered. 'We'll be lucky to come through this in one piece. When they attack, we're going to lose people, and possibly ships. By appointing Ardonyx fleet commander, Imoshen is one step removed from the disaster that is about to happen.'

'She's sacrificing him?'

'Possibly.'

Aravelle bent her head over the writing desk. Was the causare really so calculating?

* * *

IMOSHEN WATCHED THE sling-shot stones fly between the ships, trailing their message ribbons like the plumage of exotic birds. A Malaunje sailor caught her ship's message-stone and came running up to the rear-deck to deliver it to Imoshen.

She read Ardonyx's first message as fleet commander, then handed it straight it to Egrayne.

It pleased her to finally see his worth acknowledged. But more than that, if their secret bonding was ever discovered, his only hope of surviving the all-fathers' vengeance was if his stature had risen high enough to make it impossible for them to touch him.

But it was not all good news. Reoden had examined the scryer, and there was nothing the healer could do for her. Lysitzi's gift had corrupted. This was something every T'En feared.

'You've named Voice-of-reason Ardonyx commander of the fleet?' Egrayne gestured sharply with the message stone, making the ribbon fly. 'A brotherhood adept?'

'He's the best person for the job.' Imoshen held out her hand and Egrayne returned the stone. She beckoned the ship's master. 'A message from Fleet Commander Ardonyx.'

He read it and headed off, calling orders. Imoshen looked around the fleet and saw the other ships were also reducing sails. Taking a deep breath, she felt her skin prickle. Was there a storm coming?

'What is it?' Egrayne asked.

'There's an oppressive power in the air.'

'A storm?' Egrayne sounded hopeful. 'It could break up the sea-vermin's fleet.'

'It could. But it could also break up our fleet.' She studied the sky. 'Looks like it will blow over and spend its force elsewhere. Send for Hand-of-force Kiane, we must prepare to repel the sea-vermin.'

Chapter Thirty-Seven

ARAVELLE DISCOVERED SHE liked being in the all-father's cabin, in the centre of things, as everyone prepared for the attack. All afternoon, warriors had been coming and going in answer to Hand-of-force Reyne's summons.

'We're as ready as we can be, for now,' Reyne said, seeing the last initiate out. 'The Malaunje warriors and initiates are all eager to win stature, and our adepts know what is expected of them.'

'Time to prepare our minds and bodies,' Hueryx said.

As the all-father and his seconds went through to the bathing chamber, Aravelle glanced to Saskar.

'In case they die tonight, they'll meditate to prepare their minds for the higher plane. That way they stand a better chance of crossing to death's realm.' He saw she didn't understand. 'Violent death confuses the shade. If the all-father and his seconds fall, there will be no one to escort their shades to death's realm.'

'If they die?' Panic filled her chest. She couldn't imagine Hueryx and his seconds dying, they seemed so powerful and in control.

'When they won leadership of the brotherhood, they swore to protect us. They'll be in the front ranks when the sea-vermin attack.' Saskar resumed oiling the leather straps of Reyne's armour. 'If they fall and the brotherhood survives, the high-ranking brothers will be too busy challenging each other to decide the leadership to worry about the shades of the fallen.'

And if Reyne was killed, he'd take Saskar with him.

It wasn't fair.

What would she do without Saskar?

Shocked by the thought, she returned to the task at hand, preparing the armour. Concentrating on each minute detail, she polished and oiled. Something about the armour drew her, maybe because it was both beautiful and designed to deal out death. The chest and back pieces were made of linked plates covered in brilliant enamel that glistened like fish scales. According to Saskar, the brotherhood's armour had been passed down from one all-father and his seconds to the next, for hundreds of years. And soon it would be worn again, in defence of their people.

All-father Hueryx returned from the bathing chamber. Through the half-open door, she saw Reyne and Dragomyr's broad backs as they knelt to mediate.

Dressed in supple leather breeches and a cotton vest, Hueryx knelt so that Saskar could help him into his armour.

'Here.' Hueryx called Aravelle, raising his right arm so she could buckle the straps down the join side.

This close, she could feel the gift readiness coming off his skin in waves. With her own awareness heightened by contact, her fingers flew through their task.

'Good.' Hueryx came to his feet and checked his range of movement. 'Since my hair's so short, I'll have to pad the helmet.'

Aravelle glanced to Saskar.

'Reyne and Dragomyr will plait their hair and wind it around their heads to cushion their helmets. Hueryx, of course, cannot do that.'

As he spoke, he'd been winding cloth around Hueryx's head. Hueryx reached for the helmet, with its neck and cheek guards, set it in place, and checked the fit.

With his features partially hidden, he ceased to be All-father Hueryx and became every brotherhood warrior from the sagas – beautiful, dangerous and vengeful.

Deadly.

Aravelle took an instinctive step back.

Seeing her expression, he pulled the helmet off and drew her closer. 'Don't look so worried. I've planned for every contingency. You won't suffer at the hands of Mieren again.'

Reyne and Dragomyr returned; solemn and silent, they radiated intensity, and their power seemed to struggle to escape their control. Saskar helped Dragomyr into his armour, then did the same for the hand-of-force.

Aravelle's heart raced as she realised the stark reality of what was about to take place. She was glad the brotherhood had so many warriors. But the sisterhood ships only had their Malaunje warriors, the empowered lads and those sisterhood T'En who had chosen the warrior's path. 'My brothers are on the causare's ship with Healer Reoden. How will the sisterhood defend...'

She ran down as Hueryx and his two seconds turned to her. Last time she'd dared to ask after her T'En kin, Charsoria had slapped her.

'Do not fear, Vella,' Hueryx said. 'The brotherhood ships will bear the brunt of the attack. I want you to go below to Charsoria's cabin and, whatever happens, do not fail me. Promise?'

'I promise.'

'Good.' He tapped Saskar's shoulder. 'Take Vella down.'

Saskar nodded, strapped a belt to his hips and slid two long-knives into the sheaths.

'I thought only T'En could carry knives,' she said.

'I protect the hand-of-force.' Saskar's face had grown so hard and cold, she barely recognised him. 'Come with me. I must review the Malaunje defences.'

Dry-mouthed, Aravelle followed Saskar out onto the mid-deck and down the hatch to the lower-deck, where she found the Malaunje youths who had just begun their warrior training.

Saskar signalled for their attention. 'If the sea-vermin get down to this deck, it means the more experienced warriors on the upper deck are dead. Don't show them any mercy.

If they take this ship, they'll kill all of you. They only want the pretty women and small children who they can enslave or sell...'

Aravelle's stomach clenched with fear. The sea-vermin would kill Ronnyn for sure, although they would probably spare her little brothers.

'The babies they'll throw overboard,' Saskar said. 'Babies are too much trouble to care for.' Aravelle felt sick. She hated being apart from her brothers. At least she could protect Itania.

Aravelle slipped through the young Malaunje warriors to Charsoria's cabin, which was packed with all the Malaunje children.

Charsoria turned as Aravelle entered. Like the other women, she wore the leather arm guard of an archer. Aravelle hadn't known she'd been a warrior, but it made sense. The same determination that drove her and her mother, also drove Charsoria.

'I'm going up on deck now. While I'm gone, Hariorta is in charge.' The all-father's-voice gestured to her half-sister, who nodded grimly. 'You all know what you must do.'

The warriors filed out. Last out the door, Charsoria hugged Hariorta, then left. She didn't give Aravelle and Itania a second look. Aravelle told herself she didn't care. In fact, anything else would have been hypocritical.

Only babies, toddlers and children remained, with Hariorta, three elderly women, and Aravelle.

'Prepare a hot posset, Redravia,' Hariorta ordered.

As the old woman began to prepare the hot milk for the children, Aravelle did a quick count. There were twenty-nine children under fifteen. That couldn't be everyone. She suspected many of the thirteen- and fourteen-year-olds had joined the warriors on the lower-deck. She realised that Nariska was missing. Shy, silly Nariska – how would she fight?

'An early night for you, my dears,' Redravia said to herself, as she prepared the childrens' possets.

With growing misgivings, Aravelle watched the old woman uncap a small bottle and add the contents to the milk.

'Add double the honey, to hide the taste,' Hariorta advised.

Aravelle joined them. 'What's going on?'

'The hot milk is to settle them.' Hariorta touched the knife at her belt. 'If the sea-vermin take the ship we're to kill the children.'

Aravelle stared at her, horrified. 'Does All-father Hueryx know?'

'He ordered it. He doesn't want the children enslaved.'

'What if our ship falls but the others survive?'

'They won't come to our aid. They'll be too busy defending their own vessels. Each ship stands or falls alone tonight.'

'Come, the posset's ready,' Redravia announced. 'Drink up, children.'

Obediently, the children drank their hot milk. Aravelle watched, her heart racing, tears of anger pricking her eyes. She wanted nothing more than to protect these children. She didn't want them to fall into Mieren hands, but she did not believe killing them was the answer. Then she thought of what their lives would be like if the sea-vermin took them. Perhaps a quick death was preferable.

'Everyone line up. Big children take the little ones.' Hariorta ordered.

Then she led the children down the hall to the central section. Confused and heartsick, Aravelle took Itania's hand.

Below their deck was the hold, and below that the bilge. The stench of stale water made Aravelle wince as Redravia opened the hatch to the hold where their food, animals and belongings were stored.

Hariorta gestured. 'Go first with the lantern, Vella.'

She climbed down. The deck's ceiling was so low the beams brushed her head. The goats called and the chickens cackled. Above her, she heard several of the children complain about the smell.

Hariorta snapped at them, but Redravia made a game of it. 'In you go. We're playing hide and seek. Find a dark quiet place and stay there. We'll tell you when the game's over.'

The children climbed down, one after the other. Unaware of the danger and the plans for them should things go wrong, they giggled and set off exploring.

The infants and babies were passed down. The older children and Aravelle settled them on bales, tucking them in their blankets.

Redravia and Hariorta climbed down, along with the two other old women. Several toddlers of around Itania's age grizzled tiredly.

'Settle them,' Hariorta told the other women. Redravia led them to a dim corner, where Aravelle heard her singing a bedtime song.

Hariorta withdrew a knife from her belt, offering the hilt to Aravelle. 'Here.'

Aravelle stared at the blade. She didn't know if she could do this.

Just then little Itania escaped from Redravia and ran over to tug on Aravelle's arm. She looked down at her sister's upturned face. Brilliant mulberry eyes fixed on her and vivid red lips parted in a question.

Itania was perfect. Innocent of guile, she trusted Aravelle unreservedly.

'Do you want her sold into a brothel?' Hariorta's voice was harsh. 'Do you want Mieren to use her as they used you?'

Aravelle accepted the knife.

Hariorta did not let it go. 'This is a harder task than the one the warriors face.'

'I know.' But Aravelle still took the blade.

IMOSHEN TUCKED HER drowsy children into the bedding they'd set up in the hold and kissed their foreheads, Umaleni first then Deyne, who stirred and smiled at her before drifting off to sleep. Her heart turned over in her chest. She loved them so fiercely. If love alone could save them...

With lingering wonder, she stroked baby Arodyti's cheek as the infant suckled at her devotee's breast. Barely half a year old, this little girl had already survived being hidden in a chicken coop when her parents were murdered. Deyne had found her and fed her, cared for her when the Mieren found him and taken him across Chalcedonia, delivering them to Imoshen for the reward. Having survived against all odds, surely the baby girl was meant to grow up to do great things?

Tonight Imoshen wished she believed in a benevolent god who protected the innocent. But she'd seen what the Chalcedonians believed were gods, and they were only the mindless predators of the empyrean plane.

'Here.' Frayvia undid the clasp of her neck torc. 'I want you to wear this.'

'But Sorne gave it to you.'

'Wear it.'

Imoshen leaned forward. Frayvia fastened the torc around her neck and kissed her lips. 'May this protect you, as it has protected him all these years.'

Imoshen thought Sorne's wits had protected him, but she didn't protest.

Frayvia looked up. 'What if –'

'If the ship is taken?'

She nodded.

Down at the far end of the hold, Imoshen could hear Reoden's people settling their sisterhood's children.

Imoshen took her devotee's hand and held her eyes as she gift-infused her. 'I believe, while there is life, there is hope. Whatever happens, you must live to protect these children.'

'I will never let you down,' Frayvia whispered fiercely. 'But they say I'll die if you die.'

'Only if you believe it.'

'How can you be so certain?'

'You carry my treasured memories for Uma. Would I give them to you if I didn't think you'd outlive me?' In truth, Imoshen could not be certain. She knew only that gift-working was not an exact science.

She kissed her devotee's cheek and came to her feet.

She did not have the strength to look on her children one more time. If she did, it would undo her.

From now on, she had to be cold and strong.

Ducking a low beam, Imoshen threaded her way through the bales to the steps.

RONNYN SAID GOODBYE to his little brothers at the mid-deck hatch. Baby Ashmyr slept in the devotee's arms. Dropping to one knee, Ronnyn hugged Vittor and Tamaron. 'I need you two to be brave.'

'I wish you were coming with us,' Vittor whispered, pulling out of the hug.

'I have to help defend the ship. I promised Ma I'd protect you.'

'I'll stay and fight,' Vittor said.

'Me too,' Tamaron echoed.

'You will, when you are big,' Ronnyn said, throat tight with pride and love. 'Now, go below and watch over Ashmyr for me.'

'We'll protect him,' Tamaron promised.

Vittor caught Ronnyn's eye and they shared a smile. Then Vittor took Tamaron's hand and they both climbed down.

'They're good boys,' the devotee said, her voice thick with emotion.

Ronnyn touched Ashmyr's downy head – so small, so vulnerable – and looked into Meleya's mulberry eyes. 'Thank you.'

She stood on tip-toe to kiss his cheek. 'Ree will probably send you both down to the hold anyway.'

He and Sardeon had refused to drink the hot posset or

go with the rest of the children. The devotee climbed down and his little brothers waved from the deck below.

As Ronnyn crossed the mid-deck, everything seemed clearer and more intense. Even the air was fresh and sharp. Malaunje warriors from both sisterhoods prowled the planks; most spoke softly, but some laughed too loudly, hurting his ears.

The hands-of-force from both sisterhoods had gathered all the empowered lads considered big enough to hold a weapon, and were lecturing them on what to expect. Ronnyn listened for a moment. There was no jostling or joking from the lads this evening. They were eager to prove themselves and win stature.

When Ronnyn inhaled, he could taste the tension in the air. It wasn't just the T'En gifts rising; it felt like a storm was coming. Yet there wasn't a cloud in the sky.

Although it was not quite dusk, the cabin was dark. They'd closed the shutters and bolted them. Ronnyn found Sardeon helping the two gift-warriors into their armour. As he joined them, he could feel their power rolling off their skin. It made his heart race and his mouth go dry. This evening, their usually sweet gifts held a sharp undertone, as if the threat changed them in some way.

Tasasne thanked Sardeon. Grimly efficient, she turned to Ysattori. 'Ready?'

Ysattori nodded and they kissed solemnly, then left the cabin.

Sardeon swallowed audibly and Ronnyn glanced to him. His choice-brother looked like he might faint at any moment. It struck Ronnyn that he was more afraid of Sardeon disgracing himself, than of him being killed.

'I won't falter when it counts,' Sardeon assured him. 'Although I may pass out, afterwards.'

Ronnyn felt a smile tug at his lips. The bathing chamber door opened as Gift-tutor Sarodyti and her devotee came in. Ronnyn hadn't seen them since the incident on deck, and he was so relieved he could have hugged them both.

Devotee Parnia's head was bandaged and Sarodyti looked a little pale, but they were both on their feet.

'Did Ree say you were to help us defend the cabin?' the gift-tutor asked.

Ronnyn glanced to Sardeon.

'I see. Then it's off down to the hold with the rest of the children.'

Before they could object, Hand-of-force Cerafeoni strode into the cabin, herding the injured empowered lad ahead of her. She gave Ronnyn and Sardeon a sharp look, but when she spoke it was to Sarodyti. 'This is Vittor, Saro. He'll help you defend the cabin.'

The lad drew breath as if to argue.

Cerafeoni silenced him with a look.

He nodded, clearly unhappy.

'More balls than brains,' the hand-of-force muttered. But she thumped his good arm as she went to leave, only to find Reoden had come in behind her.

The healer gestured to Ronnyn and Sardeon. 'What are these two boys doing here, Saro?'

'They refused to go below.'

'They might as well fight,' the hand-of-force said. 'If the sea-vermin take the ship, they're going to kill them anyway.'

'Cera...' Reoden protested.

The hand-of-force shrugged. 'When we face death, it's time for plain speaking.'

'So it is.' Reoden took Sardeon's face in her hands and kissed his forehead. 'You have always made me proud. Always.'

He nodded, wine-dark eyes glittering with tears.

Then she cupped Ronnyn's face in her hands and kissed his forehead. Amusement glinted in her eyes as she looked on him. 'You have made such a difference to all our lives. Lucky was the day you came to us.'

He wanted to throw his arms around her, but the hand-of-force led her away, discussing the deployment of warriors. Ronnyn glanced to Sardeon. He looked pale and startled, as if he hadn't really expected to win the battle of wills and now that he had, he wasn't sure he wanted to.

'I like your choice-mother,' Vittor said.

'Come here, boys.' Sarodyti led the three of them over to a pile of weapons. She gestured to the windows. 'If the sea-vermin break through, we are to beat them back. We don't want them attacking our defenders from behind. Understood?'

They nodded.

'Spears would be more use than knives,' her devotee muttered. 'With spears we won't need to get too close.'

Sarodyti nodded. 'Go fetch some staves from the Malaunje supplies, Parnia. We'll tie the knives to the end.'

She slipped away.

When she had gone, Sarodyti turned back to them. 'Check the shutters.'

They'd already been checked more than once, but Ronnyn was happy to have something to do.

As they made sure the last shutter was secure, Vittor said, 'I should be outside, with the other empowered lads.'

'At least they didn't try to make you drink a hot milk posset,' Sardeon said.

He snorted.

Ronnyn grinned.

Sarodyti's devotee returned with half a dozen stout wooden staves. She and Sarodyti began strapping knife hilts to the ends, their gnarled old hands flying. It seemed wrong for these two elderly women to be frantically preparing weapons, but the sea-vermin wouldn't spare them.

Ronnyn swallowed. He glanced to Sardeon. 'Come on. We should help.'

They joined in, and the task was completed all too soon.

'I hate waiting,' Vittor said. 'How long before they attack, gift-tutor?'

'We'll hear them attempting to board the brotherhood ships first,' she said. 'The all-fathers have formed a circle around the three sisterhood ships.'

'There's only four of them,' Sardeon said. 'It can't be much of a circle.'

The gift-tutor conceded this with a nod. 'The smaller brotherhood ships will be in the most danger.'

At that moment they heard an eerie, echoing horn. To Ronnyn it sounded like the mating challenge of a sea-boar. Dimly, through the ship's wood, they heard shouting, and the clatter of metal on metal.

'It's begun,' Parnia whispered.

Ronnyn glanced to Sardeon. His new choice-brother trembled ever so slightly. Ronnyn hoped, for Sardeon's sake, that he wouldn't faint and disgrace himself.

If Ronnyn was honest, he hoped he wouldn't disgrace himself either.

Chapter Thirty-Eight

TOBAZIM SHRUGGED HIS shoulders, feeling the brotherhood's all-father armour lift and settle. The helmet restricted his vision and dulled his hearing, but the sight of him and his two seconds in their traditional armour would inspire his warriors.

He gripped the rail as he watched the sea-vermin approach the fleet. There were so many vessels of all shapes and sizes that they had no trouble surrounding the fleet. A wall of sound grew as the sea-raiders' vessels manoeuvred into position, every deck crowded with chanting, screaming Mieren. Some of the vessels were so small Tobazim wondered how they dared sail out of sight of land.

'Pond scum...' a Malaunje sailor muttered.

'Don't underestimate the pond scum. They're brilliant sailors and they're desperate,' Ardonyx said. He caught Tobazim's eye and gave the slightest of nods, the agreed-upon signal.

Ardonyx might be commander of the fleet, but Tobazim was all-father of the brotherhood. The order to attack should come from him. Tobazim appreciated the courtesy.

'Norsasno!' Tobazim yelled down to the mid-deck. 'Fire at will.'

The hand-of-force strode across the deck, yelling to the archers in the rigging. 'You heard him. Make every arrow count.'

Hueryx's hand-of-force echoed his command.

A rain of arrows flew towards the crowded decks of the sea-vermin's vessels.

The enemy shouted abuse and waved their weapons, their faces painted to resemble vicious animals. It didn't seem to matter how many were struck down with arrows; others filled their places, screaming defiance. The sea-vermin seemed hardly human.

Fear crawled around Tobazim's belly like a hungry worm. Sweat broke out on his skin.

They'd prepared the ship as much as possible. Ceyne was below deck in one of the Malaunje cabins with the injured. Valendia had rallied and was at his side. Athlyn had volunteered to support the Malaunje on the lower deck.

Ardonyx nudged Tobazim and pointed. On the decks of the nearest enemy vessels, sea-vermin swung grappling hooks in preparation for boarding and archers let loose a rain of arrows. These rose, hissing through the air. Some hit the rigging, some overshot and a few landed on the deck.

Norsasno strode towards Tobazim and Ardonyx, the many panels of his armour glinting like fish scales. An arrow skidded across his shoulder.

'Why don't they let the grappling hooks fly?' Tobazim asked Ardonyx.

'I think they're waiting for...'

A horn sounded. It echoed across the sea as it was repeated from boat to boat.

Impossible as it seemed, the volume of sea-vermin's howls and screams increased. Grappling hooks soared, whistling through the air.

Thunk... thunk.

The hooks hit the rails, bit into the wood and caught, weighted down immediately by eager raiders trying to scale the higher ship.

Axe in one hand, long-knife in the other, Tobazim severed the nearest rope, sending Mieren toppling into the sea between their vessels. But almost immediately, another three hooks bit into the rail within arm's length of where he stood and more agile raiders clambered up.

It was always the same with the Mieren. No regard for life, not even their own.

How would he hold the *Victorious*?

Paragian's ship had taken position on the far side of the causare's. The two smaller brotherhood ships had manoeuvred to the prow and stern of her ship. The two small sisterhood ships nestled in close to the causare's, but there was still enough space for the sea-vermin vessels to worm their way between the T'Enatuath ships.

There were so many raiders, all willing to die. How would they save their people?

As he thought this, Tobazim realised he'd begun to think like Ardonyx. He fought not just for his brotherhood, but for the T'Enatuath.

ARAVELLE SAT WITH her back to a bale. Through the ship's sturdy oak planks, she could hear the roar of the sea-vermin's attack. Although muted, it was terrifying; like a great storm, battering the vessel.

Her two-year-old sister lay stretched out beside her as she drifted off to sleep. Singing softly under her breath, Aravelle trailed her fingers over Itania's back. This was how her mother used to sing the little ones to sleep. But the gentleness of Aravelle's touch and the sweet melody were a lie. She seethed with anger.

They'd lost their home and their parents. They should have been safe once they joined the T'Enatuath. Instead, they had known only danger. Would the Mieren never leave them alone?

She'd tucked the knife into her waistband. Its pressure was a constant reminder of her promise. All-father Hueryx expected her to kill the children to save them from the raiders. It was no consolation that if the worst came to pass, he would also be dead.

A shout and running feet on the deck directly overhead made her look up. Redravia met her eyes then glanced to Hariorta, who looked grim but determined. Aravelle wondered if her face was just as grim.

Hariorta beckoned them both.

Aravelle checked that Itania was fast asleep. She tucked the blanket around her little sister, wondering if the next time she touched Itania, it would be to kill her.

Could she do it?

She'd been shocked when her father killed that unconscious fisherman who'd washed up on their beach. Da had wrestled with himself, but in the end, he'd done it. Now she understood why he'd had to. Hard times called for hard decisions, and this made Aravelle wonder if her parents had had a contingency plan in case they were attacked by their people's ancestral enemy.

Would her parents have smothered their children, rather than let them be taken by the Mieren? In the end, they'd been taken from their beds, their father murdered and their home burned.

Despite everything she had undergone since that night, Aravelle wanted to live.

More running boots on the deck above. Something had stirred up the young Malaunje defenders.

'Turn down the lamp, Vella,' Hariorta whispered.

Aravelle did so. They were plunged into a dim twilight.

She glanced to the sleeping children. Some were stirring. What if they woke, despite the drugged drink? She had a vision of chasing screaming children around the cramped storage hold as she tried to kill them before the Mieren could get in, and the horror of it made her nauseous.

'TOBAZIM?'

He waved to Ardonyx and plunged down the steps to the mid-deck. Meanwhile, his shield-brother forged through the fighting to join him. Tobazim hacked through another grappling hook rope, sending more sea-vermin back to the deck of their own vessel. One fell in the sea and the waves heaved the attackers' ship against the *Victorious*, crushing him.

As Tobazim grabbed the grappling hook, a painted, screaming creature appeared over the ship's side and launched itself at him. He buried one of the hook's prongs in the warrior's eye. With a cry, his attacker toppled backwards, taking the hook with him.

Something moved in the corner of Tobazim's vision and he turned in time to see his shield-brother deflect a blow that would have slid in under his arm and through his ribs. The armour had its weak spots and these sea-vermin were quick to spot them.

'How're the two smaller brotherhood ships holding out?' Tobazim asked

'Sea-vermin are swarming over them like maggots on a carcass.'

'We could –'

'We can't. We're only just holding our own. We don't –'

Shouts and screams carried on the wind.

Tobazim spun around. 'The sisterhood ships.'

Ardonyx turned.

At the same moment, a wave of raiders came over the sisterhood side of his ship. With their strange, painted faces it was hard to tell male from female, or old from young. For each one Tobazim struck down, another two appeared in their place. They drove him apart from his shield-brother.

He fought through to rejoin Ardonyx. Together, they struck and backed up, and struck again. And still the raiders came.

Screaming Mieren forced Tobazim towards the wall of the rear-deck cabins. Only isolated pockets of Malaunje and T'En still battled on the mid-deck.

'To me! Norsasno, to me!' Tobazim roared, and the remaining mid-deck defenders surged towards him.

His hand-of-force made a desperate bid to join them, dragging several injured young initiates with him.

'Hold here,' Tobazim told him. 'I'm going to check the rear-deck.'

Tobazim caught Ardonyx's eye and they fought their way to the steps, then up to the lower rear-deck. Here Tobazim found Ionnyn and Haromyr, among others, backed up against the door to the cabins. Raiders, four deep, surrounded them.

With a roar that went unheard in the din, Tobazim charged. He ploughed through the attackers' undefended backs, scattering them left and right.

The sea-vermin parted long enough for him to reach the defenders. Haromyr dragged Eryx to his feet. Haromyr was bloody, yet appeared unhampered by his injuries. Plucking a wicked curved blade from a dead attacker, he shoved the hilt into Eryx's hand. Eryx blinked blood from his eyes as he swayed, but he stayed on his feet.

Tobazim almost tripped over bodies piled two deep. Ardonyx steadied him. They'd reached the others just in time as a fresh wave of sea-vermin came up the steps, armed with weapons scavenged from every kingdom.

Soon they were pressed so tightly there wasn't room for skill, only furious blows. When Eryx fell again, Tobazim shoved the injured brother behind him and their circle contracted.

Something collided with the door at their backs. Tobazim thrust the door open. One of the attackers lay dead in the passage, and Iraayel was running back to the captain's cabin. Beyond his head and shoulders, Tobazim saw leaping flames and Deimosh's thin body as he struggled with two attackers.

Ardonyx shoved him. 'Go, take Eryx.'

With a curse, Tobazim grabbed the injured adept's arm and headed down the passage to the cabin. Shattered shutters let in more raiders. Flames ran across the planks, licking at the oil spilled from an overturned lamp.

Iraayel struggled with several attackers and there was no sign of Deimosh.

Tobazim charged the nearest raider, driving his blade through the man's chest from behind. As the man fell, Tobazim kicked the long-knife free, then ducked a blow from a second attacker. Iraayel brained his assailant. Another sea-vermin leapt for Tobazim.

Eryx cut the man down and sank to his knees.

For the moment, there were no more attackers.

Without a word, Iraayel leapt into the flames and emerged, carrying Deimosh across his shoulders. He laid the gift-tutor down next to Eryx. Tobazim snatched a blanket and, between them, they smothered the fire.

In the dimness, he could just make out what Iraayel was doing as he wrapped a cloth around Deimosh's head.

'They're coming again,' Eryx yelled.

Two more painted raiders appeared at the broken windows, even as a third smashed another window.

As Iraayel surged to his feet and stood guard over Deimosh and Eryx, Tobazim thought surely, after this, the brotherhood would accept the causare's choice-son.

Then there was no time to think, only react.

IMOSHEN STOOD ON the rear-deck, searching the *Victorious* for Ardonyx and her choice-son. Attackers swarmed over the brotherhood flagship. She'd spotted warriors in full armour, who had to be the two all-fathers and their seconds, but from this distance she couldn't tell who was who. At her side, Egrayne said nothing, but she felt the voice-of-reason's gift trying to break free. Unfortunately, the instinct to grab an attacker and drag him to the higher plane was useless in this situation. There were too many attackers, and their physical bodies would be vulnerable while they were on the empyrean plane.

'The brotherhoods aren't going to keep them out, Imoshen.' Egrayne gestured to All-mother Melisarone's small three-masted ship, which had already been overrun. 'They'll be on our deck in a matter of moments.'

Down on the mid-deck, Hand-of-force Kiane strode about, shouting. 'Prepare to repel boarders!'

Imoshen surveyed the fleet. Every ship was now overrun with raiders.

'Oh, dear,' Egrayne muttered, pointing to the mid-deck.

It was such an inappropriate response, Imoshen almost laughed. She looked down to find Tancred sauntering across the mid-deck, dressed in mismatched armour. 'How did he...'

She'd sent him to the hold with the children, but he must have come back and scavenged discarded armour. It would not have been so bad, if the geldr hadn't begun to follow Kiane around, mimicking her actions.

'Tancred? Come here.' Imoshen beckoned. 'I need you.'

He trotted over and climbed the steps.

'Stay here,' Imoshen told him, then turned to her voice-of-reason. 'Can you sense if there's a power-worker amongst the sea-vermin?'

'Let me see.' Egrayne closed her eyes, summoning her gift.

'Tancred play, too.' The geldr promptly reached for Egrayne. The moment his hand closed on hers, he gave a cry of pain and crumpled forward.

Imoshen tried to catch him, struggling with his weight and the amour's. This close to him, she could detect that his gift defences were down and his power activated.

She glanced to Egrayne.

Her voice-of-reason frowned, pity twisting her lips into a grimace of regret. 'He touched me at precisely the wrong moment.'

'Not your fault.' Imoshen glanced around. 'Help me get him into the cabin. Then you can try again.'

As they took Tancred's shoulders and feet, power that was neither male nor female but something 'other' exuded from the geldr.

'He's gift-working,' Egrayne whispered, her face turned away, mouth tight with distaste. 'How can he, when he's never been trained?'

'Tancred knows the higher plane. He fears it,' Imoshen revealed. 'He told me in one of his more lucid moments.'

'Fiant take him,' Egrayne cursed. 'Someone will have to stay with him.'

They carried him down the passage to Imoshen's dimly lit cabin, then laid the big geldr on the floor in the corner. The four empowered lads defending the bolted shutters across the stern windows looked to Imoshen and Egrayne in surprise.

A scream echoed from the mid-deck. Deep, eager voices roared as the sea-vermin boarded. Although she'd known their attackers were almost upon them, Imoshen flinched.

The lads shifted uneasily. Imoshen sensed their fear.

Saffazi ran in from the bathing chamber. 'Did you hear...' She stopped, seeing the geldr laid out in all his borrowed glory. 'What's he doing up here?'

'What are *you* doing up here?' Egrayne demanded. 'I sent you below.'

Saffazi raised defiant eyes to her choice-mother. 'I'm warrior-trained. This is where I should be.'

'We've lost so many initiates, we can't afford to lose you.'

'If the ship falls, you lose me. You lose everything.'

Running footsteps on the high rear-deck above made the empowered lads duck their heads and eye the ceiling uneasily.

Imoshen grabbed Saffazi's arm, pulled her close and gestured towards the lads, skittish as colts. 'Safi, I need you to put some steel in their spines.'

Saffazi nodded and brushed past her choice-mother. 'Watch the windows, lads. If the sea-vermin force the shutters and try to get through, poke their eyes out!'

The lads took heart. Aged thirteen and fourteen, they were used to taking orders from the sisterhood's hand-of-force.

'Don't tear the veil...' Tancred slurred his words. 'Something will come through. Don't... too late. Watch out. It's hungry!'

Egrayne grew pale. 'He's not on the higher plane, he's on this one. And I think he's found the power-worker.'

Imoshen dropped to her knees beside the geldr. 'What's hungry, Tancred?'

There were different classes of empyrean predators, some more dangerous than others. Some hunted in packs, some could be tricked or evaded and some not even the most skilled gift-warrior could escape.

The geldr's eyes darted about behind his closed lids. 'Here it comes...' He whimpered.

Imoshen looked over the geldr's body to Egrayne. 'I'll try to bring him back.'

'No. I'll see if I can do it.' Egrayne placed her palm on his bare skin and closed her eyes.

Imoshen waited anxiously.

'The god of the sea,' Tancred mumbled. 'Pretty, blue fire. So pretty...'

'A fiant!' Egrayne pulled back as if burnt, eyes springing open. 'It's not the sea god. It's a fiant. It's casting illusions on the higher plane.'

Imoshen took the geldr's hand in hers. 'It's an illusion, Tancred. That pretty image is what the Mieren power-worker sees. The fiant has plucked the image from the power-worker's mind so it can get close to him. Don't let down your guard. Don't let the fiant see you, Tancred!'

The geldr smiled. 'He's going to let the sea god ride him –'

'Foolish Mieren!' Egrayne lifted horrified eyes to Imoshen. 'The power-worker thinks it will make him powerful, but it will consume him.'

'Come back, Tancred,' Imoshen whispered in his ear. 'Come home before the fiant notices you.'

No response.

She dropped her defences and reached for him just as the geldr arched, eyes rolling back in his head.

Egrayne grabbed Imoshen, dragging her away.

'He needs me.' Imoshen twisted, trying to escape, but Egrayne was stronger.

They both gasped as Tancred went still.

Imoshen gasped. 'Is he...'

Tancred gave a grunt of pain and woke. He sat up, blinking. For a heartbeat, the geldr looked startled. Then he doubled over, dry retching.

The instant Egrayne relaxed her grip, Imoshen darted over to kneel and rub his back. 'You did well, Tancred. You –'

'Leave him, Imoshen.' Egrayne pulled her to her feet.

On the deck above them, they heard running footsteps, shouts, thumps and the clash of metal on metal.

Tancred lifted his head, eyes red-rimmed with tears. He frowned. 'What's that?'

'Raiders,' Imoshen said.

The geldr's eyes widened. 'The sea god's coming!'

He scrambled away from them. Flipping open a chest, he tossed everything onto the floor, then stepped in and tried to make himself fit, but he was too big. Next he ran to the changing screen and ducked behind that. It fell over.

The empowered lads laughed.

The geldr whimpered.

In frustration, Imoshen strode across the cabin, grabbed a staff and shoved it into Tancred's hands. 'Use this. Hold them off.'

'Nothing can kill what's coming.' The geldr stared at the staff, then dropped it. 'It's going to devour us all!'

Imoshen slapped Tancred's cheek. But it didn't clear his mind; the geldr dropped to the floor with his arms over his head and began to rock back and forth as he sang a nursery rhyme.

The lads didn't laugh this time. They shuffled their feet and looked away, terrified.

Imoshen spun around to confront them. 'Ignore him. The geldr's lost his wits again.' But this time he hadn't. 'It's your job to hold the windows. I'm relying on you. Safi's in charge.'

Then she strode to the cabin door, where Egrayne waited.

They stepped into the passage.

'Tancred's right,' Egrayne whispered. 'Only a gift-warrior can force a fiant back to the empyrean plane. If it comes aboard, I'll deal with it.'

'You're my voice-of-reason.'

'I was a gift-warrior before I was anything else. I took the vow.'

'No.' Only the greatest gift-warriors from the sagas had killed fiants and returned to tell the tale. Banishing the fiant would kill Egrayne. 'But I need you.'

'Need me? I'm out of my depth. I feel useless, have done since I left the Celestial City. Nothing makes sense anymore.'

'We're all scrambling to keep up.'

'True, but you thrive on it.' Egrayne looked pale. 'I hate it. I know I can do this. Anyone weaker will be consumed before they can drag the fiant back to the higher plane.'

Imoshen didn't want to lose Egrayne. The big woman had befriended her when she first joined the sisterhood, had guided her and advised her these last thirteen years.

The hinges screeched as a shutter was torn loose. The sound of breaking glass followed.

They both turned. Through the half-open door they saw Saffazi drive her staff into an attacker's face. The lads leapt to her aid and cheered when they drove the sea-vermin back.

'Someone must do this, Imoshen.' Egrayne was implacable. 'The fiant craves our power. How many T'En will you sacrifice before you let me deal with it?'

Imoshen's heart sank. Egrayne was more than her voice-of-reason. She was her friend.

Hand-of-Force Kiane thrust open the door from the deck. 'We need you, causare.'

'I'll be right there.'

'We need to entice the fiant onto this ship,' Egrayne said. 'We need a display of power.'

'I know just the thing. The air is rich with the foretaste of lightning. I'll call the blue flame. It's wild power. It'll attract the fiant.'

Chapter Thirty-Nine

RONNYN JUMPED AS something thumped against the exterior wall of the cabin. They all turned to face the shuttered windows.

'Lower the lamp, Parnia,' Sarodyti whispered.

They stood silent, in the dim cabin. Waiting.

Ronnyn glanced to Sardeon.

Another soft thump and scuffle. Ronnyn's heart pounded uncomfortably.

'They're climbing up the ship,' Sarodyti whispered. 'Let's hope they pass us by.'

A thud interrupted her, followed by the creak of wooden panels being prised apart.

'Those shutters won't hold for long,' Sarodyti muttered.

Shouting from above told them the raiders had reached the foredeck.

More wooden shutters creaked in protest. There was a grinding of wood as the first shutter's hinges were torn loose. A fierce, strangely-painted face looked in through the window. For a heartbeat, the sight was so incongruous, no one moved.

The sea-vermin punched in the window's glass, smashing the fine wooden frames.

Vittor sprang forward, driving the makeshift spear into the man's head. The empowered lad was a little clumsy with his right arm, but the sea-vermin grunted and fell backwards. Immediately, another appeared in his place.

Two more shutters were peeled away and the windows shattered, quickly followed by a third and fourth.

Sardeon froze.

The gift-tutor and her devotee dashed forward, driving the Mieren back before they could come through.

More windows filled with strange, fierce faces painted with savage designs. Ronnyn was kept busy driving the raiders back, but there were so many and they didn't stop coming.

One of the Mieren got his shoulders through, another slithered like a snake onto the bunk below the window and rolled to his feet. Sarodyti and her devotee closed in on them.

With a cry Sardeon sprang forward to protect the gift-tutor. Hacking and slashing at the nearest Mieren, he drove the man to his knees. Ronnyn should never have doubted him.

'To me, Ronnyn!' Vittor cried.

He spun around to see the big lad trying to keep three sea-vermin from climbing through the windows, and him with one arm strapped to his chest. Ronnyn thrust the makeshift spear into the face of the closest raider. The Mieren's scream was drowned by the screams from the deck above. The sea-vermin fell backwards, taking the knife from the end of Ronnyn's staff as he went, and pulling Ronnyn off balance.

Sardeon caught Ronnyn around the waist and hauled him out of reach of more Mieren as they forced their shoulders through the windows. Now there were half a dozen painted faces trying to break in.

Ronnyn's heart faltered. So many... How could they hold them off?

'Only six?' Vittor jeered, his gift surging. 'That leaves none for you two boys!'

Sardeon laughed. Ronnyn could feel his choice-brother's gift, sharp and intense.

Ronnyn looked around for another weapon. He would have liked an axe like the one back home, but he spotted a brazier poker and grabbed it. With no time to think, he lashed out at the nearest raider, hitting the back of his head, then attacked another as he appeared in the next window. The foul smell of burning hair filled the cabin. The Mieren screamed and fell back, only to be replaced by another.

Ronnyn stabbed and jabbed at heads as they appeared. Sardeon joined him with the brazier tongs, a live coal clutched in its claws. Grimly, he thrust it into the face of an attacker who already had his shoulders through the window. Ronnyn followed up with a blow from the poker that knocked the man out. He remained wedged in the window, blocking it.

'Help!' Sarodyti called, struggling with an assailant. Parnia leapt to her assistance, stabbing the raider in the back. A burly sea-vermin pulled her off the dying man, swung her around and stabbed her in the stomach.

Sarodyti screamed, clutched her own belly, and toppled to her knees.

Vittor skewered the burly man on the end of his make-shift spear, driving him into the wall. The empowered lad had to plant a boot on the sea-vermin's body to pull the weapon free.

Sarodyti crawled to her devotee's side, rolling her over. Dark blood blackened the front of Parnia's robe. Blood frothed on her lips. The gift-tutor rocked back and forth, repeating her devotee's name over and over.

'Gift-tutor?' Ronnyn called.

No response.

Someone collided with him and he found himself dodging a blade. It was only Ronnyn's reflexes that kept him ahead of his attacker's knife.

His choice-brother leaped on his assailant's back. The Mieren pulled Sardeon over his shoulders and slammed him down on the deck, raising his knife to plunge the blade into Sardeon's chest. Ronnyn shoved the descending arm, diverting the knife so that it sank into the deck next to Sardeon's head.

Vittor caught the Mieren by the hair with his injured arm and cut his throat. Sardeon scrambled away from the fountaining blood. As Vittor threw the dead man aside, Ronnyn saw that his injured arm was bleeding again.

Three screaming sea-vermin sprang through the windows. Sarodyti remained on the floor, beside her dying devotee.

'Ronnyn.' Vittor grabbed his arm. 'Get help from the empowered lads in the next cabin.'

Ronnyn ran to the door and down the passage. When he threw open the next cabin door he found the lads grappling with more raiders. Bodies littered the floor. It was the same in the cabin opposite.

Desperate, he ran down the hall to the mid-deck. Chaos greeted him: a frenzy of hand-to-hand fighting. For a moment he thought Nerazime had left her post by the door, but he saw her over near the steps, trading blows with two Mieren. Dodging struggling combatants, Ronnyn covered the distance and brought the poker down on one of her attackers. The man crumpled to the deck. Nerazime dealt with the second and turned to Ronnyn, weapon raised.

For the moment they found themselves in a pocket of quiet as the fighting eddied around them.

She blinked, then laughed. 'What're you doing here?'

'We need help,' Ronnyn said. 'Sarodyti's devotee is dying.'

Nerazime winced. She glanced around, grabbed the nearest empowered lad and told him to hold the passage door. They ran into the cabin, where they found Sardeon and Vittor struggling with the Mieren, while Sarodyti knelt, keening over her devotee.

'Leave her, Saro, we need you,' Nerazime yelled.

No reaction.

A raider had Sardeon boxed in the corner. Ronnyn slammed his poker across the man's back. The raider spun around, his sword arcing for Ronnyn's throat. Ronnyn deflected the blade with the poker, but his bad arm spasmed and the poker flew from his hand. He dropped, and the blade whistled over his head. Ronnyn scuttled back. The man stepped in for the kill.

Nerazime caught him from behind and snapped his neck, then sent him flying into another raider. As a third came at her, she kicked him in the face, breaking his nose. Then she smashed their only chair over a fourth.

Vittor and Sardeon dealt with the injured Mieren.

They'd bought a moment's respite. Sardeon bent double, trying to catch his breath.

'What about Saro?' Ronnyn asked, gesturing to the gift-tutor.

'She's trying to hold Parnia's life force in her body.' Nerazime strode across and dropped to her knees beside the old T'En woman. 'Let her go, Saro.'

The gift-tutor shook her head. 'She's been my devotee for seventy years. I can't abandon her!'

Nerazime took Sarodyti's arm. 'You must let her go. We need you.'

'She needs me. I can hold her until Ree can save her. I know I can.'

'We need you *now*. The boys can't do this alone, and I'm needed outside. I –'

She broke off as one of the fallen Mieren reared up on his knees and tried to drive his blade into Ronnyn's belly. Nerazime shoved Ronnyn aside. She deflected the strike and snapped the man's arm bone across her thigh.

Ronnyn lay on the cabin floor, gasping for breath, amazed that he was still alive.

Nerazime dispatched the raider, then found Ronnyn's poker and handed it to him.

'Saro?' he asked, scrambling to his feet.

'Grief has clouded her judgement.'

'Here they come,' Vittor warned.

'Hold them off!' Nerazime handed out fresh weapons, some taken from the raiders. They'd only just turned to face the windows when the next wave of attackers tried to get through.

With Nerazime and Sardeon at his side, Ronnyn raised the poker. And it started all over again.

* * *

IMOSHEN FOUND HER hand-of-force rallying the defenders on the mid-deck. She grabbed Kiane and drew her close.

The hand-of-force stared at her in astonishment. 'What's that?'

Imoshen glanced down and realised the blue stone on Sorne's neck torc was glowing. 'A fiant has possessed the sea-vermin's power-worker. This means it's nearby.'

Kiane blanched. 'Fiant take them.' Then she heard herself and gave a short sharp bark of laughter.

Attackers forced their way onto the deck, screaming, striking and dying. But even as they fell, more took their place, in a seemingly endless wave. Imoshen realised her people were falling back across the mid-deck, congregating at the cabins to each end of the ship as the sea-vermin overwhelmed them.

Egrayne grabbed Imoshen by the arm, swinging her around. 'Call down the blue fire. You must lure the fiant to me, so I can drive it back to the empyrean plane. There's no other way.'

Knowing she was right, Imoshen nodded. 'Watch my back.'

Lifting both arms, she called down the power that had been building all day. Eagerly, it came to her.

So much restless, untamed power.

Blue flames clung to her raised arms. Nearby Mieren gasped in fright, even as her own people backed away.

Imoshen laughed and turned on the nearest raider. He scrambled away from her, screaming in fear.

If just one sea-vermin was brave enough to strike her, they'd discover blue fire was harmless. But they backed off. Two of the raiders even took shelter behind the T'En warriors they'd been fighting, calling on the sea god for protection.

Imoshen had a flash of inspiration. 'Behold! The sea god abandons you. He favours me and my people!'

With a moan, half a dozen of the Mieren staggered away from her. She veered towards the raiders on her right and they surged back. She advanced, driving the sea-vermin before her. Her ship fell silent.

All the while she wept inside for there were no gods to bless anyone, only mindless predators hungry for power, and her success meant Egrayne's death.

She advanced on another group and they fled, only to be forced towards her again by more attackers clambering on deck. As soon as the new attackers saw her, they fell silent.

Striding along the mid-deck, towards the foredeck cabins, Imoshen drove the sea-vermin before her. A circle cleared around her as everyone drew back.

From the way Sorne's torc was glowing, the fiant was close. But where?

Any of the sea-vermin she confronted could be the power-worker that the fiant was riding. The problem was, she had no idea what the dead power-worker looked like.

A scream of horror came from up near the foredeck cabins.

It had to be the fiant.

RONNYN CAUGHT HIS breath. When he lifted his head, the windows were still empty of raiders. He lifted a trembling hand to rub his face.

Sardeon glanced to Ronnyn. Nerazime and Vittor waited, weapons raised. Still no attackers. What was that strange noise?

Silence...

'Are the sea-vermin in retreat?' Sardeon whispered.

'I think so.' Elated, Ronnyn ran down the hall to the mid-deck. The empowered lads from the other cabins followed.

Ronnyn threw open the door to find attackers and defenders alike standing in a circle, staring in stunned silence at a naked, skinny old man.

The crowd was packed so tight that when the old raider came near them, they scrambled over each other to get out of his way.

Stretched out around the old man were half a dozen bodies, with not a wound on them.

'What's going on?' Nerazime pushed past Ronnyn, striding a couple of steps out onto the mid-deck.

The empowered lads pushed forward, eager to see, driving Ronnyn and Sardeon out onto the mid-deck.

'Stay back,' Egrayne called. She was a head taller than the raiders and could see over them, but she was still a good distance from the foredeck cabins. 'It's a fiant, riding a Mieren power-worker. Out of my way!'

Nerazime gasped.

The power-worker turned towards them, revealing deep gashes on his chest that went to the bone without bleeding.

'Back.' Nerazime gestured fiercely as she and the empowered lads scattered like geese before a wild dog.

The fiant gave a silent laugh, head thrown back. Ronnyn saw its throat and gullet exposed by a horizontal cut that went as far back as the spine.

'Don't try anything, Nera,' Reoden cried from the deck above. 'It's attracted to power.'

'Saro's focused her gift to save her devotee, Ree,' Nerazime said. 'It's attracted to her.'

The fiant turned from Nerazime at the base of the steps, to Reoden at the rail above, as if following their conversation. It seemed to Ronnyn the beast was sensing their power.

'Keep your gifts contained,' Nerazime warned, shoving Vittor and the other empowered lads behind her. A dozen terrified people packed the steps, watching.

'It's finally come for me,' Sardeon whispered, and his gift surged in terror.

Ronnyn felt Sardeon's body go rigid as he fought for control. In desperation, Ronnyn clutched Sardeon's arm, only to feel his choice-brother's power run through his body. It was raw and elemental, and beyond his ability to channel or contain.

And his gift sprang to life, as if a dam had broken.

Power flooded Ronnyn's body, making his heart pound, his sense sharpen and his mind race. It felt as if his gift drew on Sardeon's. The more he tried to contain his power, the more it surged to protect him.

His sight shifted and he saw the fiant as it truly was: a seething source of hunger wearing borrowed flesh.

The horror of it held him immobile as the fiant reached for them.

'No!' Vittor shoved Nerazime aside, charged across the deck and drove his sword through the fiant's back, right through its chest.

Quick as a cat, the fiant turned and caught Vittor's face in its hands. Ronnyn watched, horrified, as the fiant consumed the lad's gift, along with his life-force.

Nerazime screamed, and sprang towards the fiant.

'No, Nera.' Reoden jumped over the rail, dropping to the deck. She landed lightly and caught her voice-of-reason, holding her back.

The fiant's head swung towards them as it cast Vittor's body aside. The lad collapsed not far from Ronnyn, an empty husk. Reoden released Nerazime, who fell to her knees, crawled to Vittor and cradled him in her arms.

Dimly, Ronnyn heard Egrayne trying to get through the crowd. His head pounded and his nose stung with the force of their combined gifts.

The fiant rolled its head towards Ronnyn and Sardeon. Dead eyes focused on them.

'Leave my boys alone,' Reoden ordered, calling on her power.

Her words held visions for Ronnyn: visions of love and sacrifice. She glowed like a beacon as she stepped forward.

'No!' The causare forged through the crowd, as people drew away from her. No wonder... She wore blue fire like a cloak. Flames flickered up her arms, across her shoulders and through her hair, which writhed as if alive. 'Come this way. I'm the one you want.'

'No, Imoshen. Wait!' Egrayne called, trying to shove through the crowd.

Gift-tutor Sarodyti appeared in the passage doorway, hands stained with her devotee's blood.

The fiant turned its head towards her, sniffing the air, tongue flicking out.

'Over here,' Imoshen said, coming closer, wreathed in blue fire.

Egrayne finally thrust free of the crowd. 'Over here, this way.'

The fiant looked from Imoshen, to Egrayne, to Reoden and then back to Ronnyn and Sardeon.

It chose them. Ronnyn could not move. It was as if Sardeon's terror held them both immobile.

A cry of protest left Reoden's lips as she leapt towards the fiant, but she was too far away to do anything and Egrayne and Imoshen were even further.

Gift-tutor Sarodyti sprang out of the passage.

To Ronnyn's gift-aware eyes she trailed streamers of power as she ran towards the fiant. It lifted its arms in welcome. Instead of the fiant consuming her, a flash of white filled Ronnyn's vision and his skin stung as if he'd been slapped.

He must have blacked out for a moment, because the next thing he knew, Reoden was dragging him and Sardeon away from the old raider's body.

Ronnyn scrambled back, shaking.

'It's all right,' Reoden said.

At least, that's what he thought she said. He couldn't hear for the rushing in his ears. Ronnyn lifted a hand to his nose. His fingers came away dark with slippery, hot blood. The roaring in his ears ebbed and he could hear Sardeon speak.

'...the beast?'

'Gone. The fiant's gone,' Reoden said.

'That's what hunted me when I went to save Lyxie.'

'Oh, Sar.' Reoden cupped his face in her hands. 'You're safe now. Sarodyti took it back to the empyrean plane.'

Ronnyn looked for her body. 'Where –'

'She's gone,' Reoden said. 'She didn't just send her awareness, she took her whole body to the empyrean plane. She won't be coming back.'

As Ronnyn stared at the raider's body, he recalled Sarodyti in that last moment, streaming power so that the fiant would be drawn to her.

The ship was strangely silent. Everyone had edged away from the causare, who was still covered in eerie blue flame.

Nerazime looked up from the dead lad in her arms. 'He took on a fiant, Ree. He had no chance. Why didn't he listen to me? I should have saved him!'

Ronnyn felt Sardeon shudder and moan in sympathy.

Nerazime slid Vittor's body from her lap and sprang to her feet. Empowered by fury, she grabbed the dead power-worker's body by his hair, lifting him up.

The surrounding raiders gasped and muttered. Ronnyn saw the causare reach out to Nerazime. He thought she was going to tell her to stop. But she didn't. Instead, the causare's blue fire leapt from her fingertips to Nerazime, racing over her head and shoulders as she shook the power-worker like a doll.

'Is this the best you can do?' Nerazime demanded of the dead raider. Lifting the body above her head, she ran to the ship's side and tossed it into the sea.

The sea-vermin moaned as one. In a panic, they shrieked and deserted the ship. Some leapt overboard, others scrambled down the ropes.

The ship's defenders turned on them as they fled, hacking and stabbing.

'It's over,' Sardeon whispered. Now that they were safe his power had drained away.

Ronnyn could feel his own gift humming deep inside him like it used to. He knew it would not take much to raise it again.

Sardeon turned to him. 'When I saw the fiant, my gift surfaced, and I couldn't control it.'

'Can you call it now?'

He concentrated, then shook his head. 'It's there – it makes me feel wild and restless – but I can't bring it to heel or rein it in when it rears up to defend me.' He exhaled slowly. 'I'm worse than useless. I'm a liability. My lack of control nearly got us both killed. I'll understand if you don't want anything to do with me.'

Ronnyn ignored him and offered his hand.

'What?'

'Just take it.' The moment Sardeon touched him, he let his gift rise. It travelled through him and into his choice-brother, rousing Sardeon's power. 'There. Now can you call your power?'

Sardeon closed his eyes and when he opened them his face was alight with joy. 'You know what this means? You're a summoner.'

'What?'

'You're the male version of an empowerer. You can't actually empower the gift, but once it has manifested, you can summon it in others. This must be why my gift returned.'

'That would explain why I couldn't create illusions back on the island,' Ronnyn said and felt a weight lift from him. 'I was trying to push my gift in a direction that it didn't want to go.'

Sardeon hugged him. 'We should tell our choice-mother.'

But when they came to their feet, they saw the deck littered with the dead and the injured. Now was not the time to trouble the healer.

'IMOSHEN?'

She turned to see Egrayne and Reoden watching her. Nerazime stumbled over, dropping to her knees beside the empowered lad's body.

All around them the crowd dispersed as the sea-vermin fled, chased by the ship's defenders.

Imoshen had been ready to take the fiant to the higher plane and kill it, or die trying.

Now that she didn't have to, her control flickered as her gift surged and her vision wavered.

'Imoshen?' Reoden approached her, hands raised as if she was gentling a skittish horse. Egrayne skirted around to come at her from the other side.

What was wrong with them?

She went to gesture them back only to find her hand still shimmered with blue fire. When she tried to disperse it, she couldn't.

'Do you need help?' the voice-of-reason asked, speaking slowly and carefully. Clearly, Egrayne was afraid of the harmless blue flame; yet she'd been ready to confront the fiant. The absurdity of it made Imoshen laugh. Tears stung her eyes.

Egrayne and Reoden exchanged worried looks.

The thought of losing control and disgracing herself made Imoshen feel ill. Sucking in a shaky breath, she went to the nearest mast and embraced it. Using this as a focal point, she sent the power up the mast, along the spars and ropes.

Once it started, it poured out of her in a rush.

At last she felt drained and safe.

Taking a step back, she looked up to discover blue fire dancing from all the masts of her ship, making the vessel glow.

Hand-of-force Kiane came to report. 'No more sea-vermin remain on the ship. Those in the sea around us are jostling to escape.'

The sea-boar horn sounded, again and again, wailing in retreat.

'They think their god has abandoned them,' Egrayne said with satisfaction. 'Well done, Imoshen.'

'Your orders?' Kiane asked.

Imoshen tried to think, but her body seemed disconnected from her mind.

'Throw the bodies of the sea-vermin overboard,' Egrayne said. 'We'll have to purify the ship and hold the farewell ceremony for our dead. But first send Safi down to tell our devotees they can bring the children up. We're safe.'

Chapter Forty

TOBAZIM STAGGERED OVER a body. His shoulder slammed into the cabin wall. He could barely draw breath. His armour felt incredibly heavy.

No more sea-vermin came through the windows and, above the din, he heard wailing horns.

Eryx tilted his head, listening. 'I think they're retreating.'

'We've won.' Iraayel grinned, then dropped to his knees, exhausted. He bled from numerous small wounds, none life-threatening. But now that it was over, he hugged his ribs and winced with each breath.

Tobazim leant on the desk. With shaking hands, he pulled off his helmet.

Norsasno appeared in the cabin door. His head was bare and his plait had come unravelled. 'All-father?'

Somehow, Tobazim straightened up and squared his shoulders. Where was Ardonyx? Surely, if his shield-brother had fallen, he would know? Perhaps this was why he felt utterly drained. 'What is it?'

'The sea-vermin are retreating. There's...' Norsasno struggled to find the words, then indicated Tobazim should come with him.

Out the mid-deck the only Mieren left behind were dead, and the defenders had gathered near the far rail to watch the causare's ship. Its seven masts glowed with an unearthly blue fire.

Tobazim blinked. 'What is that?'

'The Mieren believe it's the sign from their sea god,' Ardonyx said, joining him.

Relief made Tobazim light-headed and Ardonyx steadied him.

'It's spreading,' Norsasno warned.

The blue flames now licked the masts of All-mother Athazi's ship, the *Endurance*.

'I've never seen anything like it,' Tobazim said.

'A natural phenomenon, untamed power.' Ardonyx shrugged. 'All sailors know about it, but I've never seen it behave like this before.'

'It's almost as if one of us called it,' Tobazim whispered.

The other two looked at him.

'It started on the causare's ship.' Anger ignited Norsasno's gift. 'Why did she wait so long? Why let the brotherhoods suffer?'

'Our enemy is fleeing,' Ardonyx said, and Tobazim sensed power behind his words. 'We have to put the ship in order, see to the wounded and prepare the farewell ceremony for our dead.'

Conviction filled Tobazim as he strode to the rail that overlooked the mid-deck and raised his voice. 'We've routed the raiders and sent them packing. Time to purify the ship, farewell our dead and celebrate our survival.'

His brotherhood cheered.

He ordered the enemy bodies thrown overboard, the decks scrubbed clean and injured taken to sick bay. He set the carpenters to repair the broken shutters and started the purification ceremony.

And all the while he had the feeling there was something important he'd forgotten, just beyond his grasp...

But there was so much to think of.

ARAVELLE SAT ON the bottom rung of the ladder, below the hatch. Above her, she heard a shout and running feet. She waited, dreading the moment the hatch opened.

Redravia met her eyes, glancing significantly to Hariorta, who stood fingering the hilt of her blade.

The air in the hold was stale, and the light dim. Aravelle felt as if she'd been down here forever.

Through the deck they heard shouting and more running boots, charging along the deck towards the hatch.

'Could they have overcome our people?' Redravia whispered.

'Of course they have,' Hariorta snapped. 'I knew our exile was doomed, knew we'd come to a tragic end.'

They all glanced to the sleeping children. Several were stirring, roused by her harsh voice.

Someone began undoing the hatch.

'The Mieren must not get our children!' Hariorta's hand went to her knife hilt. 'Quick, before they can stop us.'

She turned towards the little ones, knife drawn.

'No.' Aravelle sprang to her feet, grabbing Hariorta's arm. 'We can't be sure.'

Hariorta flung off her straining hand. 'Charsoria put me in charge. And I say it's time.'

Aravelle glanced to Redravia, who was no help. No one had the nerve to speak up.

'You're a coward, just like your mother,' Hariorta told Aravelle. 'She could have been the all-father's devotee, but she ran away.'

Aravelle ignored the insult and grabbed Hariorta's arm again. 'What if you're wrong and our people have won?'

Hariorta jerked her arm free and reached for the nearest child, Itania.

Without hesitation, Aravelle kicked the woman in the back of the knee. Hariorta's leg went out from under her, and she tipped forward. Flinging her hands forward to prevent her fall, she hit the deck with a grunt.

No one moved.

'Now you've done it,' someone muttered.

But Hariorta stayed right where she'd fallen.

'What have you done?' Redravia ran to Hariorta and rolled her over. The knife hilt protruded from under her ribs.

At that moment the hatch was flung back.

Aravelle turned to face their attacker, knife drawn.

Someone leapt down. Disregarding the steps, he swung from the hatchway, colliding with her. Recognising Saskar at the last moment, she turned her blade.

'We've won!' he cried, laughing as they both staggered, then recovered their balance. He caught her shoulders. 'We've won, Vella!'

And he planted a kiss on her surprised lips.

'Thanks be,' Redravia whispered, then she looked down on the dead woman. 'What will Charsoria say?'

Saskar stared. 'What happened?'

'I... she...' Aravelle swallowed. She lowered her voice, aware that some of the youngsters were waking. 'She wanted to kill the children. I told her to wait. We had to be sure, but she thought the sea-vermin had won.'

'So you killed her to protect the children?' Saskar did not bother to hide his admiration. 'Remind me never to get on the wrong side of you!'

'I didn't mean to,' Aravelle protested. 'She fell on the knife. Charsoria...' Would never forgive her.

Saskar sobered. 'You did the right thing, Vella. Hariorta's duty was to protect the children, not panic and...' He shrugged. 'She's not the only one we've lost this night. But first...' He took Aravelle's hands, his eyes alight with wonder. 'The most amazing thing has happened. The ships are aglow with blue fire. You must come up and see!'

The oldest of the children had woken now, and they were coming out of hiding, bringing drowsy little ones with them.

'Bring them all up to see,' Saskar told the old women. 'Come on.'

Aravelle collected Itania and they all climbed out of the belly of the ship.

They crossed the Malaunje deck, stepping over bloody patches where bodies had been removed, then climbed up to the mid-deck where everyone had gathered. The

Malaunje welcomed the children with hugs and pointed to the blue flames that danced atop their ship's masts.

'What is it?' Aravelle asked, hardly able to believe her eyes.

'The ship's master says it's a sign the sea god favours us. At least, that's how the sea-vermin see it.' Saskar laughed at the absurdity of this.

He seemed very ready to laugh. Everyone did.

'Come on.' He took her hand. 'Hueryx sent me to make sure that you were all right.'

To make sure that we hadn't killed the children, Aravelle thought grimly.

She passed Itania to Redravia. Her little sister was still drowsy, and went to the old woman without complaint. Struck by Itania's vulnerability, Aravelle felt a fierce love fill her chest as she kissed her little sister's forehead. Not for a heartbeat did she regret protecting Itania, and she could not really be blamed for Hariorta's death. But she was certain Charsoria would hold it against her.

Following Saskar across the mid-deck, she climbed the stairs to the foredeck. He led her through the celebrating warriors towards their all-father.

When Hueryx turned around, his hair was plastered to his head, revealing the sharp blades of his cheekbones. His armour was stained with dried blood and his gift was riding him. The rippling reflection of the blue light danced on his pale features, making him appear strange and fey.

'Vella.' That familiar grin, Ronnyn's grin, tugged at his lips and crinkled his forehead. 'See, I told you not to worry.'

'No, because you meant for us to kill the children.'

'To save you from the Mieren. But you didn't have to. We –'

'Hariorta's dead. She panicked and tried to kill the children. I had to –'

'Vella killed her to protect the children,' Saskar reported.

'It was an accident,' Aravelle protested.

But Hueryx laughed then hugged her, lifting her off the ground. He put her down and planted a kiss on her forehead.

The physical contact made his gift surge through Aravelle like warmth on a winter night. She refused to let down her guard, no matter how sweet it was.

The all-father pulled back to study her. 'If only you'd been born pure T'En. I would have been tempted to hide you like Rohaayel hid Imoshen!' He hugged her again.

This time she had no trouble maintaining her defences.

She hated being second-best.

In fact, she refused to be second-best.

IMOSHEN UNROLLED THE last message-stone ribbon and began to write, but a whimper stopped her. She lifted her head. Another whimper followed. The children were being bathed. Who...

'Tancred?' Guilt struck her. He'd been forgotten. She crossed the cabin and found him huddled behind the changing screen. She crouched down to his level. 'It's safe now, you can come out. Gift-tutor Sarodyti killed the fiant.'

Chin on his knees, arms over his head, the geldr refused to meet her eyes.

'The power-worker is –'

'Gone, but...' – Tancred shivered – 'angry shades are everywhere.'

Opening her gift senses, she glanced around the cabin. He was right. Although the bodies of the sea-vermin had been thrown overboard, their shades remained.

Soon they would be called to the empyrean plane. But right now they were frightened, angry and vindictive, and they wanted to seek out those who'd killed them. If the T'En responsible for their death still lived, they would try to drag them through to the empyrean plane. If they had died, the vengeful shades would seek them on the higher plane. The empyrean predators would have a feast tonight.

'That's why we must purify the ship. Do not fear, Tancred.' Imoshen stood. 'The most experienced of our sisters will stand guard tonight. We'll be safe from these shades.'

He looked up at her with growing hope.

'Here we are, children,' Tiasarone said, as she led them out of the bathing chamber into the cabin. 'Time for bed.'

Imoshen took baby Arodyti from Frayvia, while her devotee settled Umaleni and Deyne. They were drowsy from the hot posset, and drifted off quickly.

Looking down on her sleeping children, on all the sisterhood's children, Imoshen could have wept with relief.

Once the baby was fed, she passed her to Frayvia and returned Sorne's neck torc before resuming her seat at the desk.

Egrayne entered, spotted her and headed across the cabin.

Imoshen lifted a finger to her lips. 'Almost done.'

She completed the last message and waved it in the air to dry.

'You've been busy.' Her voice-of-reason gestured to the temporary shutters over the broken windows and the clean cabin.

'The children needed to be settled. They've had more than enough disruptions.' Imoshen rolled the ribbon around the last message-stone and placed it in the basket with the rest, one for each of the other ships. 'There. I've claimed stature for Gift-warrior Sarodyti. Told them how she sacrificed herself to save the fleet from a fiant. And I told them I called down the blue flame to honour our dead. That should satisfy everyone.'

Egrayne accepted the basket and handed it to her devotee, who hurried away.

'We lost three T'En warriors, Imoshen,' Egrayne said, 'one empowered lad and seven Malaunje warriors. And we may yet lose two more. There are simply too many injured for Reoden to help. The losses on the brotherhood ships will be much worse.'

'I know.'

Egrayne took Imoshen's arm. 'They want you to lead the farewell ceremony.'

'Wait.' She went across to where Tancred watched them from the shadows. 'Come out and see the blue fire dance on the masts. Come out, before you miss it.'

Childlike, Tancred forgot his fear and came to his feet.

The women of her sisterhood lined the lower rear-deck rail. Beyond them, blue fire clung to the mid-deck masts. Wordlessly, they parted for Imoshen.

The Malaunje of her sisterhood had gathered on the mid-deck. They murmured her name, over and over. Bathed in the eerie blue light, their mulberry eyes and copper hair appeared black.

Tancred laughed and held his hand to catch the light. 'Pretty.'

Like a moth to a candle, blue flame gathered on his fingertips.

Egrayne glanced to Imoshen. Until this moment, they had believed only Imoshen could call the blue fire.

Frightened, Tancred waved his hand about, blundering into Imoshen. She steadied him, running her fingers up his forearm and over his fingers so that the blue flame transferred to her hand. 'There, I have it now.'

A smile trembled on his soft-cheeked face.

Just then, Reoden and her seconds came out of the foredeck cabins.

'I invited them to join us for the farewell ceremony,' Egrayne said. 'It should have been me, not Saro, who died.'

Imoshen squeezed Egrayne's hand, then beckoned the healer. 'Ree, bring your people up to join us.'

As they did this, Imoshen looked down on her ship, then out across the fleet. The seven ships sat with their sails lowered, drifting on the current. A multitude of stars illuminated the sky. Though both moons were waning, there was still enough light to cast shadows.

'Ready, Imoshen?' Egrayne asked.

Had she ever been ready for what life had thrust upon her?

'Ready.' She took a deep breath then began to honour their dead.

SORNE WOKE WITH the sense that something was not right with the boat. The first thing he noticed was the sail, hanging loose on the mast. The wind had dropped, which would explain why the boat was moving so sluggishly through the sea, but it still felt wrong.

Not sure what the problem was he looked up at the sky. It was night and he had asked to be woken just after sunset. Judging from the position of the moons, the night was half over. Both moons were on the wane, but there was still enough light for him to see that every child on the boat was fast asleep.

He rolled to his feet, stiff from sleeping for so long. Making his way across a deck littered with sleeping children, he went past the small cabin to the stern, where he found the two brothers fast asleep, with Yosune curled up next to them.

He adjusted the sail and tried to pick their course by the stars. Then he woke the children. They were most apologetic. He sent Yosune to Tiasely to see if there was anything warm he could eat.

Taking the rudder, he felt the boat respond as the sail caught what little wind there was, but the vessel was still strangely sluggish.

A few moments later, Yosune came running back to him.

'Come quick.'

He left the rudder in Vivane's hands, with Vivore advising him.

A light glowed in the small cabin. The toddlers slept packed in the two bunks. Tiasely had lifted the hatch to the hold, and she knelt beside it, holding a lantern.

'Look.' She lowered the lantern into the hold. It wasn't deep. It shouldn't have been filled with dark water. 'There wasn't any water last time I looked. All our stores are ruined.'

Sorne sank to his knees. This was why the boat wasn't responding properly. She was too heavy and riding low in the sea. The water flowing back and forth in the hold was crippling her. 'When did you last check the hold?'

'When I cooked dinner at dusk.'

And it was only halfway through the night.

'The ship's sprung a leak,' Yosune whispered.

Sorne nodded and signalled for silence. At the rate the hold was filling... It was hard to tell, but he suspected they had until around midday tomorrow before she sank.

'We need all the pots, pans and buckets you can find,' he said. 'We're going to have to bail. Get the bigger children onto it.'

He wasn't sure how far they were from the coast of Ivernia. He wasn't even sure if they had passed the tip of the north island yet. So much for his plan of sailing south-west until they hit land.

They had to attract the attention of a fishing vessel or a merchant ship. Hopefully they should be nearing Ivernia now, and entering the shipping lanes.

He left Tiasely and Yosune to organise bailing the hold, and went back to the rudder.

'What is it?' Vivane asked.

'I want you two to light every lantern you can find and hang them on the mast and the cabin. I want the boat lit up bright as day. Then I want you to look around and see what you can find to make a raft.'

Their eyes grew very wide.

'We're sinking?' Vivore asked.

'Very slowly,' Sorne said. 'So don't frighten the little ones. Just take a look and report back to me.'

They nodded and ran off.

If the worst happened, they could put the smallest of the children on the raft and the others could hold onto it and drift with it. But the water was cold. They would not be able to keep that up for long.

Sorne watched the sail, the horizon and the sky, concentrating on the feel of the boat as she struggled through the seas, and willed the craft to stay afloat.

Chapter Forty-One

TOBAZIM UNROLLED THE message. 'The causare says the sea-raiders had a fiant!'

'What?' Norsasno had been inspecting the temporary shutters. Now he held out his hand.

Tobazim handed him the scroll.

The hand-of-force frowned as he read the news, then looked up. 'When I joined the brotherhood I was taught that every dead sister weakened a sisterhood and made our brotherhoods stronger, but now...'

'Every dead T'En weakens the T'Enatuath,' Ardonyx said from the doorway.

That reminded Tobazim. Something had been bothering him since he saw the blue fire. It was something important, and the sick feeling in the pit of his stomach told him it was something he did not want to confront.

'Tobazim.' Ardonyx crossed the cabin. 'Our dead have been laid out on the mid-deck. Everyone's waiting for you.'

Tobazim did not want to go out there. Every loss diminished him, every loss felt personal. He did not know if other all-fathers felt their brotherhood's grief so deeply. He suspected they didn't, and wondered if the new facet of his gift left him vulnerable to his brotherhood's losses.

Ardonyx's hand settled on his shoulder, firm and warm. 'They want you to lead the farewell ceremony, Tobazim. The attack was devastating. They need words to inspire them, words to make their loss worthwhile, to justify their loved ones' deaths and validate their grief.'

At Ardonyx's words, a rush of conviction filled Tobazim. And in that same instant he realised the nature of Ardonyx's gift.

He was the rarest of kind of word-smith. Not only could he choose the right words to say, but he could imbue them with power. Tobazim had heard of only one other living T'En with this power. According to rumour, the playwright who wrote under the penname of Rutz had had this gift. He'd been from Chariode's brotherhood, too. But no one had known this identity because...

Because he was Ardonyx.

With realisation came understanding. Since the night they formed the shield-brother bond, Tobazim had sensed that Ardonyx was hiding something.

The very nature of his gift.

He gestured to Norsasno and the Malaunje. 'Some privacy, please.'

'What is it?' Ardonyx asked, as soon as they were alone. 'What troubles you?'

He wasn't using his gift now. He didn't need to. He instinctively knew the right words to say. It was only when he sensed his words would not be enough that he added the little push of power, as he'd done earlier when Norsasno complained that the causare had held off calling down the blue fire to let the brotherhoods suffer.

For all Tobazim knew, Ardonyx had been doing this all along. During brotherhood confrontations the gifts always ran high, so no one would notice if Ardonyx enforced his words with power.

'Our shield-brother bond is based on a lie of omission,' Tobazim said. 'There's something you haven't told me.'

'What're you talking about?' Ardonyx let his arm drop, looking ever so slightly wary.

'You're lying to me now.'

'That's rich, coming from you. You're the one who wouldn't admit to your own shield-brother that you were suffering from gift-addiction.'

'We weren't shield-brothers then, and I've overcome it. Besides, this isn't about me. It's about you and our shield-brother bond. The night we took the oath, I revealed my gift. You showed me a glimpse of your power, but not enough for me to understand its nature.'

Ardonyx went very still for a heartbeat, then Tobazim thought he appeared relieved.

'You should be the one to lead the farewell,' Tobazim told him. 'You're that rarest of word-smiths. You can imbue words with power. You're the playwright Rutz.'

His shield-brother's mouth twisted in a wry smile. 'Took you long enough.'

But Tobazim refused to be charmed. 'It was your gift that helped you convince Kyredeon to take you into his brotherhood, even though you came from the inner circle of another brotherhood. Tonight, when we talked about the blue fire, you used your gift to divert Norsasno. Why?'

'Anger and blame are pointless. We had work to do.'

It was true, but...

'Ask yourself this,' Ardonyx said. 'Have I ever used my gift for anything but the good of our people? And it's a flawed gift at best. I could not save my ships and cargo when I returned from the Lagoons of Perpetual Summer.'

'Why didn't you tell me?'

'For precisely the reason we stand here now, having this conversation.' Ardonyx shrugged. 'Honestly, how could I have told you back when I first entered your brotherhood? Then, I did not know that you were going to become my shield-brother. And if Kyredeon had suspected the true nature of my gift, he would have had me killed.'

Everything he said made sense, but Tobazim still felt betrayed.

'Have I offended you, shield-brother? I don't want this to come between us,' Ardonyx said. 'You can trust me.'

'To say the things you think I want to hear.'

'No. I say the things I believe you need to hear even if they are not welcome. That is what an all-father's voice-of-reason does.'

But even this was what Tobazim wanted to hear.

There was a knock on the door.

Tobazim raised his voice. 'Come in.'

'They're ready for you,' Norsasno said. 'And the warriors have been asking if you'll arrange trystings.'

'Tonight?'

'We've survived death's shadow. We want to bathe in sisterhood power.' Norsasno had trouble controlling the rise of his eager gift. 'It's natural after what we've been through.'

'We'll see.' Tobazim headed for the door.

'Tobazim?' Ardonyx called.

He paused, shut the door on Norsasno and turned around. Ardonyx was the person he most admired. The gift his shield-brother had been cursed with was one of the rare, dangerous powers that could get a T'En killed just for having it. No wonder he'd hidden its nature even from his shield-brother.

'Are we all right?' Ardonyx asked, his voice raw.

'Yes.' Tobazim saw his shoulders relax. 'But don't ever lie to me again. It must be all or nothing.'

Ardonyx looked down, then up. 'All or nothing it is.'

And they left the cabin together.

Hueryx and his brothers filled the foredeck, while Malaunje from both their brotherhoods shared the mid-deck. They remembered the fallen, celebrated their lives and then they sang. The voices from both brotherhoods combined, deep and powerful, as the blue fire flickered on the masts above them.

When this was done, there was silence, then a soft murmuring as the Malaunje parted for Hueryx and his inner circle.

Tobazim came down the steps to meet the all-father on the mid-deck.

'I hear you're arranging for trystings,' Hueryx said. There was cheering from the brotherhood warriors. 'I expect the causare will be honouring you with a trysting, to recognise your voice-of-reason's role as fleet commander. Or will she strip Ardonyx of his command, since we've suffered such terrible losses?'

A ripple of angry muttering travelled through the gathering. Tobazim thought they'd come through the attack pretty well, considering the odds, but his brotherhood expected him to fully support Ardonyx. Anything less would appear weak.

And just like that, he had to approach the causare's ship or admit that Ardonyx had failed.

'We're changing course now,' he said, and caught Ardonyx's eye.

His shield-brother returned to the high rear-deck to speak to the helmsman.

'Excellent.' Hueryx grinned. 'I wonder if I can lure the healer into my arms. They say she can control a man's body to prolong pleasure.'

Tobazim blinked, his mind a jumble of images.

Hueryx laughed and headed back to his end of the ship.

From this day forward, Tobazim would never look on the healer the same way. Not sure if he had been played, he joined Ardonyx to watch the celebrations. The pipers had struck up a lively tune and the dancing had already begun.

'You can't lay yourself open to the causare's power so soon after fighting off gift-addiction,' Ardonyx said softly.

'I have to approach her. If I don't, it weakens our leadership.'

'I know.' Ardonyx said the words as if they left a bitter taste in his mouth.

Tobazim gripped the rail as his eager gift tried to break free. He wanted nothing more than to open himself to the causare's power. He wanted it so desperately, he knew it would be a mistake.

'Fiant take Hueryx,' Ardonyx muttered. 'Kyredeon's adepts will be watching us. You'll have to approach her.'

Tobazim nodded. He did not trust his voice. Did not trust himself. Then it came to him. 'The gift-benediction.'

'What about it?'

'I didn't have the skill to carry out the gift-benediction, you guided me that night. Tonight you aren't injured. Tonight you can join me and help shield me.'

'You want me to share a trysting with you and the causare, and shield you from her power?' Ardonyx's voice sounded strained.

'Can you do it?'

Ardonyx swallowed.

'Can you? Because I can't go to her alone. I want her too much.'

Ardonyx hesitated.

Tobazim laughed. 'Come, when are two shield-brothers, so new to leadership, going to get a chance like this to tryst with the most powerful female of our generation?'

Still Ardonyx hesitated.

'What possible reason could you have for not wanting this?'

'None, none at all.'

And their ship edged closer to hers.

RONNYN LEANED AGAINST the ship's rail. Down below on the mid-deck, the empowered lads danced to wild piping. On the upper decks, the T'En women had shared the spiced wine ceremony and the older ones had gone to bed, but now the young ones seemed restless.

'So beautiful...' Sardeon stared up at the masts.

The blue light played across his upturned face, making Ronnyn, who had grown used to his beauty, aware of it all over again.

'Nerazime couldn't have saved Vittor,' Sardeon whispered. 'Sometimes, things are beyond our control.' He turned to Ronnyn. 'I couldn't have saved Lyxie.'

'Just like I couldn't have saved Da.'

They sat watching the blue flame in silence.

'I had no idea that Gift-tutor Sarodyti was a gift-warrior,' Ronnyn said.

'Most gift-warriors become gift-tutors, if they live long enough. They know the most about the higher plane.'

'Why would anyone want to be a gift-warrior?'

'Stature. Gift-warriors are respected. They take an oath to accept true death.'

Ronnyn swallowed. 'Stature doesn't mean that much to me. Nothing could convince me to be a gift-warrior.'

'It's not a matter of choice. The empowerer identifies your gift.' Sardeon gave a dry smile. 'If your gift-tutor tells you that you don't have the right kind of gift and mental discipline, you're supposed to be disappointed but I'd be relieved.'

Ronnyn grinned. Sometimes Sardeon reminded him of Aravelle. She was just as sharp.

He search the fleet for All-father Hueryx's *Victorious* and was surprised to find the brotherhood ship right beside theirs and growing ever closer, bringing with it lively, joyous music.

'They're dancing on the mid-deck.' Ronnyn pointed.

'Celebrating our survival,' Sardeon said.

Ronnyn frowned. 'I see Malaunje amongst the dancers. I thought you said we had to keep our distance?'

'It's different with the brotherhoods. Their Malaunje have a more intimate relationship with the T'En.'

They both gasped as one of the brotherhood warriors swung across from the *Victorious*, dropping lightly onto the mid-deck. The empowered lads spun around in surprise, then circled him warily. Two more brotherhood warriors followed, one landing on the foredeck only a body length from Ronnyn.

Their arrival caused a ripple of surprised comment from the young sisterhood warriors.

'What're you doing here, Toreon?' Nerazime asked.

Her voice struck Ronnyn as odd. For some reason, it made his heart race and tension sing through his body.

Toreon said something soft and his teasing tone made Nerazime give a low, throaty laugh.

Several more brothers swung over. Down on the mid-deck, the empowered lads retreated, and a shiver of excitement travelled through the sisterhood warriors.

'Come down and join us?' one of the brotherhood warriors cajoled. 'Come down and dance.'

The pipers produced a wild tune. Toreon held out his hand and Nerazime took it, leading him down to the mid-deck. The rest of the T'En women followed, their voices breathless and excited.

Ronnyn glanced across to the deck of the *Victorious*, thinking his sisters were somewhere on that ship. If only he knew where.

As if in answer to his need, Aravelle came out of the foredeck cabins. She carried a pan and tipped the contents over the side, before weaving through the remaining dancers as she headed back to the cabins.

His heart lifted and he ran down the steps to the mid-deck, searching for a rope.

'What're you doing?' Sardeon darted after him, watching in dismay as he tested the rope. 'You can't do this.'

'Why not? They've come to visit our ship.'

'It's different.' Sardeon rolled his eyes. 'If you're caught, you'll get in so much trouble.'

'I'm not asking you to come with me.' With that he climbed onto the rail and swung across, landing lightly on the mid-deck. No one noticed. Both decks were filled with dancers, the music growing ever faster.

A soft thump made Ronnyn turn.

Sardeon rose from a crouch. 'I don't know why I let you do this.'

Ronnyn laughed. 'Because you can't stop me.'

And he darted through the dancers, aiming for the door to the foredeck cabins. When he looked down the passage, only the door at the far end was ajar. Lamplight glowed through the gap. He headed for it.

Sardeon followed on his heels.

* * *

Aravelle shook the bed-mat, to be sure there were no more glass shards in it, and refolded it.

'Vella!'

It couldn't be. She froze with a pillow in both hands and then spun around. It was. 'Ronnyn!'

He gave that cheeky, forehead-crinkling grin he'd inherited from All-father Hueryx. 'Miss me?'

She ran and threw her arms around him. He lifted her right off her feet, swung her around, and planted a kiss on her cheek. How could she ever have doubted him? She hadn't realised how much she missed his gift until she felt it again.

Ronnyn put her down and she pulled back to look at him. The Mieren had broken his nose, but it was fixed now. 'Show me your arm.'

The twisted muscles had been smoothed out. It was not perfect, but it was not as mangled as it had been. Recalling how he'd suffered without complaint, she was glad. A sudden surge of emotion made her throat feel tight.

She looked up at him. 'I swear you've grown.'

'Are they treating you well?' he asked. 'My choice-mother said you'd be fostered with the all-father's-voice.'

Someone moved behind him and she noticed a beautiful T'En girl. A stab of jealousy surprised her. 'Who's that?'

'Him?' Ronnyn laughed. 'That's just Sar, my choice-brother.'

The youth inclined his head ever so slightly. 'Sardeon Choice-son Reoden, son of All-father Paragian.'

Ronnyn did not give her time to respond. Placing his hands on her shoulders, he urged her to turn a full circle so that he could admire her. 'Don't you look fine all dressed up? But why did you cut your beautiful hair? You should have seen it, Sar. It hung like dark red silk to her knees.'

'Malaunje aren't allowed to grow their hair past their waist. Ma should never have –'

'What?'

The beautiful youth rolled his eyes. 'Don't tell me you've never noticed? No Malaunje has a plait past their waist.'

Ronnyn shrugged this aside. 'Well, I liked it. I thought it was pretty.'

Aravelle shrugged this aside. 'How are Vittor and Tam? How's baby Ashmyr? Oh, I wish I could see him.'

'You will. I'll find a way to bring them all to see you.'

'Ronnyn...' Sardeon muttered, radiating disapproval. 'If you acknowledge your Malaunje kin, it must be done in private, with care for their autonomy.'

'Tell you what, Sar.' Ronnyn crinkled his forehead in annoyance. 'Why don't you go stand in the hall and keep watch? Warn me if someone comes.'

Aravelle hid a smile.

'Very well.' Sardeon sent Aravelle a warning look, as if to say, *you know better, we must protect him from himself.* And the strange thing was, she agreed.

Aravelle waited until Sardeon had stepped into the hall. 'He's not happy with you. Is it hard, living with the sisterhood?'

'No, not at all. Healer Reoden is so kind that at first I felt disloyal for liking her. Where's Itania? Can I see her?'

'Not without everyone knowing you've come aboard. She's down below in the cabin with the all-father's-voice.'

'I'm glad you're her choice-daughters. Is she as nice as Healer Reoden?'

'I don't think anyone's as nice as the healer.' What else could she say? She didn't want to tell him about Charsoria. As there was nothing he could do to help it would only upset him.

Maybe she was a bad person, but it pleased Aravelle to know that she still meant the world to Ronnyn. Even if she had to be careful of his gift.

'Ronnyn?' Sardeon darted through the door. 'There's a brotherhood warrior coming. We need to leave.'

'Over here.' Aravelle caught Ronnyn's hand and ran to the door to the bathing chamber. 'Hide in here. As soon as he enters this cabin, go out the other door and down the passage.'

She shoved them both in and closed the door, just as Voice-of-Reason Dragomyr entered.

He searched the cabin as he strode towards her. 'I saw a beautiful young T'En woman come in here. What are you up to, Vella?'

She shook her head, remaining silent. No believable lie presented itself.

His gaze went to the only other door.

Instinctively, she spread her hands to prevent him passing her.

He slapped her so fast she didn't see his hand move. Her feet left the ground and she landed on a pile of bedding with enough force to knock the wind out of her.

Her lip stung. She pressed her hand to her mouth and her fingers came away bright red with blood. 'Wait.'

Too late, the voice-of-reason threw the door open.

Chapter Forty-Two

RONNYN LAUGHED AS he landed on the mid-deck of his ship, rolled and came to his feet. He felt his gift empower him; felt like he could do anything. Sardeon followed one beat behind him. They steadied each other and looked back.

A brotherhood warrior charged out of the foredeck cabins.

Sardeon tensed. 'That's him.'

Ronnyn dropped to the deck, taking Sardeon with him. The pair of them lay there, hearts slamming against their ribs. Underneath the laughter, he could feel Sardeon's gift, responding to the danger.

After a moment, Ronnyn came to his knees, crawled to the side and peered onto the deck of the brotherhood ship. Sardeon joined him.

'Is he still looking?' Sardeon whispered.

'No.'

They both collapsed, laughing. Ronnyn laughed so hard that tears came to his eyes. Through blurry vision, he saw a pair of elegant bare female feet on the boards in front of him. Wiping his eyes he looked up at Nerazime. The brotherhood warrior she'd been dancing with came over.

The voice-of-reason put her hands on her hips. 'Just what have you two boys been doing?'

Ronnyn glanced to Sardeon and they both dissolved into laughter again.

Nerazime shook her head. 'Go to your cabin.'

The brotherhood warrior curled an arm around Nerazime's waist and lifted her off her feet, drawing her back into the dance, and she didn't protest.

Sardeon sobered up. 'We should do what she says.'

'Why?'

'It's like midsummer feast.' He saw Ronnyn did not understand. 'A time for unsanctioned trystings.'

Ronnyn tilted his head, intrigued. 'In what way does trysting differ from shagging?'

'Shagging is what animals and the Mieren do. Trysting is something else entirely.' He tugged Ronnyn to his feet. 'Come on.'

As they neared the door to the foredeck cabins, Reoden stepped out. She studied the revellers, searching for someone.

Nerazime paused in full swing, and the laughter stilled on her face.

Reoden said nothing.

Nerazime completed the circle, slipping under Toreon's arm and into his embrace.

'Go inside, boys,' Reoden ordered sharply, proving she had noticed them. 'Now.'

'I told you,' Sardeon whispered.

They ducked past her and she herded them down the passage to the empowered lads' cabin, even as the music and laughter called to Ronnyn, stirring his gift.

'Wait.' She placed a hand on the door they'd been about to open. 'Is that your gift I can sense, Sardeon?'

'It's back. I can call it.' He lifted his hand, offering her a taste.

'That's good, but...' She turned her face away. 'That's not appropriate. Besides, this power felt different.'

'Then it was Ronnyn. Show her.'

He took the healer's arm and called her power.

She pulled back, outraged. 'How dare you!'

He lifted his hands, frightened by the force of her reaction. 'I'm sorry, I didn't –'

'He didn't mean anything,' Sardeon insisted.

She grimaced and rubbed her arm as if something repulsive had touched her. But when she lifted her eyes to them, she was the choice-mother Ronnyn knew and loved.

'I would never do anything to hurt you,' he said. 'I'm sorry.'

'I know. It's just...' She reached out to reassure him, but stopped before touching him. And Ronnyn realised there would be no more hugs from adult T'En unless they were both prepared.

'He's a summoner. It's why my gift came back,' Sardeon said. 'He's really lucky. It's a high-stature gift.'

'So it is,' she said. But she seemed sad for him. 'Off you go.'

'IMOSHEN?' EGRAYNE CALLED. 'You need to see this.'

'A moment.' She tucked the blanket around Umaleni, then came to her feet.

Imoshen joined her voice-of-reason at the door to the deck. Wild music reached them. 'What's the problem? We all risked our lives tonight and the warriors paid the highest price. They deserve to celebrate.'

Her voice-of-reason said nothing, leading her over to the rail where they could look down on the mid-deck. Imoshen blinked. A dozen or more brotherhood warriors danced with the women from both sisterhoods.

Imoshen's mouth dropped open. It was like midsummer's night; a night for licence and daring. The music and gift readiness stirred Imoshen.

Egrayne snorted. 'What are you going to do about this?'

'Nothing.' Imoshen shrugged. 'No point fighting battles I can't win. With everything we've been through, this is a natural reaction. They need this, Egrayne.'

Her voice-of-reason turned on her heel and strode off, returning to the cabin.

TOBAZIM WATCHED THE causare from the shadows near the steps. Imoshen said something to her voice-of-reason, who went back inside.

After a moment, Imoshen left the rail, heading for the cabins. The lambent blue light of the heatless flames still clung to the masts and rigging. It made Imoshen's pale skin and hair glow. A smile played about her generous lips.

His mouth went dry with need and he nudged Ardonyx. 'You're the wordsmith. Sweet-talk her before she goes inside.'

His shield-brother laughed and pushed him into the light. 'Do your own sweet-talking.'

Quick as a cat, the causare turned to face him.

'Causare, I...' He could not go on, as raw, primitive need gripped him.

He saw understanding dawn. She'd read him. But with the way he felt, she didn't need to be a raedan to know what he wanted, not when it was written in his face and his body.

'Causare.' He managed to give a gracious obeisance. His voice dropped. 'Imoshen.'

Her lips parted as she drew in a quick breath. He wanted to kiss those lips. He'd never trysted with a T'En woman, and he wanted the most powerful woman, who could kill with a touch. He must be mad.

But he could not do this alone. One unshielded taste of her gift and he'd be craving her power again. Reaching behind him, he caught Ardonyx's arm and drew him out of the shadows. 'My voice-of-reason, your fleet commander...' If he'd been a wordsmith, he would have reminded her how Ardonyx had taken on the role of defender of the fleet, but all he could do was wait for her signal.

Her gaze went to Ardonyx and he thought she winced.

She turned to leave.

Tobazim caught her bare arm, skin to skin.

With a practised flick, she slipped from his grasp but, during that brief contact, his gift had recognised hers and it raged through him, driving him to place his hand to each side of her against the wall to block her retreat. 'You reject us? Why?'

She stared pointedly at his arms.

He dropped them, although this cost him.

So close...

They were so close he could sense her gift on her skin, and it called to his. He wanted to roll naked in her power.

'Contain your gift, all-father.'

Her words meant nothing to him. They were just strange sounds that became lost in the rushing in his ears and the pounding of his heart.

'Tobazim.' Ardonyx slid an arm around him, pressing against his back. Chin on Tobazim's shoulder, he siphoned off a little of his excess power.

The causare – she was every bit the causare now, and not the sweet sister he'd glimpsed before – glared at Ardonyx. 'How dare you bring him to me in this state?'

'It's you. You breached his walls the night you gift-infused him.'

Horrified to think his shield-brother had betrayed his weakness, Tobazim flung off Ardonyx's restraining arm and ran across the deck, heading for his own ship. Shame stung his face, burning his cheeks, driving him to seek the privacy of his cabin.

He didn't bother to light a lamp, but stood staring out the windows. How had it come to this?

His gift still raged for the causare and it took all his self-control to contain it. He didn't know how long he stood there.

Eventually, the cabin door opened behind him and he turned, furious. 'Why did you tell her? How could you shame me like that?'

'What? After you'd already shamed yourself?'

He turned away, grasped the bulkhead above the bunk in both hands and thumped his forehead on the polished wood.

'Tobazim.' Ardonyx crossed the cabin, caught him around the chest. 'Listen...'

Tobazim went to brush him off, but his shield-brother would not be diverted. Furious, Tobazim tried to overpower him. But, fast as he was, Ardonyx countered him. Neither went for painful blows, it was all quicksilver skill – even so, a chair went flying and Tobazim ended up pinned to the wall, panting with exertion and emotion.

Short of hurting himself or Ardonyx, he could not break free. He groaned and threw his head back, skull thumping against the wall. 'She'll think me a fool.'

'She apologised.'

'What?'

'She apologised for breaching your walls. Said she would never have gift-infused you if she'd realised you had a concussion.'

'Really?'

Ardonyx nodded.

They heard running feet, feminine laughter and a slamming door in the hallway outside.

'She also said there was no privacy for trysting on board ship,' Ardonyx said.

'She's not angry with me?'

His shield-brother shook his head. 'She was angry with me for not protecting you as a shield-brother should.'

Tobazim took a moment to think this through. 'We weren't shield-brothers when I was gift-infused.'

'No.' Ardonyx grinned. 'But I should have been looking out for you.'

Tobazim pulled him close, forehead to forehead. 'I'm sorry I didn't trust you. I...'

Ardonyx kissed him.

And he forgot what he was about to say. He forgot everything, because he felt the causare's gift riding his shield-brother.

He pulled back. 'She –'

'Gift-infused me. Her apology to you, through me. Don't worry. Her power's safe for you. I've taken the edge off it.'

But that wasn't what Tobazim truly wanted. He wanted to immerse himself in her gift until he lost all sense of self.

Just as well his shield-brother was here to protect him. It was the last coherent through he had, as he reached for Ardonyx.

ARAVELLE PRESSED HER hand to her split lip, tears of pain stinging her eyes. She hoped Ronnyn and Sardeon had escaped Dragomyr and made it back to their ship.

If they had slipped away, the voice-of-reason would be coming for her. Even though there was more to clean up, she darted out of the cabin, running down the passage towards the door to the mid-deck.

Only to meet up with Dragomyr as he flung the door open.

He grabbed her arm and dragged her back to the cabin, where he spun her around and shook her. 'They got away, the empowered lad and young sisterhood initiate. What were you up to?'

She was glad they'd escaped. Glad, even if it meant she was in trouble.

'What's a sisterhood initiate doing in here?' He raised his hand, threatening to slap her.

She didn't answer. Dragomyr had never liked her. He'd find a way to make this her fault.

He shook her. 'Who were they?'

'I'm not telling you. I'll tell the all-father.'

'Hueryx is busy. So tell me.'

She pressed her lips together and shook her head.

He glared at her, then flung her away from him. 'Clean up, then get out. They'll be back here to tryst before long.'

Face burning, she finished cleaning up and left.

Tomorrow she'd tell Hueryx the truth. She had a suspicion that even though Ronnyn had left the sisterhood ship and entered brotherhood territory without permission, Hueryx would be proud of his daring.

Slipping through the dancers, she climbed down the ladder onto the Malaunje deck and headed for the cabin. She was proud of Ronnyn. He hadn't forgotten her and Itania. He...

As she opened the cabin door, Charsoria's hard palm connected with her cheek, splitting her lip further and knocking her sideways.

Aravelle staggered several steps and hit the cabin wall.

Charsoria stalked towards her.

For a moment, she had no idea why the all-father's-voice was angry.

Then she saw Redravia's worried face in the background.

And it all came back to her. 'I didn't mean for it to happen. Hariorta panicked. She was going to –'

Charsoria covered her mouth, stepped in close, shoved her against the wall and spoke in a voice so thick with hatred it was almost unintelligible. 'So you killed her.'

Aravelle couldn't speak. Could hardly breathe.

'It was an accident. Hariorta fell on the knife,' Redravia pleaded. 'I was there. I saw it all.'

'And she boasted of it to the hand-of-force's devotee, so now the all-father knows and he'll stand by his brat, even if she is Malaunje. Where does that leave me?' Charsoria demanded. 'Alone without my female kin!'

Aravelle could have pointed out that she and Itania were Charsoria's nieces. But even if her mouth hadn't been covered, she wouldn't have bothered.

Charsoria's eyes narrowed. 'You think you're so smart. You think you can't be touched. But I know your weakness. If you take one step out of line, your little sister is going to pay, and keep on paying.'

Aravelle tried not to panic. But, if a tragic accident could happen to Hariorta, then how much more easily could it happen to vulnerable little Itania?

She wanted to protest that her sister was innocent, but fear froze her.

Using Itania to punish her was wrong; the injustice of it burned. Tears of fury filled her eyes.

Charsoria leant in closer. 'Yes, cry. Weep for yourself. You're going to wish you were never born. You think I was hard on you before? That was nothing – *nothing* – to what's coming.'

And she reached up under Aravelle's robe, caught her right nipple and pinched, twisting as hard as she could.

Aravelle made a high-pitched moan of protest.

Satisfied, the all-father's-voice released her, wiping her hands down her sides as if they were dirty. 'Go.'

Aravelle ran over to her bedroll, undid it and cuddled Itania. Her split lip stung and her cheek throbbed, but that was nothing compared to her breast. It hurt so much she dare not touch it.

But even that was not her biggest worry. How was she going to protect Itania?

Chapter Forty-Three

SORNE COULD FEEL the boat settling deeper into the sea as it began to wallow between the swells. Since long before dawn, every child big enough to carry a pot or bucket had been bailing, but it did no good.

Tiasely sent around one of the smaller children with a basket of carrots. Sorne took one. He was heartily sick of eating carrots, especially as they had started to go soft.

Vivore and Vivane had begun dismantling the cabin fittings to build a raft. They'd taken the bunks out and built a frame, lashing planks together with ropes. A few moments ago they'd come to him for permission to remove the planks from one of the cabin walls. Orza and two Malaunje boys were still on the roof, feet spread, hands shading their eyes as they searched the horizon for sails.

The boat's nose slid down a swell into the hollow before the next wave. Sorne felt the water in the hold slide down to the nose of the boat. It was still down there when the prow cut the rise of the next long swell. The nose did not rise enough and cold, green sea water lapped over the sides of the prow. It splashed on the deck, rolling towards him as the nose finally lifted and the boat rose to ride the incline.

The children gave a yelp of fright and began bailing faster.

As the stern of the boat reached the belly of the swell, Sorne felt the weight of the water in the hold weigh it down and the boat battled valiantly to climb the next wave.

'See anything, Orza?' Sorne called.

He checked with the other two. 'Nothing.'

'Vivane, take the rudder.'

Sorne handed over to him and took the mallet from Vivore. He aimed precise blows along the nail line of each plank on the cabin wall. The boat was old and the nails had rusted, but it didn't take him long to remove a pile of planks.

Returning the mallet, Sorne felt the boat shudder and water splashed over the nose, running up the deck in a small wave. 'Hurry up with the raft, boys.'

Vivore nodded and Sorne resumed his place at the rudder. They didn't have until midday. They didn't have long at all.

ARAVELLE HERDED ALL the children into the bathing chamber. Some were choice-children and some were the natural children of Charsoria's inner circle. And they were due to have their hair washed and combed to prevent nits, according to the all-father's-voice.

'Right,' Nariska said. 'Strip off, then line up.' She winked at Aravelle. 'This way their clothes won't get wet. No point in making work for ourselves.'

The bigger children undressed themselves, but the little ones needed a hand. As Aravelle helped the little ones strip, she chafed at the delay. She was eager to go up to the all-father's cabin. Voice-of-reason Dragomyr would have reported her transgression to Hueryx by now, and he would have painted it in the worst possible light.

But of course, Charsoria seemed to sense this and had invented a task for her. It was pure spite.

She sent another toddler towards Nariska and reached for the next child.

Each time Aravelle moved, she was reminded of Charsoria. Her right breast was so sore she couldn't bear material brushing across the nipple. But she wasn't about to complain, not when so many were nursing injuries from the sea-vermin attack.

Itania was the last child to be stripped. Aravelle reached for her little sister's nightgown, pulling it over her head. Itania's curls bounced on her bare shoulders, shoulders covered in bruises. Aravelle lifted her little arms to inspect the bruises, some old and fading some livid on her pale skin.

'Tani...' Aravelle moaned.

Her fingers shook with fury as she turned Itania around. There were more bruises on her thighs and buttocks as well. All were situated where they would be hidden under her clothing. Who would...

Charsoria, of course.

So angry that she didn't trust herself to speak, Aravelle picked up Itania and headed for the cabin.

Nariska jumped in front of her, fingers covered in nit oil. 'Don't –'

'But her bruises.' Aravelle lifted Itania's plump little arm. 'Charsoria –'

Nariska didn't even glance at the evidence. 'Don't give her the satisfaction. The more she knows you care, the more she'll hurt Itania.'

Aravelle knew she was right. 'But...'

Nariska held her eyes and slowly rolled up her sleeve. Her upper arms were patterned with new and fading bruises.

Aravelle gasped. 'It's not fair.'

'Who said life was fair?' Nariska whispered. 'Come on. If we don't hurry up, she'll be angry.'

Aravelle returned to the task, combing the children's hair. By the time she was done, she was ready to wash the first child. Working as a team, she and Nariska were soon finished.

Still seething, Aravelle returned to the cabin with the children. She could hardly bring herself to look at Charsoria, who sent her off to fetch the grownups' breakfast.

In the passage, she met Redravia with the remains of the children's breakfast.

This was her chance. Aravelle blocked the hall, the memory of Itania's bruises fresh in her mind. 'You have to help me.'

'I don't have to do anything.'

Aravelle knew she'd phrased it badly. 'I don't have anyone else to turn to. Charsoria threatened Itania, and she's already covered in bruises.'

The old woman grimaced. 'You killed –'

'That has nothing to do with Itania. She's only two. Please help.' She knew she was begging, but she didn't care. 'I need you to watch over her while I'm serving the all-father.'

A sly light lit Redravia's deep-set eyes.

'What?' Aravelle asked, warily.

Redravia's mouth worked. 'Bring me something infused with the gift, something small that I can wear next to my skin.'

Aravelle hid her disgust. If someone had asked her for help to prevent an injustice she would never have bargained for something in return. 'Very well.'

'Something that contains concentrated power is best.'

Aravelle nodded, unable to meet Redravia's eyes.

'Don't look down your nose at me, girlie. When I was young and beautiful, I had a T'En lover. He willingly shared his power with me. I –'

'Why?'

'Silly girl. He did it to ensure my absolute loyalty. I was not his devotee, but I was the next best thing.'

'Where is he now?' She suspected she knew.

'Dead. They're all dead. All those beautiful, bold young men...' Redravia stared off into space, seeing the faces of long-dead brotherhood warriors, Aravelle suspected. Then the old woman recollected herself. 'Few T'En warriors live long enough to grow old, and my lover wasn't one of them. That's why I need your help. I bathed in his power until it sank into my bones. And now my bones ache. Not a day goes by that I don't feel hollow and needy. And don't go thinking you're so much better than me. One day you could be in my shoes.'

Aravelle bit her lip. Then giggled.

'What?' Redravia stiffened.

'I'm already in your shoes.' She lifted one foot.

Redravia smiled reluctantly.

'I'm sorry.' Aravelle met her eyes. 'I didn't know.'

The old woman accepted the apology. 'Then we're agreed.'

Aravelle nodded and returned to the cabin.

Itania ran over to her.

Aravelle scooped her up. Kissing her sister's copper curls, she carried her over to a quiet corner and knelt with the toddler in her arms.

'Ronnyn's safe, so's Vittor and Tamaron, and baby Ashmyr,' Aravelle whispered fiercely, determined that Itania would not forget her brothers.

'Tam,' Itania repeated. They had been close in age and Aravelle knew her little sister missed him most, just as she missed Ronnyn.

A familiar knock at the door made Aravelle's stomach cramp with anticipation. She carried Itania on one hip as she answered the door.

'The all-father wants you.' Saskar gestured to Itania. 'Put her down and come now.'

Aravelle spotted Redravia coming up the passage and waited for the old woman. Redravia held Aravelle's eyes as she accepted Itania.

Aravelle nodded once. She wouldn't forget. And now that she knew, she would be doubly careful to maintain her defences against the T'En gift.

When the cabin door closed on Redravia, Aravelle joined Saskar in the dim hall.

'What happened last night?' he asked. 'Dragomyr is trying to convince Hueryx you're a sisterhood spy.'

Aravelle laughed.

'Vella!' He took her shoulders in his hands. 'If the all-father doubts your loyalty, he'll have you executed in a heartbeat.'

Her stomach knotted. She had no loyalty to Hueryx. Her only loyalty was to her family.

Saskar looked so concerned for her she felt annoyed, which just proved she wasn't a very nice person. She slipped out from under his hands. 'Don't worry. Hueryx won't be angry when he hears who visited me.'

'Now you've got me curious.'

'You'll just have to wait,' she said over her shoulder, darting down the hall.

Inside the all-father's cabin, a single lantern illuminated the gloom. The windows were all covered with temporary shutters, and the cabin was filled with Hueryx's inner circle.

Aravelle dropped to her knees and gave the correct obeisance. 'You sent for me, all-father.'

'My voice-of-reason tells me when our ship came alongside the causare's, you had visitors and one was a sisterhood initiate?'

'It wasn't a sisterhood initiate.' She threw Dragomyr a contemptuous look. 'It was Sardeon, All-father Paragian's son.'

'If Paragian's son was one of them, who was the other?' Hueryx asked. His sharp eyes told her he'd already guessed.

'Ronnyn. He came to check up on Itania and me.'

'How dare he enter brotherhood territory without permission?' Dragomyr muttered, but Hueryx grinned, as she knew he would.

'So what was Paragian's son doing here, in our brotherhood cabin?' the hand-of-force demanded.

'Sardeon was Ronnyn's lookout.'

Hueryx gave a bark of laughter. 'My son is ordering Paragian's son about? This is priceless!'

The others joined in and Aravelle knew she was safe, safe from everyone except Dragomyr, who glared at her. The last thing she needed was another enemy.

'WHAT NEWS?' IMOSHEN asked, as Egrayne joined her on the rear-deck. The children were playing in the sun and

Imoshen was just grateful to be alive, but all was not well on Melisarone's ship. The small, three-masted vessel had suffered terrible losses during the sea-vermin attack.

Around dawn, Melisarone's ship had drawn alongside, and they'd requested the healer for the all-mother. Imoshen was expecting the worst.

'Nothing from Reoden, yet,' Egrayne said. 'But this has just come.'

Imoshen accepted the message. As she read it, her heart sank. 'We've lost All-father Egrutz.'

'According to Dretsun, he was killed by the raiders, along with his seconds and inner circle, making his brotherhood unviable.' Egrayne's voice dropped. 'I think Dretsun used the sea-vermin attack to cover his attack on Egrutz. Now Dretsun's brotherhood is no longer a lesser brotherhood.'

'Poor Egrutz... and to think, he offered Dretsun safe passage on his ship.'

'Dretsun's always been ambitious. He'll stir up trouble, and nominate himself for causare.'

'We'll deal with that when we come to it.' Imoshen returned the message.

As Egrayne stalked off, muttering, Imoshen found herself recalling those stolen moments with Ardonyx, after Tobazim had gone.

'You'd better go after him,' she'd said. 'He –'

Ardonyx had caught her face in his hands. 'If he finds out I've lied to him about us, he'll kill me. Gift-infuse me now. I'll use it to win him over.' And he had kissed her.

Gift-infusing Ardonyx gained her nothing, but she gave willingly. She'd been afraid the raiders would kill him, and she was just so relieved to finally have him in her arms, if only for a moment.

Then he'd pulled away, with the force of her gift glowing in his wine-dark eyes.

Leaving her there, he'd returned to his shield-brother and a night of celebration in Tobazim's arms.

No wonder she was jealous.

The sound of weeping reached Imoshen. She went to the rail and saw Reoden return from the smaller ship. Egrayne ran up the steps to join Imoshen.

'Bad news,' her voice-of-reason reported.

'Melisarone's heart gave out.'

'Yes, how did you know?'

Imoshen didn't answer. 'Ree looks exhausted.'

'She is. She did what she could, but Mel's sisterhood has lost too many adepts to be viable. When we get to port, we'll have to absorb her people.'

'We should have taken all of her people on board our ship before the attack.'

'And put them where? Besides, that would have meant ordering Mel to abandon her ship. Imoshen, we may have a problem.'

She bit back a laugh. 'You mean other than marauding sea-vermin and an overambitious all-father who would use the Mieren attack as cover to murder a fellow all-father?'

Egrayne did not smile. 'Reoden didn't consign her scryer's body to the sea.'

'The scryer lives?'

Egrayne nodded. 'Her shield-sister, Sarodyti, is dead and her gift was already corrupting.'

Imoshen thought this through. 'So she's –'

'Her body is alive, but her mind will be ravaged by her gift.' The big woman's mouth twisted with regret. 'It would have been kinder for Reoden to have her suffocated than leave her to suffer.'

'Egrayne...' Imoshen was shocked.

'Would you want to live, if your gift was destroying your mind?'

Imoshen shuddered. 'You could be right. Killing would be a kindness, especially as gift-corruption may be contagious.'

'I've never heard –'

'It's one of Scytheon's theories.'

'But he was discredited.'

'Not in this matter. It was never proven, one way or another.' Imoshen turned to face Egrayne. 'I believe the gifts affect each other, and I don't just mean the tug of male and female gifts. I suggested Ree put Sardeon in with the empowered lads to see if it would bring his gift on. And it has.' She glanced down to the fore-cabins. 'Poor Ree, what should I do?'

'You can't interfere. Reoden rules her sisterhood. We'll watch and wait. Reoden is sensible. She will listen to reason.'

'Reoden is a healer. She cannot bring herself to kill. It goes against her nature.'

Two MESSAGE-STONES HAD arrived in quick succession, and Aravelle caught herself listening for the all-father's reaction to the news. It surprised her to realise she trusted Hueryx's insight, and this annoyed her. After a brief mental wrestle, she decided she could admire his intelligence without liking him.

'I'm just glad our brotherhood wasn't assigned the same ship as All-father Dretsun,' Hueryx said.

'You think he used the sea-vermin attack as cover to displace Egrutz and acquire his brotherhood?' Dragomyr asked.

'Almost certainly.'

Unnoticed and unimportant, Aravelle tidied the cabin, collecting clothing they had simply shed as they disrobed. You'd think they could put their clothes away instead of dropping them on the floor.

She'd promised Redravia something small, infused with the gift. It had to be something she could take without anyone noticing, something unimportant.

But it still made her uncomfortable. No matter how you looked at it, this was stealing. If they caught her...

They'd laugh.

She flushed. They'd think she was taking the gift-infused object for herself. They'd think she'd succumbed to the lure of their power.

With jerky angry movements, she plucked discarded garments from the floor. As she picked up a vest, her fingers brushed a button and she felt the concentrated T'En gift in the pewter button. Her heart leapt.

Without pausing in her work, she collected more clothing. When the basket was full, she sorted the things, putting most away and some in the mending pile.

Her mother used to say that mending her brothers' breeches was a never-ending task. The same could be said for the T'En warriors. They were rough with their clothes and casual about damage, as only those with servants could be. None of them had ever worn their fingers to the bone making-down old clothes for their children, or darning until the breeches were more darning than cloth.

While the inner circle continued to discuss All-father Dretsun and his growing stature, she sat cross-legged in a corner. Heart pounding, she picked up the vest. It belonged to the hand-of-force. She would have known, even if she hadn't seen him wear it. She could sense his distinctive gift.

Snipping off one of the gift-infused buttons, she slipped it in her pocket, then sewed on a new button.

It was as easy at that.

Chapter Forty-Four

WATER CAME IN with every swell, now. It was ankle-deep on deck and Sorne had decided to launch the raft and tie it to the boat. First, he would send Tiasely across with what stores they could scrounge and the blankets they'd managed to keep dry. Then he'd transfer the little ones across...

'Sails! I see sails,' Orza cried.

Sorne sprang onto the cabin roof with the boys and shaded his eyes. 'Five masts. A merchant ship.'

He'd been afraid it would be a sea-vermin ship and they'd end up where they'd started. 'Tiasely, pass me up the red blanket.'

Bracing himself, Sorne waved the blanket above his head. The three boys jumped and waved their arms, shouting at the top of their voices, regardless of the fact that the ship was too far away to hear them.

At first, Sorne feared they would not notice them. Then he kept waving the blanket, aware that the captain was probably studying the boatload of children through his spy-glass.

When he was certain the merchant ship had veered towards them, he jumped down into the knee-high water washing across the deck.

He grabbed Tiasely and Yosune. 'Sit the little ones on the raft and hold onto them. Everyone who can't swim, get onto the raft now.'

The boat shuddered, barely rising to meet the swells. Sorne turned to the boys on top of the cabin. 'Can you swim?'

They shook their heads. He lifted them down, one after

the other. 'The boat's going to sink. You need to hold onto the raft. Understand?'

They nodded and moved over to the raft, which would not carry any more.

He shaded his eyes, judging the speed of the approaching ship.

'What do you want us to do?' Vivore asked, Vivane at his side.

'Find anything that floats. Rope everything together and tie it to the raft.' He didn't want the children getting separated. Some of the little ones wailed as a wave rolled onto the deck, lifted the raft and nearly swept it into the cabin wall. In a mad scramble, Sorne and the boys tied several barrels and a chest together.

They'd barely finished when the boat's nose plunged into a swell and the water swallowed it. A wall of water moved towards them. Sorne shoved the raft to one side so it wouldn't collide with the cabin, and held onto the ropes. The children cried out, some in excitement, others in fear.

He felt the deck go out from under his feet as the boat sank. Icy cold water climbed up his chest. The barrels and the raft tried to drift apart; Sorne felt the ropes tighten around his wrists.

And they were all in the sea, squealing, crying, shouting and splashing.

Several children fell off the raft and had to be hauled back on. Others just held on. The raft rocked as one of the children tried to stand up and wave to the ship.

Tiasely pulled him down.

Sorne glanced over his shoulder; the barrels bobbed along behind with four of the bigger children holding on to them. He unwound the rope from his wrist and drew the barrels closer to the raft.

Now that it was clear everyone was safe, the children laughed, even as their teeth chattered with cold.

Orza cried out and pointed to the ship as two rowboats were lowered. The children cheered.

Sorne wondered what their rescuers would say when they realised they'd picked up a pack of Wyrds. He tried to see the ship's flag, but the sails were in the way.

'Hold on,' the sailors in the nearest rowboat called. They spoke Chalcedonian, but that could have been because the children had been calling out in that language.

One of them threw a coiled rope. 'Catch this.'

Sorne caught hold and tied it to the raft. The sailors started to haul in their catch. As soon as they were close enough, the sailors urged the children to climb into the rowboat. The second boat collected the four children clinging to the barrels. Sorne was last on board.

Teeth chattering, Sorne thanked the sailors. By their colouring and their accents, they could have been from anywhere north of Dace.

As they rowed back to the ship Sorne counted heads, then counted them again to be sure. No one was missing.

He felt like weeping with relief, but was kept busy reassuring the little ones. Now that they were amongst Mieren sailors, the children became subdued; their recent experiences with Mieren did not give them hope. Several wept.

When they reached the ship, the bigger children scrambled up the rope netting while the little ones went up in a large sling with Tiasely to watch over them.

By the time Sorne climbed aboard, the children were wrapped in blankets, sitting wide-eyed on the deck as the sailors gathered to watch them. Sorne suspected the children feared the sailors would throw them back, now that they realised they were Wyrds.

A moment later, the cook and his helper arrived to hand out mugs of warm soup and chunks of bread. At this, the children relaxed a little and those who could speak Chalcedonian thanked them.

Teeth chattering, Sorne accepted his mug with thanks. He wrapped his hands around it, grateful for the warmth.

'You're in charge?'

Sorne turned to see a grizzled, but well-dressed sailor he took to be the first mate, or even the captain.

'Yes,' Sorne answered, trying to assess the man's honour. He'd been sold into sea-vermin hands by a man much like this one. What merchants valued was gold, and right now Sorne had none.

The man stepped aside to reveal someone dressed in the traditional robes of the Sagoras. 'This is Merchant Sahia of House Vulpii.'

Sorne's mind raced. He knew that Imoshen had approached the Sagoras for sanctuary and had not heard back. Sahia wore a floor-length robe and veil that covered all but the mouth and chin. He couldn't tell the merchant's gender; they were either a woman, or a youth not old enough to have a beard.

Putting his mug aside, Sorne gave the deep obeisance of gratitude. 'We are in your debt, Merchant Sahia of House Vulpii.'

'Yes, you are. How did you come to be sailing a sinking raider boat with two dozen Wyrd children?' Sahia asked, in excellent Chalcedonian. She was a woman, and older than the mouth and chin made her appear.

'They were captives of the sea-vermin, meant for sale in southern brothels. That leaky boat was the only way we could escape.'

'You gloss over much. Before that there was a fire.'

'Yes, how...' Sorne lifted a hand to his head. 'My hair.'

'And your eyebrows. So you escaped and sailed for Ivernia? Or did you lose your way?'

'No, I was sailing for Ivernia, when I was captured by sea-vermin.' He did not want to sound desperate, but the more he said, the more vulnerable he appeared. 'All Wyrds have been exiled from Chalcedonia.'

'We heard something to that effect, Warrior's-voice.'

'Whatever you may have heard about me, it is incorrect, an exaggeration or an outright lie,' he said. 'I am Sorne, ambassador of the T'Enatuath, sent by Causare T'Imoshen to negotiate with the Sagora Seven, and these children are under my protection.'

She studied him.

Sorne held his breath.

'Captain, prepare a cabin for the ambassador and another one for his companions.'

Sorne thanked her, as if he had never thought she might doubt him.

IMOSHEN LEANED ON the rail of the high rear-deck, watching the west and the last of what had been a piercingly-beautiful sunset. According to Ardonyx's latest calculations, they should reach Ivernia late tomorrow, or early the next day. And then she would have to convince the Sagoras to offer them sanctuary.

'Worrying about the Sagoras?' her voice-of-reason asked.

Imoshen nodded.

'You should be worrying about the scryer. I've been thinking. Lysi lives, but she and Sarodyti had been shield-sisters for seventy years. When Saro died, the shock should have killed her.'

'Normally, but the gift-corruption could have interfered with their link,' Imoshen said. 'I've been reading the gift treatises.'

'Did you also read up on healers?'

'I didn't get as far as the chapters on healers,' Imoshen admitted.

Egrayne's expression told her it was not good news. 'I did. The part about healers and gift-corruption makes particularly interesting reading.'

'Is Ree more susceptible to gift-corruption because she's a healer?'

'No, but her healing gift is a problem.' Egrayne sighed. 'I know you are fond of Reoden.'

Imoshen nodded. She could not bring herself to reveal just how deep her feelings went. 'Ree would never do anything to endanger her sisterhood. She holds her honour high.'

'It's because she's both a healer and an all-mother that we have a problem.'

An all-mother was sworn to protect her sisterhood. Imoshen looked up in horror. 'Lysi is draining Ree to sustain herself.' A rushing filled Imoshen's ears. 'Ree's sisterhood link with the scryer could kill her.'

'Eventually.' Egrayne looked grim. 'That, or Ree's gift could sustain the scryer indefinitely, but that would be bad. The longer Lysi lives, the more chance her gift-corruption will spread –'

'...to Ree.' Imoshen swallowed.

'You must intervene. You must speak with Ree, the sooner the better.'

Imoshen met Egrayne's eyes. 'If I interfere with how she runs her sisterhood, our friendship will never be the same.'

'That's Imoshen talking. You must think like the causare.'

She was right. Imoshen's heart sank. 'Poor Ree. Coming to the realisation that you must kill one of your own sisterhood is a terrible thing.'

ARAVELLE WAITED IN the passage for Redravia to come back.

'Here.' Aravelle gave her the button. 'This is for you. It's –'

'I know what it is.' The old woman accepted it and pressed it to her chest. She closed her eyes and inhaled deeply, then sighed with relief. When she opened her eyes, they were brighter and more alert. 'Perfect.'

'So a button is all right?'

'Pewter is good, so is bronze. Silver and gold are better.' Redravia hung the button on a leather thong around her neck, tucking it inside her bodice. 'Best of all is electrum, that's why their torcs are made of it.' Those sharp eyes fixed on Aravelle. 'Some of them wear electrum rings through their ears or on their fingers.'

'You want me to steal electrum jewellery for you?'

'Their gift settles in it and emanates slowly.'

'But I could get caught.'

'There's no need to steal.' Redravia tilted her head. 'A pretty girl like you, you'd have no trouble convincing an initiate or an adept to give you jewellery. A ring in exchange for a kiss, it means nothing to them.' Aravelle stiffened, offended.

Redravia laughed. 'How is a trinket in exchange for a kiss worse than stealing?'

Aravelle couldn't explain. 'It just is.'

'You're your mother all over again. Too proud and too clever. And look what happened to her.'

As the old woman walked off, Aravelle wanted to shout after her, wanted to tell her that she was proud of her mother, who had chosen to live free rather than give in to Hueryx's gift enticement.

She would be just as strong. She'd never give in.

SORNE STOOD AT the rail as the ship entered the headlands of Port Sorvernia. He had bathed, dressed and eaten, and now he looked like an ambassador. He'd checked the children, who were all bunking down together. The younger ones thought their troubles were over. The older ones had made him promise not to abandon them.

'I am curious,' Merchant Sahia said, joining him. 'Why did the causare send a Malaunje as her ambassador? Don't the T'En rank higher than half-bloods in T'En society?'

'Yes, but this half-blood has lived amongst True-men for many years. As the Warrior's-voice, I served King Charald.' Who would have taken one look at this port and thought he could crack it wide open. Did the Ivernians believe that because theirs was an island kingdom, they were safe from invasion? Perhaps they had been, so far. There was no Ivernian king, just a number of provinces, each ruled by a city-state. This was the Sagoras' province. 'But now I serve the causare. She believes that True-men and women will be more comfortable with a Malaunje who is used to their ways.'

As he spoke, he searched the ships anchored in the bay for the distinctive blunt-nosed profile and segemented sails of the T'Enatuath ships, but did not see them. He had beaten Imoshen's fleet to port.

'So you know the ways of True-men. But do you know the ways of the Sagoras, ambassador?'

'I know your people came from across the Endless Ocean over three hundred years ago, on one ship containing seven families, or "houses," as you call them. Starting with almost nothing, you built that.' He pointed to the sandstone edifice that ran along the crest of a ridge behind the port. 'The Halls of Learning are renowned across the Secluded Sea. The greatest scholars come here to study, experiment, debate their findings and teach. If they're clever enough, the poorest child can win a scholarship and study alongside future kings and queens. All they need is a true love of learning.' Sorne smiled. 'In truth, I know very little about the Sagoras themselves, other than that they live segregated lives in the hidden city, at the southern end of the Halls of Learning, and guard their privacy closely.'

'And what makes you think the Sagoras would offer the T'Enatuath sanctuary?'

'Two things. Like you, we have fled persecution.'

'Who says we fled persecution?'

'You sailed across the Endless Ocean in a single ship that sank just off the west coast of Ivernia. You must have been desperate to make the journey; no other ships have succeeded in the three hundred years since.'

'And the other thing?'

'Like my people, you value knowledge.' When he saw her smile, he suspected he had fallen into a trap.

'You say scholars come from all the mainland kingdoms to study with us. What possible knowledge could the T'Enatuath have that we do not already have?'

'That is something I must discuss with the Sagora Seven,' Sorne said, wondering just what Imoshen planned to offer. Hopefully, he could delay until her ship arrived.

The merchant ship dropped anchor, and the sailors prepared to lower a boat.

'I'm going to report to the Sagora Seven right now. Come with me, Ambassador Sorne. I'm sure they will be fascinated to meet the half-blood who served the Mieren king and now serves Causare T'Imoshen.'

'I would be delighted.' Sorne hesitated. 'But the children... They saw their friends and families massacred. They had lost all hope when I found them. They'll panic if they see me go.'

'Then we will have to make sure they don't see.'

Sorne swallowed and turned to her. 'Do I have your word that they will be safe until I return?'

Now she hesitated. 'It would have been much easier for you to escape alone. Yet you didn't.'

'I couldn't live with myself if I had left them there.'

'Yet there must be other Wyrd children in other Mieren cellars.'

'The world is full of injustice,' he acknowledged. 'I had the chance to save these children.'

'And they call you the Butcher of Maygharia.'

Sorne laughed.

Chapter Forty-Five

IMOSHEN WAITED FOR Reoden on the high rear-deck. It was time to confront the healer about her scryer. Unnerved by the thought, Imoshen checked the spiced wine she had prepared. Behind the ship, their wake spread out across the swells of the rolling sea, gleaming in the moons' light. This time last night they had been fighting for their lives.

'You sent for me,' the healer said.

Imoshen turned. Hopefully, they would come out of this with their friendship still intact. She studied Reoden's familiar face. The healer's features were close to the T'En ideal of beauty: long nose, strong jaw, high cheekbones. But Imoshen saw past the beauty to her dear friend and lover, who seemed fragile today.

Not surprising, considering.

'You look tired, Ree. Is something bothering you?' *Tell me about your scryer. Ask for my help. I don't want to back you into a corner.*

The healer shrugged. 'More than a dozen of my people were injured and I was still working with the burn victims from the first night we were attacked.'

Imoshen poured two glasses of spiced wine and offered one to the healer. 'After everything you've been through, you need this.'

Reoden accepted hers and sipped. 'Hmmm, citrus peel. I like your mix, Imoshen.'

'Ree, I know you prize healing above all else –'

'But there's never enough of me to go around. I haven't had a chance to work on Ronnyn since we left Shifting-sands Bay, and I know his crippled arm still gives him pain.'

It was typical of Reoden to worry about others. Imoshen gave up being subtle and came straight to the point. 'Sarodyti's dead. Lysi should have died with her, yet she still lives. She's suffering from gift-corruption. What have you done with her, Ree?'

'That's what this is about?' Reoden put her wine cup aside. 'Lysi's being cared for where she cannot infect other T'En. Don't worry.'

'So you also believe it can be communicated?'

'When it gets this bad.'

'How can you be sure she won't infect others?'

Reoden's gaze shifted ever so slightly.

Imoshen pounced. 'You can't be sure. With two sisterhoods packed onto one ship, we can't risk contamination. As her all-mother, it's your duty to see that she cannot infect others. If she was in her right mind, she would agree. As it is, her gift is out of her control. Seeing the futures... think how frightening it must be. It's your duty to ensure she no longer suffers.'

'She's unconscious.'

'Good.' Imoshen drew breath. Now came the tricky part. Had the healer made the connection, or was she too close to see what was going on? 'How is it that Lysi still lives, Ree?'

The healer looked down.

'Ree, you haven't been –'

'No. I don't have the power to spare to sustain her.'

'But she's one of your inner circle. You share a deep sisterhood link.' Imoshen caught her friend's hand. 'Ree, she's draining you of your healing power to stay alive. That's why you're so tired.'

'She's not conscious.'

'It's instinctive. Her gift may be corrupted, but it will live as long as she does. Ree, I don't want to see you corrupted...' The healer would have broken away, but

Imoshen refused to let go. 'No, hear me out. Your gift shapes the way you think, the ability to heal defines you. If your gift is being drained and subtly corrupted through the sisterhood link, how do you know you can trust your own judgement?'

'I'm not corrupted. Test me and see. I'll drop my walls.'

'Both our gift-tutors are dead.'

'You'll know. You'll feel it.' Reoden caught Imoshen's face in her hands and kissed her, dropping her defences.

Skin on skin, lips to lips was the quickest and surest way to communicate gift to gift, but they had been lovers, and her body recognised Reoden's on this level. The warmth of desire pooled in Imoshen's belly. At the same time, she savoured the purity of the healer's gift and her own gift rose in response. If only...

Reoden pulled back, a half smile tugging at her lips. 'You're supposed to be testing my gift, not trying to seduce me.'

Imoshen blushed. She had to take a step back to gather her thoughts.

'Is my gift pure?' Reoden asked.

'Pure and perfect.'

'Then –'

'For now,' Imoshen admitted. 'But the scryer is linked to you. She's not going to fade away and die, not while you live. And it's only a matter of time before she corrupts you.'

'I swore an oath to protect Lysi. I cannot kill her.' Reoden's beautiful wine-dark eyes grew brilliant with determination. 'I cannot kill anyone, my gift won't let me, and I'm glad of it!'

'I know, Ree.' It was part of why she loved her. 'But I can kill.'

'Imoshen...' Reoden took a step back.

'Would you let her suffer? Would you see the whole ship go mad with gift corruption?'

'I can't ask this of you.'

'You don't have to ask.'

'Oh, Imoshen.'

'It must be done, and the sooner the better.'

'Then let it be tonight.' Reoden's voice broke on the last word.

'Tonight,' Imoshen agreed. 'Up here, out in the open.' Where the lingering gift-corruption would be blown away by the wind.

'I don't know how you can do this,' Reoden whispered.

'I do it because I must.' Imoshen searched her friend's face, afraid Reoden would despise her.

But she didn't.

Not yet, anyway.

'I CLAIM THE sisterhood.' Ronnyn revealed his cards. 'I have the all-mother, the voice-of-reason, two gift-warriors and a gift-empowerer.'

'Not so quick,' Sardeon challenged. 'I have the hand-of-force, a gift-tutor, two gift-warriors and a wild-card raedan. She can become an all-mother, so I think we're even.'

'How does this game differ in the brotherhood? Are there powerful gifts amongst the males that...' Ronnyn ran down as he saw Sardeon's expression. 'Don't worry. Now that our gifts have surfaced, we'll be empowered soon and begin training. We'll make our fathers proud.'

'I wish I was like the others. I wish I didn't know who my father was.'

'You're worried you won't be able to live up to his reputation,' Ronnyn guessed. Although he didn't feel he owed All-father Hueryx anything, he still felt the pressure. 'I'm in the same boat.'

'There's more to it.' Sardeon glanced around the empowered lads' cabin and lowered his voice. 'Once we join the brotherhood, if someone challenges our all-father and wins, the new all-father will execute us. They can't afford to let us live long enough to grow into our gifts and avenge our fathers' deaths.' He shrugged. 'If our fathers truly loved us, they wouldn't have claimed us. They only claimed us to shore up their leadership. With our loyalty, they gain the loyalty of the next generation of initiates. That way they can hold onto the leadership for thirty or forty years instead of fifteen or twenty.'

Ronnyn's mind reeled as he ran through the ramifications.

'Boys?' The hand-of-force beckoned them. 'I need you to help Ree's devotee look after the children while the rest of us are at a ceremony.'

'What ceremony?' Ronnyn asked.

'Scryer Lysitzi's farewell.'

'She's dead?' Ronnyn was aware of a rush of relief.

There was the barest hesitation. 'Yes. Now go help Meleya.'

When they reached the cabin door, Vittor let them in.

'I'm glad you're here,' he said and gestured to the pile of sleeping toddlers. 'All day long I'm surrounded by little boys. It's driving me crazy. What are we going to do?'

'Well...' Ronnyn thought quickly. 'How about I teach you to play cards?'

'I can already play cards,' Vittor insisted. 'I'm good at it.'

'This isn't the memory game we used to play back home. It's a grown-up card game, about forming sisterhoods and brotherhoods.'

Vittor's eyes widened. 'I'd like that.'

Ronnyn grinned. 'Sardeon will explain the rules, and I'll get the cards.'

While crossing the cabin, Ronnyn paused beside the devotee. Ashmyr dozed in her arms; Ronnyn cupped his baby brother's soft head. Then he left for the empowered lads' cabin.

As much as Ronnyn resented being separated from their sisters, he knew his family couldn't survive on their own. The deaths of his parents had proved that.

When he retrieved the cards, it struck him that this set wasn't as fine as the cards his father had painted. His Da had been a manuscript illuminator, who gave up his high stature to run away with his mother and live like the poorest Mieren on their island. Back then, Ronnyn had just accepted the exquisitely-painted cards and delightful carved toys as normal. Now he knew they were as good as, or better than, the ones the sisterhood's children played with.

No, they were better. Asher had made them with love for his family.

Ronnyn felt like something had hit his chest.

'You all right?' one of the empowered lads asked.

He nodded and ducked into the passage, where he leant against the wall, dragging in great gulps of air.

They'd left Da's body on the beach for the wild dogs to devour.

Ronnyn thrust open the door and staggered out onto the deck. Some instinct for self-preservation prompted him to dart under the steep steps to the foredeck.

There he gasped and bent double. What was wrong with him?

He had to hang onto the steps and drag in one breath after another.

Gradually, his breathing slowed and his vision cleared. Before him, through the steps, he saw the women of Reoden's sisterhood gathered around the Malaunje hatch as the scryer's body was brought up from below.

Poor thing. Just as well she was dead.

When they carried her past his choice-mother, one of the scryer's hands reached out for Reoden.

She was alive? They were going to throw the scryer overboard alive? They'd never...

But he recalled Cerafeoni's slight hesitation when he'd asked if the scryer was dead. They wouldn't throw her overboard alive. They'd kill her first, then farewell her, the practical part of his mind told him.

Outrage reverberated through him. His gift surged; he wanted to accuse them of savagery.

At the same time, he was torn. It was not that simple. Her gift had corrupted. It was dangerous. But...

To kill her?

Sardeon would help him make sense of what was happening. Clasping the cards in one hand, he ran back to the cabin, where he found the devotee singing to a fractious toddler.

Meleya and Sardeon both looked at him, startled by his abrupt arrival. The devotee lifted her finger to her lips.

Ronnyn caught Sardeon's eye. They needed to talk. He picked his path carefully through sleeping toddlers.

But Vittor had also been waiting. 'What's wrong?'

Ronnyn thrust the cards into his brother's hands. He didn't want to trouble Vittor with what he'd seen, so he said the first thing that came to him. 'These cards reminded me of Da.'

Vittor's eyes widened as he stared at the cards.

Remorse made Ronnyn drop to his knees and hug his little brother. 'I'm sorry. I shouldn't have –'

'No. I want to remember.' Anger lit Vittor's dark eyes and hardened his little mouth. 'Da didn't deserve to die that way. I should have –'

'There was nothing you could do. Nothing any of us could do.' And as Ronnyn said this, he felt the truth of it, bone-deep. He hadn't failed his father, or his family.

Ronnyn hugged Vittor again. 'Go to the desk and shuffle the cards. I'll be over in a moment.'

While Vittor did as he was told, Ronnyn stood up and met Sardeon's eyes.

'What is it?' his choice-brother whispered.

Ronnyn led him to the bunk under the window. He sat, leaned one arm on the window frame and stared out. Stars filled the night sky.

'The scryer's not dead,' Ronnyn whispered.

Sardeon's lips compressed in a grim line. He didn't appear surprised. Saddened, but not shocked.

'You knew?'

'I suspected. They try to keep the truth from us, but power comes at a price.'

'So they're going to kill the scryer –'

'To prevent the gift-corruption spreading.'

Ronnyn rubbed a shaking hand across his mouth. He could feel his gift churning in his belly, urging him to action. Last time, it had snuck under his guard and driven him to do things that had shamed him. This time he would not let it ride him.

Sardeon put his hand on Ronnyn's shoulders. 'Sometimes, the right thing can seem wrong.'

'I'm not a child.' Ronnyn met his eyes. 'I've killed... we've both killed to defend the ship. But this is different.'

Sardeon nodded. 'Back then there was no choice. This is deliberate.'

Ronnyn felt betrayed. As if he'd found a safe harbour, only to discover it filled with hidden rocks.

Meleya joined them. 'What's wrong, boys?'

'Nothing,' Sardeon said.

The devotee was not fooled, but she didn't press the issue.

'You have good hearts,' she said and went to kiss Sardeon on the forehead, but pulled back. She did the same with Ronnyn. And he knew their gifts made her uncomfortable.

Too bad. This was what he wanted. More than that, it was what he needed, if he was to survive in the brotherhood.

The devotee returned to the little ones, while Ronnyn and Sardeon taught Vittor how to play the sisterhood card game. It was preparation for real life, when they would be forming alliances to increase their stature and power with the ultimate goal of winning a brotherhood.

But neither of them would get the chance, if Hueryx and Paragian lost control of their brotherhoods. Their futures were tied to the all-fathers'. He hoped Hueryx was as cunning as the sisters claimed, and Paragian as well-loved.

Chapter Forty-Six

As SORNE JOINED Merchant Sahia in her carriage, he decided two things: he would not agree to anything until Imoshen arrived, and he would have to be very careful. If Sahia was an example of a Sagorese merchant, then the leaders of the Sagoras were going to be a real challenge.

The carriage travelled up the sloping road from the port to the ridge behind it and stopped just inside the entrance to the Halls of Learning.

Sahia gestured to another Sagora waiting by a door. 'This is the Most Venerable Uda of House Felinii. She will show you around until the Sagora Seven are ready to see you.'

Sorne thanked the merchant and climbed out of the carriage. Two servants, also Sagoras, held hooded lanterns, which cast golden pools on the paving.

No one spoke as the carriage pulled away in its own circle of light. Sorne caught a glimpse of an avenue easily wide enough for two carriages to pass. Then the carriage turned left.

'This way, ambassador.' His escort was small, slight and very old.

She led him through the door into what appeared to be one of the gate towers. They climbed four flights of steps, with one servant in front, one behind. Despite her age, his escort managed the stairs without trouble.

Sorne waited until they'd reached the top floor and another door before attempting conversation. 'What is your area of study, Venerable Uda?'

'*Most* Venerable,' one of the lantern bearers corrected. From his protective tone, Sorne suspected he was her student. 'The Most Venerables are the Heads of Halls. Ven Uda is the Head of the Halls of Philosophy.'

'Apologies, Ven Uda.' Sorne gave the obeisance of contrition. 'What does the Most Venerable of the philosophers teach?'

'I teach how to think. If we cannot think logically, we cannot begin to make sense of the world.'

'So you seek to make sense of the world?'

'In as far as it is possible for our minds to grasp.'

He had the impression she was amused, but whether it was by him or her indignant student, he could not tell. The veils revealed only the mouth and chin, hiding the eyes which usually revealed so much.

Ven Uda gestured to the door and the servant opened it.

Sorne stepped out onto the wall-walk, and a view that took his breath away. They were perched high above the silvered bay. Beyond it the sea stretched to the horizon. Much closer, around the edge of the bay, light spilled from doorways and windows in the port. 'It's...'

'Isn't it?' she agreed. 'You must bring T'Imoshen up here. When will she arrive?'

'I'm not sure. I lost track of the days in the sea-vermin cellar.'

'We'll see what tomorrow brings. This way.' She led him along the wall. It followed the ridge, which was roughly triangular in shape, and higher at the southern base. He was headed north to the lower point of the triangle but even here, the walls were high and they rose straight up from the ridge. King Charald would approve; it was eminently defensible.

The hooded lanterns illuminated the wall-walk under their feet, but the moons illuminated the night beyond the wall.

'As you can see' – Ven Uda gestured to their right, where the wall dropped four storeys, before the ridge fell away into the countryside – 'the Halls of Learning hold an enviable position.'

He could see why they were giving him this tour.

'And on our left, safe behind our walls, are the Halls of Learning themselves. For hundreds of years we have guided the minds of the greatest thinkers and military advisors to kings. Mainland royal families and great merchant families send their best and brightest to study under us. So you can see, although we live out here on the rim of the world, we keep in touch with every corner of the mainland.'

As they had reached the end of the wall-walk, he noticed there was another tabletop ridge to the north. It was almost as high as this one, but posed no threat as the distance was too great to span. The Sagoras were right to think their eyrie impregnable.

Looking south, the halls and the Sagoras' private walled city were laid out before him. All spires and domes, the hidden city reminded him of the Celestial City.

'This way.' Ven Uda went south along the wall which gradually climbed, in a succession of long steps, towards the triangle's base. 'On our right, you see the fertile plains of Ivernia, stretching all the way to the mountains. North and south of us we have alliances with the city-states that rule those provinces.'

There was enough moonlight for him to make out a chequerboard of fields, farms, sinuous rivers coming down from the mountains making their way to the sea, glinting silver.

Whether they knew it or not, the Sagoras were in the same position as the Wyrds had been. If they were besieged, then their lands and people were vulnerable. An army could live well off these fertile southern plains. In fact, they could simply move in, set up their homes, subdue any incursions from the provinces to the north and south, and ignore the Sagoras.

But he was not leading King Charald's army, intent on carving a kingdom for himself. He was the T'Enatuath ambassador, representing barely two thousand survivors. And they were frighteningly vulnerable.

'Ah, the Sagora Seven are ready,' Ven Uda said.

Sorne turned around to see someone with a lantern, signalling from the street below. They went down the steep steps and were escorted into one of the buildings to a verandah, overlooking a courtyard.

The smell struck him. Vaguely familiar, feral and effulgent, it made his heart race. The primordial part of his brain screamed danger and he turned to Ven Uda. 'What is this – ?'

A strange, raw scream split the night. He felt for his sword, but of course his only weapons were his wits and his words.

'Be still, it is not what you think,' Ven Uda whispered.

A moment later her students removed the hoods from their lanterns as they hung them at each end of the verandah to reveal three of the Sagora Seven. There was no sign of Merchant Sahia.

In place of veils, the Sagorese leaders wore extraordinary masks. With their arms folded, hands tucked under their long, full sleeves, they were even more of an enigma than their fellow Sagoras.

Each stylised mask was a work of art, representing a creature from the natural world, its features picked out in swirling striations of different metals, embossed to represent fur or scales and embedded with jewels. One mask was based on a peacock, its crest picked out in finest filigree silver. Brilliant enamelled plates represented the peacock's eyes. Another was a feathered cat, and its tufted ears moved in response to sounds. The last was a serpent, covered in iridescent scales. Delicate wings fanned out behind its head. The work was so exquisite Sorne longed to study each mask in detail. As it was, he had to take them in at glance.

He made the deep obeisance. 'Ambassador Sorne, representing Causare T'Imoshen of the T'Enatuath. Thank you for seeing me. I also have to thank Merchant Sahia for coming to our rescue.'

'Yes, we heard you'd had an eventful voyage,' the feathered cat said.

Another woman. Sorne's mind raced. Had they thought he would be disarmed? Or, did they think that since Wyrd women were more powerful than men, he would instinctively obey a woman?

The woman in the feathered cat mask inclined her head. 'I am House Felinii.'

Sorne bowed, then turned to the serpent-masked Sagora.

'House Vulpii.' His voice was deep and rich.

Sorne gave him the obeisance of greeting then turned to the peacock.

'House Pavoii.' Her voice was clipped and formal. Sorne had the feeling she did not like him.

He bowed. 'Forgiveness, but what is that smell?'

'Come and see.' Felinii beckoned.

All the Sagoras went to the edge of the verandah and Sorne joined them. He made out cages and realised it was... 'A menagerie.'

'Exactly,' Felinii said. 'These are the Halls of Beasts, where we study the animal kingdom.'

As she finished speaking, lanterns were lowered so that the caged beasts were illuminated. At one end was an aviary that ran the height of the two-storey building. Disturbed by the light, all manner of birds fluttered about, calling and screeching.

This set off the beasts below. Sorne spotted two silver-backed wolves from the high southern mountains, a crested bear and a nest of snakes, scales glinting in the light. But it was the prowling panther which attracted his gaze. It was directly below them and it knew they were up here. This was what had screamed and this was what smelled so bad.

'It's a female and she's in heat,' Sorne said. He'd once seen King Charald throw an arrogant captive in a pit with a panther. After that, the rest of the captives had cooperated.

'We've sent away for a mate,' Felinii said. 'But panthers are lone hunters. She may think the male is trying to take over her territory and tear him to shreds.'

Sorne swallowed, not sure if he had interpreted their meaning correctly. 'That would be a pity when the male seeks only something to their mutual benefit.'

'How can she be sure?' Pavoii countered. She gestured sharply.

Metal clanged and a lamb bleated. The panther stopped prowling. Sorne saw there was a passage between the cages. A keeper had put the lamb into the passage and closed the outer gate. He knew what was coming. He'd seen worse.

The panther's cage door slid open. It slunk into the passage. The crested bear reared to its full height and gave its distinctive trumpeting growl. Next thing Sorne knew, the panther was dragging the dead lamb into its cage and the door clanged shut.

'Such is the nature of beasts,' Sorne said, turning back to the three Sagora leaders. 'But we are not beasts. The T'Enatuath seek sanctuary, nothing more.'

'So you say. Tell the causare we will deal with her and no one else,' Pavoii said. Again, she signalled and this time a servant arrived with a lantern.

Sorne had been dismissed. If they would not negotiate with him, why had they agreed to this meeting?

He was taken back to the ship, where there was no sign of Merchant Sahia. As he lit a lamp and stripped in his cabin, he heard scratching at his door and opened it up to find Tiasely, accompanied by several teary children.

'They would not sleep until they knew you'd come back,' she said.

He spread a blanket on the floor and lay down. The children settled around him like puppies, snuffling and wriggling until they were comfortable.

'You don't mind?' Tiasely asked. 'I did almost have them asleep, but when the Sagoras came –'

'What Sagoras?'

'After you left, several Sagoras came to see us. They brought toys and treats. They told stories and played games and got the children all excited. Then I couldn't get this lot back to sleep.'

So that was why they'd agreed to see him. The Sagoras wanted to question the children. Guessing rightly, he suspected, that the youngsters would reveal what they wanted to know.

'Did the Sagoras ask questions?'

Tiasely nodded and knelt on the floor near the door. 'They asked us how we'd come to be captured and how you saved us. They asked so many questions...' She shrugged and yawned. 'Our people will arrive soon, won't they? And then we'll have a new home.'

'Yes.' He sincerely hoped so.

After Tiasely returned to the children's cabin, Sorne stared at the ceiling. He wasn't sure what the Sagoras hoped to learn from the children, but he suspected it was how desperate his people were.

The Sagoras had put on a display of strength and gauged his people's strength... it could only mean one thing. They wanted to negotiate. This meant they wanted something from the Wyrds, wanted it enough to try to intimidate him before negotiations started.

IMOSHEN DIPPED HER fingers in the scented water and bathed her face, hands and feet. Formal gift-working required ceremony and the execution of one of their own required the most solemn of ceremonies. She placed a hand on Egrayne's shoulder as her voice-of-reason dried her feet.

Egryane stood, folded the cloth and placed it on a tray. The purification over, it was time to begin.

But as Imoshen went to step forward, Egrayne caught her arm.

'Make it quick. Take her straight to the higher plane and leave her there. The empyrean predators will feast on her power. And...' – Egrayne's hand tightened on her arm – 'whatever you do, don't lose concentration. If you do, her gift will feed on your power, gain in strength. It could infect you.'

Imoshen nodded. Tonight, she was pure purpose.

Egrayne kissed her forehead. 'Do this because it needs to be done. Do it without faltering and come back safe to us, because we need you.'

Reoden met Imoshen's eyes across the high rear-deck, the scryer's body between them. More than Imoshen's life was at risk here tonight. If the healer was not strong enough to control her gift's instinct to preserve life and sever the link she shared with her scryer, she would be dragged onto the higher plane as well.

Reoden nodded once, her meaning clear. *Do what I can't do.*

No one spoke. Imoshen knelt by the scryer's head. Despite being in the open air, the gift-corruption was so strong Imoshen felt nauseous.

She centred herself, lowered her defences, placed her fingertips on the scryer's temples and reached...

The scryer's gift sank its claws into her. Discovering that Imoshen's power was not defended, the gift severed the connection with Reoden and sought to link with Imoshen.

The moment the connection to Reoden was closed, Imoshen segued to the higher plane. There was nothing gentle about it. The move was brutal and abrupt.

And she was lost.

Normally, the higher plane was bone-numbingly cold. Normally, she would impose form on it, but the scryer's gift had been ascendant over hers at the moment of change and so it had shaped the plane.

Everything was formless and confused. Shapes flickered around Imoshen, snatches of conversation, a laugh, music...

She sensed something move behind her and spun around, expecting one of the empyrean predators. It was her choice-son, Iraayel. He opened a window. And just like that, they were in a high tower. All she could see past his shoulder was clear blue sky.

It was Iraayel, but not as she knew him. This was the adult Iraayel, in full control of his gift. He radiated anger, which was directed at her.

'If that's how you feel, then there's no more to be said.' He turned his back on her and walked out.

She could not believe it. Iraayel would never turn against her.

She felt his rejection to the core.

Devastated, her concentration wavered.

In desperation, she refocused and segued onto... the higher plane. Immediately, she felt the cold in her bones.

Then where had that last place been?

The only explanation was that she'd ridden the scryer's gift, which revealed a future where Iraayel would turn on her.

She refused to believe it.

In this moment of distraction, the gift-enhanced essence that was the scryer escaped from her.

On the empyrean plane, the T'En shaped themselves. In this case, the scryer was not in control of her gift, and shattered into a dozen shadowy creatures. Part cat, part mongoose, they screamed like newborns, terrified and indignant. And Imoshen recognised them as scraelings.

Did this mean the beasts that hunted them on the empyrean plane were products of their own misfortune?

She stared in horror as the scraelings fought and hissed amongst themselves, utterly vulnerable to the predators of the empyrean plane.

She could have left then, but she didn't. She wanted to make it quick, so she let her power flare to attract the hungry predators. The scraelings circled her, curious and growing bolder by the moment.

She had hoped there would be a moment's peace at the end for the scryer, a moment when she recovered her senses, but it was not to be. Lysitzi had degraded to these feral creatures, which hunted Imoshen and were in turn hunted. Already something large and dangerous had reached the crest of the nearest dune.

Imoshen recognised her surroundings.

Shocked by the future Iraayel's betrayal, she had come home to the lighthouse island of her childhood. In the west, the island had been cliffs and crashing waves, while the eastern shore had been silken dunes and sheltered inlets. And it was to one of these private dune hollows that she had fled.

The predators approached, slinking up the sides of the dune, coming from all directions.

She could feel the cold of the higher plane creeping up through her feet, into her bones, as it tried to leach the power from her. Imoshen's instincts told her to flee.

One of the scraelings screamed in terror as something streaked over the lip of the dune, snatched it and dragged it out of sight.

The others screamed in horror, sharing its pain as it was devoured.

One scraeling tried to run back to Imoshen. Something moved under the sand like a wave, catching the creature. Sand slid towards Imoshen, as the scraeling struggled briefly and was engulfed.

Shrill cries from the others, cut off abruptly, one by one.

She stayed to see the last one dragged off and devoured.

Then, as the remaining predators turned their attention to her, she reached for Egrayne.

And found her; found herself cradled in her voice-of-reason's arms.

'You're back. Good.' Egrayne's voice was hard and no-nonsense, in direct contrast to the tenderness Imoshen had felt a heartbeat before. 'You need to purify yourself.'

'What?' She had no idea where she was, or even who she was. She knew only that she could trust Egrayne.

'Your gift has been tainted. You need to purify yourself.' Egrayne helped her sit up.

They were alone on the deck.

'Where is everyone?

'Watching the horizon. The lookout just sighted land.'

Imoshen scrambled to her feet, then had to bend double as she fought a wave of nausea. At last, she lifted her head. A dark shadow lay across the silvered sea, dividing it from the stars.

'Ivernia,' Imoshen breathed.

And she remembered her vision. Her beloved choice-son would turn his back on her.

No, the scryer's gift was corrupted. It had plucked her deepest fear from her mind and presented it as the future to make her suffer.

Or so she told herself.

She had to believe it, because if Iraayel ever turned against her, it would break her heart.

Chapter Forty-Seven

IMOSHEN'S FLEET ARRIVED in Port Sorvernia mid-morning. As they sailed through the headlands, she studied the Sagoras' Halls of Learning. She had seen etchings, of course, but the reality was much more impressive. Golden sandstone glowed against the rich blue of the southern sky. And below the ridge lay the port, red-tiled roofs bright in the winter sunshine.

The harsh cry of a seagull made Imoshen look up. It landed on the ship's rail not far from her, watching hopefully. It was said seagulls made their own luck. Her people were going to need to be like the seagull, quick and adaptable.

Imoshen beckoned her hand-of-force. 'As soon as we drop anchor, send word to the harbour-master. Let them know that the causare is here and wishes to see the Sagoras. Arrange a meeting before this evening, if you can.'

Kiane hurried off.

'What are you going to do if they refuse us sanctuary?' Egrayne asked softly.

'Now that we're here, it will be much harder to refuse us in person. The Sagoras are philosopher-scholars; their coin is knowledge. They know what it is like to come to a new land looking for a home. I hope –'

Saffazi came running up the steps, eyes bright with wonder. 'You have to see this.'

She led them down to the mid-deck and over to the ship's side. As their fleet dropped anchor, two long rowboats navigated between the ships. Both boats were laden with

children, mostly Malaunje, a sprinkling of T'En and...
'Sorne?'

Imoshen turned to Saffazi. 'Quick, fetch Ree.' Then she
beckoned the ship's master. 'Drop the rope ladder over the
side and prepare the sling.'

As this was done, Imoshen noted rowboats being
lowered from the other T'Enatuath ships. It seemed the
all-fathers and All-mother Athazi would be joining them
for an impromptu all-council.

'This is not good, Imoshen,' Egrayne said. 'This will be
the first all-council since Melisarone's death. There are
only three sisterhoods left and six brotherhoods. If the
brotherhoods force a vote...'

Meanwhile the children clambered over the side and ran
about the deck, calling out for their loved ones and their
all-fathers or all-mothers.

'Imoshen!' Healer Reoden came running over with a
T'En girl of about ten years of age. Tears of happiness
spilled down Ree's face as she hugged the girl. 'Look, it's
Yosune, Parazime's daughter. We thought her dead, but she
was captured and sold, only to be rescued by Sorne.'

'You poor things.' Imoshen's heart went out to them.

Yosune nodded. 'Then our boat sank and the Sagoras pulled
us off our raft. It was lucky we were with your ambassador,
or I don't know what would have happened to us.'

'Ambassador?' Egrayne repeated, as Sorne climbed
aboard.

'Ambassador Sorne,' Imoshen greeted him.

He gave a wry grin. His hair had been shorn and his
eyebrows had been all but burned away but he was richly-
dressed and he'd delivered these children unharmed,
despite their ordeal.

'I met with the Sagoras last night.'

Before he could say more, the children clamoured for his
attention. They'd found their all-fathers and all-mothers,
and now they dragged Sorne along to present him as their
saviour.

The all-fathers and their seconds, who had been so dismissive of Sorne at the all-council in Shifting-sands Bay, soon discovered they were now in his debt.

Gradually, the chaos subsided as the children were sent below, or to their ships, to be with their loved ones.

Frayvia appeared at Imoshen's side with a tray of spiced wine, and this time no one protested when Sorne was served first.

Imoshen accepted her glass with a kiss of thanks. 'To Ambassador Sorne, who rescued our children from the sea-vermin and returned them to the T'Enatuath.'

Her words were repeated and the toast drunk.

But not by All-father Dretsun. 'Since when do we appoint a Malaunje as an ambassador for our people?'

'Imoshen appointed me because I've had so many years dealing with True-men, and she thought the Sagoras would find a half-blood less threatening than a T'En,' Sorne replied.

'Dealing with True-men?' Dretsun repeated. 'Last we heard of you, you were riding to battle a rebel baron and save Chalcedonia. Next thing we know you've been captured by sea-vermin. Is that how you deal with True-men?'

'Baron Eskarnor had been dealt with. His army was defeated and I executed him on the battlefield. I was on my way here to act as ambassador when I was captured by the raiders.'

'I have no objection to Sorne speaking at an all-council,' Reoden said.

'You would accord a Malaunje the stature of a brotherhood leader?' Dretsun asked, as if he couldn't believe what he was hearing.

'Sorne is an ambassador,' Imoshen said. 'He's already spoken with the Sagora Seven. He –'

The T'Enatuath leaders interrupted her. They wanted to know if the Sagoras had given them sanctuary. Before Sorne could answer, Kiane returned.

She gave Imoshen the causare's obeisance. 'The Sagoras invite you to meet them within the Font of Knowledge, when the large moon is four fingers risen. They will accept no more than three delegates.'

On hearing this, there was celebration. Then the advice flooded in. Her hand-of-force wanted Imoshen to take two bodyguards, and offered to organise it. Hueryx claimed his background as a historian and an interest in the history of the Sagoras entitled him to a place at the meeting. Dretsun insisted, since he had compiled the list of inventions suitable for trade, he should attend the meeting.

'The Sagoras are wary of us,' Imoshen said. 'I'll take Ambassador Sorne and –'

'Me. I have the list.' Dretsun patted his robe.

'Excellent.' Imoshen held out her hand. 'Give it to me.'

'I compiled it. I should go with you.'

'Because you have already met the Sagoras and have insights into them, like Ambassador Sorne? Or, perhaps, because you've studied their history, like Hueryx?'

'No,' he conceded. 'But I –'

'What else can you contribute to the negotiation? Can you speak Sagorese?'

'Who speaks Sagorese?' Dretsun snapped. 'They don't even use a civilised script. Only the most learned scholars of the seven kingdoms have bothered to study their obscure language.'

Imoshen inclined her head. 'You honour me.'

'You speak Sagorese?' Dretsun snorted. 'I don't believe it.'

'I am not in the habit of lying,' Imoshen told him, her voice cold.

Silence fell as Dretsun took a step back. He should apologise, but it was clear he had no intention of doing so.

'You amaze me, Imoshen.' Hueryx smoothed over the awkward pause. 'When did you learn the Sagoras' private language?'

'I started taking lessons from Merchant Mercai nearly five years ago. At one point, I planned to come here to study. I've had work published in Sagora treatises, so I am known to their scholars and I've made a study of their history. I'll take Ambassador Sorne, who can scribe for me, and one more person. If there was someone able to understand Sagorese while appearing not to, that would be helpful.'

The T'Enatuath leaders glanced to each other.

'Do none of you speak the Sagoras' language?' Imoshen asked, knowing full well that only one person present could speak it.

Ardonyx whispered something to Tobazim, whose eyes widened.

'My voice-of-reason speaks Sagorese,' Tobazim announced.

'What?' Dretsun lifted his hands as if he could not believe what he was hearing. He turned on Ardonyx. 'He's a sea captain, not a scholar.'

'An explorer needs a facility with language,' Ardonyx said. 'I speak five languages fluently and I can get by in another three.'

Imoshen hid a smile. 'Very good, Captain Ardonyx. You will accompany me.'

'As you wish, causare.' He stepped back into place at Tobazim's side. For a fraction of a heartbeat his eyes met hers. She had to look away before she betrayed herself.

'Promise the Sagoras nothing until we have discussed the terms,' Dretsun said. 'On no account must you give them access to the higher plane.'

'He's right,' Reoden said. 'The Mieren cannot be trusted with the dangers of the empyrean plane. That sea-vermin power-worker called down a fiant. Sarodyti sacrificed her life to destroy it and restore the balance.'

But Dretsun was remorseless. 'No access to the higher plane, Imoshen.'

She met his eyes. 'I will negotiate the best possible outcome for the T'Enatuath, under the circumstances, All-father Dretsun.'

Would he insist on more?

He reached into his robe. Imoshen tensed, gathering her gift.

'The list you requested, causare.' He presented her with a scroll.

But his eyes were mocking. She read him. He'd meant to alarm her and he intended to challenge her. Maybe not at this all-council, but...

'We could deal with these Sagoras,' All-father Saskeyne said. 'They are few in number and their province is full of Mieren used to serving a powerful elite. We could replace the Sagora leaders with –'

'Leaders of our own, and invite the wrath of the mainland kingdoms, not to mention the other Ivernian provinces.' Imoshen's voice was sharp as a lash.

Silence fell.

'Does anyone else harbour secret plans to turn on those who have offered us the hand of friendship?' Imoshen asked. No one spoke. She turned to Saskeyne. 'Then I will hear no more of this.'

'All-father Saskeyne speaks sense,' Dretsun said. 'We need a defensible homeland, and an island is more defensible than Chalcedonia ever was. Where will your causareship lead our people, Imoshen? To a home of our own, or to extinction?'

'All in good time. First we must secure sanctuary, then –'

'Is that all your causareship will be, stop-gap measures?' Dretsun demanded. Then he strode off before she could counter by asking him what his plans were.

'I call an all-mother-council,' Athazi announced, stepping into the silence. 'We must deal with Melisarone's survivors.'

At this, the rest of the brotherhood leaders left.

When the sisterhood leaders were alone, Athazi turned to Imoshen. 'Now that we have sanctuary, I should take in Mel's survivors. I'm –'

'Let's deal with the Sagoras first. Then we can organise the sisterhoods,' Imoshen told her.

Athazi's mouth tightened, but she said nothing, stalking away with her seconds.

'The survivors are due to go to her,' Reoden said softly.

'Would you wish to join her sisterhood?' Imoshen countered.

Nerazime snorted, then covered her mouth.

Reoden took Imoshen's hands and kissed her cheek. 'Good luck tonight. You carry all our hopes.'

And with that the others left, so that only Imoshen and her two seconds remained on the carpet, with Saffazi a few steps behind them.

Imoshen glanced to Egrayne and Kiane. 'I hate to admit it, but Saskeyne has a point. Back in Chalcedonia, despite the sacrifices our gift-warriors made to protect this plane, all the T'Enatuath ever received from the Mieren was grudging tolerance. Should we seek a kingdom here in the physical world, one we can hold with force?'

'Yes!' In her eagerness to be heard, Saffazi stepped onto the all-council carpet. 'If we'd ruled Chalcedonia instead of greedy King Charald, we could have looked after our people.'

'Kept the Mieren under our thumbs like slaves?' Imoshen asked.

'No, not slaves. They –'

'They outnumber us ten thousand to one. How would we contain them?'

'Ruling ourselves is hard enough, without factoring in thousands of Mieren.' Egrayne shook her head slowly. 'Our kingdom is mystical.'

'We can't live on the empyrean plane,' Saffazi objected.

'I was speaking metaphorically.'

'I know that.' Saffazi flushed. 'I'm saying our power on the empyrean plane has not won us the respect of the Mieren, or kept us safe from them.' She gestured to the *Triumphant*. 'All-father Saskeyne is right. Only strength in this world will protect us from Mieren. We used to rely on their fear of our gifts to keep them at bay, but they called our bluff. Now we must grow as powerful on the earthly plane as we are on the empyrean plane. Then they will fear us.'

'Mieren kill what they fear,' Imoshen said.

'Then what's the answer?' Saffazi asked.

'I wish I knew.'

SORNE SLIPPED FROM Frayvia's bed and began to dress. Now that he was about to join Imoshen's sisterhood, they should formalise their relationship, but he wasn't sure how to go about it.

When Frayvia came up behind him and ran her fingernails down his back, he forgot what he'd been about to say.

She laughed and kissed his shoulder. Then she turned him around, suddenly solemn. 'You did well, bringing those children home to us. But I can read between the lines. You were nearly sold to Maygharians, who wanted to kill you slowly, under torture.'

He kissed her upturned face. 'It didn't happen, so –'

'But it could have.'

'If I worried about all the things that could happen, I'd never get anything done.'

She thumped his chest and he grinned, absurdly happy.

There was a knock on the door.

Frayvia helped him dress, sighed over the state of his hair and presented him with a scribe's satchel, with paper, ink and pens. She tugged him down to kiss his lips. 'Don't do anything brave.'

He was smiling when he joined Imoshen on the mid-deck. She seemed distracted. He'd already told her his observations based on the meeting last night.

Imoshen glanced around to make sure no one could overhear them. 'There's a rumour that behind the walls of the Sagoras' hidden city, there is an elite group of mystics called Sensitives. These males supposedly have innate power. They say the Sagoras blind them and geld them. Have you heard anything?'

'I've never heard of Mieren having innate power, let alone anything about these Sagora Sensitives.'

'Few have. The T'En race arose in Chalcedonia. It's possible a similar race arose in the Sagoras' home land, beyond the Endless Ocean. You say the philosopher...'

'Ven Uda.'

'...hinted that we would arrive today.'

'That's how it seemed. The way she put it was ambiguous.'

Imoshen nodded. 'Tonight you may see things that should go no further, Sorne.'

'Now that's ambiguous.'

She smiled, but there was only determination in her eyes. 'Come on.

Chapter Forty-Eight

IMOSHEN'S HEART RACED and her gift tried to break free as she climbed into the rowboat. Tonight she would bargain for the future of her people.

She nodded to the two Malaunje rowers. One was a young warrior, whose name she had to work hard to recall. 'Meloria.' She dredged it from her memory. The other rower was Redraven. He'd been with Iraayel and Saffazi the night Safi dragged Iraayel onto the higher plane and nearly got them both killed. Imoshen wondered if Redraven was still in love with Saffazi. 'Redraven.'

Both rowers were warriors; Kiane had seen to that. They lowered their eyes and put their backs into the oars, guiding the boat across to the *Victorious*, where Ardonyx was already waiting to join her.

As her secret bond-partner climbed down the rope ladder and stepped lightly into the small rowboat, something deep inside Imoshen clenched. She wanted him. She never got enough of him. And she never would, unless things changed.

But tonight there was no time for pleasure. She kept their link closed and focused on what had to be done.

'Causare.' He took his seat beside her in the stern. With the two Malaunje rowers facing them and Sorne in the prow, they were hardly alone, but her body didn't care. A rush of awareness moved over her skin. Again she closed down the instinctive urge to link with him.

As they rowed away from the *Victorious*, Ardonyx waved farewell to his shield-brother. Imoshen turned to see Tobazim standing on the deck.

Alone.

A surge of joyous spite shocked her. She hadn't known she could be so petty.

Tonight, she took Ardonyx away from Tobazim; but their shield-brother bond was acknowledged and approved of, while the bond she shared with Ardonyx had to be hidden. In all of the T'Enatuath, only her devotee knew the identity of Umaleni's father.

Imoshen swallowed. 'It's fortunate that you speak Sagorese, Ardonyx. We may need that advantage.'

He smiled, for they'd met and fallen in love at the Sagorese language lessons. They'd made the deep-bonding, cementing it later with physical intimacy of such exquisite depth that she wondered how her people could have rejected this. Maybe one day...

'Learning another language requires dedication,' Ardonyx said.

'I'm a little rusty,' she admitted. 'Shall we practice?'

He nodded.

Imoshen launched into the language of the Sagoras. The only thing she had to be wary of was using T'En names that would betray who they spoke of. 'Was your new brotherhood leader satisfied with the gift-infusion?'

'I walk a fine line. I must have his complete trust, yet he must never know about us. He would be devastated if he knew I lied to him, but I have no choice.'

She wondered if he lied to her, as well. It startled Imoshen to realise that she was no longer certain of Ardonyx's loyalty.

His love, yes, but his loyalty?

'What of my choice-son? Does he suffer because of his connection to me?'

'The other brothers were wary of him, but since the sea-vermin attack they've accepted him. I know you want me to use the pretext that I cannot speak Sagorese to spy,' Ardonyx said. 'But what if the Sagoras consult our old tutor?'

'Merchant Mercai is probably halfway across the known world, trading and spying in some other centre of commerce and power.' She looked up. 'We're nearly there.'

The Malaunje shipped oars and the boat glided on, carried by momentum.

Meloria leant forward, dropping her voice. 'Causare, permission to speak?'

'Speak.'

'Hand-of-force Kiane told us to wait at this wharf. That way, if there's trouble, we can row you back to the ship.'

'Or we could go with you, causare,' Redraven offered. 'As your servants.'

'You honour me. But the Sagoras have specified a delegation of no more than three. I thank you for your concern.'

'We live to serve.' They both said the words, but Imoshen's gift surged, telling her Meloria's motivation sprang from ambition, not dedication.

Ardonyx sent Imoshen a smile. They were so young and eager for stature.

At the wharf two Sagoras waited. They held lanterns and their light pooled on the still waters of the bay. Wisps of fog clung to the cold sea, curling around the poles of the nearest wharves.

Imoshen's party stepped onto the floating jetty, and the Sagoras welcomed them in Chalcedonian.

As they left the wharf, Ardonyx walked on her left and Sorne on her right. Either Sorne didn't know a Malaunje should walk one step behind a T'En, or he didn't care.

She felt safe with Ardonyx and Sorne, and was tempted to comment in T'En, but there was no guarantee that the Sagoras wouldn't use the same ploy on them. In theory, only Malaunje and T'En knew the private language of the T'En, and they would die before they betrayed their people, but you never knew.

Imoshen and her two aides were escorted to a waiting carriage. As their vehicle climbed up the long slope to the

Halls of Learning, Imoshen noticed that there was not a single tavern open. The port folk had closed their homes and businesses against the T'Enatuath. It made her wonder what terrible untruths had spread ahead of them, and if the T'Enatuath's arrival was going to cause trouble for the Sagoras.

As their carriage entered the Halls of Learning, Imoshen caught glimpses of formal sandstone buildings. Then they turned left and continued up the rise to the hidden city. The carriage came to a stop and they climbed down.

One of the Sagoras waited to greet them just outside the gate. Only her mouth and chin were visible below the veil, and her hands were tucked under the long folds of her gown.

'Welcome.' The waiting Sagora spoke T'En and gave them the appropriate T'Enatuath obeisance. 'You are Causare T'Imoshen?'

'I am. Greetings, Venerable.' Replying in Sagorese, Imoshen took a guess as to her title. The veil hid everything but her mouth and chin, and Imoshen could not tell if the woman had dared to meet her eyes. The Sagora probably thought herself safe from the T'En gifts. Imoshen would be very surprised if the Sagoras did not possess natural gift defences.

'You speak our language, causare?' The Sagora smiled.

Imoshen had the impression that their eyes had met. 'As you speak ours. I had once planned to come here and study. My people prize knowledge above all else. We have much in common with the Sagoras.' Imoshen switched to the Chalcedonian tongue. 'These are my assistants: Voice-of-Reason Ardonyx and Ambassador Sorne.'

The Sagora welcomed them. 'This is the hidden city. Outsiders enter only on invitation.'

'We are honoured,' Imoshen said.

Within the hidden city, the buildings were all shuttered and dark, and there was no one in sight. The road continued to rise until they came to a set of wide, shallow steps. Straight ahead was a circular wall, pierced by a simple arch.

'The Font of Knowledge.' The Sagora hesitated, but Imoshen did not need to be told. She was already removing her shoes. The Sagora scholar smiled and backed away. 'I'll wait here.'

Imoshen took a deep breath and prepared herself.

ARAVELLE CLEANED UP after the brotherhood's inner circle had finished their evening meal. She had just sent the last tray back to the ship's galley when Saskar entered. He did not knock or wait for the all-father to acknowledge him, but tugged on Reyne's arm and whispered something to him in an urgent tone.

'What is it?' Hueryx asked. He was shuffling the cards and did not get up.

'Dretsun is here, with his hand-of-force,' Reyne said.

Aravelle felt their gifts surge and the air in the cabin became denser, pressing on her ears.

The all-father gestured to her. 'Spiced wine, Vella.'

Hueryx and his most trusted advisors settled themselves on the cushions in a half circle, and Reyne signalled Saskar to open the cabin door.

As Dretsun strode in with his hand-of-force, gift energy rolled off him, infecting everyone. He came straight to the point. 'I offer an alliance, Hue.'

'We were choice-brothers, All-father Dretsun, but that was a long time ago,' Hueryx said. 'Don't presume to know my mind.'

'I know you are smarter than anyone else I've met. I know you are impatient with pointless formality and I know you despise Imoshen the All-father-killer. Tonight I move against her. I have All-fathers Saskeyne and Abeliode ready to take up arms. Are you with me?'

Aravelle's mouth went dry with fear. The cabin became utterly still.

'What's the plan, Dret?'

Dretsun dropped to kneel across from Hueryx. 'We all-fathers are going to take our seconds and meet Imoshen when she returns to the wharf. We'll kill her along with that upstart half-blood and the arrogant sea captain. We'll dump their bodies in the bay, then come back to our ships. Tomorrow morning, when Imoshen doesn't return, I'll call an all-council, and claim the Sagoras have betrayed us and killed Imoshen. I'll nominate myself for causare and lead an assault on the Sagoras. They won't be expecting it. We'll sweep through their hidden city, put everyone to the sword and install our own people in there. Saskeyne's right, the Mieren of this province are used to serving foreign leaders. They'll capitulate.'

'And you'll be causare?'

'Of course. The plan is mine. But the causare needs seconds. I've offered Saskeyne the role of hand-of-force. I'm offering you the chance to serve as my voice-of-reason.'

Hueryx nodded slowly. 'It just might work.'

'So I'll see you there on the wharf?'

'You'll see me there.'

Dretsun nodded and left. The taint of his aggressive gift seemed to linger on the air after him.

Hueryx and his inner circle sprang to their feet, some protesting that the all-father had not consulted them, others insisting they did not trust Dretsun. The elderly gift-tutor and historian advised caution.

As they argued, Hueryx beckoned Saskar. 'Did he seek out Tobazim before me?'

'No. He came straight to you.'

'Go now and see if he's gone to Tobazim or left the ship.'

Aravelle put the spiced wine chest away and removed the pot from the brazier. There had been no time to prepare it, let alone serve it.

Everything felt unreal. She could not believe Hueryx would do this. She felt personally betrayed by him, as if turning on Imoshen meant he was turning on her.

She realised in a horrible moment of clarity that she loved her T'En father. When had he slipped under her guard?

It didn't matter. He was going to betray the causare and everything she'd worked for.

A familiar knock sounded on the door.

'That'll be Charsoria, here to give her report,' Hueryx said. 'Answer the door, Vella.' He caught her hand and kissed her forehead. 'Don't look so worried. Go below and say nothing.'

The last time he had told her not to worry, he'd meant for her to kill the children.

When she opened the door to Charsoria, Hueryx dismissed the all-father's-voice, saying, 'We'll speak tomorrow, when we know what's going on. Take Vella below with you now.'

Aravelle could tell Charsoria was annoyed with the all-father for cancelling their meeting. When they reached the cabin, Charsoria gestured. 'Since you're with us, you can help Nariska put the children to bed.'

So Aravelle was stuck singing nursery rhymes, while above her Hueryx planned a brotherhood uprising.

Someone should warn the sisterhoods. Someone should...

She should do it. There wasn't anyone else. She'd always been a good swimmer, and it wasn't far to the causare's ship. It didn't matter if her heart was breaking. She had to betray her T'En father for the greater good.

THE STONE WAS dry, warm and dusty under Sorne's bare feet as he followed Imoshen and Ardonyx up the shallow steps. They paused in the shadowed archway of the Font of Knowledge.

There was no 'font' as such, and no lanterns. The large moon had yet to rise high enough to shine into the courtyard. The pale paving stones glowed softly, illuminated by the small moon and the stars.

On the far side, seven kneeling figures formed a semicircle. An eighth figure lay face-down in the centre, swathed in long white robes.

Imoshen shivered, and Sorne felt her gift rise and Ardonyx's respond. They knelt and gave the deep obeisance.

Imoshen greeted their hosts in Sagorese. 'The causare thanks the Sagora Seven for agreeing to see us.'

Although the night was cool, the stone was still warm from the day. Sorne felt the warmth seep into him. He took out his scriber, ink and paper board. He wasn't sure how he could write anything but chicken scrawl in the semi-dark. Sorne knew the two T'En would have gift-enhanced their sight to make the most of the slight glow coming off the white stone, but he did not have that advantage. He had expected there to be a table and lamps.

No one spoke.

The Sagora Seven all wore masks in place of veils, leaving only their mouths visible and, with their hands tucked under their formal robes, they gave nothing away. Sorne wondered if Imoshen could still read them.

She waited.

Not one of the Sagora Seven spoke.

Last night he had met the Sagoras representing Houses, Pavoii, Felinii and Vulpii. Tonight there were four more Sagoras, two wearing masks based on birds, the third a fox and the fourth a crested mountain bear.

In front of the Sagoras, in the centre of the courtyard, the figure continued to lie face-down on the stones, arms extended, head towards the Sagora leaders. Whoever it was, they appeared to be bald. Perhaps they were one of the mysterious Sensitives Imoshen had mentioned.

'I am the causare,' Imoshen started again, this time speaking Chalcedonian. 'This is my assistant, Voice-of-reason Ardonyx, and Ambassador Sorne. He'll take notes of our discussion in the Chalcedonian tongue, so there can be no misunderstandings.'

Her words hung in the courtyard as she waited for them to respond.

Then the prone figure came to their knees, bowed and stood. Graceful as a willow, the stranger danced to music only he – or she – could hear, long triangular sleeves swirling around, hands obscured, hairless head gleaming in the starlight. The figure's eyes were in shadow, and their face was mask-like in its beauty and stillness.

As their arms lifted, the large moon crested the wall and a finger of silver light struck the white-robed figure.

She, or he, dropped.

The moonlight hit Sorne and the two T'En in the face. For a heartbeat he was blinded. He felt both Imoshen and Ardonyx's gifts rise.

When he could see again, Sorne realised the courtyard's white stone was inlaid with silver, reflecting the moons' light. The three of them had been placed so that they were fully illuminated, while the Sagoras, on the far side of the courtyard, remained in shadow.

Subtle and secretive, the Sagoras lived up to their reputation.

The robed figure rose with exquisite grace. Sorne was convinced this was a Sensitive. How could they blind and geld one of their own people?

The figure glided towards Imoshen. As the Sensitive approached, Sorne realised the dancer's eyes were shadowed because they were empty. His stomach turned in revulsion.

Without warning, the Sensitive seized Imoshen's arm, then released her just as swiftly, and backed away.

'The causare thinks us barbarians,' the Sensitive announced in T'En, voice revealing he was male.

'I deplore the maiming of healthy males,' Imoshen said. 'And I deplore the wilful blinding of perfectly good eyes.'

'Ah, but you don't know what I can see,' the Sensitive crooned.

'I believe one should respect the customs of others,' Imoshen said. 'Amongst the T'En only those we trust have the right to touch us.'

'Apologies, causare. Our Sensitive is young and he "seeks stature," as you would say,' the raven-masked Sagora said.

Imoshen inclined her head. 'And your name?'

'I am House Hrafnii,' he answered.

The Sensitive retreated to kneel behind the Sagoras. He tilted his head and sniffed the air every now and then in a manner that was not quite human.

'When we said we would meet you, causare, we did not expect you to arrive with all your people. The invitation was for you alone,' Felinii said. 'Why did you not come to negotiate when you first received our reply?'

'I was in Port Sorvernia with my fleet when I received your invitation,' Imoshen said.

'Not this invitation. The first one.'

'This is the only invitation I have received.'

'So you have come to us,' Pavoii said, 'seeking sanctuary.'

Sorne could tell Imoshen didn't like her tone.

'As you came here over three hundred years ago seeking asylum,' Imoshen said.

Sorne had the impression that the Sagoras stiffened under their robes and masks.

'In your original message, you spoke of offering knowledge,' Hrafnii said.

'In exchange for sanctuary. It is said the Sagoras value knowledge above all else.'

'We do. But we also know the value of knowledge,' Pavoii said. 'In exchange for sanctuary, we ask that you train three of our Sensitives to operate on the higher plane.'

It all fell into place. The Sagoras had knowledge of all things except the higher plane, and this was a source of power. Their Sensitives might have a little innate power, but a little was never enough, when someone else always had more.

'The higher plane is dangerous.' Imoshen spoke slowly, as though choosing her words with care. 'What you ask could kill your people.'

'It's true. I lost my brother to the higher plane.' Sorne gestured to his face. 'And the night I lost this eye, four

Mieren died. Over the years, I've lost count of the number of Mieren who have been killed because they thought they could manipulate stolen power.'

'Our Sensitives are more than Mieren,' Pavoii said. 'This one just read the mind of a T'En.'

'A market-day trick, compared with gift-working on the higher plane,' Imoshen said.

'Then you refuse?' The Sagora in the crested bear mask was terse.

'We did not say that,' Ardonyx said smoothly. 'Even the T'En cannot operate on the higher plane without training. We train for twenty years, yet we still lose some to the dangers of the empyrean plane.'

'Just a few days ago,' Imoshen's voice was raw with remembered pain, 'we lost Gift-tutor Sarodyti, when –'

'Are you saying it would take twenty years to train our Sensitives?' Felinii asked, her voice neutral.

'Would you hand a naked flame to a child and turn them loose in a hayfield?' Ardonyx countered.

'I would give them a lantern, that they would find their way.'

'What if the lantern attracted beasts, which hungered for the light?' Ardonyx asked.

Sorne nodded; he had been about to bring up the predators.

'We know about the predators of the higher plane,' Felinii said. 'Our Sensitives have –'

'Been taken,' Sorne guessed.

Imoshen let her breath out in a long exhale. 'I agree. We'll teach them. No one should venture onto the higher plane unprepared.'

RONNYN HEARD SOMEONE shouting his name out on the mid-deck. He glanced to Sardeon, and they both ran out, to find everything shrouded in fog and Aravelle being restrained by two of the night-watch. She looked like a drowned rat, teeth chattering as she insisted she had to see him.

'What's wrong, Vella?' He ran to her side, fearing the worst. 'Did they –'

'No.' Aravelle reached for him.

Cerafeoni separated them. 'Ronnyn, I know you grew up with your Malaunje kin, but you can't associate with them now. And besides, we can't have brotherhood Malaunje creeping onto our ship. This is sisterhood territory.'

A crowd had gathered and Ronnyn could hear the empowered lads snickering. He felt a stab of annoyance with Aravelle. She looked ridiculous, being held off the ground by two of Cerafeoni's warriors, all dripping and bedraggled. She made him look ridiculous. Then he was ashamed of himself for thinking this.

Aravelle glared at the snickering empowered lads. 'I've come to warn you about the brotherhood uprising. Perhaps I shouldn't have bothered!'

Cerafeoni took a step closer and tilted Aravelle's chin so she could see her face. 'This is not something to joke about.'

'I know. I serve in All-father Hueryx's cabin. Dretsun came to see him tonight. They –'

'Send for Egrayne and Kiane,' Reoden said, as she pushed through the crowd. 'Everyone else inside. This is all-mother business.'

The empowered lads grumbled. Ronnyn planted his feet; he wasn't leaving. Sardeon went inside, only to return a moment later with a blanket for Aravelle. By then, Imoshen's voice-of-reason and hand-of-force had joined them in the circle of light cast by the lantern. The fog was so thick he could not see beyond the next mast.

'So what's this about a brotherhood uprising?' Egrayne asked.

And Aravelle told them about Dretsun's meeting with All-father Hueryx.

'...and if you don't hurry, you'll be too late to save Imoshen.'

Chapter Forty-Nine

As Imoshen travelled down the road to the port, the carriage was swallowed by fog. She was filled with the conviction she could not have done other than she had. To leave the Sagorese Sensitives vulnerable to the empyrean predators was wrong.

'And besides,' she said, although they hadn't been speaking. 'If our people are to stay here, we can't have Sensitives unleashing predators and leaving it up to our gift-warriors to risk their lives to make this plane safe.'

'The fact that the Sagorese Sensitives are already in contact with the higher plane changes everything,' Ardonyx said. 'Dretsun and the others will understand.'

The carriage came to a stop, and they climbed out into a world of mist. They could not see more than a body length in front of them.

The Sagora unhooked one of the two lanterns and handed it to Sorne. As they made their way towards the wharf, they moved in a pool of golden light. They walked in silence. Imoshen's mind was full of questions about the Sagoras and their innate power.

Sorne hesitated.

'Give me the lantern,' Ardonyx said. 'I can find the way.'

'I thought I sensed male gift,' Sorne whispered. He reached to his hip, as if going for a sword, then cursed when his hand closed on the scribe's satchel.

Imoshen opened her gift awareness. 'Sorne's right. Put out the lantern.'

'Too late,' Saskeyne said, stepping into the circle of lantern light with his two seconds.

'You?' Imoshen had not expected him to turn on her. He was impetuous and eager for stature, but she had not thought him devious. Her gift surged as she read him. Determination. She could talk her way out of this. 'There's no need –'

'But there is. What we need is a leader of vision,' Saskeyne said.

'And you're that leader?'

'No, I am.' Dretsun stepped into the circle of light.

Her gift surged as she sensed others closing in on them. Dretsun's supporters meant to kill them here. She sought Ardonyx's eyes; so much time wasted.

He moved forward, drawing their gaze to him. 'There's no need for this. We share a common enemy. We...'

And Imoshen felt the force of his power, as words laden with gift-resonance poured from him. She couldn't have repeated what he said, but she knew as long as he spoke, she was spellbound. A calm descended on her, on all of them.

Yet one small part of her mind shrieked a warning. Ardonyx had lied to her. He was more than a clever wordsmith, able to select the right thing to say. He could imbue his words with power. And all this time she had trusted him, believing everything he said.

Of course.

A dog barked. The sharp sound cut through Ardonyx's voice. At the same time, All-father Abeliode stumbled out of the mist with his two seconds.

'Kill the wordsmith first!' Dretsun shouted and attacked, long-knives drawn.

'Run, Imoshen!' Ardonyx stepped in, deflecting Dretsun's blow, but before he could escape, Dretsun's hand-of-force stabbed him in the back.

Sorne swung the lantern, scattering burning oil across their attackers. 'Run, Imoshen.'

She ran blind through a dark grey featureless world, the waning moons barely illuminating the fog.

Her foot caught on a step a fraction of a heartbeat before her hands connected with a fog-damp stone wall. She felt along the wall until she came to a wooden door. There were people on the other side, she could tell. But they weren't going to open the door and let her in.

She gasped and quietened her breath, listening. Running footsteps approached, carried on a wave of acrid male gift. She felt her way along the building until she found an alleyway and stepped into it.

Heart thundering, she waited.

If she could just touch her attacker's skin before he stabbed her, she could wrench his life force from his body and send it to the empyrean plane.

Mouth dry with fear, she waited for him to reach her.

A dark shadow solidified as it ran out of the fog towards her. She let her gift surge.

He stopped, stunned.

That slight hesitation gave her the chance to reach out and touched his face. Saskeyne. She knew a moment's remorse. But they'd stabbed Ardonyx. She tore the life from him. He was so surprised he didn't even try to drag her with him.

He fell and she saw another brotherhood warrior only a step behind him. Saskeyne's companion drew his blade. Imoshen sensed the strike coming. She dropped to her knees, meaning to crawl past, but his thigh collided with her shoulder. She clasped his leg, and ran her hands up, trying to find skin.

He caught her hair, pulling on it. Tears of pain burned her eyes. She saw his other arm swing down, heard the blade whistle. Her hand slipped past his belt, slid under his vest, onto the hot skin of his belly. It was Saskeyne's hand-of-force. She ripped the life from him too.

Momentum carried his arm along its strike and the flat of his blade hit her head, even as he dropped. They both sprawled on the cold, damp stones.

Disoriented, Imoshen lay there, panting.

Then she heard shouts and running feet.

Coming to her knees, she felt around for the knife. Took it and ran down the alleyway into the fog. She had to get back to the wharf, find the rowboat, return to the ship and bring help.

SORNE EXPECTED TO die. The irony was that it was his own people who would kill him. He swung the lantern, spilling burning oil. His attackers cursed as they beat out the flames.

Shouldering into one of them, he pulled the man's knife from its sheath and ran off into the fog. Ardonyx was down, and Imoshen had run the other way. There were nine armed assailants. Unless they were very lucky...

He wasn't lucky. His boot caught on a wooden bench and he fell over it, dropping the knife.

The dog barked again, setting off others. But the wall of sound was too late to disguise his whereabouts.

As he felt for the weapon, two men caught him, hauled him to his feet, and slammed him up against a cold stone wall. All he could see was dark man-shaped shadows to each side of him in the grey fog.

He could feel power coming from his captors, but it was the power coming towards him that terrified him.

Dretsun paused at arm's length. 'What have we here?'

'Just kill me and be done with it,' Sorne ground out.

'Kill a half-blood who can command armies?' Dretsun laughed. 'I think not, I have something much better planned for you.'

He tore open Sorne's shirt and placed his palm over Sorne's racing heart. Knowing what he intended, Sorne fought with all his strength to break free. He was not going to spend the rest of his life as this T'En's devotee.

Then the power hit him, wave after wave.

Once before, a T'En warrior had tried to break his walls and Sorne had retreated to his childhood, to the scouring frame, where he had learnt to bear pain under the lash. Each burning lash-stroke was a wave of painful gift power, but he had never broken under the lash. Never...

The hand left his chest and he sagged in his captors' grip. He felt like laughing. He'd beaten Dretsun.

Hands caught his face. A mouth covered his. Dretsun kissed him, pouring power directly into him.

And he drowned.

TOBAZIM CLIMBED OUT of the rowboat, onto the dock and raised his lantern. 'Curse this fog. We'll never find them.'

'It might help them escape,' Hueryx said.

Who would have thought he'd ally himself with Hueryx? But the all-father had come to him and revealed Dretsun's plan, knowing he would want to save his shield-brother.

A dog barked.

Tobazim's hand-of-force, Haromyr, Eryx, Ionnyn and Iraayel joined him on the dock, bringing another two lanterns. Norsasno had objected to Iraayel's presence, saying there were other, more experienced warriors. But it was Iraayel's choice-mother who was in danger. So Iraayel came with them.

Hueryx had his two seconds, a devotee and four T'En warriors with him. They were all armed, but it would do no good if they couldn't find Ardonyx and the others.

'Open your shield-brother link,' Hueryx urged.

Tobazim opened his gift awareness, seeking Ardonyx, and... staggered as pain stabbed into his back between his ribs. He almost dropped the lantern.

'We're too late. They've already attacked,' Hueryx said. 'Quick.'

Haromyr slid an arm around Tobazim and they headed up the dock. He thought he saw figures beyond the golden circle of the lantern-lit fog, but he must have been mistaken.

He heard cursing and running footsteps up ahead.

Somewhere there was clattering, and then the dog barked again, setting all the other dogs off. With the fog and the unknown terrain of the port town, it was hard to tell where the sounds came from.

The circle of golden fog moved with them, illuminating damp cobbles under their boots, a huddled figure in a pool of blood.

'Ardonyx.' Tobazim staggered the last few steps and dropped beside him. Still alive. 'We're here. You're safe.'

He rolled Ardonyx over, only to discover he wasn't conscious. They had to get him back to the ship and to Healer Reoden.

'Help me.' Tobazim looked up to see Hueryx organising search parties.

When the others ran off into the fog, Hueryx came back and knelt beside him.

Tobazim took Ardonyx's shoulders. 'We must get him back to the ship.'

'We can't let you do that,' Abeliode said, walking into the circle of light with his two seconds. Aggressive male gift radiated from them.

Abeliode's two seconds circled them. Tobazim lowered Ardonyx, put the lantern down next to him and drew his knives. Hueryx unsheathed his knives, putting his back to Tobazim.

'Over here!' Hueryx yelled. 'To us, Reyne.'

His hand-of-force called in response, then called again, but this time he was further away.

Abeliode's voice-of-reason darted in, slashing for Tobazim's groin. Tobazim avoided the strike and pinned his attacker's knife-arm against his body. They were so close he could see the sweat on the warrior's top lip. Tobazim headbutted him. It had been one of his choice-brother's favourite moves. He heard the other man's nose break.

Releasing him, Tobazim pulled back. As Abeliode's voice-of-reason doubled over, trying to stop the blood gushing from his nose, Tobazim drove a knife into his belly.

He staggered a few steps and fell to his knees.

Tobazim turned in time to see Abeliode's hand-of-force trip over Ardonyx's unconscious form. Tobazim followed the man down, giving him no time to recover. The back of the warrior's head slammed into the cobles, and a heartbeat later, Tobazim's knife slid into his chest.

He looked up to see Hueryx climb off Abeliode and wipe his knives. By now the miasma of roused gift was so pervasive, Tobazim was numb to it. He stripped off his vest, folded it up and pressed it against Ardonyx's wound.

Somewhere nearby a man screamed. There was a scuffle, and then nothing. A moment later Haromyr, Eryx and Ionnyn returned, dragging Dretsun's hand-of-force. They dropped him next to the other bodies and ran off again.

Meanwhile, two of Hueryx's warriors came back with Saskeyne's voice-of-reason. One of them was injured. They added Saskeyne's second to the growing pile of bodies.

Iraayel ran into the pool of light. 'Any sign of Imoshen?'

'No.'

'Look what I found.' Hueryx's voice-of-reason returned with two Malaunje.

'We were waiting to take the causare back to her ship,' the youth said.

'They were creeping around –'

'Redraven?' Iraayel grabbed the youth and hugged him. 'And... Meloria.' He turned to Tobazim. 'I can vouch for them.'

Tobazim nodded and Iraayel took them with him as he went in search of Imoshen.

Hueryx's hand-of-force approached from the other direction. His devotee lit the way for two T'En warriors, who carried Saskeyne and his hand-of-force.

'Funny thing is,' Reyne said, holding the lantern over the bodies, 'there's not a mark on them.'

'Imoshen,' Tobazim said. 'I've seen her rip a Mieren's life force from his body with a single touch.'

'These were not Mieren,' Reyne objected.

Hueryx grimaced. 'If you see Imoshen, don't approach her. She's dangerous and she won't trust us. Dretsun and his voice-of-reason are still out there.'

Someone screamed.

'That's one less,' Reyne muttered.

'Unless it's one of ours,' Hueryx said. 'Go carefully. Search the port street by street.'

Iraayel returned, lighting the way for the two Malaunje carrying Sorne's body.

'Dead?' Tobazim asked, heart sinking.

'Not quite, but there's not a mark on him,' Iraayel said.

Tobazim met Hueryx's eyes. Had Imoshen mistaken him for an attacker in the fog and almost killed him before she could stop herself?

Iraayel looked around. 'Any sign of –'

'Imoshen, no. I need to get Ardonyx back to the healer,' Tobazim said.

Just then Haromyr and the others returned with Dretsun, wounded but alive. They were followed by Reyne's warriors, who carried the body of Dretsun's voice-of-reason.

Tobazim gestured. 'I want the all-father here.'

Ionnyn drove Dretsun to his knees.

He glared up at his captors. 'Fiant take you, Hue. I should have known you'd take the causareship for yourself.'

'Why did you want him alive?' Hueryx asked Tobazim.

'I just want to know one thing,' Tobazim said, coming to his feet. Eryx knelt to keep the pressure on Ardonyx's wound. 'Come here, Iraayel. I'm going to ask him a question and you can tell me if he's lying.'

'He can taste the truth?' Hueryx asked, coming over to join Tobazim.

Iraayel put his hands on Dretsun's temples. Ionnyn and Haromyr held him still.

Tobazim stood over him. 'Did you break your vow? All-father Egrutz gave your brotherhood safe passage on his ship. Did you use the sea-vermin attack as an excuse to kill him and steal his brotherhood?'

Dretsun just stared up at him.

'He's laughing at you,' Iraayel said and pulled back, wiping his hands, then his mouth. 'He tastes foul.'

Tobazim reached for his knife.

'No...' Hueryx drew his blade and stepped around behind Dretsun. 'We were choice-brothers. I always knew this day would come.'

'Oh, get it over with,' Dretsun sneered, 'before I tell them what an irritating little sh –'

Hueryx cut his throat, then stepped back.

'What's going on here?' Hand-of-force Cerafeoni demanded.

They turned to see a dozen sisterhood T'En warriors and a dozen Malaunje. The fog had lifted a little. The women's gifts were roused and dangerous.

The brotherhood warriors reached for their weapons.

'Where's Imoshen?' Kiane asked, drawing her knives. 'If you've hurt her...'

Iraayel stepped between the two groups. Unarmed, he walked towards Kiane. 'We can't find Imoshen. We've put down the uprising, but Ardonyx is wounded. Sorne looks half-dead and no one's seen my choice-mother.'

'You put down the brotherhood uprising?' Cerafeoni repeated.

'All-fathers Hueryx and Tobazim did,' Iraayel said.

Cerafeoni and Kiane exchanged looks.

'I'll take the injured back to the ship,' Reoden's hand-of-force said.

Kiane nodded. 'I'll look for Imoshen.' She glanced to the pile of bodies. 'Get rid of those and clean up all the blood. We don't want to frighten the Mieren.'

Hueryx started to laugh.

Chapter Fifty

'IT'S THE CAUSARE!'

A dozen hands helped her over the ship's side onto the mid-deck. Imoshen found she was shaking so badly she could hardly talk. At least the blood wasn't dripping into her eyes anymore.

Egrayne called for Reoden, who came running and knelt next to her.

Imoshen pushed her healing hands away. 'I'm fine. It's Sorne and Ardonyx I'm worried about. They're still out there. I know Ardonyx was stabbed. Dretsun ambushed us. We have to –'

'We know. We've already sent a party to rescue you,' Egrayne said, then hugged her. 'I swear you have more lives than a cat!'

'One of the boats is returning,' the lookout shouted, and everyone ran to the ship's side.

Imoshen thought about getting up, but she felt too shaky. Frayvia knelt next to her with a bowl of water and bandages, and started to clean her face.

'I don't know if Sorne got away,' Imoshen confessed. Tears filled her eyes. 'They stabbed Ardonyx, and then Sorne told me to run...'

Frayvia wept softly as she wiped the blood from Imoshen's head wound and bound it. Her touch gave Imoshen strength.

What Egrayne had said finally sank in. 'You knew about the ambush? How did you know?'

Her devotee tied off the bandage then gestured to

a Malaunje girl who was standing with Ronnyn and Sardeon. 'Aravelle swam across to warn us.'

Imoshen got to her feet and beckoned the youngsters. She took the Malaunje girl's hands, gift-infusing her. 'Thank you. That was very brave.'

'I hate him,' Aravelle whispered, and Imoshen read the heartbreak in her. 'I thought I could trust him, but I hate him.'

'Hueryx?' Imoshen asked.

Aravelle nodded.

'He wasn't with Dretsun.'

'But...' – Aravelle looked confused – 'he said he'd see Dretsun there!'

'Iraayel!' Saffazi ran to him as he climbed aboard.

He laughed, hugged her, then drew her out of the way as Reoden's hand-of-force climbed aboard with her warriors.

'You!' Iraayel strode over and enveloped Imoshen in a hug. 'I should have known you'd be all right. And there I was, running all over port, afraid I'd find your body around the next corner.'

Imoshen felt his hot tears on her skin. She kissed his cheek and pulled back with a shaky laugh. 'How did you know I was in danger?'

'Hueryx came to Tobazim, revealed Dretsun's plans. We went to stop –'

'That's what he meant?' Aravelle gasped in horror. 'And I betrayed him. He'll never forgive me.'

She was right. Imoshen caught Ronnyn's eye. 'Take your sister up to my cabin.'

Several brotherhood warriors had climbed aboard while they were speaking. Ronnyn and Sardeon avoided them, as they guided her to the far set of rear-deck stairs.

Aravelle had betrayed her all-father to the sisterhoods. Imoshen didn't know what she was going to do with the girl. Malaunje had been executed for less.

'Gently,' Tobazim said.

Imoshen turned and spotted him, guiding the sling into place as a wounded man was lowered onto the deck. She knew it was Ardonyx. Still alive, but...

She looked around for Reoden.

The healer dropped to her knees at Ardonyx's side as the sling was removed.

Imoshen knelt beside her secret bond-partner. Reoden ran her hands over his wound. Imoshen reached for Ardonyx's hand at the same time as Tobazim. He beat her to it and didn't even notice that he had, his attention was so focused on his shield-brother.

Imoshen felt the healer's gift at work on Ardonyx's injury. After a moment, Reodeon's power eased.

Tobazim looked up. 'Will he...'

Reoden nodded and left them to see to others. Someone came by, distributing blankets and Tobazim gently tucked one around Ardonyx. Imoshen wanted to weep with relief, but she had no right to intrude. Tobazim met Imoshen's eyes across Ardonyx. She should go before he began to wonder.

'How is he, Fray?' Reoden asked and Imoshen spotted them with Sorne.

Frayvia knelt over him. She'd been listening to his chest, now she lifted her head. 'He's breathing and his heart is beating, but only just. There's not a mark on him.'

As Imoshen joined them, Reoden rubbed her hands together and ran them over Sorne. She pulled back. 'I recognise this. Valendia was in the same state when Graelen died.'

'But Sorne isn't a devotee,' Frayvia protested. 'He would never –'

'Then someone forced their gift on him.' Reoden wrinkled her nose. 'There's so much residual male gift, I can't tell...'

Imoshen opened her senses and grimaced. 'It was Dretsun. I know his taint.'

'Dretsun's dead,' Tobazim said. He was helping Ardonyx to sit up and lean against the ship's side.

'Hueryx executed him. He'd broken his vow and betrayed Egrutz's trust.'

'How can you be sure?'

Tobazim gestured to her choice-son, who was over near the mast with Saffazi. 'Iraayel can taste the truth.'

'But he's a gift-warrior,' Imoshen said, then heard herself. She, of all people, should know a T'En could have more than one gift.

'Imoshen.' Frayvia caught her arm. 'You have to save Sorne.'

'She's right,' Reoden said. 'Only a powerful infusion of the gift will bring him back.'

'But then he'll be my devotee,' Imoshen said. 'He'd hate that.'

'He'd hate being dead,' Frayvia snapped. 'Do it now, before it's too late.'

Imoshen hesitated.

Frayvia took her hand and placed it over his heart, palm to skin. 'Do it for me.'

'Let's try this.' Imoshen removed her hand and replaced it with Frayvia's. Covering her devotee's hand with her own, she gift-infused Sorne through Frayvia until she thought she'd pass out.

'Will that prevent him from becoming your devotee?' Reoden whispered.

'I've no idea,' Imoshen admitted.

But Sorne did not stir.

They knelt in silence, watching for any sign of consciousness.

Finally, Frayvia took Sorne's shoulders and shook him as she berated him. 'I told you not to do anything brave. How could you –'

Sorne woke, rolled her under him, pinned her and reached for her throat, before he registered who she was. 'Fray?'

He slid off her, stunned, and she came to her knees to embrace him, weeping with relief.

Imoshen glanced to Ardonyx. He leant against the ship's side, watching the gathering. Thankfully, Tobazim was not with him.

As she approached Ardonyx, he gestured behind her. 'Looks like you're about to hold an impromptu all-council.'

She saw Egrayne, Reoden and Athazi making their way towards her from one quarter, and Tobazim and Paragian from another. Hueryx had just climbed aboard.

The all-father appeared tense. Her gift surged as she read him: he was furious. Someone must have told him Aravelle's part in all this.

'It'll be a small council with three all-fathers missing,' Ardonyx said and tried to get up.

She helped him, then turned just in time as the others reached her.

Paragian gave the obeisance of contrition. 'Causare, I swear I knew nothing of Saskeyne's plans.'

His emotion was transparent to her gift.

'I know,' Imoshen said. She gestured to the three all-fathers. 'I want you to go to the three brotherhoods that lost their leaders tonight and ensure there's a smooth transition of power. Then come back here with the new leaders.' They hesitated. 'We have to be organised, if we are to make the most of sanctuary.'

'Sanctuary? The Sagoras have given us sanctuary!' Reoden hugged Egrayne, then Athazi.

Imoshen smiled, but the three brotherhood leaders didn't and she realised they expected her to exact retribution for the attempted coup. 'Tell the new brotherhood leaders; if they come with contrition in their hearts, there will be no punishment. There have been too many lives sacrificed on the altar of stature and ambition, both ours and King Charald's. We must look to our people's future.'

'Causare T'Imoshen.' Tobazim gave the deep obeisance, then lifted his head. 'I'll see to Abeliode's brotherhood.'

He strode off, calling for his hand-of-force.

'And I'll see to Saskeyne's brotherhood, Causare T'Imoshen,' Paragian said and headed off.

'I guess that leaves Dretsun's brotherhood,' Hueryx said, turning to leave.

'Wait...' Imoshen met his eyes. 'I owe you a debt. You made a choice tonight that went against tradition. You chose the T'Enatuath over the brotherhoods. This required both vision and bravery.'

He inclined his head, but his expression remained grim.

'You should be proud of your Malaunje daughter, Hueryx. She chose the causare over her all-father.'

'She should have trusted me.'

'Have you given her reason to trust you?'

He went to say something, hesitated, then squared his shoulders. 'She betrayed me, and my warriors know it. Soon everyone will know. I must disown her.'

Or he would lose the respect of his brotherhood. He gave Reoden the obeisance of supplication. 'Will you take her in?'

'Of course. I'd be honoured.'

Hueryx nodded once, and walked off abruptly.

'What a rude man,' Athazi muttered. 'I want to talk to you about Melisarone's survivors –'

'Not now, Athazi.' Imoshen cut her off.

'When, then?'

Reoden swept an arm around the small all-mother's shoulders. 'Imoshen's exhausted. Come with me.'

As the healer led her off, Egrayne said, 'You'll have to hand Mel's sisterhood over to her eventually.'

'I was thinking of letting them choose.'

Shocked, Egrayne went to protest, but glanced to Ardonyx. Clearly, she was uncomfortable discussing sisterhood business in front of a brotherhood's voice-of-reason.

'Later, Egrayne,' Imoshen said. 'I need to discuss the T'Enatuath's future with my fleet commander.'

'Why do we need a fleet now?' Egrayne asked. 'The Sagoras have given us sanctuary.'

'We need wealth to establish our new home. I'm going to send Captain Ardonyx on a trading mission to the Lagoons of Perpetual Summer. One successful voyage would go a long way towards setting us up.'

Egrayne's eyes widened and she appeared shattered. 'Of course. I should have seen –'

'You can't think of everything.' Imoshen felt for her voice-of-reason; things were moving too fast for her. She slid her arm through Egrayne's, and led her away from Ardonyx. 'Right now, we need to organise a celebration: food, spiced wine and music.'

'He's DISOWNED ME?' Aravelle repeated.

The healer's devotee nodded. 'You no longer belong to All-father Hueryx's brotherhood. Reoden sent me to say she's taken you in. You'll be the choice-daughter of her all-mother's-voice.'

Aravelle hesitated.

'There's no point pleading with your all-father,' the devotee said. 'He's not even on the ship. He's gone to settle things with Dretsun's brotherhood.'

As soon as the devotee left, Aravelle turned to Ronnyn. 'I have to go back to the *Victorious*. I have to get Itania. If you don't help me, I'll do it myself.'

'Vella.' Ronnyn shook his head. 'How can you doubt me?'

She felt a wave of relief.

Ronnyn turned to Sardeon. 'You don't have to come.'

'I know. I should talk you out of it. But... someone has to keep you out of trouble.'

They found the mid-deck full of T'En and Malaunje, and the celebrations well underway.

'How are we going to lower the boat without anyone noticing?' Ronnyn muttered.

Aravelle went to the side and spotted a rowboat. Two Malaunje rowers were waiting.

She tugged on Ronnyn's arm. 'Come on.'

They simply climbed in and told the Malaunje to take them to the *Victorious*.

The night-watch were surprised to see Aravelle being escorted by two lads, but Hueryx had not been back to the *Victorious*, so they believed her when she said she was running an errand for the all-father.

Ronnyn and Sardeon waited on deck as she went down to Charsoria's cabin. Stomach churning, she crept up the passage and slipped into the cabin. She needn't have worried; the women and children slept.

Stepping over them, Aravelle reached Itania and picked her up, blanket and all. Her little sister stirred, then snuggled into her arms.

As Aravelle made her way back to the door only one head lifted. Nariska blinked sleepily.

Aravelle lifted a finger to her lips. The other girl nodded and said nothing.

After that, it was a matter of watching for Ronnyn's signal, then passing Itania up to him, and scurrying across the deck before the night-watch returned.

Itania woke as they passed her down to the rowers, but settled again when Aravelle took her.

Back on the *Resolute*, they crossed the mid-deck, where everyone was celebrating. They'd almost made it as far as the hatch when Cerafeoni stopped them.

'What's this?' As she took in Ronnyn and the way Aravelle held the toddler, her eyes narrowed.

Aravelle's heart sank. She searched the deck for the causare or the healer, and spotted them together near a trestle-table laden with food.

'If that's your little Malaunje sister, Ronnyn, you've overstepped the mark. You too, Sardeon,' Cerafeoni said. 'You can turn right around and...'

Aravelle ducked behind Ronnyn and ran across the deck, weaving through the dancers. Itania whimpered and held on. If she could just reach the causare...

Someone caught arm, swinging her around. Aravelle clutched Itania to her chest.

'How could you?' Saskar demanded, mulberry eyes brilliant with hurt and anger. 'How could you betray us, Vella?'

'I had to.' Tears stung her eyes. 'I had to do the right thing, no matter what it cost.'

'Here, you. Malaunje.' Cerafeoni gestured to Saskar. 'Hold her.'

Aravelle glanced over her shoulder and saw the hand-of-force ploughing through the crowd. People parted for her.

Desperate, Aravelle turned back to Saskar. 'Please let me go.'

He hesitated.

She could wait no longer. Aravelle pitched her voice to carry over the music. 'Causare Imoshen, Healer Reoden, I claim sanctuary for my sister!'

The hand-of-force caught her just as Imoshen and the healer reached her.

'I claim sanctuary for my sister,' Aravelle repeated.

Before they could tell her this was impossible, Aravelle let the blanket drop and pulled Itania's nightdress off her shoulder to reveal the bruises. 'I'm not taking her back. She deserves better than this!'

'Fetch a lantern,' Causare Imoshen ordered.

'Bring her over here.' The healer led them to the nearest table, and pushed plates of food aside.

Aravelle stood Itania on the table and undid the drawstring. Ronnyn arrived with a lantern. Itania's chin trembled, but Aravelle held her little sister's eyes, willing her to be strong.

As the two powerful all-mothers inspected Itania's back and upper arms, Aravelle looked for Saskar. He stood back, watching, and she knew this would all be reported to Hueryx and his seconds. Good.

Imoshen and the healer were shocked and distressed by the story written on Itania's pale skin. Their outraged comments were everything Aravelle had hoped. This close, she could feel their roused gifts. Female power was different, but not unpleasant.

'Who did this?' the causare asked, eyes glinting with anger.

'All-father's-voice Charsoria. And Itania's not the only one she mistreats.' Remembered pain made Aravelle shield her breast.

'Why didn't you go to your all-father, child?' Reoden asked.

Aravelle found it hard to explain. Why had she failed to protect Itania? She felt terrible. The causare's gift surged.

'It's all right,' Imoshen said, touching Aravelle's arm and easing her pain. 'You've come to us. We'll deal with Hueryx and Charsoria.' She noticed Reoden rubbing her hands together. 'Don't heal her yet, Ree. Hueryx needs to see this.'

THERE WAS A moment between dealing with sisterhood business, Ronnyn's abused sisters and preparing for the all-council, when Imoshen spotted Ardonyx standing alone at the ship's side.

As she went over to him, she wanted to pull him into her arms and give thanks for their escape. But tonight she'd discovered the true nature of his gift, and it changed everything. 'You lied to me.'

'Yes. And I'd do it again in a heartbeat. You would never have let your guard down, if you'd known.'

He was right, but... 'I'm still angry.'

'How can you be angry? Look at what happened tonight. Two brotherhoods united against three all-fathers to save you, Imoshen the All-father-killer. We would have said this was impossible only a year ago.'

He was right. They had come a long way but... 'I still can't acknowledge you as my bond-partner. Brotherhoods still have to give up their T'En children to the sisterhoods.

And T'En choice-mothers still have to declare the lads they loved for seventeen years dead to them –'

'It's a start.'

'It's never enough. And now I have to hold an all-council to explain the conditions of our asylum here.' Imoshen sighed. 'Most of our people think sanctuary means going back to what life was like before, but it will never be like that. And I haven't even told them about the Sagoras' Sensitives.'

'One problem at a time, Imoshen.'

She wanted to acknowledge him as her bond-partner, right now, right here in the open where everyone would see. She wanted it so much, she had to walk away; she didn't know if the feeling sprang from her heart, or if he had planted the compulsion, playing on her dreams for their people.

RONNYN WAS FINALLY happy. His family were back together, and his gift had returned. He was the male equivalent of an empowerer. As a summoner, he would have high stature. He'd be able to protect his brothers and his sisters.

Aravelle and Itania had stretched out on the bunk, in the secret nook where Sardeon used to live. He was proud of Aravelle, and also a little in awe of what she'd done tonight.

'What?' Aravelle whispered.

'Nothing.' He pulled the blankets up and kissed her forehead. 'Sleep. You're safe.'

As he drew back, she caught his hand, squeezed it then let go.

He took the lamp and turned to leave, only to find Sardeon leaning against the panel, grinning.

'What?' Ronnyn whispered.

'I've grown.'

'We're still the same size.'

Sardeon rolled his eyes. 'You've grown, too, you idiot.'

'How do you know?' Ronnyn asked.

Sardeon straightened up and pointed to the panel.

Ronnyn lifted the lamp. All he could see was a scratch at about eye level. He shrugged. 'So?'

'That's the mark I made the day we came aboard. That's how tall I was.'

Ronnyn glanced at him and Sardeon nodded, then grinned again. Ronnyn thumped his arm. He thumped back. They wrestled.

'Careful of the lamp,' Aravelle muttered. 'Boys...'

AS SORNE WATCHED Frayvia dress, he marvelled at his good fortune. She was his and he was hers, and this time he did not have to leave her and ride off into danger. From the mid-deck, he could hear music and laughter, which seemed appropriate.

She sank onto the bedroll beside him. 'Are you hungry? I'll fetch some food.'

'No. I'll come out. Just let me hold you for a little longer.'

'How can I argue with that?' She snuggled down next to him and spoke of sanctuary, the Sagoras and her hopes for the future.

He did not have the heart to tell her, when Imoshen's power poured through him, he'd had another vision.

Epilogue

IGOTZON PACKED HIS notes away and made sure the lids were tight on his ink bottles. 'Are you ready?'

'I'd be ready sooner if the noise hadn't kept Soihana up all night.' Masne finished rolling her small bundle and tied it off. 'Now she'll be asleep all day.' She slipped the baby into the sling and adjusted the infant across her body.

Igotzon added Masne's bundle to their pile, then helped her to her feet.

As they stepped out into the sunshine on deck, he was already planning how he would describe this day when he wrote of it in his journal.

The T'Enatuath's first day of sanctuary.

Masne smiled. 'It's so warm for winter.'

'Port Sorvernia is approximately as far south as Maygharia, but the weather can turn cold.' He offered his arm.

She took it and they stepped off the ship, into a new life.